4th Degree

THE FIGHT GAME: BOOK FIVE

NIKKI CASTLE

Cover Design: Dark City Designs

Editing: NiceGirlNaughtyEdits

✳ Created with Vellum

To those who carry the world on their shoulders.
It's okay to be selfish with your happy.

AUTHOR'S NOTE

If you've read the other books in the Fight Game series, you probably know what to expect here: a fun, spicy time with an obsessed MMC. Which is still true (Coach really ran away with the spice in this one...). But this one also contains some heavier topics. To avoid spoiling Skylar's story, all **Trigger Warnings** are listed in the Afterword at the end of this book.

1

SKYLAR

"Where are *you* going looking all excited?"

I turn to my brother, not even trying to hide my grin.

"I have my first kickboxing class tonight," I tell him, tossing an extra t-shirt into my gym bag. "I'm going over to the gym after my shift at the restaurant."

"Ohhh, so that's today." Joey throws himself onto the couch at the sound of his video game starting. "Thank God you'll finally have someone else to try out your YouTube moves on."

I snatch a third t-shirt from the laundry pile and chuck it at my brother. "Shut up. You used to love it when I padded you up and kicked you onto the couch."

"Yeah, when I was six and thought it was cool to fly. It's not that fun when your nineteen-year-old strong-ass sister is trying out a choke on you and accidentally makes you pass out."

I shoot him a sheepish look. "I apologized for that." When something occurs to me, I frown and throw a fourth t-shirt at him. "Hey, you got an Xbox out of that! You don't get to use it as a guilt trip after I've evened us out."

Now it's his turn to look sheepish, but it's only for a split second before his attention goes back to the game on the TV screen. "Sure I do. It's in the brother-sister handbook."

I let out a growl and launch a fifth shirt at him. "I'm leaving. I set your basketball uniform aside, so make sure you pack that up for your game tomorrow. And fold the rest of the laundry before you go to bed."

"Hey, *you're* the one that just unfolded it!"

Giving my teenage brother a smack on the head as I pass him, I ignore his pout as I do it.

I'm just about to walk out the door, when my mom hobbles into the living room.

"Hey, Mom," I say, helping her into a seat at the kitchenette. "I thought you were sleeping."

"I was. I just woke up." Her voice is just as sleepy as her bedhead that's sticking up at the crown of her head.

I grab her a glass of water. "Did you have a good nap?"

"It was fine," she answers. When I place the glass in front of her, she grips it in her hand, studying it before slowly lifting it to her lips. "Seems to have stopped the tremors I was having this morning."

I'm pleased to see she's right, that her hands are no longer shaking as she holds the glass on her own.

"That's great news, Mom." I smile. "If you're having a good day, maybe you could try that puzzle you were working on last week?"

She clearly likes that idea, because she returns my smile as she says, "That's a great idea. I think I'll do that."

Relief deflates the tension in my shoulders, and I lean down to kiss her temple. "I'm gone for the rest of the day; I have work and then I'm starting at that new gym tonight. Maria is coming in a little bit to check on you, but if you need anything before then, just ask Joey."

"Okay, honey. Have a good day!"

I press another kiss to her aging face. "Thanks, Mom. I'll be home tonight."

Joey waves as I start toward the door, pausing only to grab my water bottle from the fridge. And when I see that magic piece of paper stuck to the fridge door, my eyes zeroing in on the words *Medical Grant*, I'm reminded of what made it possible for me to finally do something for myself.

When I leave the apartment, it's with a pep in my step that I haven't felt in a long time.

"Hey, Skylar, you coming out with us tonight?"

I finish ringing up my table's added dessert before turning to my new coworker. "What's tonight?"

"We're going to Graffiti after work for some drinks," he answers. "You coming with?"

"Skylar doesn't drink," comes my other coworker's dry tone from behind me. "And she has no idea how to have fun."

I grin at her over my shoulder. "Trust me, I had plenty of fun with your dad last night."

She rolls her eyes but turns back to her work. Once upon a time, her words would have hurt—being seen as the anti-fun one because I keep my distance doesn't make for a great reputation in the workplace. Especially because everyone here *loves* to go out together after their shifts. They're like a family unit that I've purposefully ostracized myself from.

But I've since hardened myself to both the teasing and the guilt. There are more important things than fun in the shape of shots.

"Why not?" the nosy new guy asks. "I mean, I have plenty of friends who don't drink, so I get that part, but you won't even come out with us to hang out?"

I shrug, turning my attention back to the silverware I've started to roll. *Always stay busy.* "I just don't have time." *Or money.* But I wave that thought away. "I have school, and work, and—"

"You can't spare time for *one* drink after a shift?" he asks in a shocked voice. Guess that's what I get for working in a bar-heavy restaurant. I stand out like a sore thumb.

"Nope," I say, popping the p. "I'm a full-time student with two jobs. Extra time isn't my strong suit."

I don't want to admit the real reason I'll never join them. The one that keeps me away from not just these coworkers, but also from the ones I have at the coffee shop, where I work in the mornings.

I don't see coworkers as friends. Being anything less than professional with other employees is risky, and *risk* and *job* will never go in the same sentence for me. I refuse. Too much of my life is affected by money, and I've carefully constructed every piece of my week so that I have some semblance of control over it. Risking my paycheck for a convenient friendship isn't worth it. An after-shift drink is definitely not worth it.

"Jesus, that sounds awful," he says, finally giving up the argument. "I don't know how you do it. When I lived on-campus, I had *one* part-time job, and I barely survived. When do you do anything for yourself? Or do you just never sleep?"

I barely hold back a sardonic laugh. "Something like that."

Sleep? What's that? If I'm not working or studying, I'm cooking, taking care of my mom, and helping my brother

4

with homework. I can't even remember the last time I got eight hours of sleep. Self-care isn't exactly on the schedule.

But then my thoughts flit to my plans tonight, and I realize...that's not quite true anymore.

It wasn't just the financial assistance of Mom's medical grant, though that was huge. Being able to hire Maria as a home nurse to help with Mom so Joey and I weren't on 24/7 duty was a change to the quality of our lives. Knowing that my brother and I have a little more freedom is invaluable.

I glance at the clock on the wall, mentally calculating how much time I have left before my MMA trial class tonight, feeling a rush of anticipation.

The rest of my work shift drags by. But somehow during the course of it, my excitement morphs into anxiousness. By the time I'm walking into the gym, my nerves have bubbled to the surface.

Beyond gym class, I've never done a sport in my life. I wouldn't say I'm unathletic, but there's also zero muscle knowledge in my body. Watching this sport and studying YouTube videos don't give me much of a boost.

"Hey, Skylar," I hear called out when I step through the gym entrance. I turn to the left and find Jax, the guy who signed me up last week, sitting behind the reception desk with a big smile on his face. "Glad you could make it."

"Nothing would've kept me away from this," I say with a grin.

"We'll start in ten minutes, so feel free to set your stuff down under any of the chairs. Or there are cubbies in the locker rooms. Wherever you're comfortable."

"Sounds good," I answer, my jitters dissipating. "I'll just wait for your word to start."

As I move through the warmup, and then the lesson with Jax, I experience about a dozen emotions. Wonder, as I learn the techniques. Relief, that I'm enjoying it as much as I always hoped I would. Glee, that I can feel my muscles straining, knowing I'm going to be pleasantly sore tomorrow because my body is putting in good, hard work.

By the time the class is over, I'm drenched in sweat, breathing hard, and I have a huge, goofy grin on my face.

"Awesome work today, Skylar," Jax says. "You're a natural."

I must be beaming at his praise, because he chuckles when he sees my expression. "You seem surprised. You didn't think you'd be good at this?"

I shrug, rolling my shoulders back in a stretch. "I've never done this before, so I didn't know *what* was going to happen."

"You seem knowledgeable about the sport, though. You've *never* trained?"

I shake my head. "I enjoy watching fights, and I've... watched videos, but I've never actually trained. I never had the opportunity to take that step."

"Until now," Jax finishes my sentence, the statement sounding more like a question.

"Until now," I confirm without adding anything else.

Jax opens his mouth to say something, but before the words come out, his eyes dart over my shoulder.

"Hey, Coach," he says.

"Hey," comes a gruff voice from behind me. "You guys all finished here?"

Jax nods. "Skylar just finished up her first lesson. She did great."

I turn around to face the owner and head trainer of the gym. I had researched him—and the other instructors—before I decided to join, but knowing his record and watching a few of his fight replays is not the same as seeing him in person. Because just like it did last week when I met him, the sight of Coach Dominic drives the breath from my lungs.

He's older, with serious blue eyes and dark facial hair, his face battle-worn from life and a decade of fighting. But despite being retired from his sport, I can tell even through his t-shirt and gym shorts that he's kept himself in peak physical condition—one glance at his bicep has me wondering if he could crush a man's skull in his hand.

Combined with the fact that he carries himself with all the confidence of a man who knows his place in the world, and he's easily one of the most commanding people I've ever stood in front of.

He looks at me in a way that makes me realize he's got the kind of eyes that don't give away what he's thinking, or how he's feeling.

"Did you like your first class?" he asks me.

"So much," I answer with a grin. "It was so fun."

"You sure you've never trained before? You looked like a natural out there."

I shake my head, trying to tamp down on my excited smile so he doesn't know how his compliment affects me. "Nothing beyond slapping my brother around a little bit."

I think I see a glimmer of amusement in his eyes. Then he's turning to Jax and saying, "Run the fighters through their warmup. We're doing defense drills today."

Jax returns a stiff nod. "Yes, sir." Facing the fighters who are starting to stretch and warm up on the other side of the room, he yells out, "Everyone on the mat! Five minutes of shadow boxing. Let's go!"

Everyone snaps to follow his command. Since it's only the warmup, people are still chatting and focusing more on loosening muscles than technical perfection. But I'm fascinated by it all the same. I watch as they move through kicks, punches, knees, and elbows.

"Don't worry, there's no final exam."

I'm snapped out of my thoughts when I hear Coach Dominic's voice, my head jerking in his direction. He's still standing next to me, still observing me with an expression I can't read. And when the timer goes off that signals the end of the round, I realize I've been staring at the fighters for five whole minutes, and Coach has been watching me do it.

"I just like getting things right," I say unapologetically as I turn my attention back to the mat. "If I'm going to do something, I might as well try my best while I do it."

I can sense him still studying me. After a moment, his gaze turns back to his fighters. "So why so interested in training? You have plans to fight before you get too old or something?"

When I look at him this time, my brow is furrowed in confusion. "What? What does that— No, of course not."

He lets out a puff of air that I think is meant to be a chuckle. "Every so often we'll have someone sign up who wants to train every single day because they're almost forty and they want to get at least one fight in before they die." He sends me another sidelong look. "It was a joke, since you're obviously not even close to forty." His eyes narrow as he takes another look at my face. "I wouldn't put you a day over thirty-four."

My laugh bursts out of me, and I have to smother it with my hand when some of the fighters look to me with curious eyes. Coach has already schooled his expression by the time they do.

"So," he says after a minute. "Why so interested?"

I think about the first fight I ever watched on TV, when that spark of passion first ignited. I think about how I felt

8

watching it, how amazed I was that a sport like this even exists. How I remember thinking...I want to try that. I want to experience that kind of excitement.

How do I explain any of that?

But instead of explaining that a life of routine and safety has made me desperate to feel some kind of safe, inexpensive high, I just grin and say, "Because if I'm going to get in a fight, I might as well be good at it."

2

COACH

It takes me a second to look away from my new student. We've had plenty of overeager people sign up at the gym, but there's something about Skylar that makes me want to understand her motivation.

"Am I allowed to watch the advanced class for a little bit?"

Even with the little I know about her, I'm not surprised that she asks. Normally, I would say no. This is the invite-only fighter-specific training session, and I don't need students trying out the advanced stuff I teach before they've reached the correct level of skill. And if Tristan were here, I would definitely say no, as his status in the UFC guarantees that I need to keep his training private. But Tristan's training at the boxing gym tonight, and Skylar's expression is so hopeful that I find I don't *want* to deny her.

"I don't want to see you try any of this on your own," I say brusquely. "These are advanced moves that need to be practiced safely. This is just to watch."

Her nod is quick. And the smile taking over her face makes me feel good about my decision.

I point toward the chairs on the far side of the room where they're lined up along the mat. "Take a seat, and I don't want to hear a peep from you while I'm teaching."

"Yes, Coach," comes her bubbly reply. And then she's hurrying around the mat to take her place in one of the seats.

"Alright, we're doing offense versus defense drills today," I call out to my fighters, forcing my attention back to the class. "Partner up. We're starting with boxing."

My fighters separate into pairs, and as I wait for them to ready for the round, I chance a glance back at Skylar. She's riveted by the class; there's no other way to describe her expression. It doesn't even look like she's breathing.

What *is* it with this girl?

We get a lot of different kinds of people signing up at the gym, for a variety of reasons. Some want to fight, some want to get healthier, a lot want to learn a new sport. I make it a point to talk to every new student, not just to keep my finger on the pulse of my gym, but to also understand people's motivations. It helps me cultivate the kind of environment and program that people want.

But looking at Skylar... I have no idea why she's here. I believe she's always wanted to try the sport, but there's something deeper driving her level of excitement.

I study her for a moment. Based on the backpack full of books, she's clearly young, though she doesn't carry herself that way. But it's her appearance that I let myself take in.

The red hair is the first thing I noticed when she walked in. Then when she looked at me, my attention went straight to those green eyes, the spattering of freckles over her creamy skin, the sparkle of excitement that lit her gaze as she looked around the gym. She's skinny enough that I don't think she has much muscle on her, or has ever done any kind of sport, but that didn't stop her through Jax's intro class. She put everything she had into every move.

Which takes my brain right back to wondering why she's so into this, while also being impressed.

"Coach, you gotta hit the timer."

Aiden's voice breaks through my thoughts. When I turn to look at him, his grin is shameless as always.

"Just for that, Reeves, we're going no timer today."

The entire gym groans at the knowledge that there will be no end in sight to these rounds. That they'll only be over when I say they are.

I don't miss one of the fighters, Remy, punching Aiden in the arm way harder than necessary. But I do ignore his yelp and the glare he sends her in return.

"Get to work. I'll tell you when to stop."

I watch the pairs as they start to work the drill. Walking around the gym, I make small adjustments here and there, giving everyone at least one thing to work on, but not more than that. Teaching is a delicate balance of instruction. Not too much commentary, not too little. Not too harsh, but also not too soft.

"Remy, your combos look good, but you're waiting too long between them. Pick up the urgency."

"Max, I want you to work on your footwork the entire class. Your sole focus today should be on not staying glued to the same spot. Move more."

"Lucy, I see you've been working on that cross. Nice work. Keep it up."

Only when I see everyone improve on my instructions do I call the end of the round and have them switch roles. And then we do it all over again.

The class becomes a blur, just as it always does. I've been teaching for almost two decades and I can't remember a time that I *didn't* get completely sucked into a lesson. I started teaching because it was an easy way to train for free —teach in exchange for a free membership—but at some point, I fell in love with helping others achieve their goals. And when I quit fighting, it was a healthy way to keep my love for the sport alive.

By the time the two hours are up, we're all exhausted— the fighters physically, me mentally.

I disappear into my office to finish some admin work while the fighters clean themselves up after their workout. It doesn't take long for the gym to empty completely. When it finally does, I quickly shower and change into street clothes. Then I take an Uber to my favorite cigar bar in the city.

My friend Pete is already waiting for me when I arrive. As soon as I climb the steps to the second-floor lounge, I see him sitting on one of the couches.

"Hey, man," I greet with a fist bump. Nodding toward the cigar in his hand, I take my coat off and settle in the seat across from him. "What'd you pick?"

He studies the dark cigar. "I went with the Perdomo Champagne Noir today. It's not bad."

Just then, the waitress appears next to our table. "Can I get you something to drink, sir? Or do you need help picking a cigar?"

"I'll have an El Dorado 21, one rock." I glance at Pete's cigar. "And I'll take the same cigar."

The girl smiles and nods. "Very well. I'll be right back with those for you."

Pete watches her walk away. "One of these days she's going to get tired of waiting for you to ask her out."

I huff a laugh. "She should already be tired of waiting. It's been weeks."

"Remind me again why you won't go for her?" he asks, moving his focus back to me.

My sigh is heavy. "I don't know, I just don't think I'm a relationship guy. Last time I tried, it blew up in my face."

Pete lets out a snort. "I didn't say to marry the girl, I'm just saying you could ask her out for a drink."

I shrug. "Even that. I've got so much other stuff going on, I don't really *want* to go on any dates."

"So you're just going to live out your days as a bachelor?"

Another shrug. "I like being single. Seems stupid to disrupt my life when I've already got everything I want."

He looks skeptical of my answer, which doesn't surprise me—Pete is happily married with two kids. But I'm not lying. I got married because after five years of dating my ex-wife, marriage felt like the obvious next step. And when it fell apart, not only did it feel natural to settle into single life, but I *liked* it. I could focus all my energy on fighting, and then on opening the gym. I could create exactly the kind of life that *I* wanted to live, with my dog by my side as my best friend.

Why would I want to change anything about that?

When the waitress appears with my drink and cigar, I look her over as inconspicuously as possible. She's young, very pretty, and very obviously giving me bedroom eyes. Pete's right, I could definitely have her under me at the end of the night.

But I don't feel any desire for it. Yeah, it'd be fun to get her off, but whether or not that happens, I'm still sleeping alone, and I'm still going to wake up excited to get back to my daily life.

"Thanks," I tell the waitress, not meeting her eyes and not letting our fingers touch when I take the cigar from her. I can sense the moment her smile droops.

Pete's chuckling when she walks away. "One of these days some girl is going to turn your whole life on its head."

I take a few puffs on the cigar to get it started. "She better not. It took me a long time to build the life I have. I'd like to keep it that way."

He's still shaking his head when I change topics. "So what's going on with you? How's the gym?"

He doesn't balk at the deflection. Talking business is one of the reasons we get together like this, and although we won't admit it out loud, we both look forward to it every month. "Gym's good. I've got a few guys competing in Worlds next month, so I'm pushing them hard." A grin stretches across his face. "Do you remember when you, me, and Sean did Worlds when we first got our black belts? All three of us cramped in that shitty little motel room because we were dead broke?"

I huff a laugh at the memory. "Worst sleep I ever got. *But* I did get that big win against Rivera, so I can't exactly complain."

Pete chuckles. "Hard to believe that was ten years ago. Our lives were so different."

My agreement is only a silent nod, but his voice takes on an excited edge. "No, but seriously, think about it. We used to *dream* about doing this shit as a career. Opening a gym, training all day—actually making money with it. And I don't know about you, but I thought this was a pipe dream."

"Honestly, I did too," I mumble.

"And now you've got a guy in the UFC, and I've got so many students, I had to move into a bigger building to fit them all—twice. Everything that we dreamt our twenties, we made happen. How crazy is that?"

I let out a heavy breath, absorbing Pete's words. I've had my head down working as hard as I can for so long that sometimes I forget to look at how far I've come. What I've built with blood and sweat and tears.

How proud I am of what I've built.

"Yeah," I breathe. "It's crazy."

3

SKYLAR

"Okay, class, that's it for today. Remember, midterm review starts next week!"

I hurry to type out one last note from the lesson before closing my iPad and packing up my bag. Since I always sit toward the front of the class, it's easy to push my way to the professor before anyone else. He seems to be expecting me when I appear in front of his desk.

"Hi, Skylar. What can I help you with?"

I adjust the books in my arms. "I was hoping to ask you for a recommendation, sir."

He quirks an eyebrow. "To medical school?"

I swallow roughly to clear my suddenly dry throat. *If only.* "No, for the university's RN program."

He hums a non-answer, the sound almost disappointed.

"You'll make an incredible nurse, Skylar," he says, thankfully saving me the painful moment of explaining—or lying about—*why* I chose the nursing path. "I'm always happy to write a recommendation for someone who I think will make the healthcare world a better place. Especially with your passion."

I give him a grateful smile. "Thank you, sir. I really appreciate it."

"When do you need it by?"

"Any time this month would be great."

"I'll have it for you by midterms," he responds, straightening the papers on his desk. But then he looks up and meets my eyes. "By the way, have you decided what you're going to write your research paper about?"

"I'm going to write about the specific effects that Parkinson's disease has on younger brains, and the treatments that current studies are pursuing," I answer automatically.

His eyes widen slightly. "That doesn't seem like it took you long to decide."

I don't answer. *Because it didn't.*

He studies me for another moment, and I start to wonder if he can see right through me. If he can read my truth between the lines. About medical school, about this assignment—about everything.

Instead, his attention drops back to his papers. "Well, I look forward to reading it. Who knows, maybe you could use parts of it for an admissions essay."

My brow furrows. There is no essay for nursing programs, only for—

I once again shove down the idea of medical school. I don't have the time, and I can't afford it, so even the thought of it doesn't belong on the table.

"I really appreciate you writing a rec for me, Professor," I say. "Just let me know if you have any questions about it. Otherwise, I'll see you in class on Thursday?"

He doesn't react to my abrupt change of tone, just nods his answer. "I'll see you Thursday, Skylar."

Despite the conversation with my professor being a positive one, I feel a little empty when I settle on a couch in the quad. It's rare that I question the path I've chosen for my career, but I guess today is one of those days.

I wish Dad was still here to talk to. He would've helped me pick the right path.

When I hear a chuckle, I startle. "I *thought* that was you chatting with Teach. Let me guess, you were asking for an extra-credit assignment."

Looking up, I see one of my classmates standing beside me. "Hey, Craig. No, I just wanted to pick his brain about something. Are you ready for midterms?"

He ignores my question and takes a seat beside me, stretching his arm along the back of the couch and making himself comfortable. As his fingers brush against my shoulder, I shift subtly so we're not touching.

"I can't *wait* for this semester to be over," he groans. "I'm ready to move into the frat house and spend my mornings doing wake and bakes instead of taking shitty 8 a.m. English classes. I mean, I know we *have* to take all the bullshit GenEd courses, but God...when am I ever going to need to know why John Milton wrote *Paradise Lost*?"

I don't answer him. I rarely see life the way that Craig does, which includes how he views college. Where he sees it as a chore, I see it as a privilege. Which I know isn't his fault, or mine. It's just another reason why I struggle to relate to my peers.

As a kid, my after-school hours were spent with nurses and doctors and sometimes our seventy-year-old neighbor lady. So even surrounded by kids in my grade, it never came with the option to deepen any of those friendships once the bell dismissed us for the day. And that only continued into my teenage years.

I just... I don't know how to have conversations with people my own age *now*. It also explains why Craig is pretty much my only friend, despite these near-constant awkward moments.

"You should rush Greek life," Craig continues, oblivious to my desire for him to leave. He sends me a big grin and adds, "I bet sororities would kill to recruit you. You'd be like the perfect magnet to bring the frats in. I swear, Sky, you look better every day."

I manage a tight smile. "Aw, thanks, Craig. The dark circles really bring out my green eyes, don't you think?"

"You look more fit, too," he says, completely ignoring my efforts to joke my way out of an increasingly uncomfortable conversation. It's rare that anyone takes the time to hit on me, and Craig has never been one of them. "Did you start a new workout routine?"

"Yeah, kinda," I respond carefully, shifting a little farther away on the bench.

He perks up with interest. I should've known talking about the gym would be the thing to steer him back to safer territories. As a personal trainer, Craig *loves* talking about the gym.

"What're you doing? If you picked up a trainer that's not me, my feelings are going to be hurt, Sky."

I swallow my laugh. "No, of course not. Actually, I started doing MMA."

His interest turns to confusion. "What, like karate?"

"No, it's jiu-jitsu and Muay Thai."

"Muay—what? What is that?"

Excitement bleeds into my voice; I can't help it. "It's like kickboxing, only way cooler because it uses knees and elbows. And jiu-jitsu is like wrestling mixed with chess."

Craig doesn't match my excitement. "What's the point of that? That doesn't really sound like a workout."

My lips purse slightly in annoyance. "Of course it's a

workout. I can barely move my arms and legs after the classes. And I'm doing it because it's fun."

Craig still looks baffled. And honestly, I'm kind of baffled by *his* reaction. I always thought MMA was the coolest sport ever, how could someone *not* be interested in it?

But clearly, Craig is done with this topic. His focus drifts away from me and toward the people walking by us. "You should stick with lifting, it's way better for you."

I clench my jaw to hold back from snapping at him that he's an idiot. "I'll keep that in mind."

"Seriously, if you ever want someone to work out with, or even to write your workout plan for you, you know who to call." He looks back at me with a grin. "I wouldn't mind spotting you. It'd be like a fun little date."

And that's enough for me. I stand from my seat and sling my backpack over my shoulder—life's too short to waste time on this. I don't even look at him as I say, "I appreciate the selfless offer. I have to get going. I'll see you for midterm reviews next week."

"Yeah." But something must have made him brave today, because then he adds, "If you want someone to study with this weekend, give me a call."

"You got it," I respond stiffly. "See you around, Craig."

I cross campus toward the bus stop that will get me to the gym. I don't even care that I'm almost an hour early for my class—even sitting outside the gym doors waiting for them to open would be better than listening to some guy shit on something that brings me joy.

But when I reach the gym, it's not locked. There's nothing on the schedule for 4 p.m., but as I walk through the doors, I see Coach sparring with Kane.

Standing in the doorway with my jaw on the ground, I can only stare in complete shock at the scene before me.

I've seen plenty of fights on TV. With many different sizes of men, strategies, and endings. But I have *never* witnessed something like this.

It's not just that I'm watching two large grown men trying to hurt each other. It's not even that they're both so fast, and their shots so powerful—when the punches land, I swear I can feel the impact reverberate through my own body. Neither is going easy on the other; they're both genuinely trying to win. But that's not what has me staring, unable to formulate any thoughts, unable to make an escape before they notice I'm here.

They're shirtless and drenched in sweat. They both look like models in their own way, shiny with oil and ready to step onto the cover of GQ. And directly into reader fantasies.

Kane looks like the bad boy that every good girl wants, covered in tattoos and with a look on his face that says he'll kill anything standing in his path. He's not usually my type, but I can't deny that he's insanely attractive right now.

But Coach... Jesus, he might be the hottest thing I've ever seen.

I'd never guess he isn't the same age as Kane. He's absolutely shredded, to the point that I can't decide if I'm more drawn to his strong arms, broad chest, or the washboard abs. I'd probably have a different answer every time. The only thing that *might* make me think he's older—besides the dusting of dark chest hair that I like way more than I ever thought I would—is the fact that he doesn't have a single tattoo inked onto his skin. In MMA nowadays, that's basically nonexistent. But beyond that, nothing about him screams *thirty-six-year-old*. Even his speed and power can keep up with Kane.

It isn't until my attention finally drifts to his face that I see his age.

It's the beard and facial hair, yes, but mostly it's the wisdom in his eyes and the patience in his expression. He's not attacking Kane in the same desperate way that his fighter is coming after him. He's clearly relying on his experience and technical knowledge, and beating Kane with his smarts rather than his physical abilities.

And he *is* beating Kane. It's slight, but Coach is edging out Kane with the number of shots landed.

I don't know how long I stand there and stare. Normally, I'd be fascinated by the fight itself, analyzing the techniques and trying to see the strategy behind them, but for the life of me I can't tear my gaze away from *him*. From his rippling muscles, the sweat sliding down his skin, the primal feel of his movements. I'm so mesmerized by the sight before me that my body heats and my breaths come quicker, and—

The shrill sound of the bell snaps me out of my haze. I'm essentially stuck in quicksand as the guys bump gloves, because I haven't moved an inch by the time they notice me.

Coach's brow furrows. "Skylar? What are you doing here?"

"I'm sorry," I blurt out. I feel like a deer caught in the headlights—if the deer felt true attraction for the first time in its life. "I didn't mean to interrupt. I know I'm early, and that the gym isn't technically open, but the door was unlocked, and I was coming in to ask if it was okay to—"

"Skylar," he interrupts. "It's okay, we're done. I didn't realize I had left the door unlocked. Not your fault." Turning toward Kane, he tells his fighter, "I want you to finish up with ten minutes with the weighted jump rope and fifty sit-ups on the incline bench. You'll spar again on Saturday, but after that, we're doing bag work and conditioning only until the fight. Got it?"

Kane nods his acknowledgement, then turns and stalks toward the heavy bag room.

Leaving me with a shirtless and sweaty coach.

"I really am sorry for interrupting." *Where on earth is this nervousness coming from?*

Dominic—*Coach*—turns to me as he starts to unwrap his gloves, holding my gaze. And when he lifts one of them to his mouth and bites into the leather so he can pull it off, I swear my heart stops beating.

"Skylar, it's fine." He tugs the other glove off. "Excited to train again?"

I'm too flustered by the sight of him to do anything but nod.

Tossing his gloves to the side, he moves over to the sidelines where his water bottle is. I try not to watch as he chugs it, but that becomes next to impossible when some of it drips from his lips. My attention zeroes in on the water drop as it slides down his neck and chest.

"Which class do you like better?" he asks, reaching into his gym bag again. "Muay Thai or jiu-jitsu?"

"Uh...I don't know. I can't pick."

When he straightens, his expression is amused. "You're not even *trying* to pick a favorite."

"Of course I'm not trying. That's like picking a favorite kid."

He chuckles, shaking his head. And I shouldn't feel as bummed as I do when I realize he's pulled a shirt out of his bag.

I bid a silent farewell to his beautifully toned, sweat-drenched muscles as he quickly tugs it over his head.

"Seeing you excited makes me remember why I started coaching," he muses.

I focus back on his face, hoping he didn't catch me ogling. "Why's that?"

His eyes lock with mine. "To make people love the sport as much as I do and to help them achieve all of their goals within it."

Admiration twines with attraction. I knew when I signed up that I was going to be learning from someone with a lot of knowledge, but seeing that Coach cares just as much about his students' successes as they do is special.

Our eye contact snaps when the sound of leather hitting a heavy bag starts up. Coach's attention travels to the other room, then back to me. "If you want to get started early, you can warm up out here. I'm teaching class tonight."

He waits for my nod of affirmation, then walks to the other side of the room to grab a foam roller. Lying down on the mat, he starts to massage his muscles, effectively ending our conversation.

Which is just as well, because the sight of him flipping onto his front and rolling out his quads, his hips moving in a thrusting motion, has my mouth drying and any coherent thoughts leaving my mind.

4

COACH

I don't let myself talk to her, but I still watch Skylar out of the corner of my eye.

I'm not surprised that she's early, given how late she stayed the other day. There's something about her genuine excitement that has me wanting to make sure she meets every single one of her goals. I wasn't lying to her when I said that's the best part of being a coach—and I'm entirely certain that helping *Skylar* meet hers would be that much more satisfying.

I continue to wonder about her reasons for being here as I roll out my hamstrings. She sets out her gear on one of the chairs in my peripheral, taking a final swig of water before stepping onto the mat. At the last second, she decides to take off her sweatshirt.

As she pulls it over her head, her clothes underneath start to go with it. Whatever she's wearing rides up her taut stomach, all the way up until the edge of her purple sports bra is visible.

My blood heats from the sight of her exposed skin.

I hurriedly turn away. It's not that I'm opposed to people

training or walking around shirtless—plenty of the traditional gyms have that rule, but I pride myself on making sure my fighters feel comfortable. I've heard horror stories about girls being made to fight in their sports bra by their coach, or being forced to strip down almost completely for weigh-ins. Being a girl in this sport is undeniably harder than being a guy. So I've always ensured that I'm the respectful old man they can count on, not run away from. It's the same reason I put a shirt on when Skylar came in— even though pulling the fabric over a layer of sweat is making me want to scratch every inch of my skin.

Giving up on my last stretch, I stand from the mat and head into my office. Whether it's Skylar seeing me shirtless or me seeing *her*, I need to put some distance between us. She hasn't even been here two weeks, and I'm already thinking about her more than any of my other students.

I busy myself for the next fifteen minutes. It isn't until I hear the gym filling with students that I leave my hideaway and venture back into the mat room for the Muay Thai class I'm about to teach.

I look around for Lucy, since she's the one who helps me with the beginners, and spot her working with Skylar.

Lucy's lips move with instructions, and Skylar follows them. They're standing in front of the mirrored wall so Skylar can watch herself as she goes through the motions. The pair seem to be comfortable working together.

"Coach."

I pull my attention away from the girls and focus on Kane.

"All done?" I ask him.

He nods. "Thanks for giving me some extra work today. And for fitting me in early."

"Of course. I'm happy to do it. You feel good?"

Another nod, but the look in his eyes is distant. "Yeah, I feel strong."

I quirk an eyebrow. "That's not what I asked."

When he looks directly at me, I watch as the wall over his expression drops.

When Kane first signed up here, that wall was a thousand feet tall and made of steel. It never moved, could never be breached. For the longest time, we had no idea who Kane really was behind it. It was how he kept the whole world out, us included.

Nowadays, he lets us see more on a regular basis.

I see him now. I see that his self-assured front was a partial lie, because there's fear, and nervousness, and uncertainty in his eyes as he stands before me. He's got a fight next week, and if having an old, shitty teammate for his opponent wasn't enough, this is also his first fight since he's changed his mentality. It used to be kill-or-be-killed, but in the past few months, he's learned to see the beauty in the sport. It doesn't surprise me that it's having an effect on his preparation.

"I feel good," he confirms, honestly this time. "It just feels weird going in with no injuries and an actual strategy."

I clap him on the back with a chuckle. "Welcome to being a real fighter."

Kane lets out a huff, which is as close to laughter as I've seen from him.

"Go home," I tell him. "Go see your girl, take a night off. You've earned it."

That gets me a look of obvious gratitude. And it strikes me that being on the receiving end of a look like that, from a man like Kane, feels just as good as any win I ever had as a fighter.

"Alright, if you're here for Muay Thai, I want you lined

up on the mat," I call out, clapping my hands together. "Let's get class started."

I lead the class through this week's drills, separating them into pairs within intermediate and advanced groups. Lucy takes the new students into the cage.

I keep my focus on the groups I'm coaching, but occasionally I feel it drifting back to Lucy's group.

Besides Skylar, there are two young guys in the beginner group, both moving as if they've done plenty of sports before. They're muscular and have not only the strength but the gracefulness of athletes. The punches they're throwing are perfectly acceptable for first timers.

And yet, their movements are lazy. They're relying on their athleticism, and not really trying to make the adjustments that Lucy is calling for.

On the other hand, Skylar is trying ten times harder and honing in on technique instead of power. She doesn't have the same fluidity that the guys have, but she's hanging on Lucy's every word and tweaking her punches after each one. Between her first class and this third one, she's gotten exponentially better.

I can confidently say I'd take a student like Skylar over the guys any day.

The timer sounds out, signaling the end of the round.

My attention drifts back to her a few more times over the course of the class. But because I'm looking at Skylar, I start to notice something about Lucy. She keeps wincing and rubbing her head.

We only have ten minutes left, so I decide to wait until the end before I separate her from the students and ask, "Lucy, what's with your head?"

I half expect her to play it off. But if there was any doubt about the severity of her injury, it disappears in a wisp of smoke when she gives me a no-bullshit answer.

"I'm not sure," she admits quietly. Her hand reaches up to rub her temple. "I just can't get rid of this headache."

"How long have you had it?"

She shrugs. "It's been coming and going for a couple days."

"Anything different in your life? Diet? Stress levels? Did you stop drinking coffee?"

"Nothing's out of the ordinary," she says on a heavy sigh, her shoulders dropping in defeat. "I mean, I'm not at fight camp level, but my diet's pretty clean and I'm not any more stressed than usual." She winces again and reaches for her head. "I don't know what it could be. I thought it might be a concussion, but I've never thrown up after sparring. And I've never been knocked out."

"It could still be a concussion," I tell her. "Those are the worst and most obvious tells, but there are plenty of other, smaller signs, too." I study Lucy for a moment, knowing she has to be done for the day. "Why don't you take some time off, anyway. Drink a lot of water, no sugar, and get some sleep. I'll check back with you next week."

She nods, looking miserable. Telling a fighter to take time off is the last thing any of them want to hear, but their safety comes first.

"I don't want to interrupt, but I might be able to help," comes a soft voice from behind me. I turn to see Skylar stepping closer to us and give her a questioning look. "Does anything else feel like it's changed physically?" she asks Lucy. "Any dizziness, grogginess, problems sleeping—?"

"I *have* been waking up in the middle of the night lately," Lucy says thoughtfully. "I don't usually have issues sleeping seven hours straight."

Skylar nods, as if Lucy just confirmed something for her. "Anything else feel different?"

Lucy slants a nervous look my way. "It's nothing big, but...I feel like I've had some trouble remembering things. I've never had the best memory, but I had a few moments this week where I completely blanked."

Skylar turns to me. "She's concussed. And I know you have no reason to listen to the new girl who just interrupted your conversation, but I've got a lot of experience with this kind of stuff." She looks at Lucy and adds, "There's no 'cure' for a concussion, but I can give you some exercises that will help it heal."

Lucy looks surprised, but not skeptical. "Like physical therapy?"

Skylar nods. "Exactly like physical therapy. The brain is a muscle, so you have to work it out to get it back to peak physical condition." She glances at the clock on the wall. "I can run you through a few now, if you have some time."

"Weren't you going to take jiu-jitsu?" Lucy asks.

Skylar waves it off. "I can take jiu-jitsu anytime."

Compared to how badly she obviously wants to train, she just gave up the opportunity for it without any hesitation, all for someone she doesn't even know.

Respect outshines my fascination for my new student.

"Okay then," Lucy answers. "Thanks, Skylar. I really appreciate it."

"Don't even mention it," Skylar says with a smile. Then she faces me again and asks, "You're okay if I do this? I don't want to assume you don't know how to treat a concussion, but if I can help in any way—"

"Skylar," I interrupt. "I'm never going to be anything less than appreciative of you helping a teammate. Because I *don't* know how to treat a concussion. We're still catching up on TBI knowledge in this sport. Back in my day, I'm pretty sure our coaches didn't believe concussions were even a thing." I check the time. "I have to start jiu-jitsu class, otherwise I would listen in. But maybe you and I could chat about it another time. I'd love to hear what you know about it."

Skylar smiles. "Of course. Whenever you'd like, I'd be happy to share."

"Good. Do what you need to, then. And let me know if I can help with anything."

I leave the two girls and step back onto the mat for class. Between demonstrating the moves and it being more packed than normal, I can't pay much attention to Skylar's exercises, much as I'd like to. The most I can do is glance over at them a few times and try to make sense of what they're doing. Once, I see Lucy moving her head from side to side, slowly at first, then quicker, until eventually she winces and stops the motion. Skylar has her do it again, this time moving her head up and down.

Once I realize my student pairs have all figured out the drill and are simply going through repetitions for the rest of the round, I take the opportunity to cross the room and catch the tail end of Skylar's instruction.

"Those three exercises where you got a headache? Do those every day for a few minutes, just until you have a slight headache. Not a bad one, just somewhere around a 3-4 on the 10 pain scale. Slight pain represents muscle soreness, which is why we don't want actual pain. But each day you should be able to do them for longer without getting a headache. That's how you help a concussion heal." She gives Lucy a look that's reminiscent of a parent scolding their child. "The worst thing you can do with a concussion is get another one before it's healed, so don't brush this off.

Do the exercises, take it easy, and stop anything that makes your head hurt."

"Which means no sparring," I interject.

"Obviously," Lucy says with an eye roll that screams *thanks, Dad.*

But then she looks at Skylar and sobers. "So how do you know all of this? You have doctors in your family or something?"

Sadness flashes through Skylar's expression. But it's there and gone so fast, I wonder if I imagined it.

"Oh, you know, I'm just your typical overachiever," she jokes. "I had a professor I wanted to impress last semester, so I read the brain chapter a few times."

I don't know if Lucy buys it, or if she just senses Skylar's evasion of the question, but she nods and reaches for her gym bag.

"Alright, doc, I've got my orders: three exercises every day. I'm going to head home and get some sleep." She grins at me. "Get it? *Head* home?"

I roll my eyes right back, but there's a smile tugging at my lips. "Your dad jokes are getting worse. Go home, Lucy."

"Yessir," she says with another grin. But right before she turns around to leave, she snaps her fingers and says to Skylar, "Oh, I meant to ask. You're coming to Kane's fight this weekend, right?"

Another smile hiding a glimmer of sadness. "I can't, I have to work."

"Come *on*, you should come! The whole gym will be there. It's so much fun."

Skylar hesitates for another half-second, but then blurts out, "Okay, I'll see if I can get off work," and then immediately looks shocked by her own answer.

Lucy's too excited to notice. "Great! When you get your

ticket, make sure you tell them you're with Bulldog MMA. We get a whole section to ourselves." Skylar still looks stunned as she only nods.

"Alright, that's enough from the welcoming committee," I interrupt, clapping my hands together. Lucy sends me a grin that shows just how pleased she is with herself. "You, get out of here. Go rest up."

With a final salute my way, Lucy's out the door. As soon as we're alone, I'm facing Skylar and asking, "Do you still want to take class? I can fill you in on what you missed after."

She chews on her lower lip in thought. "Tonight's the one night I have to get home early, unfortunately, but I appreciate the offer."

I hate doing privates, and I *never* offer them. Yet it feels effortless to say, "Another time, then."

Her eyes brighten when she smiles. As she holds my gaze, something inexplicable moves between us. "Another time, then."

5

COACH

Later that week, I'm sitting in my office when I hear the sounds of fight footage right outside of my door. It's not an uncommon sound, so at first, I ignore it. But then the commentators catch my attention.

"Jamal really needs to start defending those leg kicks, John. He may have won the first round, but this round Dominic is stepping up his pressure. I don't know how much more of this Jamal's leg can take."

Frowning, I stand from my desk and walk out of my office. I find Skylar sitting on the couch in the reception area, an iPad in her lap.

"What're you watching?" I ask before I can think better of it.

Skylar's head snaps up from the screen. When she realizes that I'm watching her, a wide grin splits her face. She lifts the iPad and turns it to face me.

And suddenly I'm watching a younger version of myself punching another guy in the face while the crowd goes wild.

I wince before I can smother it. Then I'm giving Skylar a blank stare and asking in a dry voice, "Seriously?"

She shrugs, her shameless grin still in place as she goes back to watching *my* fight.

I should be double-checking contracts. Organizing my business. Not staring at this girl who's so interested by an old fight of mine that she's silently mouthing the combos that my corner is calling for.

She hears something that makes her brow furrow. When she looks up at me again, she looks confused.

"What were you trying to do with the leg kicks?" she asks. "He's not really throwing punches, so I'm assuming the leg kicks weren't to stop his striking. Were you setting something up?"

I try to think back to my game plan for that fight, and how it ended up, but I can't for the life of me remember what my thought process was. "Start the round over," I instruct in a gruff voice as I settle on the couch beside her, a safe distance between us. She looks surprised, but does as I ask.

We watch the fight in silence for a few moments. "I was focusing on leg kicks because I wanted to throw him off of his takedown game," I explain eventually. I point at my opponent's stance on the screen. "He was going for double legs the entire first round, so all of his weight kept shifting forward onto his front leg. Every leg kick made him second guess another takedown, or even punches to *set up* a takedown."

Skylar nods in understanding, never taking her eyes off the action. "And what was *your* game plan going into the fight?" she asks.

"Tire him out. Wear him down. I knew I would be in better shape than him." She snorts at my answer.

"Look. See that?" I lean forward in anticipation of what's coming next. "He's reached the point where he's starting to get pissed. He can't get to his takedowns without getting hit, so he's trying to figure out what he'll need to sacrifice to get me to the ground."

"Holy shit," she breathes after a moment.

My grin breaks through as we watch one of my inside leg kicks force a stumble, enough to make Jamal trip forward so I can wrap an arm around his neck in a choke.

"That looks tight," she murmurs under her breath, leaning closer to the screen. She cocks her head and asks, "Wasn't Jamal known for his submissions, and for never getting submitted himself?"

Amused, I quirk an eyebrow. "Did you look *me* up for that information or him?"

Her cheeks pinken as she shrugs. "I wanted to know who I was learning from," she admits.

I chuckle, but decide not to tease her anymore. Instead, I wait for the inevitable end of the fight.

My choke tightens, until my corner starts yelling and Jamal squeaks in my hold. I think Skylar and I are both holding our breaths as we wait for Jamal's hand to twitch on my thigh. For him to tap.

And he does.

"Damn," Skylar says with a laugh. "You beat him with his own move."

"After he kept taking me down in the first, I told my corner between rounds that I was going to submit him with a guillotine if he kept doing it. My coach laughed in my face and told me to be serious, but I knew I could get it. I could feel it."

When she turns to finally look at me, I'm grinning from ear to ear. "You like talking about your fights, don't you?" she asks as her eyes search mine.

I shrug, trying to tamp down my rush of confidence from her curiosity. "The ones I won, sure."

"What about training?"

"To an extent," I admit. "Why, you have questions?"

"Always," she quips with a light laugh, almost to herself.

I debate going back to my office. I don't mind answering student questions about techniques, but I usually try to keep a solid line between coach and athlete in the gym. I don't want to invite friendship.

But then I think about how excited she looked watching my fight. And that eagerness is one of the best qualities any coach could ask for, which means I can't bring myself to move from this spot.

"Fine. Shoot."

"How was training different in your first few years?" she asks, the question bursting out of her like it's been waiting at the tip of her tongue. "What do you do differently now that you didn't do forty years ago?"

"Watch it," I growl. Her smile only grows.

I settle back against the couch, draping my arm along the back of it to get comfortable as I mull over her question.

"It's more brain, less brawn nowadays," I answer after a moment. "We used to spar three times a week back when I was fighting—if you could even call it that. It was more like a fight to the death. I'm surprised we didn't have more concussions and injuries than we did."

"You probably had plenty of concussions; you were just too stubborn to acknowledge them."

"And for jiu-jitsu, our training was completely different," I continue, bypassing her comment, even though it's probably true. "We do way more drilling and teaching nowadays. Back then, most of my time was spent live rolling. It was a learn-as-you-go kind of thing."

She's wide-eyed as she tries to imagine it. "That...sounds bizarre. There were no classes?"

"We had classes, just not as many as we have now. But beyond that, our new moves came from stumbling upon them during live rolls, or having our teammates share something they picked up somewhere. There was no internet, no YouTube where we could research a technique by looking up a tutorial. I used to have to rent VHS tapes of old matches and watch them over and over again to try to pinpoint the details. No one except our main coach was breaking down moves the way I break them down for you guys."

She's silent, mulling over the picture I just painted for her. I never really stopped to think about how much the game has changed in the twenty years I've been in it, so I'm a little lost in the memories right now, too.

It means I don't expect it when she asks, "What's a VHS tape?"

It takes me a second to drag my head back to reality. And then another.

"Are you serious?"

For a moment, we only stare at each other. Her expression is one of confusion, whereas mine is one of shock. Shock at my own age, at what her question signifies, at the difference in our general life experience.

I think I'm on the verge of an existential crisis when I see the corner of her lip twitch.

She's fucking with me.

"Smartass," I growl, though it sounds slightly impressed to my ears.

And she hears it, because her half-smirk blooms into a grin.

"You calling me old?" I ask.

She doesn't even flinch. "I would never disrespect my coach like that," she quips, looking every bit the troublemaker.

"You *are* a smartass," I repeat, reaching up to tug a strand of hair that's escaped her crazy post-training hair.

I don't even realize what I've done, until I hear Skylar suck in a startled breath at the touch. It hits me then I'm way too close to her, because there's no way I should be able to see the golden flecks in her eyes.

No reason I should want to find out how many there are.

I pull my hand back and awkwardly cough into it, then quickly stand from the couch and return to the reception desk. I have no idea what to say, or how to get back on topic. *What had she asked me?*

"So, what I'm hearing is..." Skylar says, and I let out a breath of relief. When I finally meet her eyes again, she looks completely normal, not uncomfortable at all—besides the slight color in her cheeks.

"That we should bow to you for your instruction?"

My lip twitches with a grin. "I'm saying you have no idea how much easier it is to consume the sport's technical knowledge nowadays." I pause for a second, nodding. "Also yes, you should be bowing to my greatness."

Her laugh rings out, and two things become clear to me...

One: I wish I could bottle that sound and play it on repeat.

And two: that's not a normal thought for a coach to have about their student.

6

SKYLAR

When I walk into the arena on Friday night, it's with a riot of emotions.

Not working tonight feels weird. I can't remember the last time I *didn't* work a Friday night. Normally, there's no way I call out of work, but then one of my coworkers asked to swap my shift tonight with her shift on St. Patrick's Day, and it was a no-brainer to accept. The fact that it opened up my night and made it possible to come to the fights tonight was just a bonus.

A very exciting bonus.

I look around the arena, taking in the bright lights and screaming fans. I'm early, so the fights haven't started yet, but that doesn't make this environment any less chaotic. There are plenty of people already waiting for the first fight of the night, loudly making their predictions and getting drunker with every beer. I can hear the sounds of shins hitting pads in the back, and can smell the oil fighters use for warming up muscles.

I watch the first three fights by myself, alone in the

section reserved for our gym, getting giddier with each one. I'm so lost in the back-and-forth of the fifth fight that I don't realize Lucy and Remy have appeared beside me until they call my name.

"Hey," I greet with a wide smile. "You're here!"

Remy gives me a contemplative look and then grins. "I remember my first fight, too. If you believe it, they actually get more exciting from here."

I laugh. "That obvious, huh?"

"Don't worry, it's cute," she says, taking a seat next to me. "So you're still enjoying training then? Lucy said you looked really good this week."

I aim a grateful smile at the blonde who's become a good friend in the gym. "She's being sweet. I know I'm not a natural or anything, but I appreciate the help. And yeah, I like it a lot. I don't know how anyone could *not* like it."

Remy chuckles as she puts her combat boots up on the empty seat in front of us. "You already sound like a lifer to me."

"Hopefully," I breathe. Looking past Remy to Lucy, I ask, "So how long have you two been training?"

"Six years for me," Lucy answers. "I got into it in high school because I liked the idea of punching guys in the face. Then I realized I was *good* at punching guys in the face and got addicted to fighting. I only fight Muay Thai, though. Jiu-jitsu takes away too much of the violence."

"Damn, Lucy," Remy grumbles, making me laugh. "Scare the new girl, why don't you?" She looks at me and hitches a thumb in her friend's direction. "She's a pussycat, don't worry."

I turn my attention to Remy. "What about you? How long you been doing this?"

She does some mental calculations. "Five-ish years. I got into it in college because Jax was obsessed with it." She answers my questioning look with, "I grew up with the giant. We've been copying each other since we were fifteen. Meeting Tristan at the gym was just a bonus." She frowns. "Or on some days, a punishment."

That prompts a chuckle from me. I *had* noticed her dynamic with Coach's right-hand man. Honestly, it was hard to miss. Those two were either snapping at each other and trying to tear each other apart, or eye-fucking across the gym. There didn't seem to be an in-between.

"And have you ever fought?" I press, curious to see if every dedicated student eventually picks up fighting.

Remy's shaking her head before I've even finished the question. "No way. I have no interest in getting in the cage. I like training because of the techniques, not because of the fight. I enjoy a good, hard sparring session as much as the next guy, but I'm perfectly happy without the stress of fighting. I've seen what Tristan goes through, and I have zero inclination to do any of that."

"Interesting," I say. "I kind of assumed everyone who got serious about the sport would eventually fight. It seems like it's natural to get pushed in that direction."

"Nah, no one's going to force fighting on you," Remy says, her gaze shifting toward the cage. "It's definitely the most common goal for people who sign up at the gym, but Coach will support any goal you come in with."

Suddenly, she straightens in her seat, dropping her feet to the ground.

"Speaking of fighting...Kane's up."

We zero in on the archway where fighters have been entering the arena. I realize the rest of the Bulldog MMA team has filled in the seats around us while we were chatting, but I only get a glimpse of how packed the section is now before the lights dim and the music starts playing loudly over the speakers.

Then, a spotlight shines on the archway, and Kane appears.

He walks down the path, going through the ref's last-minute checks, and then climbs into the cage.

He looks...calm.

"God, he's like a whole different human," I hear Remy comment after a minute. She glances at Lucy. "Do you remember his last fight? I thought we were about to witness a murder."

Lucy nods at the memory. "He definitely looks more composed. Question is, what's he going to do when he gets hit for the first time?"

The question hangs in the air as the rest of the fight preparations happen. Kane's opponent makes his entrance, a smirking, swaggering beast of a man who clearly doesn't view Kane as a challenge. Every time he meets Kane's eyes, his grin widens, and an unspoken message of *you're dead* crosses the cage.

Kane doesn't react to it. To anything. Where I would expect a fighter's nerves—or Kane's rage—he doesn't show a hint of anything. No fear, no excitement, no hunger for the violence. He's composed as he bounces on his feet and snaps out a few punches to stay warm, but his face is stone. Unreadable.

"That's his old teammate," Lucy tells me quietly. "Kane said he's got a huge ego, and he can unfortunately back it up. Even if he has to fight nasty—which he does." Her voice lowers even further. "I got the sense that he had a big problem with Kane. It's probably why he said yes to this fight so quickly."

"And also why there's no glove touch," Remy murmurs after neither fighter reaches to touch gloves in the center of the cage. Instead, they back up to their corners.

I take those few seconds before the fight starts as an opportunity to look over the Bulldog MMA team. Kane stands, ready to go, and behind him I can see Jax and Coach Dominic standing outside of the cage. Jax looks nervous, like he's about to jump out of his skin. But beside him, Coach just looks...determined. Confident in his fighter.

I think we're all holding our breaths when the bell rings to signal the start of the round. Kane's opponent, Chevlin, couldn't appear more arrogant if he tried. His hands are down, his strides forward are lazy, and that damn grin hasn't left his face.

He waits a few seconds before snapping a few punches out, trying to bait Kane into attacking first. But Kane just defends them and continues to circle, settling into his fighting stance.

Chevlin doesn't like that. His smirk falters, and his next few combos are thrown with ill intent. Still, Kane doesn't react.

"Coach said Chevlin used to do whatever he could to piss Kane off so he would start throwing," Lucy explains. "Once Kane's punches became wild, Chevlin would use it as an opportunity to take him down and submit him." Chewing on her lip, she adds, "His whole goal this fight is going to be to bait Kane into going crazy."

Just as she says that, Kane starts to throw back. We all watch with bated breath, the tension in the air stifling.

Chevlin's expression becomes one of absolute glee. He

waits for Kane to throw one combo, and then another, and on the third one, he counters it with a *hard* right hand to the chin.

The arena gasps as the shot lands flush. It doesn't wobble Kane, but the sound of the impact is enough to have Chevlin's corner screaming, the crowd cheering, and everyone in the Bulldog section holding our breath as we wait for Kane's reaction.

Only, he doesn't give one.

His movements stutter for half a second after the punch, but it seems more like a mental hiccup than a physical reaction to the shot. And then he goes right back to circling Chevlin and looking for his opening, throwing a few more punches of his own.

The lack of reaction clearly confuses Chevlin. His smirk is nowhere to be found, and his hands come up higher, as if he's suddenly realizing that he's underestimated Kane. That this isn't an opponent he can play with anymore.

It gives Kane the opening he needs. With Chevlin's hands up, and his attention focused on Kane's punches—albeit controlled—coming at him, the last thing he expects is a takedown. And that's exactly what happens.

Faking a punch, Kane shoots forward and wraps his arms around Chevlin's legs. He scoops them out from under him, making Chevlin land on his back with a resounding crash.

The crowd cheers, but no one is cheering as loudly as Kane's cornermen. Jax and Coach are *screaming*, looking like they might climb the cage soon.

Kane starts to rain punches down on Chevlin. His old teammate still looks stunned from the takedown, so his defense against the attack isn't very effective. He eats one, two, three shots to the face before the ref sidles closer and calls for him to protect himself.

Coach is yelling something. Kane's punches have become tinged with desperation, with *victory*, but somehow, Coach's words break through Kane's growing haze. And right as he goes to throw another punch, he changes tactics.

Instead of beating his old teammate by what would likely be a brutal knockout, Kane grabs a hold of Chevlin's arm, falls onto his back into an armlock, and forces the submission by straining his arm until he taps out with a cry.

The arena *explodes*.

Around me, the Bulldog team is on their feet, high fiving each other and screaming at their teammate's victory. I've never seen people so happy for another person's success in my life.

I let myself get swept up in the celebration. This is the most fun I've had in I can't remember how long.

My gaze catches on the scene inside the cage. At first, it's because Kane is standing over Chevlin with a completely blank expression, so I have no idea if he's about to curse him out or help him up.

But after a second's hesitation, Kane extends his hand to his old teammate.

A chill covers my skin. I don't know the tattooed fighter that well, but there's a sense of gravity in the moment that tells me just how important this is for him. And when Chevlin takes the offered hand and gets pulled to his feet, and I hear Kane's girlfriend Isabella let out a happy sob behind me, I know I'm witnessing something incredible right now.

Kane claps his opponent on the shoulder and murmurs something to him before walking back to his corner. Jax and Coach are already in the cage, and it's anyone's guess which one of them is happier about tonight. They're both practically vibrating with excitement, their faces stretched wide with matching grins.

But then Jax lets out a whoop and hoists his friend into the air. Even Kane can't stop himself from smiling, though it's followed by his lips moving to say something that looks suspiciously like *put me down, asshole.*

Then it's Coach's turn to congratulate his fighter. And I shouldn't be surprised that he doesn't say anything, doesn't even hug him. He simply grabs him by the neck and brings their foreheads together. A silent moment passes between the two men, pride emanating from Dominic and appreciation from Kane.

"And your winner, fighting out of the blue corner... *Kane Whitaker!*"

After another ear-splitting round of cheers, the Bulldog fighters can barely settle for long enough to listen to Kane's post-fight interview. When he finally steps out of the cage and looks around for our group, it's like a lid being popped off a shaken-up soda can.

You'd never guess this sport is an individual one, because with the way this team is cheering for Kane, you'd think *they* were the ones who won the belt.

Kane splits the crowd as he moves toward our group. It doesn't take him long to reach us, and it takes even less time for the congratulations and back claps to start.

"You did it! You fucking did it!"

"I knew you were going to get him with that submission."

"Did you see the look on his face when you took him down?"

Kane tries to return his teammates' accolades, but his responses are half-hearted. He only has eyes for his girlfriend.

When he finally reaches Isabella, he gives up on paying

attention to anyone else. He sweeps the beautiful dancer into his arms and buries his face in her neck.

She doesn't seem at all bothered by how sweaty he is, or the fact that they're the center of attention. Right now, those two seem like they're the only ones in this arena.

She wraps her arms around his neck and hugs him closer. It's barely a whisper, but I can hear her murmuring *I'm so proud of you* over and over again. Kane's grip around her waist tightens at the words.

When I feel a presence beside me, I look away from the couple's intimate moment and find Coach standing beside me. He's got a hint of a smile on his lips as he looks at Kane, and then at his other fighters who are still excitedly chattering away around him.

"You look like a proud dad," I comment with a smile of my own.

He lets out a sound of agreement. "Some days I feel like one. I don't know what it's like to have kids of my own, but I want to imagine it feels something like this."

Warmth blossoms in my chest. *He's such a good coach.*

"They love you, too, you know," I tell him quietly, so no one else can hear. I might be overstepping my brand-new boundaries, but I'm a firm believer that people should be told they're loved and appreciated as often as possible.

"They're a good group." He sends a glance my way, smiling fondly. "We're lucky to have you be a part of it."

That warmth spreads to every piece of my soul that's been cooled for so long. Being a part of something I love— being a part of it with *these* people—is bringing me alive in a way I didn't know was possible.

Coach's expression softens when he sees mine. But he doesn't comment on it, just squeezes my hand with the tiniest, quickest touch and says, "I'm glad you came out tonight, Skylar."

My hand is still tingling when he turns and walks away. I knew when I signed up at the gym that Coach Dominic is a talented, respectable coach, but I never thought about who he might be outside of that label.

And as I watch him leave, I wonder if I'm entirely unprepared for the type of *man* he is.

7

SKYLAR

If I thought I was hyped about training before, it's nothing compared to how I feel on the Monday after the fights. Between Kane's lightning-quick takedown and the knockout that ended the main event, I'm itching to get back in the gym to practice those moves.

My night starts with the cardio kickboxing class, which has me depleting my restless energy. By the end of the forty-five-minute bag work class, I've completely sweat through my shirt and my legs shake from the exertion.

Still, it's not enough to keep me from taking jiu-jitsu. Or from ducking away to the heavy bag room after so I can work on the techniques from the fights. I move over to the open mat space beside the heavy bags to start with Kane's takedown.

Taking up a wrestling stance, I shoot forward for the takedown, lowering one knee to get low as I mimic wrapping up someone's legs. But even doing it by myself, I can tell I'm not low enough. I make sure my knee touches the ground as I shoot forward during my next rep.

Unfortunately, I end up almost faceplanting in the process. I barely catch myself with my hands on the mat.

I let out a huff of annoyance. But then I'm back up and trying it again.

And again, I'm falling forward at the end of it.

"It's because you're leaning forward."

I spin toward the door and see Coach at the top of the steps, leaning against the doorframe with his arms crossed.

My cheeks burn instantly. Partly because I'm embarrassed he caught me messing up, but also because I'm suddenly very aware of the fact that I look like a hot mess. I'm drenched in sweat and my hair probably looks like a bird set up shop in it. Yet there he stands, like he just walked out of a Sports Illustrated photoshoot.

Seriously, who looks like that after a two-hour workout?

"It's the most common mistake people make and the hardest thing to adjust when you're doing double leg takedowns," he says as he starts down the steps. "The good news is, once you get a feel for how it *should* be done, it'll feel natural."

"I don't think anything feels natural in this sport," I murmur.

The corner of his lip twitches. "Hasn't stopped you yet."

I let out a heavy sigh. "I know but it's incredibly irritating."

His full grin appears. "Come on, I'll help you fix it. Get in your stance."

I do as he says, feeling the heat of his presence when he stops beside me on the mat.

God, I hope I don't fall on my face again.

"You have to slow the move down. You're trying everything too fast," he says. "When you step forward, drop your knee down to the mat. Step, knee, then swing your other foot around the side to stand up. Focus on not leaning forward." Taking up his own fight stance beside me, he demonstrates the move.

I suck in a deep breath. *Step, knee, swing the other leg around. Got it.*

Forcing myself to go slow, I do as he instructed. I step forward, then bring my knee down, trying to ignore the wobble in my leg. But by the time my other leg swings around and I stand up, I'm no longer in danger of falling on my face.

"Good. Now do it again."

I do another rep, my movements slightly less shaky this time. On the third rep, I go a little quicker.

"Atta girl. Nice job."

An unfamiliar tingle spreads through my body. I'm hesitant to lift my eyes and check his expression, but his words are so intoxicating that I can't *not* see how he's looking at me right now.

Sure enough, his expression is pleased. His eyes twinkle with pride, and his smile is genuine. If he's aware of what his praise is doing to me, he doesn't let on.

Maybe this is what every student feels when they please their coach?

The shot of confusion—and maybe some jealousy—tamps down on the heat running through my body. Slightly.

Enough that I work up the nerve to ask my question.

"Can I try one on you?"

His body goes rigid, tension lining every muscle. He glances at the door, and I wonder if he's thinking that we're alone in here, the gym probably close to cleared out by now.

But he nods stiffly anyway. And takes up a stance in front of me.

"Focus on your balance," he instructs.

I nod, suddenly nervous. But I move into my stance and mentally work through it. Stepping forward, I go to my knee and reach to wrap my arms around Dominic's legs.

"You're too far away," he says, his voice like gravel. "You have to be close to me to grip me up."

God, is it always this hot in here? Why does this feel so different than when I do it during class?

Forcing myself to *focus*, I go through the move again: step, knee, drive my weight into him as I step up on the other side. And this time, I follow him down, determined to get the move right no matter how nervous I feel about being this close to the man.

He lets out a grunt from the impact.

"Oh my God, I'm so sorry!" I exclaim, scrambling off. "I was trying to stay close—"

"It's okay, you did exactly what I said," he says from his back. Leveling a hard look at me, he adds, "Don't ever apologize during training. There's no place for that here."

I clasp my hands in my lap where I'm still kneeling on the ground. "Yes, sir."

His eyes flare with something I don't understand. It's how every student refers to him, other than "Coach," but right now, he's looking at me in a way he hasn't before.

Before I can analyze it further, he's standing to his feet. "Again."

This time, I execute the takedown without flopping onto his stomach. I go through the steps the way he just showed me to, and I end up with him on the ground and me in side-mount position on top of him, chest to chest. Grinning, I push up onto my hands—and then suck in a breath when I come face to face with a coach I've never seen before.

There are only a few inches between us. His hand is still gripping my hip, bracing against me the way you're

54

supposed to in this position. Suddenly, this sport is the furthest thing from my mind as I swear I see something flash in his blue eyes.

But I can't read anything on his face. He's stone, in his expression and in the way he's frozen on the mat. I distantly wonder what he sees on my face, as I stay as still as him and try to take in the sight of him like this.

By the time he blinks and breaks the spell, the tension between us has become suffocating. I suck down a greedy breath as I scurry to my feet.

"That was good," comes his gruff voice. I can't bring myself to meet his eyes, so I just nod my silent thanks.

"You can always practice that on your own, or grab someone after class and rep a few on the mats," he continues. "Don't stress so much. You're getting way better."

Frustration bleeds into my veins, and I plant my hands on my hips. "Doesn't feel like it. With the amount of time I put into watching fights and breakdowns and seminars, I should be way better by now."

"Extra work is always going to be a good thing," he assures me. "Repetition and attention to detail is how any of us get good at this sport. You just need a little structure." His jaw hardens as he comes to a decision. "If you want some extra help, I could always give you a few pointers after class."

"Oh, no, you don't have to do that," I say quickly. Even though I very badly want to say yes. For one obvious reason and for another I'm not ready to admit to myself. "I can just keep working on my own, it's no problem." Clearing my throat, I add, "I can't really afford to pay you for private lessons, so—"

"I wouldn't charge you," he interrupts. "This is a thank you for helping Lucy the other day." A sheepish grin appears on his face. "Besides, it's good to have someone in here who knows anything about medical things. I have fighters who can sell me computer software and write me a thriller, but none of them could pop a shoulder back into place. You'd be doing me a favor."

I laugh at that. "To be clear, I'm not a nurse *yet*, I'm just in school for it. Legally, I have no liability here."

"Sounds like something a medical professional would say when she's off the clock."

I release an exaggerated breath. "I feel like you just offered me a job. Am I the gym nurse now? I signed up here to learn *how* to hurt people, not to heal them."

He chuckles and raises his hands in surrender. "No job. No pressure. Just an honest offer. Besides, you didn't seem to hesitate when you helped Lucy last week. I'll bet you didn't even notice you said something, am I right?"

My mouth opens to argue, then closes, then opens and closes again. Finally, I sigh. "Guilty. I'm a perpetual caretaker. It's my flaw."

His gaze sears into mine. "That's pretty far from a flaw, Skylar," he says.

I don't know how to respond to that, so I don't even try. I want to say *no, it's not a flaw. But it's tiring. So tiring that I come in here just to feel something in my bones that isn't exhaustion.*

But I don't. And for some reason, I think Dominic might know without me even having to say it.

"How about this," he says. "On days when you can stay after class for a little bit, and when I don't have to teach a class, we'll review what you did in class, and I'll give you a few pointers for what you need to work on. Nothing huge, just a helpful nudge." When I thoughtfully chew on my bottom lip instead of jumping at the offer, he says, "Come on. Are you really going to turn me down for some YouTube videos? I'm way better. And smarter."

"Who said fighting makes you humble." I roll my eyes, but there's a smile on my lips. "Okay, yes. I'd love the extra help." My last words are quiet. "Thank you."

He looks a little relieved that I've accepted. And when he smiles, it doesn't feel like any of his other smiles.

And I don't know what that means.

8

COACH

I'm sitting at the front desk when one of my high school students walks into the gym, looking both unsure and curious.

"Nate? What're you doing here?"

His gaze, which was wandering around the gym, snaps back to mine. "I wanted to talk to you after today's workout, but you were gone by the time I turned around. I hope it's okay that I came here."

I wave him into the gym. "Of course it's okay. What's going on?"

Sliding his backpack off his shoulder, he digs around inside of it for a second before pulling out a sheet of paper and handing it to me. "I'm applying for scholarships, and I was wondering if you could write me a letter of recommendation. You know, if...if you want."

I take the paper from his hand, suddenly needing to swallow down the mess of emotions threatening to choke me. I met Nate when he was twelve years old and on the verge of going down a dangerous life path. With his dad not around and his mom working three jobs to make ends meet,

Nate spent a lot of time on his own. And because he was at such an impressionable age, he ultimately got mixed up in a bad friend group. Before long, he was going with them as they did risky, and often illegal, activities. It wasn't until I caught them in the middle of one such activity that anything changed.

I bet every single person in their group that I could make them look like Mike Tyson on mitts if they gave me an hour each week. They scoffed at me, but I saw the curiosity light in Nate's eyes. He was the first one to take me up on my offer to learn real boxing. And even though he was the only one following my instructions in the park that day, the other kids were intrigued enough to linger on the basketball courts and watch out of the corners of their eyes as I taught basic footwork.

But it was the day I brought gloves, and showed Nate how to hit focus mitts, that I really got their attention.

Over the next month or so, every one of the boys ended up drifting over to the corner of the park I had claimed as our training area. I met them there once a week and I taught them footwork, head movement, and how to be sharp with their punches. They loved it the most when I held mitts for them. And whenever they showed me a good grade, I'd hold for a few extra rounds.

My days with them became my favorites—their hoots of laughter and playful teasing was my reason for coaching.

Unfortunately, because I was fighting at the time, there came more and more times when I couldn't make it to the park. Most of the kids eventually faded out—only Nate and one other boy kept showing up every single week. And if I wasn't there, then they'd work together.

In the span of less than a year, I watched Nate go from a lost, troubled kid, to a responsible, driven teenager. He started to take school seriously, he joined after-school teams, and he found a good group of friends. Seeing him applying to college so he can continue his education and work for a future he wants is the best ending I ever could have hoped for.

I read over the scholarship details, taking a few extra seconds to compose myself. "Of course, I'll write you a letter of recommendation. When do you need it by?"

"Within the next few weeks. There's no rush."

"Did you decide what you want to major in?"

"I was actually thinking I'd go for business," he admits with a nervous shrug. "Figured there's a lot of things I could use it for, and you know I've always liked numbers."

I nod, my mouth twitching with a smile. Every good grade Nate showed me was at the top of a math test.

"I'll write something up and get it over to you next week," I tell him. Hesitating, I add quietly, "I'm proud of you, Nate."

His focus drops to his feet, hiding any expression from me. The only thing I can make out is his subtle nod. He turns around to leave with a mumbled *see you next week*, but right before he pushes the door open, he freezes.

And then he spins and throws his arms around me.

"Thank you," he chokes out, his cheek buried into my shoulder. "For everything."

I barely get my arms around him to return the hug before he's pulling back. I catch him trying to blink his tears away, but just as quickly as he turned around, he's through the door and out of the building. And I'm left staring after him.

My conversation with Nate stays on repeat in my head, filling me with pride and making me even more excited to help students than I usually am. I decide to teach class after all, despite Tuesdays being my usual night off.

There's a lightness in my chest by the time people file out of the gym. "Awesome class tonight, Coach," one of my students calls as he leaves, and there's a rumble of agreement from everyone around him. I give them all a smile and nod of thanks.

Skylar's the only one who seems to be dragging her feet. She's mostly packed up, but her gym bag is still open, and she hasn't put her sweatshirt on yet.

Tristan notices it, too. When everyone is packed up and shooting the shit, he slings an arm around Remy and hollers, "Hey, Skylar, we're going out to the pub to grab burgers and beers. Want to come? I'll let you ask Max all the jiu-jitsu questions you want."

Max glares at my second-in-command, even though he doesn't look all too bothered by the idea.

Skylar smiles but shakes her head. "Thanks, but I already ate. And I don't drink."

There's a stray thought in the back of my head that says the only food she had with her was half of a protein bar, but I'm too stuck on trying to figure out why she doesn't want to leave and what she's going to do next.

Tristan looks a little confused, too, but he's not going to push. He just nods and says, "Alright, well, the invite is an open one. You're more than welcome to come with us any time."

She gives him another smile, this one softened by gratitude. "I appreciate that."

He nods again, then drops the strap of his gym bag over Remy's shoulder. She lets out a grunt as the weight of it suddenly lands on her, and then glares at her boyfriend. Who just winks and blows her a kiss.

"Aiden, Max, you ready?" he calls out. "I'm starving, let's *go*."

"Coming, Dad!" comes Aiden's chipper voice from the locker rooms.

Tristan rolls his eyes and gestures for the other fighters to follow him. "We're waiting outside. Quit messing with your hair and get out here."

I can't make out Aiden's grumbled response, but Max's laugh is loud.

And then I'm left alone with Skylar.

She's staring so intently at the gym door that it allows me to study her for a moment. Her entire demeanor has changed in the past few minutes. Normally, she's lit up and excited when she's in here. But for whatever reason, now her posture has become tense and exhausted.

She doesn't want to leave. And I don't want her to.

I stride over to the couch and take a seat, then reach for the remote to turn on some fights.

I make sure I pick an exciting, technical fight from the UFC library. It's not a wild guess that something like that will pique Skylar's curiosity.

Sure enough, one minute into the fight, Skylar's craning her neck to see the TV screen.

"Is that the Chimera fight?" she finally asks.

"It is," I confirm. "My favorite one to watch."

She takes a step closer to the couch. "This was the one that set him up for the title fight, right?"

I wipe my hand over my mouth to smother my grin. That's not amateur knowledge—Skylar clearly knows her stuff.

"Yup. He fought for the title two months later."

Skylar mouths *"wow"* as the fighter in question moves through a series of advanced transitions on the screen. I don't think I've ever seen anyone as riveted by a fight as she is.

But she's still straddling the invisible line of *stay or go*. Even though she's moved over enough to be standing beside the couch, close enough that she's absentmindedly petting Brutus's big bulldog head where he's taken over the arm of the couch.

I open my mouth to say something that might make her sit down. I have no idea what that might be; I just know I want her to stay. But before I can voice anything, a door slams.

Two seconds later, Aiden zips by in a cloud of blonde hair and some kind of exotic cologne.

"Bye, Coach," he calls as he reaches the front door. "Bye, new girl, whose name I don't remember!"

And then he's gone, and Skylar is left blinking after him.

After a moment, she asks, "Is he always...?"

"Yup."

The corner of her lip tugs up in a smile. "A class clown probably isn't a bad thing to have in a gym."

"Unless you're cutting weight and don't have the energy to tell him to shut up," I comment dryly.

She lets out a laugh, the sound light and airy, and my desire for her to stay intensifies.

I turn back to the fight, making it a point to put my legs up on the coffee table and settling more comfortably into my seat.

"You're not leaving?" she asks.

I shake my head. "Nah, sometimes I like to watch the fights here."

She hesitates, and I turn my attention back to her.

"Do you want me to go?" Her brow furrows as she looks down at me.

I simply shake my head again.

But she still looks like she's about to cut and run, so I turn back to the TV and say, "Look at this submission he's about to hit. It was his go-to move for the longest time."

That brings her closer. She can't see the details of the move from where she's standing, so she finally takes a seat, leaning forward to brace her forearms on her knees.

"How is he able to set that up *every* time?" she asks, her voice awed. "His opponents *have* to know it's coming, right? And he still pulls it off?"

"He's just that good." We both watch in silence as the fighter onscreen locks in the submission, puts pressure on the choke, and gets the tap from his opponent.

"Insane," Skylar breathes. "How does someone get that good at something?"

The question seems to be spoken automatically, but then she turns her attention to me and asks more seriously, "As a coach, what would you say is the secret to getting good?"

I brush a hand over my beard as I mull over her question. "To getting good or to winning fights?"

"Getting good. I don't care about winning fights."

That makes me forget her question for a second. "You don't want to fight?"

"I have no interest in fighting. That's not why I'm here."

I cock my head as I take her in. "Why are you here then?"

She quirks an eyebrow. "Are you avoiding the question?"

Chuckling, I turn my attention back to the TV, where the hype trailer has started for the next fight.

"Consistent training focused on skill development," I answer after a moment.

Skylar frowns. "What else would it be focused on?"

"Winning. You'd be surprised how many people come in here who don't care about getting better; they just want to beat everyone they go against."

I can tell she's mulling something over in her head before she asks, "Was Kane one of those people?"

I nod. She's clever to have noticed that.

"He's gotten way better. Used to be he wanted to kill everyone in here, Tristan and Jax included, just to prove he *could*. Took a few life changes to get him to see this as a sport that relies on more than just force of will."

Skylar leans back against the couch, her hand still on Brutus's head.

"So, he changed the way he trains?" she asks, and I nod again.

"He sparred less and took more classes. He always trained a lot, so consistency was never his problem, but he spent more time drilling. Remy is actually his best training partner now because their size difference forces him to be slow and controlled. Their rounds are focused on getting better technically."

"Consistent training focused on skill development," she parrots back.

"That's all it is," I confirm. "Nothing earth-shattering, if that's what you were expecting."

She turns her head to face me as she asks, "Is that how you got so good? Just trained often and drilled a lot?"

"Nah, mine is just raw talent."

She lets out a snort, the sound surprising us both. I open my mouth to tease her about it, but suddenly her stomach growls, cutting me off.

That pinkens her cheeks in embarrassment. Her gaze snaps up to meet mine.

I want to ask why she lied to Tristan about eating

already. I want to ask her when she last ate. I want to ask her *why* she's not eating. But some kind of sixth Skylar sense tells me she won't want to talk about it.

Not just that, but I'm her coach. The only thing she needs from me is to show her how to punch harder. It's not my place to ask any more of her.

So between that and her very obvious *don't ask* expression, I stand from the couch and walk over toward the gym's tiny kitchen, throwing a different question over my shoulder.

"Do you like chocolate or vanilla?"

There are a few seconds of silence, and I can sense her confusion without looking back at her.

"Umm, chocolate?"

"Correct answer. It's the elite flavor." I reach for the chocolate protein powder tub, then for the coconut milk in the cabinet. When I plug in the blender, I hear Skylar's voice again.

"Are you making me a protein shake right now?"

I don't respond, at which point her voice becomes panicked—the first time I've ever heard it take on that pitch. "You really don't need to do that—"

I interrupt her protests by turning on the blender, having put all the ingredients in while she was talking.

"I'm serious, I'm not that hungry—"

Once again, I turn on the blender. When the shake is the consistency I want, I take two cups from the cabinet and pour the mixture into them evenly. By the time I grab two spoons and turn back toward Skylar, she's glaring at me.

I tamp down my grin at the sight of it.

"Do you like blueberries?" I ask instead.

Her expression turns baffled. "*Blueberries?* What kind of weird concoction are you making?"

"Just trust me. Protein shakes are my specialty. You're not allergic to blueberries, are you?"

"No, I'm not allergic..." she says with narrowing eyes, her curiosity winning out.

Pleased with her answer, I take the frozen blueberries from the freezer and dump a healthy heap into her glass. Dropping a spoon in, I hand one to Skylar, and then I take my spot beside her on the couch. And promptly dig into my own shake.

After a few seconds, I sense Skylar do the same.

"Oh my *God*," she moans.

It has me freezing in place, too nervous to look at her and risk seeing an expression that matches that sound.

"What *is* this?" she asks, hurriedly dipping back into the cup and searching for more blueberries. "This tastes nothing like Muscle Milk. This is like a straight up milkshake."

I can't help it; my smile breaks free at her excitement.

"You're just hungry from two hours of training." I chuckle, going back to my own shake.

"No, I'm serious," she says with wide eyes as she turns toward me. "How is this so good? And who knew frozen blueberries would go so well with a chocolate milkshake?"

I eat a spoonful before I answer. "I feel like I've been eating that for half my life. I forget that people usually have a negative association with protein shakes."

Skylar snorts. "That's because they usually taste like wet sand." And then eagerly digs in for more.

I try to understand the warm feeling in my chest from seeing her eat something that *I* made her. But it also comes with the knowledge that she was hungry, which immediately cools any pleasure. I can only hope like hell that the only reason she didn't want to go out to eat is because she's frugal enough to limit extra spending.

Even though I know she doesn't want to talk about it, even though it probably crosses the professional boundary I've always drawn between myself and my students about their personal lives, I open my mouth to ask.

Except, the words die on my tongue, because when I look over at her again, she's wiggled more comfortably into the couch cushion and pulled her legs up to cradle the cup in her lap. There's a genuine, *happy* smile on her face as her attention returns to the fights on the screen.

And as I sit back and relax in my own seat, I comfort myself with the knowledge that I made her full and content *now*.

9

SKYLAR

This protein shake is so good that it takes until I've scraped the cup clean and placed it on the coffee table with a content groan to realize I haven't spoken in minutes. That Dominic is still eating his, much slower than I did, and is occasionally glancing over at me.

I feel a slight blush warm my cheeks. He's right, I *was* hungry, but I try to eat at home as much as I can to avoid wasteful spending. I guess I haven't been packing enough food on the nights that I train.

It takes me a moment to muster up the courage to say thank you. I'm not used to someone taking care of me. I'm usually able to joke my way out of it before anyone can notice I *need* help.

Yet somehow, Dominic's been able to see right through me every time.

"Thank you," I say, meeting his eyes. "That was delicious."

His gaze lingers on me a little longer this time. "You're welcome."

"What weight did you walk around at when you were fighting?" I blurt out, both curious and wanting to take the attention off myself. And then I'm blushing again, because the question *should've* been 'what weight did you fight at?' but now I've given away that I've stalked him enough to already know the answer to that question. I hurry to cover up my slip. "I mean, is this the kind of stuff you ate when you were fighting?"

His lip twitches, and I think he might be having the same thought. But he doesn't call me out on it.

"My diet was really clean when I was fighting," he answers. "More protein than anything, but I never bulked up between fights, if that's what you're asking. I felt the best when I walked around at my fighting weight." He shoots me a look that lets me know he's basically reading my mind. "At middleweight."

I turn my attention back to the dog sitting beside me to hide any lingering blush. *Why do I blush so much around this man?*

"I meal prepped a lot," he continues. "I liked having control over the food I put in my body, and knowing exactly what it was and how it would benefit my nutrition. I didn't enjoy going out to eat either."

And the comment is just odd enough, just random enough, that a small frown twists my lips.

Without looking at him, I say, "I've never been an athlete, so I can't say I meal prep for nutrition, but I can agree with the control part. I just prefer controlling where my money is going, as opposed to where calories are coming from." My voice softens. "There are things I'd much rather spend my money on that's not a burger or a beer."

My response must be what he expected, or was looking

for, because out of the corner of my eye, I see Dominic nod to himself and then finally return to his protein shake, his posture no longer stiff.

Seeing him relax makes me relax, and I find myself asking him another question.

"Why did you stop fighting?"

He places his empty cup on the coffee table, then leans back on the couch and makes himself comfortable. One arm is on the arm of the couch, and the other stretches along the back of it, letting him recline in that alpha, kingly pose that only the most confident men are able to adapt.

My mouth goes dry at the sight.

I'm entirely aware of the fact that Dominic is an attractive man. A very attractive man. Not just because he's in ridiculous shape, but also because...his age looks good on him.

Because there's a smattering of dark hair on his chest that sometimes peeks through his gi jacket when he teaches. Because every line on his face, every word out of his mouth, speaks to experience. Because every move he makes, whether he's teaching or working out or doing paperwork, is so sure of himself, so *confident*, that he could never be seen as anything other than a man who's spent a lifetime garnering that confidence. That assuredness.

I've never once thought of myself as being attracted to older men, but with Dominic...it's not even a question.

As I watch him contemplate his answer, I wonder if this is a bad idea. Me being here. With him. *Alone.* I wasn't originally going to stay past the last class, but there's something about this place that draws me in. Makes me feel at peace—like I'm already home when I'm here.

I wonder if Dominic is a part of that.

I shouldn't be thinking of him in this way. He's my coach. *Coach* Dominic.

I'm pulled from my thoughts when he starts to talk, and suddenly I'm singularly focused on learning more about this man. Good idea or not, I want to know everything.

"I was tired," he says simply. "I had been fighting for so long, and technically I had already accomplished the goal I went into the sport with, so I couldn't find a very good 'why' by the end. And in this sport the 'why' is everything."

I pull my legs up so I can wrap my arms around them. But when I lean back against the couch cushions to settle more comfortably into my seat, my shoulder bumps against Dominic's hand where it's stretched out along the back. And heat sparks through my body at the place of contact.

I hurriedly shift my body so we're not touching, going back to petting the dog's head to cover the reason for my adjustment.

Once I have my heartrate under control, I turn my attention back to Dominic. I assumed he'd put more distance between us after the accidental touch, something more appropriate for a coach and his student, but to my unending surprise, he hasn't moved an inch. He's still reclined like a king, focused entirely on me. Though I have no idea what thoughts hide behind those eyes.

I don't allow myself to guess.

"What was the goal you wanted to achieve?" I ask, my voice sounding scratchy to my own ears. "The one you went into the sport with."

After a moment, he faces back toward the TV. "I just wanted to see if I could do it."

I frown at that. "You wanted to see if you could fight?"

He shrugs. "Pretty much. I got into this sport for the

same reasons you did. It seemed exciting. I wanted to learn all of it. But wanting to learn the techniques of fighting and wanting to learn how to *fight* are two very different things. Once I got good at the techniques, I wanted to see if I'd actually be any good at fighting."

"Well, you definitely answered that question," I mumble. "You won your first seven fights and made it to one of the biggest MMA organizations in the world. I'd say you achieved your goal."

One dark eyebrow rises at my comment, a smirk settling on his lips. "You really *did* do your research when you signed up here."

Busted.

"I wanted to know who I was learning from," I say with a shrug, refusing to feel embarrassed about my interest.

"Tell me something: which belt does Lucy hold right now? Which win is she known for in the circuit?"

I rifle through my brain for the research I did on the coaches here.

"Umm, I know the belt is green..." I stumble over my answer. I can't remember anything beyond that. "It's...a state championship belt?"

He shakes his head, a knowing grin on his face. "National belt. She posts about it once a week. Guess your research wasn't that thorough, huh?"

That earns him a glare. He's teasing me. He's perfectly aware of the fact that he was the only one I researched.

He chuckles at my expression and turns back to the fight. We watch silently through the first round, but by the second, I'm fully immersed and can't stop myself from asking questions about the fighter strategies.

He's patient as he answers each one. He even seems to

enjoy my curiosity. When the fight ends and I finally relax against the couch again, he lets out an amused huff at my laser focus.

"You sure you don't want to fight?" he asks. "At this rate, you'll know more than my fighters."

I drop my head back against the couch and let myself imagine it. "I wasn't planning on it, but never say never, I guess. Maybe a jiu-jitsu tournament. Training is exciting enough, and as far as fighting goes... I've spent too much time inside of hospitals to ever want to purposefully risk ending up there."

I suck in a breath at my honesty. I hate talking about my mom's condition, and the struggles that come with it, because it always leads to reactions that I'd much rather avoid. I don't need to complain about my life. I don't need the looks of pity.

Dominic is too sharp to not catch my admission. But he's polite enough to not ask more about it.

"Do you ever miss it?" I turn the conversation back to him.

He's shaking his head before I can even finish. "No. I don't miss getting stitched up at 2 a.m. after a victory. Even seeing the good parts of the sport when the guys win, the hard days don't make it worth it anymore."

"Do you like coaching more than fighting?"

"Definitely," he says. "Coaching is like the best parts of fighting *without* all the bad parts. Where the worst part of fighting was bad losses with bad injuries, the worst part of coaching is... I don't even know. Caring more about a students' progressions than they do, I guess. That always frustrates me."

My admiration for Dominic was already high, but it grows even more. "You really were meant to teach," I say thoughtfully.

The compliment seems to make him uncomfortable. And suddenly, I want nothing more than for him to see himself the way I see him.

"I'm serious," I hurry to reassure him. "I may not have had coaches before this, but I've had teachers, and you have the best teaching style. And not just because you have a shit-ton of knowledge and experience. Your teaching is just so easy to ingest. It's detailed, but not overwhelming, and you make it easy to apply it and actually get better in the gym." I stumble over my last thought. "Or at least, I think I'm getting better. I guess I don't know. But it *feels* that way."

He's seems to appreciate my feedback, easing a bit as he responds, "Don't worry, you're definitely getting better. I've never seen someone pick things up as quickly as you have these past few weeks."

The returned compliment fills my chest—and probably cheeks—with warmth as I smile.

"Some days, I'm not sure if I'm getting better or worse. This sport is a little chaotic."

He barks out a laugh at that. "That's an understatement. My first year of training, I had to give myself a pep talk every time I stepped on the mat. I would tell myself that I'm going to get smashed, but that I still needed to give 100% effort. My first year was all losing."

The image of a young, green Dominic has me twisting in my seat to face him, my excitement likely visible.

"Really?" I ask. "I can't picture you losing, and especially not all the time."

"Oh, trust me, I lost *all* the time. And a lot of my losses were against this one guy who showed up to all the jiu-jitsu tournaments, same as I did. We were in the same weight class, and we probably got matched up twenty times that first year. Guess how many times he was the victor."

"Twenty," I answer on a laugh.

"Such little faith you have in your coach," he scolds. But he's smiling as he says it. "Nineteen. Our twentieth match was the time I finally got angry enough to throw all caution to the wind and let my instincts take over. I think I was more surprised than he was when I won. In the picture that someone snapped of my hand being raised, I look like a child who was just told Santa isn't real: shell-shocked and a little bit horrified."

By now, I'm fully laughing. I love getting these little bits and pieces of his mind and his life story. I think I could sit here and listen to him talk for hours.

But when the loud sounds of cheering pull our attention back to the TV, and we realize that the fight card we were watching is over, it hits me that we've been sitting here for well over an hour.

It seems to occur to Dominic at the same time. "We should probably get going." He sounds reluctant, but that might just be wishful thinking. "You said you have classes in the morning, right? I don't want to keep you late."

I give him a stiff nod. Leaving is the last thing I want to do, but he's right. I need to get home.

"I'll walk you to your car," he adds. "You shouldn't walk alone at night. No matter how terrifying your chokes are."

I grin at that. "High praise, indeed." Standing from the couch and walking over to my gym bag, I add, "No need, though. I'm taking the bus."

He doesn't respond as I pull on my coat and gather my bag. When I turn back to him, he's standing frozen beside the couch, frowning in my direction.

"You're taking the bus at 11 o'clock at night?" he asks sternly.

I glance at my phone. "It's barely 10:30. But yes. Public transport is great in the city. Takes me twenty minutes and it doesn't cost me a car payment."

His unhappy expression morphs into something resembling unease. "But this late? That doesn't seem safe, Skylar."

"I have my pepper spray and taser, and it's not like I'll be the only one on the street. I'll be fine."

His discomfort starts to turn slightly more panicked. "Why don't you let me give you a ride home?"

I give him a hard stare. "This is hardly the first time I've had to travel the city by myself. I'm perfectly fine on my own."

"I'd just feel better if—"

"I don't need you to take care of me," I say in a tone that leaves no room for an argument.

After a moment, he gives a stiff nod and retreats to his office to gather his things.

We're silent as he shuts down the fans and turns off the lights. When he locks the doors behind us, the sound of the lock clicking is loud in the cool city air. And when it's finally time to go our separate ways, there's no sign of the relaxed, easy-to-talk-to man I just spent over an hour watching fights with.

I shine a smile to hopefully force some levity back between us. "Have a good night, Coach."

For a moment, I only receive a hardened stare in response. Then, "Goodnight, Skylar. Please be safe getting home."

My smile stretches into a wide grin. "Yes, Coach."

When that finally softens him into giving me a scolding look, I lean down to pat Brutus's head.

"Don't worry, buddy, those scowl lines aren't directed at you. That's just his face."

He lets out an exasperated breath. "Skylar."

I straighten and shoot him a wink. "See you later, Coach."

He doesn't say anything else, but I can sense him watching me the entire walk down the street. And I think I like his eyes on me way too much.

10

SKYLAR

"You good to close up, Skylar? I'd like to duck out a little early if possible."

I look up from where I'm sweeping the coffee shop floor. "Yeah, of course. Get out of here. I'll take care of it."

My coworker mouths a relieved "*thank you*" in my direction, already reaching for her purse and coat. "You're a life-saver, Skylar. See you next week!"

Shaking my head with a smile, I go back to sweeping under the tables. I still have twenty minutes before I have to leave for class, and this is the last thing I have to do for my shift-end tasks.

My thoughts return to the same place they always seem to wander to nowadays: the gym. Starting with the new submission I learned last night, mentally working through the ten steps necessary to lock it up, before drifting to the takedown that we set it up with.

Which means it doesn't take long for my thoughts to turn to Coach Dominic.

My skin warms at the memory of us working on my double leg takedown. He's spent some time working with

NIKKI CASTLE

me since that night, but it's always on the heavy bag, working on punches and elbows after a grueling Muay Thai class. Part of me wonders if he's keeping it to striking for a reason. If he regretted watching those fights with me and is trying to keep some distance, physical or otherwise.

My company didn't feel unwanted that night I sat down to watch the fights with him because it was obvious he was baiting me to do it. I might not have a lot of experience with the opposite sex, but I can still read their social cues. Dominic wanted me to sit with him. *So then why has he been putting space between us over the past two weeks?*

I think back to our conversation, frowning when I can't remember us talking about anything unprofessional or inappropriate. We talked about fighting. At no point did anything feel like we crossed an invisible line in the conversation. The only thing potentially odd about our interaction was the fact that I was alone in the gym with my coach at ten o'clock at night.

But...he initiated that. And it's *his* gym.

I let out a heavy sigh. Maybe I really am overthinking this. It's entirely possible that the reason for us doing Muay Thai and keeping our physical contact to a minimum is because my striking is what needs the help, not my ground game.

I sweep my worries under the rug, knowing there's nothing I can do differently so choosing not to stress. Finishing my shift at the coffee shop, I head to campus for my afternoon classes.

I'm mulling over the homework we were given when Craig enters my view and leans his hip against my desk.

"I almost didn't recognize you sitting back here." He raises an eyebrow at me. "No more teacher's pet sitting in the front row?"

I barely hold back an eye roll. "I got here late, and I didn't want to interrupt Professor Calloway's lecture," I explain—not that I should need to. *Are we in middle school that we're still mocking people for being good students? Or is this his attempt at flirting?*

I stand and head toward the door, hoping Craig gets the hint that I don't feel like talking today.

He doesn't.

"Why were you late?" he presses, taking up stride beside me.

I let out a heavy sigh. "Work."

He whistles, the sound obnoxiously loud even in the busy college hallway. "You work way too much, Sky. You need to relax. Take a break."

My exasperation gives way to annoyance. "That's not really a luxury I have."

He waves off my answer—as if working more is a decision, not a necessity.

And *this*. This is why I don't get along with people my own age. His answer is completely normal: nineteen-year-olds *should* be finding time to relax and have fun. Freshman and sophomore years of college don't need to be spent buried under schoolwork and multiple jobs. They should be spent making new friends and learning how to be independent. Craig's answer isn't *wrong*. I shouldn't judge him.

And yet, it's so far from my reality that I *hate* him for it.

"You should make time," he continues, completely oblivious to the irritation simmering in my veins. "You can't pour from an empty cup, you know."

Yes, you can. When your family's lives literally depend on it, you'd be surprised where you can pour from.

He must finally sense that this is a less-than-pleasant

conversation for me, because he pulls me to a stop in the hallway, his expression softening.

"Look, I'm just trying to help. Anyone can see how stressed you are. You really can't take an hour out of your day to do something for *you?*"

My shoulders drop. He's right, of course, but I don't really feel like telling him that *training* has become my respite. Physically, mentally, in every way something can be someone's peace. Even just *being* in the gym makes me happier.

"I can't tonight. I have plans."

He quirks an eyebrow at my answer. "I'm glad to hear that. But now I'm curious to know what kinds of plans Skylar Vega makes in her free time."

"I already told you. I signed up at that MMA gym."

Why does he look just as baffled as the first time I told him? "How does *that* make you *less* stressed? Wouldn't you rather go to a movie or something? Spend time with friends, instead of some juiced-up, angry guys?"

My eyes narrow in his direction, finally latching onto the part that bothers him.

"You mean, wouldn't I have more fun with *you?*"

He only shrugs. "I can pretty much guarantee I'm better company."

Adjusting the bag strap on my shoulder, my body suddenly feels ten times heavier with exhaustion. "I don't have time tonight, Craig." And I'm not the kind of person to apologize if I don't mean it, but a small part of me is wondering if this is just his awkward way of asking me out, and I'm blowing it out of proportion. "I'm sorry."

It's enough to make a relieved grin appear on his face. "Another time, I guess."

I turn to continue toward the exit. "Yeah, sure."

I've reached the doors when he calls out to me, his words sending a shiver of foreboding through my body.

"Maybe I'll sign up at your gym. Will you be able to avoid me then, Skylar?"

———

It takes a textbook on anatomy to get my mind off Craig's parting words.

Not his blatant come-on, but his comment about how everyone needs *something* in their lives to ease their stress. When forced into it, I can handle anything my family needs, stress relief or no, but having an outlet somewhere really does seem to make a bigger difference than I'd anticipated. I can't remember ever thinking I *needed* an outlet, or assuming one would make a difference, but looking back, I don't know how I survived without the gym. How did my brain get a break, and my body a release?

With gratitude in my chest and a smile on my lips, I settle deeper into the big chair and power on the iPad in my lap. I have an hour before my next class, then it's straight to the gym. *Thank God. I need it today.*

I'm just about to dive into my anatomy notes, when I see an email notification pop up on my screen. It's from the Bursar's office, so I switch over to my email immediately.

Dear Skylar. We regret to inform you that due to funding changes in the university, we are unable to offer you the full amount of your academic scholarship. This change will not take effect until next semester, but at that point, the new amount of your scholarship will be...

I stare at the screen for what feels like hours. Maybe if I don't move, I can pretend like the last minute didn't happen, that my life didn't just get flipped upside down.

My brain is slow, moving through the mental calculations. The new amount is about half what it was, which is still something, but it still completely changes my financial situation.

I blink away the tears forming in my eyes. I was *just* getting to a good place financially. While Mom's disability check was only enough to pay for rent and utilities, the paychecks I earned from my two jobs kept us afloat otherwise. I covered groceries and clothes and every other necessary cost of two teenagers. Not to mention, the costs that come with having a disease like Parkinson's. I can't remember a time that I *didn't* keep track of every dollar, just to keep us safe and fed and healthy.

But with my scholarship covering school and Mom's new medical grant helping with hiring Maria, I was finally able to afford other things. I could give Joey some spending money to be a real kid, and I signed up at the gym. These past few months were the closest we've ever gotten to financial freedom—or whatever it's called when you can sleep without nightmares of being evicted.

This email changes all of that.

I'm so *tired*. Tired of the stress and the responsibility and the constant, soul-crushing fear that one day I'm not going to be strong enough to hold it all together. Every time I think I might be catching a break, something like this happens.

But then I think of Joey. And Mom. My two reasons for *always* pushing through the hard times. So, I shake off my moment of self-pity and move the fuck on.

I can do this. I can figure this out.

My mind starts to fly through the numbers. *I probably won't have to beg too hard for more shifts at the café—that won't make a huge dent, but it's something. If I can get more shifts at the restaurant, that could mean more tips, but tips aren't very budget-friendly so that's not a reliable solution.*

I run through my usual list of *what do I own that I could sell*. I don't have a car, my phone is about four generations old, I'm never frivolous with things that I buy—

I suck in a breath when it hits me.

The only expense I have right now that's "frivolous" is the gym.

My eyes slide closed as a breath stutters out of my lungs. *Fuck.*

I'll have to quit the gym. It was a lot of money even when I had the scholarship, but there's no way I can keep it now.

I allow myself a final moment of despair, and anger, and self-pity. It feels like a special kind of torture that this comes after my conversation with Craig, that right as things were going well, and I finally found a place of *peace*, that this would happen.

Sagging with defeat, I wake up my iPad and make the decision to end my gym membership when I go in tonight. And in the reflection of the black screen, a second before it illuminates with the email all over again, I see a single tear roll down my cheek.

11

COACH

It takes me three seconds to figure out that something is wrong when Skylar walks into the gym.

It's not just that her class has started in the room next door, the sounds of the warmup emphasizing that she isn't here fifteen minutes early the way that she usually is; it's also that she's not wearing her trademark excited expression. Instead of looking happy to be here, she seems...distressed.

"What's wrong?" I ask, my concern coming out in a barked order. I clear my throat and try again, my voice softer this time. "Everything okay?"

She nods. "Fine, everything's...fine. I just, umm, I need to talk to you about something."

That snaps me to attention. Standing from my seat, I jerk my head toward the office and silently gesture her to a more private setting. "Let's talk in here."

She follows me into the room without a word, but she doesn't look nearly relaxed enough to take a seat. So I stay standing, watching in disbelief as she twists her hands in front of her body and as her eyes look everywhere but at me.

What the fuck is happening? I can't tell if she's nervous or just reluctant, but I don't like either option.

"What's going on, Skylar?" I ask.

"I need to quit," she says without preamble. It catches me so off guard, I feel like I've been slapped. "I know your contract says to give ninety days' notice, but if there's any way you could make an exception—"

"Wait...*what?*"

Her eyes widen at my outburst. Honestly, I'm just as surprised as she is at the severity of my reaction, but...what the *fuck*. She's *leaving?*

"You don't seem like the kind of person who would quit," I explain, arms crossing over my chest as I take a breath. "I want to know why."

She seems shocked by my statement. I don't tell her that I've been in this game long enough to know when people are quitting for the right reasons, and when they're quitting for the wrong ones.

"I just don't have time to train anymore," she says, still not meeting my eyes. "My work schedule got busy, and I'm already stressed with school, so—"

"Did something happen at the gym?" I ask, suddenly worried that there's something going on under my roof that I've missed.

Her attention jerks back to me, and her eyes widen as they latch onto mine. "What? No, of course not. I love it here. I..."

"Then what is it?"

Her eyes fill with an expression of tiredness, of...defeat.

I fucking hate it.

"Do you really have to quit?" I press. "Can we tweak your membership instead? I know you're paying for the unlimited option, but most people do twice a week, or three

87

times, and it makes it easier on time and money resources—"

And that's when I realize I touched the truth. Because the second those last words leave my mouth, her body freezes and her eyes fill with tentative hope.

But only for a second, because sadness takes over again as she shakes her head.

"It wouldn't help, unfortunately." She sighs, her gaze dropping back to the floor. "It's kind of all or nothing at this point."

My brain struggles to filter through the possibilities. Time or money, right? That's what she reacted to? If it's time, I can't really do anything about that. But if it's money...

Money. I can fix the money problem.

Why am I so eager to keep her?

I've never stopped anyone from quitting before. I've never wanted anyone in the gym who didn't want to be here.

It's because she does *want to be here,* I tell myself, ignoring the whisper of my subconscious telling me that it's something else.

"How about this," I start, ignoring all other thoughts. "I've been looking to hire someone to help clean the gym. The mats have to be cleaned between evening and morning classes, so I don't have nearly as much help as I want. If you clean for me, I'll let you train for free."

And thank God that hope softens her expression. I'm so relieved to see it that I don't even mind that it's followed by narrowed eyes.

"I don't like being a charity case."

My head shake is vehement. "It's not charity. Anyone who works for me gets to train for free, just ask any of the assistant instructors."

The skepticism doesn't leave her eyes, but it does dull.

The thought that Skylar might not have the easy life that someone as kind and hard-working as her deserves is like a nail in my lungs.

"Do you actually need the help?" she asks, almost as a final, pride-filled pushback. "Or are you just making up a job for me?"

My lips twitch, and my chest finally loosens with my exhale.

"Trust me, you'd be making my life a lot easier. Right now, I'm basically doing it myself, since I only have one of the high schoolers helping me. And you don't want to know what teenage boys think counts as clean."

That gets a reaction I didn't expect. A smile blooms across her face, and it's so...*adoring* that I have to blink my surprise away.

"I definitely do," she says with a tinkling laugh. "I can't tell you how many times I've had to explain that deodorant is required, not optional. It's like they think hygiene will give them a rash."

Interesting. A younger brother? Clearly, she's very fond of him. Is she the oldest? What is she like with her family?

"So you get it then. You'd actually be helping *me* out. I'm tired of cleaning the mats myself."

Her lips purse as she tilts her head, amusement shining in her eyes. "Too good for a little cleaning, Coach?"

I wonder what my name sounds like on her lips.

Fuck, these thoughts... Who am I today?

"Hardly," I force out. "I'm just tired of doing it. I've cleaned so many mats, I've probably contributed to the hole in the ozone layer with the chemical fumes. Twenty years later, and I feel like I've paid my dues enough times over to not want to clean anymore."

Skylar lets out a whistle. "Twenty years? Sometimes I forget how long you've been in this game."

My eyes narrow on hers. "You calling me old again, Skylar?"

She bites her lip to hide her smile, but as she shakes her head, it slips through anyway. "Never old. More like...experienced."

My blood rushes hot at the way she says it. I'm well aware of the fact that I've got at least a decade on my fighters, but it's never made me feel...*old*. Especially when I can keep up with even my best competitors.

But hearing Skylar call it experience instead of age is... I don't know what it is. But it suddenly feels like I'm crackling with sensations I shouldn't be.

"That I am," I say, deeper than intended.

Sure enough, Skylar's pupils dilate at the sound, and I can't look away.

It takes her a second to snap out of the haze she fell into —that we both fell into. She clears her throat and says, "So, um, you just need me to clean the mats? Anything else?"

"Just the mats and heavy bags," I confirm. "They need to be done between night classes ending and the morning classes starting, so it's up to you if you'd rather clean them after class or come in during the day. Not sure what your schedule is like."

"I'll do them after class," she says immediately. "I have class and work during the day, so it would be hard to come in then. Unless it's at like 4 a.m."

4 a.m.? Jesus, how busy is this girl?

"After class, then," I agree with a nod. "So, any night that you're here to train, just stay after and spray down the mats and heavy bags. In exchange, I'll zero out your membership fee."

Back is the hesitation in her eyes, her teeth once again chewing on her lip. She's the poster child for not wanting to ask for help.

But I can see when the urge to train wins out, because she lets out a heavy breath. "I really do hope this isn't you doing me a favor, but"—she glances up at me from under her eyelashes, and the look is full of appreciation—"thank you for doing it. I'm really glad I'll get to stay here."

Because of training? The people? Fuck, what does that mean?

I swallow thickly. "Me too, Skylar," I say in a rough voice.

She sends me one last tremulous smile before adjusting the strap on her shoulder. "I guess I'm too late for class now, but I'll stretch out on the mat while I wait for Muay Thai to start."

"Don't worry about being late. I'll tell Max you're jumping in now. Just go get changed."

She frowns at that. "But you hate when people are late."

"I do. But this was important, and the whole point of it was to get you more mat time. So that's what we're doing." I pause, my lip curling with an errant thought. "You can make it up by doing thirty burpees and thirty shrimps across the mat after class is over. Should take you the fifteen minutes that you just missed."

Before she turns away to leave and get ready, a smile spreads across her face as she purrs, "Yes, sir."

And when blood rushes to my cock at the sound of those two words on her lips, two words that I hear multiple times every day, I realize...

Yeah, she's nothing like my other students.

12

SKYLAR

"Well, you're in a good mood today," my coworker comments as we lock the restaurant door behind the last customer.

I try for a nonchalant shrug, but my smile sneaks through anyway. "It's been a good week."

She moves toward the register to start the process of balancing. After a moment, she lets out a long whistle.

"No kidding. Whatever it is you're doing to the customers this week, don't stop. You made almost double your usual tips tonight."

"Really?" I squeak, stepping up behind her to look at the numbers myself. "I didn't do anything, I just...smiled more, I guess." She looks over her shoulder at me with a raised eyebrow, and I shrug again. "Like I said, it's been a good week. Being happy makes it easier to smile at the assholes."

She laughs loudly at that. "You got that right. Well, whatever's making you happy, I hope it keeps up. We're eating *good* tonight."

I was already in a great mood, but hearing I made extra money puts an extra pep in my step as we clean up.

Looking back, this week has been an emotional rollercoaster. It was only a few days ago that I got the email from the Bursar's office. From feeling like the weight of the world was about to crush me, to now being afloat financially *and* able to keep the things that make me happy *and* making extra money is the biggest relief.

As I start to sweep up, my thoughts trail back to the conversation that made it all happen. The *person* who made it all happen.

Dominic didn't need to offer me that deal. He can say it's not charity all he wants, but we both know he doesn't *need* me to clean the gym. He was probably fine doing it on his own—or at the very least, he could've gotten a much cheaper deal by having one of the fighters do it as a way to give back to the gym.

Usually when I'm offered help, I decline it because it comes with a look of pity. I've worked too goddamn hard in my life to have any of my successes fueled by that.

And yet...I barely hesitated when Dominic made his offer.

He looked genuinely upset when I told him I had to quit. I'm sure people quit all the time, so it shouldn't have been a big deal. I don't understand why he immediately tried to find alternatives for me.

All I know is that I saw no pity in his eyes, and no ill-intent in his gestures. Nothing he does makes me feel uncomfortable. On the contrary—he makes me feel safe.

So, whatever his reasons were for offering me free training...I only feel grateful. Because with his gesture, and the addition of a few shifts at my other jobs, I can now afford my college tuition without feeling like I'm on the verge of having to sell a kidney.

I feel like I can *breathe*.

It's late when I'm finally walking into my house. So seeing Joey sitting at the kitchen table, it causes me to slow my steps.

"You're still up?" I ask, then peek at what's in front of him. "Actually, the real question is: you're still up *doing your homework?*"

Joey looks up at me long enough to roll his eyes, then immediately turns back to his computer.

"How was work?" he asks.

I settle in the chair across from him with a tired exhale. "Pretty good, actually. I did well on tips."

For some reason, that gets his attention. He lifts his gaze to me again, this time with urgency shining in his eyes.

"Hey, I was thinking," he starts, his tone not giving anything away. "I'm old enough to work now. I could get a job, help out with the bills and stuff. So, you know, you wouldn't have to work so much."

Joey's words drive a shard of something I can't describe into my gut. "Don't be silly, you don't have to do that," I say with forced ease. I don't want to let on that his offer makes me feel like I'm failing. *I'm* the one who needs to worry about money. *I'm* the one who needs to have multiple jobs. This shouldn't even be a thought in Joey's brain.

His brow furrows in confusion. "Why not? I'm almost fifteen. Plenty of kids get jobs when they're in high school."

"That's exactly why," I snap, harsher than I intended. I soften my tone as I continue. "You're a *kid*, Joey. You shouldn't have to think about money and jobs and bills. You should be focusing on school, and after-school sports, and your friends. You should be doing what *teenagers* do. I don't want you worrying about anything beyond that."

Something like sadness enters his expression. "How

would you know anything about being a teenager, Sky?" he asks quietly. "You never got a chance to be one."

My eyes widen. And I can't gather a response to that.

He releases a heavy sigh. "Sky, I *am* a teenager. I'm doing all those things you just said. I hang out with my friends, I play basketball, I get my homework done. And I can do all those things because *you* take care of everything else. But..." I suck in a breath at the storm of emotions in his eyes. "But I'd like it if you could have some things, too. I know you started training, and that's finally bringing you some happiness, but I still don't like how stressed you are about money. Especially when you don't need to do it all by yourself."

To my horror, my eyes fill with tears. It softens Joey's expression, and he takes my hand. "All I'm saying is, you don't need to carry the entire weight of the world on your shoulders. It's okay to let other people carry a pound or two or ten. It doesn't make you any less of a person. Or a sister. Dad would've been so, *so* proud of how well you've taken care of our family, but he wouldn't have wanted you to do it alone."

I blink the tears away. *I'm* supposed to be the one in control, dammit. I should be the one doing the reassuring.

But Joey is so genuine in his request that I can't bear to just shoot down his idea. I squeeze his hand and say, "Okay, I'll agree to consider it. A job is a big deal, Joey, and a big change. It's not a light decision."

"I know. But I've been thinking about it for a while. I want to do it."

"I want you to finish your basketball season first," I say firmly. "For one, your schedule is unreliable with your games, and I know how much you love playing. I'd rather you be committed to it."

95

"Deal," he says with a quick nod. "My season's almost over, anyway."

"And I get final call on where you work," I tell him. "I don't want you getting taken advantage of by some shitty employer who thinks he can pay a kid a couple bucks and overwork him."

That earns me another eye roll. "Fine."

"Okay, then," I say on a shaky exhale. "We're in agreement."

Joey grins. "Okay, then."

And *God*...my heart can't decide if it wants to burst from pride or pain.

I clear the emotions from my throat under the guise of my chair squeaking as I stand up. Heading into the kitchen, I start my usual routine of meal prepping for us for the week. "Alright, well, since you're up, we might as well do some review prep. I know your history test is on Friday, so as soon as you're done with whatever you're working on, I'll quiz you on the material."

I'm met with the familiar sound of a teenager's groan and head hitting the table.

Training is hard enough that I have to take a few minutes to get my breath back when the bell finally signals the end of class. Thankfully, I'm not the only one struggling.

Aiden is smart enough to wait until Tristan's back is turned before he sends him an inappropriate gesture.

"Twenty burpees, pretty boy," Tristan orders without looking back.

Aiden grumbles something under his breath but gets to

his feet. He doesn't even seem surprised as he launches into the burpees.

It's the last class of the day, which means I'll be staying after to clean the gym, per my new membership agreement. I've seen other people spray the mats down, but I'm too appreciative to Coach to fuck this up, so I'll have to find him to ask a few questions about how he likes things done.

My blood rushes a little bit hotter at the idea of talking to him again.

We've passed each other in the gym, of course, and he taught one of my jiu-jitsu classes yesterday, but we haven't had another one-on-one conversation.

I don't consciously wait for the gym to empty, killing time by finishing my water and changing into dry clothes, but by the time I walk toward the office, there are only a handful of people by the locker rooms, all getting ready to leave.

When I knock on the door and push it open after a voice calls out for me to come in, I see Jax is still here as well, sorting through some paperwork. Coach is on his laptop at the desk, too immersed in whatever is on his screen to look up right away.

"Hey, Skylar," Jax greets with a warm smile. "What's up?"

I nod toward the mats. "I just wanted to check in about cleaning the gym—make sure I know what the chore list looks like."

"Oh, right, Dom mentioned you'd be doing that now," he says, looking to his boss.

My eyebrows rise. I've never heard anyone refer to him as anything but Coach or sir.

Jax huffs a laugh at my reaction. "We call him Coach during gym hours, but once everyone's gone...he's just Dom, the grumpy old man."

"I heard that."

Jax and I share a silent look of amusement.

"Just give me a minute, and I'll walk you through everything," Jax says, returning to the papers in his hands. "I'm almost done here."

At that, Dominic pushes back from the desk, his attention turning to us.

"Don't worry about looking for that contract. I'm pretty sure it's in the to-be-filed stack on my desk. If you could show Skylar around instead, that'd be great."

Jax brings the stack of papers in his hand to the filing cabinet in front of him. "You got it." He pushes past me where I'm still standing in the doorway and gestures for me to follow.

It only takes him a few minutes to show me where the broom is to sweep, the wipes for the heavy bags, and the spray bottle and mop for the mats.

"All clear?" he asks once he's finished our trip around the gym. "Any questions?"

I shake my head and reach for the broom. "It's pretty self-explanatory. I just wanted to make sure there wasn't anything that he needed done in a specific way or something."

"Nah, it's what you'd expect. It's just annoying because we have to disinfect everything after every jiu-jitsu class. Dirty mats are the easiest way to spread ringworm."

I shiver at the thought. "I'll make sure I'm thorough. Thanks for showing me around."

"Anytime." He hesitates before walking off. "I'm glad you're staying at the gym, Skylar. It would've sucked if you had to quit."

My smile is warm, and pleasantly surprised. I signed up

here because I was fascinated by the sport, but somehow... the people are beginning to mean something to me too.

"Thanks, Jax. I'm glad too."

With one last smile aimed my way, he turns and heads to the front desk, where he grabs his gym bag from beneath the chair.

"Alright, Dom, I'm done for the night," he calls out. "You need anything else from me?"

Dominic steps out of the office and says, "No, that's all. I'll see you at noon tomorrow. Aiden said he can finally start coming to the pro practices, so we'll make tomorrow a wringer."

Jax chuckles and adjusts his bag strap on his shoulder. "Sounds like a fun time." He heads toward the front door, but then pauses and turns back. "Oh, and congratulations on being inducted into the UFC Hall of Fame, you sneaky bastard."

My attention snaps to Dominic. "You *what?*"

Dominic, to no one's surprise, looks uncomfortable as he shrugs. "It's nothing."

Jax barks out a laugh. "You are *such* a humble asshole." He looks over at me. "It's only one of the most prestigious awards in the MMA community. But this guy says it's 'nothing.'" He shakes his head in mock-disappointment. "I had to learn about it from Tristan."

Dominic simply shrugs again.

Jax laughs and claps his friend on the shoulder. "Have a good night, Dom."

"Night, Jax."

And after he sends a final wave in my direction, I'm left alone with Dominic.

My gaze darts toward the man, my *coach*, as my grip

tightens on the broom. His eyes don't meet mine as he asks, "Jax set you up with everything?"

I nod. "Yup, I'm all good. I don't know how long this usually takes, but I'll try not to keep you here later than usual."

"Take your time," he says, looking toward his office. "I'll be in here if you need anything."

I feel more than hear Dominic disappear back into the office. I can't tell if he's trying to distance himself from me or if he just doesn't want to awkwardly linger out here, but I start in on my job before I can think too much about it.

It doesn't take me long to sweep up both rooms. Wiping the heavy bags down takes me a little bit, just because there are so many, but it's only twenty minutes later that I'm returning to the utility closet beside the locker rooms to get stuff for the mats.

Grabbing the bucket, I carry it over to the kitchen sink in the welcome area at the front of the gym. I can't stop myself from glancing at the couch where I spent two hours the other night watching fights that I can't remember the results of.

I fill the bucket halfway, but then it gets too heavy to hold, so I put it on the floor and try to figure out if the faucet is detachable so I can fill it the rest of the way. It's obvious that the head can come off, but I can't get it to stretch into a hose. I tug on it a few times, but it feels like it might be stuck.

"Hey...Coach?" I call out, and I hear the sound of the door opening immediately. "Is there a secret to getting this faucet to work? I can't get it to detach."

I feel his warmth as he stops behind me. It takes everything in me to keep control of the shiver that wants to run through me from his overwhelming presence.

"Yeah, it gets stuck sometimes. Just twist it a little to the left before you pull."

I half expect him to reach over me and do it himself—hell, I'm half-*hoping* for it—but he keeps a few feet between us as he moves over to the kitchenette. Swallowing my disappointment, I follow his directions.

Only, the second I twist the head of the faucet to the left, the water suddenly goes from running into the sink...

To squirting out of the break where I just twisted. Right in my face.

I let out a yelp and slap my hand down on the handle to turn off the stream. Beside me, I hear a rumble of laughter.

"Oh my God," I splutter, blinking the water from my eyes. I snap my head to the side and aim an outraged stare in his direction. "You knew that would happen!"

Leaning his hip against the counter, he crosses his arms over his chest as his chuckles trail off. "I saw Tristan do it to Aiden the other day. Wanted to see if it was as satisfying of a prank as it looked."

My eyes narrow, my glare intensifying as I feel water drip from my chin onto my tank top. "And what's the verdict?"

He lifts a hand to his mouth to cover a clearly elated smile. "It's as satisfying as it looked."

I'm almost as surprised by the admission as I am that he played an actual prank. Seeing him do something I'd expect from my teenage brother is a shock in itself.

I have no response but to flick the water from my fingers into his face.

It earns me a bark of laughter in return.

Which is enough to make me turn the sink on again—leaving the faucet in its default position—and attempt to splash the stream of water at him.

Another burst of laughter, one I match, and he lifts his hand up to shield his face—not that my attack does anything. The more I try to splash him, the more he laughs, and I can't get enough of it.

Giving up on the sink, I lean down to scoop some of the water from the bucket into my hand. I'm too frantic to get much in my palm, but I manage to hit Dominic in the face with enough water that his laughter cuts off with a surprised grunt.

A grin stretches across my lips at the victory, and I lean down to do it again. My second attack gets his arms where he's blocking his face, and my third gets his shirt wet. But by then, I distantly realize that Dom has grabbed the water bottle from the counter.

In a split second, he twists off the top, aims the opening in my direction, and squeezes both sides of the plastic bottle.

I yelp as I'm blasted by the water. It catches me straight in the face, drenching my face, my hair, my shirt.

"I *cannot* believe you just did that!" I shriek, unable to catch my breath as I laugh harder. Then, in my desperation to retaliate, I lean down and grip the sides of the bucket, fully intending to end the war by dumping the entire thing on him.

But before I can get it off the ground, arms are wrapping around me, and a deep laugh is rumbling against my back.

"Don't even think about it." Dominic chuckles. "You already have enough to clean up."

"*You* started it!" I exclaim, wriggling in his arms. "You should be the one to clean it up."

"Sorry, that's not our deal," he says, his lips close to my ear. I can feel the heat of his body—though with him wrapped this tightly around me, the heat could be coming from either of us.

I stop trying to escape. With my back to his chest, I can't see Dominic's expression, can't get a read on what he's thinking. I can only feel every pound of my heart as I wait for what he says next, because his grip around me isn't loosening one bit.

"Come on, Skylar, this hold should be easy to get out of," he teases, his voice a low rumble against my back. My suppressed shiver surfaces at the sound.

I hate the idea of getting out of the hold, but the competitor in me refuses to back down. I grip Dominic's hands, then push all my weight down on where they're clasped around my waist. The second I feel his grip loosen, I spin around so my back is no longer to him.

Which just means I'm still close enough to reach him, but now we're facing each other.

I catch a split second of pride on his face that I broke his grip with the correct technique. But then he realizes how close we are, and the smile fades.

Only a few inches separate us. I have to look up to meet his gaze, but I can still count every droplet of water dripping from his jaw. The jaw that's now clenched. His eyes blaze, never looking away from me, and I can see his chest heaving with his breaths.

I can't bring myself to move, speak, anything. I can only wait with bated breath to see what he's going to do.

Even though I know what I'm *dying* for him to do.

I expect him to either pounce or step away. He surprises me by doing neither.

Lifting a hand to my face, he gently brushes a water droplet off the bow of my lips.

I suck in a breath at the touch. It only takes a second, but my lips feel on fire where he touched them.

Before I can bring my hand to my lips to soothe the tingling he left behind, I watch as awareness comes back to his gaze. Whatever haze he sunk into that led to that touch, he seems shocked by it now.

He wrenches his attention from me and reaches for a towel to clean up the counter. For a long moment, I can only stare at him, but when he eventually mutters a brisk, "Sorry," I also snap back to reality, grabbing the mop and cleaning the floor where water had spilled.

I have no idea what to say or how to act right now, but Dominic doesn't seem to have the same problem. Putting us firmly back in the space of boss and worker, he shows me how to detach the faucet and fill the bucket at my feet the rest of the way.

"Let me know if you need anything else," he says in a stilted voice. And he doesn't wait for me to respond before he's disappearing into his office.

I stare after him as I digest what the fuck just happened.

But I can hardly stand here mulling over something I'm sure I can't find the answer to in my head, so I return to my work. I mop the mats the way Jax showed me, making sure to be thorough but quick. I'm so focused on covering every inch of the mat that I don't allow myself to think about anything else. When I'm done, I put the floor fans on a timer to start drying them and head back to the front of the gym to collect my things.

"I'm all done out here," I call into the office. "Anything else you need me to do?"

Dominic comes out of the office with the same stone expression he was wearing going in.

"You swept and mopped?" I nod. "And you wiped down the heavy bags?" Another nod. "Then that's it." He hesitates, then adds, "Thanks for...everything."

"Of course. Thanks for...the opportunity."

Shit, I need to get out of here.

"Alright, well, I'm going to get going," I mumble. "I'll see you for class tomorrow night."

Dominic gives me a stiff nod. But by the time I pull my sweatshirt on and gather my things, he's also packed up and turning off the lights around the gym.

"I'll walk you out," he says.

I don't argue. I just follow him outside.

When the door locks behind us, I stand awkwardly on the sidewalk, trying to figure out how to salvage this night and get us back to normal, since that's clearly what he wants to do. But I'm coming up empty.

Dominic's eyes look over my shoulder to the bus stop at the end of the street. He stiffens, and it's not hard to guess that he hates the idea of me taking the bus home. Memories of last week, of him trying to convince me to let him drive me, suddenly assault my brain. He sounded so worried then, and honestly, part of me wishes for that worry again, if only to get some kind of reaction out of him now.

But there's a bigger part of me that stands firm in my independence, so even though it looks like he wants to make the offer again, he takes one look at my expression that screams *don't* and clenches his jaw shut.

"Be safe getting home," is all he says.

I nod. "Of course. See you tomorrow, Coach."

And even though our separation is stilted and confusing, we're also very clearly back to being coach and student. I should be glad that our risky moment hasn't ruined or threatened my membership here, in this place that's brought me peace and happiness. My life and everything in it is back to its carefully-constructed shape.

So why does that make me sad?

13

COACH

I avoid Skylar for two weeks.

I still see her almost every day, and she's still in several of my classes during the week, but I only give her as much attention as to be polite, and to be a good coach. I even keep up our extra training sessions, but I schedule them to be at the same time as other classes to ensure that Skylar and I are never alone. And with the gym filled with people and with the sounds of shouted instructions, there's no space for us to do anything but train.

The only time the strain between us is obvious is when she stays late to clean and we close up the gym together. Those are the nights that my inappropriate thoughts appear without invite and make it more difficult to be around her.

I don't understand this pull I feel toward Skylar. My gym is not just my business, it's also my life—one I've worked damn hard to build. I protect the boundaries I've put in place to keep those things safe, including the relationships I have with the people inside of it. I've never once been interested in being anything other than a coach inside this building. Even with Tristan and my fighters, who I like immensely, I don't want to *hang out* with them. I don't want to know about their personal lives—beyond maybe their mental and general well-being—and I don't wonder about their interests outside of here. I have a clear-cut coaching relationship with them and that's it. We're not friends.

But Skylar is...different. I know she's a student, but for the first time in my life, I want to erase that distance. I don't want her to keep her questions between gym hours; I want to know exactly what thoughts are rolling around in her brain. I want to keep her late and learn about her.

As much as I tried to ignore this pull toward her, the first night she stayed late to clean made that impossible. I mean for fuck's sake, I played a *prank* on her. I can't remember a time that I was ever playful with someone. Who even am I? Why is this girl affecting me so much? There are so many reasons I should stay away from her—my age and our power imbalance being the two standouts—yet I can't stop myself from wanting to spend time with her. Last time, I almost *kissed* her...

I shut down that thought as soon as it hits. There isn't a chance in fucking hell.

Yanking off my shirt with a frustrated grunt, I remind myself of the million reasons that Skylar is off-limits as I undress and step into the shower. I'm her coach, and her kind-of boss, and even thinking about her is inappropriate.

I force my thoughts toward this week's teaching curriculum as I scrub away the day's sweat. Everyone's been doing well with the judo throws, but the wrestling take-downs have been harder for people to grasp. *I should make tomorrow's class all about wrestling.*

I start to mentally run through the drills, visualizing each step of the move and preparing for the ones people tend to get stuck on. Some drive straight forward, instead of to the side. Some don't follow through. Some have to work on dropping their knee all the way to the mat.

My focus zeroes in on this last scenario. The person practicing the takedown has to kneel and pause, specifically to emphasize that step. They stay there, on their knees, red hair splayed over their shoulder as they look up at me with wide eyes, wordlessly asking for approval—

I don't realize I've wrapped my hand around my cock until the thought of Skylar sends a sharp stab of lust through my lower body. I can't help sliding my fist over my length any more than I can stop the image in my head from crystallizing.

Skylar, on her knees before me, staring up at me like this is the only place in the world she wants to be. When I free myself from my shorts, her eyes dart down to my hardening cock, and then her tongue slides out, wetting those pouty pink lips that are just begging for me to slide between them.

My hand glides over my length, my chest heaving as I struggle to breathe through the stifling heat of the fantasy. I barely feel the water beating down on my skin anymore; all I can focus on is the friction on my cock and how badly I wish it wasn't my hand.

I grip her ponytail with one hand and guide my cock to her mouth with the other. She opens for me right away, like she's been waiting for this moment. Then she wraps her lips around me and sucks.

I jerk myself faster and faster, lost to the image of Skylar with my cock down her throat. I'm too far gone to feel the shame and guilt that usually accompanies these kinds of thoughts—the ones that make me stop before this point.

But it's been two long weeks of this. Two weeks of seeing her, of spending time with her, of keeping a firm lid on my inappropriate thoughts about her. And I've reached my breaking point.

Imagining Skylar on her knees before me, mouth full and taking my cock like the good little student she is...

I fall forward with a moan, bracing a hand on my shower wall as I come all over the tiles.

I'm fucked.

The next night, I steel myself before I walk out of the office. Because I have a private lesson with Skylar tonight, and after losing control and jerking off with her on my mind, my defenses are at an all-time low.

I stride out of my office and look around for Skylar. Her jiu-jitsu class just finished, and she usually drills moves on her own while she waits for me to be ready.

Sure enough, I find her practicing takedowns on the mats. I open my mouth to tell her she's on the heavy bag today, but before I can get a word out, I hear Tristan's voice from behind me.

"Coach, you got a minute?"

I shift my attention to the other side of the room, where the chairs are set up for people to watch classes. I find Tristan standing there with a stocky, middle-aged guy.

Twisting to look back at Skylar, I ask her, "Skylar, are you okay to wait a little bit? I need to talk to Tristan. I should be about fifteen minutes, then we can get started."

She nods. "Take your time. I'll work on the heavy bag, so don't worry about me."

I grunt out a *"thanks,"* and then I'm leading Tristan and the other man over to the seating area where we do consults with new people.

That fifteen minutes turns into thirty. By the time I'm done, my steps to the heavy bag room are rushed.

But when I open the door, I'm not even a little surprised to find Skylar completely engrossed in the combinations she's working on the bag. She doesn't notice I'm in the room until I call out her name.

Her startled gaze meets mine, and suddenly there's heat sparking through my body. It's not the first time it's happened, and it's no easier to ignore. All I can do is try.

"Out here, we're rolling today," I call out in a hardened voice.

Skylar wordlessly follows me into the other room.

"We'll focus on jiu-jitsu today," I say without preamble. I'm wound too tight lately to be any kind of polite or gentle about training. "Good?"

"Yes, sir."

Fuck, what those words do to me coming from her mouth.

I was planning on working on her guard today, but with the way I'm feeling, I'm buzzing with adrenaline, and I need to get rid of it.

Takedowns, it is.

"Let's go back to that sweep you liked last week. We did it in the gi, but you can do it just as easily in no-gi."

We settle into our usual routine. She picks things up quickly during the week, so we've been using these sessions to fine tune and make them more suited to her style.

I don't realize Max is standing beside the mat until I'm being thrown by Skylar and flying through the air. I land with a thud at Max's feet, slapping the mat to control my fall.

"Sorry, I didn't want to interrupt," he says.

I push myself to my feet. "It's okay. What's up?"

"I hate doing this last minute, but I can't clean the mats tonight," he says with an apologetic wince. "Class is all finished, and everyone's gone, but I got a text as I was pulling out the sprayer and found out my apartment has a leak. Apparently, my upstairs neighbor's tub is dripping into my living room right now."

"Jesus," I mutter. "What are you still doing here? Go home. I'll take care of the mats, don't worry about it."

"Thanks," he breathes out, visibly relieved. Then he's immediately rushing toward the exit. "I'll be in for pro training tomorrow," he calls over his shoulder.

The door slams shut before I can respond.

Sighing, I turn my attention back to Skylar. "Let's keep going."

"I can do the mats," she offers.

I shake my head. "You don't have to do that. Tonight's not your night to clean. I'll just do them when we're done here."

"Our deal was that I'd do them any night I'm here until the last class. So, I'll do them." She hesitates, then adds, "Let me earn my keep."

I deflate, too tired from the insanity of my day today to argue. "We'll split the work. We're already going to be here too late since we started late, so we might as well get it done as quickly as possible. But I appreciate the help."

Once we're done with our lesson, we separate to get started on the cleaning. I move to the heavy bags while Skylar sweeps up, and at the same time, we head to the supply closet to grab the sprayer and some mops. We're silent as we take up our space on the mats, with me untangling the hose for the cleaning solution and Skylar leaning on her mop as she waits for me to spray.

And then, for the third time tonight, the universe hands me the shit end of the stick. Because the sprayer is broken.

I let out an aggressive, muttered curse. These things are fucking expensive, but they're worth every penny because of how much quicker they make the cleaning process.

Which is now going to take forever.

"Do you have another one?" Skylar finally asks after I fumble with the hose connection for a minute.

"No," I grumble. I'm going to have to do it manually now.

"What do you need?"

I let out a defeated sigh. "I don't have any spray bottles, so we'll have to drip the cleaning solution onto the mats and spread it with the mops."

She doesn't even hesitate, she just nods and rushes to the supply closet for two mops.

It's slow going, made even worse by our painful silence. It takes us almost three times as long to clean the mats, even with the two of us doing the work, and the whole time, I find myself wishing we could talk and laugh easily again. But I can't open that door. Especially not when with every passing glance, I feel tension lingering between us.

It's past 11 p.m. when we finally finish. I'm physically tired, mentally exhausted, and I just want to get out of here.

But after Skylar and I close up the gym, I realize the universe has one more decision left to throw at me today.

14

COACH

Standing on the sidewalk where we usually say goodnight, and where I always watch her walk to the bus stop at the end of the street, it hits me that it's way later than it usually is when we do this.

I don't doubt that Skylar knows what I'm thinking, because she's already looking for an escape route. But before she can bolt, I say what I haven't said since that first night, when she asked me not to try to take care of her.

"It's late. Let me give you a ride home."

She glances toward the bus stop again.

"I told you, I don't need to be—"

"Skylar. Just let me drive you home. Don't make me beg."

That puts an end to her fight. Eyes widening, she only hesitates a moment before giving me a small nod.

"Okay," she says. "Thank you."

With her finally agreeing to my offer, the tightness in my chest loosens, and I let out a heavy breath. I'm not sure if she sees my relief, but I jerk my head in the direction of my car.

"Come on, I'm this way."

She follows along, allowing Brutus to walk beside me. When we reach my car in the designated parking lot, she waits patiently as I open the back door and nudge Brutus to climb in.

"You want to put your bag in the trunk? If you put it on the back seat, he'll probably slobber all over it."

Skylar lets out a giggle at that, the sound tinkling like bells in the cold city air and making something take flight in my stomach.

With both of our bags packed away in the trunk, we climb into my car.

"Where to?" I ask.

"I'm over in Fairmount," she answers, her hands clasped in her lap and nerves lining her body. At first, I think it's because she's uncomfortable with being alone in the car with me. Which is when I realize I didn't even bat an eyelash before offering to drive a student home, a boundary I've never crossed before.

For fuck's sake, what am I *doing*?

But before I can spiral, I glance at Skylar again, and I realize...she's not nervous about being alone with me. She looks the way she did when she almost quit: uncertain about asking for help.

That I can handle.

"I actually used to live around there," I say as I pull out of the parking lot, wanting to put her at ease with some conversation about myself. "You know Eastern State Penitentiary?"

I see her nod out of the corner of my eye.

"That's where I grew up."

That earns me a raised eyebrow. "In a prison?"

"Yup. How do you think I got started with fighting?

Those 'Muay Thai in Prison' documentaries aren't based on fiction."

She huffs a laugh, relaxing a little more into her seat.

"I'm three streets over from the prison on Poplar," she says on a chuckle. "I was actually going to use it as your landmark for getting me home."

"Prison, it is. But next time, you're sitting in the back for this ride. So you can get the full experience."

Another laugh has my stressed and tired mood starting to dissipate.

"So did you actually live around Fairmount?" she asks curiously. "Or where did you grow up?"

"I grew up in West Chester, but I've been in the city since I started fighting. I lived in Fairmount for a while. Actually, I feel like I've lived in every part of Philly."

"Well, yeah. Twenty years will give you the time to jump around."

I aim a glare her way at the reminder of my age, but she's grinning wide, so my look softens almost immediately.

"What about you?" I ask her. "Grow up around here?"

She shrugs. "It's kinda the same for me, minus growing up outside of the city. I've bounced around, but always within Philly. I've been in Fairmount the longest, but only because we're grandfathered into a pretty nice spot right now."

I rest an elbow on my window as I rub my beard in thought. I want to ask her more questions, but my meter for how much knowledge is appropriate is totally shot with this girl. When does it go from normal small talk to *I want to get to know you?*

I decide on one more.

"Restless family?"

A pause. "Restless isn't the right word. We just...lived where we could. Whatever we could afford."

Money again.

I'm starting to realize money plays a big part in a lot of Skylar's life decisions. And as much as it makes it easier to understand her and her life, it also just makes me really sad.

I've never had that kind of money problem. Sure, there were plenty of times I lived paycheck to paycheck when I was nineteen and living on my own as my fighting career started, but I never reached a point where I had to consider giving up my gym membership.

I don't even want to think about what else she was thinking about giving up for the sake of whatever money she needed.

I feel the weight of her words, and the emotions that they evoke, so I try to steer us toward a safer topic.

"If you could live anywhere in the world, where would it be?"

And *bingo*, my attempt works like a charm. A smile immediately lights up her face.

"Probably somewhere in Colorado."

"You a snow sport kinda girl?"

She shakes her head. "No, I've never tried any of that. I just love the idea of living in a small town in the mountains like you always see in Colorado pictures. Just surrounded by fresh air, gorgeous views, and none of the chaos of a city. Seems like it would be the least stressful place to live."

The last comment hooks in my brain. Any person would love to live in a place with views they consider gorgeous, but it sounds like she's focusing more on the stress-free part than anything else.

"Have you ever been out there to visit?" I ask.

"No. I've never been anywhere." The way she says it is so matter of fact, I feel myself frowning.

"Did you get to travel a lot when you were fighting?" she asks.

"Uh...you could say that."

I see her quizzical look in my peripheral. "How would *you* say it?"

"I traveled, but it was never to anyplace good."

She shifts in her seat slightly, turning to look at me. "What do you consider 'not anyplace good?'"

I let out a heavy sigh. "Back when I was fighting, they weren't exactly sending us to Madison Square Garden. The most interesting place I ever fought was in the city with the largest teapot in the world."

Skylar lets out a delighted laugh. "A *teapot?* Oh my God, where was that?"

I aim a grin at her. "Chester, West Virginia."

She dissolves into giggles in the passenger seat. "I have so many questions."

"Alright, but if they're mocking questions, I'm dropping you off at the prison."

"Yeah, yeah, okay." She waves me off. "How big is it? Did you actually see it? Did the MMA organization take you there? Did they tell you that about the city, or did you find out on your own? I would've *died* to be a fly on the wall when you found out that's the city you'd be fighting in."

I shoot her a scolding look. "Prison it is."

She falls back against the window in another fit of laughter.

"So, no cool work trips for you?" she asks with a grin.

"Not when I was fighting, no. Now I get to travel for Tristan's fights, though, so the MMA employers made up for it."

She hums thoughtfully. "I know he just fought in Vegas, but where else do you think they'll send him?"

"Technically, I can't tell you anything before the contract is signed, but..." I size her up with an exaggerated side glance, already knowing she's trustworthy enough that I could tell her anything. "We're trying to sign a fight in London for later this year."

Skylar immediately straightens in her seat. "London?! That's so cool! And they pay for everything?"

I nod in answer, hearing her age in the comment for the first time since I met her. But it's an innocent kind of reminder—one that makes me think more about giving her that kind of opportunity, rather than highlighting that she hasn't had it before.

"I guess that's one of the benefits of fighting in the big leagues, huh?" she wonders out loud. Then she gives me a mischievous grin. "Or at least, it is when you're competing during a decade when fighting is popular enough to warrant being sent to London instead of the city with the world's largest teapot."

Since I'm currently stopped at a stoplight, I make it a point to unlock the passenger door with a loud click. "Guess we're not even making it to the prison."

She chuckles. "I'm up here on the right."

The mood in the car sobers at that. It's late enough that the streets are packed with cars parked in for the night, so I have to pull over into the crosswalk.

"Thanks for letting me drive you," I say hesitantly. "I know you're capable of getting home by yourself, and of smacking down anyone who tries to start something"—she huffs a laugh, giving me the courage to continue—"but it makes me feel better to see you get home safe and sound."

Skylar glances at the townhouse we're parked in front of.

I want to look at her place, maybe get a little more insight into Skylar's life outside of the gym, but I can't take my attention off of her long enough to do that.

After a moment, she turns to face me fully. "Thanks for the ride. You didn't have to, but I really do appreciate it."

I hold her gaze and try to get a read on what she's thinking. *Does she hate that I know where she lives now? Did I overstep? Did I just become the creepy coach who pushed for something he shouldn't have?*

But when she continues to look at me, giving me the chance to memorize her expression, I know she's not uncomfortable. Not even a little bit.

That's not fear in her eyes—there are no nerves or discomfort. There's no desperation to get out of my car and out of this situation that shouldn't happen for so many reasons.

She's giving me the same look I remember so clearly.

The look that had me touching her.

Her chest is rapidly rising and falling, and her pupils have blown wide. She's staring so intently into my eyes that I have a sneaking suspicion she's really just trying not to look elsewhere. And when her focus drops to my lips, I know I'm right.

Fuck.

My own gaze travels over every inch of her face. From her striking green eyes, to her freckled cheeks, to her plush pink lips that are parted slightly.

As my grip tightens on the steering wheel, it suddenly feels like it's a thousand degrees in the car. I can't breathe, can't look away from this untouchable girl who's sitting inches away from me. Not just because she's half my age, but also because she's my student, and basically my employee, and this is so. fucking. wrong.

And yet, when I start to lean forward—because I'm mesmerized, and I want to taste her, or, *fuck*, maybe just be closer to her—there isn't a chance in hell I can fight this charge between us.

I think she's moving closer, too. And now neither of us are breathing, and there's barely an inch between our lips, and I can practically *taste* her—

The sound of a dog barking just outside of my car startles us apart.

Skylar jumps from fright, then looks around for the close sound. I can see the owner over her shoulder, the woman who's walking a tiny little dog that noticed Brutus drooling out of my back window.

The older lady pulls her dog away, embarrassed at the incessant yipping. But when she looks into the car to wave her apology, and she notices Skylar and me—alone, parked on the street at 11:30 p.m., sitting way too close together—a look of confusion, and then disapproval, crosses her face.

With a judgmental huff, she pulls on her dog's leash and keeps walking down the street.

The car feels heavy with our silence. I can't think of a single thing to say right now. I'm confused and disappointed in my lack of control, yet so fucking annoyed at the interruption. All I can do is grip my steering wheel with both hands and grind my teeth in frustration.

"I should probably get going," comes Skylar's quiet voice after a moment. I hear her shuffling her jacket in her lap, but I can't bring myself to look at her.

After another second, she pulls on the door handle to get out. That sound is what snaps me out of my frozen state, and what reminds me that I shouldn't be a total dick.

I'm out of my car and opening the trunk before she can

round the back. Pulling her gym bag out, I finally lift my gaze to hers.

She looks... uncertain. Just as confused as I am. But there isn't a hint of embarrassment or regret on her face.

"Thanks again," she says, holding my eyes.

"You're welcome," I force out, my voice like gravel.

My hands clench fists where she can't see. I'm too desperate to just fucking touch her—

A breeze blows by, and a shiver runs through Skylar. I jerk my chin toward her house. "You should go. It's late."

She nods, adjusting the bag strap on her shoulder. But before she turns to go, a small smile appears on her face.

"You're going to wait until I actually get inside, aren't you?"

I dig my hands into my pockets and give her a hard stare in answer.

Her smile widens. "I knew you'd be the type."

"What, old-fashioned?"

The look she gives me is warm and sweet and makes me want to get close to her all over again.

"The good kind," she says softly. Giving me one more smile, she turns and starts to walk up the steps of the town-house. "Goodnight, Coach."

And even though I told her I'd wait for her to get inside the house, I stand on the sidewalk for far longer than that.

15

SKYLAR

I have no idea which version of Dominic I'm going to find when I walk into the gym.

Is it going to be the coach keeping his distance? The professional who doesn't open up or test boundaries? Or will I get to enjoy the man who I feel comfortable talking to and laughing with, one who actually sees *me*.

The same man who I know is experiencing the same tension I have been.

I wasn't sure of his feelings before. But everything changed when he drove me home. Now, there's no more hiding or denying what's happening between us.

I've never been affected by someone like this. A single look has my heart racing. A simple touch might make it *stop*.

And I wasn't the only one. One look at Dominic made that obvious.

I want to say I understand why he's fighting this attraction between us, but I think that would be a lie. Sure, a coach dating a student would probably turn a few heads, but it's not like it's illegal. I've seen plenty of female fighters marry their coaches. So what's wrong with a kiss behind closed doors?

Whatever his reason for fighting this is, I expect to be greeted by a cold, distant Coach Dominic, but I'm stunned to find the opposite.

When Dominic makes eye contact with me while I'm warming up for my class, everything I think I know goes out the window. I forget about everyone around us, about the fact that it took me all day to school my emotions and promise myself that I wouldn't react when I finally saw him. I forget all about how what's happening between us might be wrong. With one glance, I forget all of it.

He's not avoiding me, he's letting me see the full force of his emotions. And I can sense every ounce of his hunger, his yearning, his hesitance.

That knowledge has me stuck in my head during my class. Thank God, it's cardio kickboxing, with mindless repetitions instead of new techniques, because the surprise of seeing Dominic's unfettered emotions has me spinning with confusing assumptions.

I thought the attraction was one-sided.

I thought he wouldn't want me even if it wasn't.

I thought he hated the idea of us because it would be against the rules.

My movement on the heavy bag stutters at the last thought.

The rules? Or *his* rules?

I never really stopped to think about where his hesitation would come from. I figured with our age and with him being in an authority position that he wouldn't take anything like this lightly, but I never thought about *how far* that would stretch. Is it frowned upon or completely against the rules with a zero percent chance of anything happening?

I glance over at Dominic where he's working with Tristan on the other side of the room. His attention is wholly on his fighter, but the second the rest timer goes off and Tristan turns away to grab some water, Dominic's eyes immediately flit to me.

And *yeah, that's not a zero percent chance look.*

The moment I reach that conclusion, this class ends and my next one begins. I don't have any time to dwell, because there's a 185-pound man on top of me trying to break my arm and I can't afford any distractions. So, I don't think about Dominic for the rest of the night.

But then the gym empties out and we're the last two left. And even when we're in different rooms, the heat between us is stifling.

The closer I get to being done with cleaning, the more nervous I become. There's just something about Dominic, something about the way he disarms me, the way he sees the real me...

I have no idea what to say to him. I know what I *want* to say, but that doesn't mean that's what I *should* say. Do I tell him I want him? Or that we can pretend nothing happened? Is it better if I don't say anything?

Dominic takes the choice out of my hands when he walks out of his office and nears the mat I'm sweeping. His expression is too unreadable to know what he's thinking, but at the very least, I can tell he couldn't stop himself from coming out here.

After a moment's hesitation, he asks, "Need any help finishing up?"

I look around at the gym. "No, I'm just about done. I'm getting pretty quick at this." My eye catches on one of the dummies on the edge of the mat. "Actually, can you help me move BOB? I apparently need to up my strength training, because I could barely get that thing two inches down the mat."

Dominic chuckles at that, some of the tension leaving his shoulders. "Yeah, I can move him."

I start toward the dummy, but Dominic beats me there. And before I can motion for him to grab one end and I'll grab the other, he wraps an arm under its middle and hoists it onto his shoulder. With one hand and zero effort.

"Did you want him somewhere specific, or just back in the corner?" he asks.

But I'm just gaping at the sight of Dominic being so effortless in his strength.

God, this man is so hot. And he has no idea.

When he lifts an eyebrow in question, I manage to stammer, "Uh...um, just the corner. Is fine."

He turns and heads toward the corner, with me following behind him with one of the smaller medicine balls that goes in the same spot. He tosses the dummy on top of the others, and I do the same with the ball in my hand, but I miscalculate where he's dropping BOB and end up tripping over its foot as the medicine ball leaves my hand. I let out a yelp and try to twist so I'll fall on my hands instead of my face.

Except, I never make it to the ground. Because I'm yanked back into a hard chest.

My chest rises and falls with rapid breaths, shock freezing me in place. But when I finally take in what happened, and where I am, my skin lights on fire from my current position.

Every part of my front is plastered to Dominic. Not only did he pull me back, but he pulled me tight enough against him that there isn't an inch separating us from chest to thighs. One of his arms is even wrapped around my waist, holding us together. The other is still clutching my arm where he pulled me.

The only part of him I can't feel or read is his face, because he's almost a foot taller than I am. But if the way his grip is tightening on my arm is any indication, he needs the contact just as much as I do.

Taking in a silent breath for courage, I slowly tilt my face up to meet his gaze.

And immediately lose every molecule of oxygen in my lungs.

His eyes...and his expression...it's like he wants to *burn. me. up.* Like he's holding himself back with a fraying thread of control. Like he wants nothing more than to give in to this heat and let it incinerate us.

I think I might be looking at him the same way because whatever he sees in my eyes, it makes his go wholly black and his grip around my waist to tighten until I can't breathe. When his gaze drops to my lips, there isn't a chance in hell that I could hold myself back.

Pushing up on my toes, reveling in every inch of my body that slides along his as I get the additional height, I bring my mouth so close to his, I can *taste* his want. And I can feel him tremble with his restraint.

So, I make the decision for us. Because I know he wants it, because *I* want it, and because, for once in my life, I want to take something good for myself without any thought of anything else.

Covering the last inch between us, I press my lips against his.

And immediately sigh at the feel of him, my body deflating with relief. He feels...*right*. If I thought this gym felt like my safe haven, it's nothing compared to how it feels to be with Dominic.

Except, the sound I let out is like a starting pistol. In a split second, Dominic's body tenses. I don't even get to feel his lips moving against mine before he's ripping away from me.

"*What are you doing?*" he says, his voice *so loud* in the silence, I can't help but frown. His expression is stunned, and a little scared. He takes another step back to put more distance between us.

His reaction cuts into me like a knife, though part of me also understands it. But I know what I felt, and I'm not going to feel bad about going for it.

"Kissing you," I say simply.

I watch his Adam's apple bob on a rough swallow. "Why?"

I pause, softening as I decide to answer honestly. "Because I wanted to."

He almost looks more surprised that I answered the question. His voice is shell-shocked and flat when he says, "I'm almost twenty years older than you. And your coach."

His chest heaves with his breaths, and there's a wild look in his eyes. Everything about him screams defensive.

"Well, the age difference doesn't bother me," I admit with a small shrug. "And I'm pretty sure I've heard of gym owners dating fighters. So I guess I just didn't think any of that mattered."

And yeah, that's definitely panic in his eyes. The only thing he manages to get out is a desperate, "Skylar, you can't just *kiss* me. It's *wrong*."

Finally, the blatant refusal knocks me back to reality. I'm not surprised I needed to push a little, but an outright rejection drives a knife of hurt into my gut that decimates any remaining butterflies.

I look down so I don't have to meet his eyes. "Sorry," I murmur. "It won't happen again."

Cheeks burning with humiliation, I start past Dominic so I can get out of here as quickly as possible. I'll worry about how I'm going to look him in the face again when I get home.

But a grip on my arm stops me, and my breath hitches.

It takes me a second to work up the nerve to turn around and face him again. Maybe because I don't know what I'll find.

Or maybe because I *do* know.

Slowly, I turn around. And where a moment ago he looked scared, now he looks...ravenous.

The air between us stills as my heart thunders in my ears. Neither of us is breathing any longer, and our gazes lock in a way that tells me it would take the world ending to break it.

The world stands still for a beat, and then...

"*Fuck it.*"

The second he slides his hand into my hair to tilt my head up for his kiss, I'm a goner.

Because he doesn't just kiss me. He *devours* me. His lips take ownership of mine, and there's none of the frozenness or hesitation from before. I don't even know if I can call what I did a minute ago a kiss, not if *this* is how Dominic kisses.

His grip on my hip tightens and my stomach clenches in response. When he tilts my head with his other hand, licking deeper into my mouth, a groan rumbles through him, vibrating against my hands where they lay flat on his chest. The sound is enough to make a whimper build in my throat and press higher on my toes to get as close to his mouth as possible.

My desperation unleashes something in him. With a feral growl, he turns us so he can press me up against the wall. I let out a gasp at the feel of his body molding so perfectly against mine, and he swallows the breath with another heated kiss.

He can't seem to get enough. His touch is possessive, his mouth hungry, and I'm starving for air when his hips push into mine. And at the feel of his rock-hard length against my stomach, I melt all over again with a needy moan.

I don't know how long we stand there, completely connected and consumed by each other. It feels like forever, but at the same time not long enough. I'm *addicted* to him. I don't know how I ever fought the urge not to kiss him. And if the look on his face when he finally pulls away to give us a chance to breathe is any indication, he's feeling the same.

"Holy shit," he gasps, sucking down air. He leans his forehead against mine, his hand still wrapped in my hair and his body still caging me against the wall. The half inch between our mouths is the only space that exists between us.

"Yeah," I breathe. Curling my hands in his shirt, I silently beg him to kiss me again.

Unfortunately, the pause seems to have brought back some of Dominic's earlier reluctance. When he pulls away another inch, I see regret shining in his eyes. And my stomach drops at the sight.

"Skylar..."

Swallowing past the lump in my throat, I loosen my grip on his shirt. It gives him the opportunity he's so obviously looking for to step away.

And he does. Taking a step back, he says, "I shouldn't have done that."

I don't have the breath to speak. I simply nod, in what hopefully looks like understanding.

"I'm sorry," he continues, sounding truly remorseful. "I'm the older authority figure, I should've never—I *never* should've—" Now he's the one swallowing, trying to work up the courage and find the right words.

My chest aches from watching him distancing himself. But I also can't really blame him for drawing this kind of boundary in his place of work, with someone so questionable. Part of me knew it was a pipe dream to have him want me back, anyway.

"It's okay," I tell him in a tight voice. "I'm the one who initiated. I read into your kindness and got the wrong idea, and I'm sorry—"

"No, Skylar, that's not—"

"I won't let it happen again."

Expression pained, his voice is soft when he says, "You didn't get the wrong idea. And *I'm* the only one to blame. But Skylar... it just... It can't happen."

After that, there's not much to say. I give him a miserable nod of affirmation and pause just long enough for him to say anything else, but when he doesn't, I walk past him to gather my things.

I'm out the door without another word.

16

COACH

The second Skylar leaves the gym, my head starts spinning.

What the fuck did I just do?

I haven't been blind to the attraction between us. In a way, I'm not surprised that I kissed her—or that she kissed me. She's so fearless, so sure of herself, that I knew, if given the opening, she'd go for what she wanted. A dazed part of me feels honored that I'm the one she wants.

But next to that amazement, there's a cocktail of other emotions: confusion, shame, hunger. My entire night is me just lying in bed with those emotions spiraling on repeat.

Confusion because I don't know how to end this.

Shame because I don't want to end it.

Hunger when I think of what happens when I don't end it.

This can't happen. This *can't* happen. I've been telling myself I need to keep distance between us because she's my student and there's a professional boundary, but that doesn't even touch the reasons why a relationship—or whatever the hell this is—couldn't work between us.

I'm almost twice her age. She's literally a teenager, for

fuck's sake. She probably doesn't even want me; she's just innocent and enamored by an older, successful authority figure, enticed by the forbidden nature of what could be. She would get looks even if she dated one of the guys in their mid-twenties, let alone her *coach* in his mid-thirties.

People wouldn't understand. They'd look at us and they'd assume I'm her father, or at the very least, a creepy older guy trying to fuck a naïve nineteen-year-old. No one would understand a relationship between us.

And if Skylar's intention was just to start a casual, physical relationship, in the end, the same things would happen. There's no way we wouldn't eventually get found out, and then I really would look like a creepy older guy just looking for ass.

Everyone would judge me. My name as a coach, my name as a gym owner—there's a good chance even my fighters would distance themselves from me. Nothing about a relationship between me and Skylar is understandable. It can't happen.

It *can't* happen.

I don't sleep a wink. By the time I walk into the gym the next day, I've got dark circles under my eyes and look about as run-down as I feel. My stomach swirls with nerves about seeing Skylar, and guilt that I essentially have to reject her all over again when I put her back in the category of any other student.

And yet...she doesn't seem bothered by it. I shouldn't be surprised that she acts completely normal the rest of the week but, for some reason, I am.

I watch her all week, but I don't find any hurt in her eyes. She goes right back to acting like nothing happened, showing up for classes and putting in the work on the mat.

She doesn't avoid my gaze or stop herself from asking her usual questions. She's just...Skylar.

The only thing I catch is a very subtle kind of knowing sadness. She's covering her hurt with a level of patience and understanding that some grown adults aren't even capable of. She knows why I made the decision I did.

She knows. She knows and she gets it.

That guilt over expecting to tell Skylar no again becomes guilt over hurting the kindest, sweetest person I know.

That feeling only grows when I walk into the gym and find her helping Lucy. They're standing in the corner of the gym, going through some of the concussion exercises that Skylar had outlined for her. Lucy's seemed way more chipper lately, so I'm assuming the physical therapy has worked.

Skylar digs around in her bag for a second, then straightens and hands something over to Lucy. I'm close enough that I can hear their exchange.

"What's this?" Lucy asks, turning the small vial over in her hand.

"They're CBD drops," Skylar explains. "My mom swore they were little miracle drops. Any time she needed something anti-inflammatory, this is what she reached for."

Lucy's eyes go wide, and she tries to hand them back to Skylar. "I can't take this, they're your mom's. I'm sure she needs them more than I do for my silly little headaches."

Skylar's shaking her head before she even finishes, and she pushes the vial back toward Lucy. "She can't take them anymore. They mess with her new meds, so they've just been sitting around the house. Take them. There's still a third of it left, so use it as you finish the rest of your physical therapy."

Lucy still looks skeptical, but she pockets the vial.

"Thank you," she tells Skylar. "You're a good teammate. And friend. I'm glad you're here."

Skylar smiles, her voice soft when she says, "Me too."

"And I'm sorry about your mom," Lucy adds softly. "If you ever need any help, with anything, you know we're all here for you, right?"

I see the sheen in Skylar's eyes even from here. She swallows roughly and nods.

Just then, Tristan calls that class is starting. As the girls take their place on the mat, I move over to the reception desk.

I work as they train. But every so often, my attention drifts over to Skylar, to where she's paired with a new girl. It's her very first class, and she's clearly nervous. She's listening intently to Max's instructions, but she's trying to fly through every step all at once and inevitably confusing herself more.

Skylar, who's partnered with her, tries to talk her through the move again. I can hear her soothing voice even from here. She's patient as she repeats the steps for the girl, as she walks her through each of them one at a time. She barely gets any reps in herself because she spends two thirds of the round letting the other girl work.

God, this girl. This wonderful, beautiful, selfless girl.

And...I'm an idiot. She knows *exactly* what she wants. She is unapologetically herself. So thinking she only wants me because we're forbidden is not only a cop-out on my end, but also an insult to her.

I become mesmerized by her for the rest of the class. I watch as she helps her partner, as she buckles down and gets her own work in—as she throws everything she has into her training, while still being a kind and helpful team-mate. She's incredible.

I don't know when it happens, but my guilt over putting a boundary between us morphs to anger that I need to. She's incredible. She's incredible as a student, as an athlete—as a person. I *want* her. I want to spend time with her, to talk to her, to be more than just her coach.

Why does she have to be everything I want?

My anger becomes directed at the universe, for taunting me with something I can't have. Because I *know* it's a bad idea to pursue anything with her. It's just a fact. And yet... I'm fully aware that I'm not going to be able to hold this professional boundary. There's just no way. She's too perfect.

And that's even before I remember that today is one of the days I give Skylar a private lesson.

After classes have ended, I find her sitting on the edge of the mat, patiently waiting for me to start our lesson. As soon as she sees me toeing my shoes off, she stands from her chair and hurries to meet me in the center of the mat.

"Your passing skills need work," I start, knowing my words are harsh but completely unable to do anything about it. I'm vibrating with the chaos that's coming from wanting to be near her but knowing I shouldn't, as well as *needing* to be near her and knowing I *can't.*

The complexity makes me meaner than I intend to be.

"I'll show you the move first, then you can practice," I say, pointing at the mat where I want her to lie down. It isn't until she sucks in a breath and goes down to the mat that I realize how much it looks like I just ordered her to my feet.

And if I had any hope of banishing last week from my brain, this moment makes that hope disappear in a heartbeat.

I've always been confused when people ask me if jiu-jitsu feels sexual. There are top and bottom positions, yes, and God knows I've been stuck in a position more than once where someone is just sitting on my head, but I've never, not once, thought about it in a sexual way. This is a sport, a *violent* sport, where I'm basically simulating murder in the form of a chess match. There's nothing even remotely arousing about it.

But right now, for the first time in my twenty plus year career, I'm fighting to keep my dick from getting hard.

As Skylar settles on her back and spreads her legs to give me space to kneel between them, I make peace with the fact that there isn't a chance in hell this couldn't be considered sexual. Because I'm now climbing on top of the girl I can't stop fantasizing about, the one invading every one of my dreams and making me wake in a tangle of sweaty sheets.

I mentally talk myself through the drill I intended when I walked in here. Mentally reciting the records and stats of every fighter in the gym. I do everything I can to put myself back in the professional headspace I've always settled into so seamlessly.

"I want you to get more comfortable putting your knee against their butt so you can break their guard," I force out. I let her lock her legs around my waist, but try to keep my weight upright to put some distance between us. Normally, space is the last thing you want in this sport, but right now, I'm praying for it. Decided on a drill *because* of it.

Unfortunately, I can't continue not touching her, which means my hands have to move to grip her waist.

"Knee behind the butt, then push your hips back until their guard breaks. If that doesn't work, sit up and reach back with one hand to break their grip that way."

She nods, but she looks winded before we've even started. When she opens her mouth to say something, no sounds come out, so she swallows thickly and tries again, her eyes staring everywhere but at me.

"A lot of times I feel like I can't get to a sitting position to do that," she admits. "If they have a grip on my neck that's keeping me tight to their body, I can't get to the position you're in right now."

Fuck, she's amazing. Even after everything, even though she's obviously distracted, she's still trying to put it all aside so she can learn.

Respect blooms in my chest, and the need to fuck her into the mat dissolves. Slightly.

"You can do it from a low position, too," I explain. "If they're holding your head down, put your hands on their biceps and push them away from there. Once you've created a little bit of space, you can put your knee behind their butt and go back to hands on their waist to straighten up."

I shift forward to move my hands from her waist to her biceps. Biceps are safe—biceps don't mean anything.

But then I have to lower my head as if I was being kept tight to my opponent's body. And typically, that means my forehead goes right on their chest.

I can't quite bring myself to do that, but I can lower my upper body to simulate it. Without meeting her eyes, and without letting anything touch that's not my hands on her biceps or her legs wrapped around my waist, I stretch out above her so there's only an inch or two between our bodies.

And yet, when I feel her hand slide behind my neck to hold me to her, my body reacts as if I were nine inches deep inside her.

She's not doing anything that isn't a normal jiu-jitsu move that we do a dozen times a class, but just feeling her skin against mine...it drives me fucking crazy.

I shove my hands against her biceps to break her grip

and immobilize her arms. I'm frustrated with her, for being so tempting, at my body for reacting.

Which makes my movements more aggressive than they need to be. I'm not gentle or teacherly as I slide my knee against her butt to brace her body while I drop my hands to her hips and push my upper body higher.

She shudders under my hands.

I freeze where I am, not quite in an upright sitting position. Which means I'm looking down at her face, only a few inches between us.

She's staring directly at me, her pupils blown black and her breaths coming quickly.

Her thoughts couldn't be more obvious if she vocalized them.

"Stop it," I order through clenched teeth, too on edge to make another move.

Her throat bobs on a swallow. "I can't help it," she whispers.

I let out a sound of surprise.

Then I'm pulling away from her and saying, "Fine, we'll work your armbar then. You going to get hot over my arm, too?"

I'm being a dick. I can't help it.

She's off-limits. Forbidden. Not mine to have.

And I'm taking it out on her.

She doesn't respond to my taunt. I'm sure she knows exactly what war I'm fighting, and being the good girl she is, she doesn't make it harder for me. She's not going to be the one to cross this line.

She waits for me to lie back, then comes around to my side and takes her place in the sidemount position. Her knees press against my side, and her chest lowers to mine.

"Remember, when you slide your leg across, you have to

stay close. You always leave too much space during your transitions."

She nods and starts the technique by tightening her grip. Her next step is to slide her knee across my chest and plant it right under my arm. I feel her weight shift and wait for her to make a move.

And she does, but...

As her knee slides across my body, she loses her balance and, instead of locking my arm in, she ends up straddling my waist.

"*Skylar.*" Her name is born on a groan torn from my chest before I can stop it. My hands go to her waist to steady her—and to keep her from moving back and discovering just how unprofessional my body is being.

"Sorry," she whispers, freezing in place. "I slipped." And I think I believe her, but she's also not moving away. Not restarting, or even continuing the move despite her mistake.

"Don't," I bite out, holding on to my last shred of control.

I see the moment she surrenders to the heat between us. Her eyes, already darkened with lust, glaze over, and she bites into her bottom lip. Then she shifts her hips backward.

And comes into contact with my rock-hard cock.

She *moans.*

My tether snaps, and I'm lost to anything that isn't *her*.

Before she can brace for it, I'm flipping Skylar onto her back and crashing my lips down onto hers.

17

DOMINIC

There's nothing gentle or patient about this kiss. As much as I need to taste her, she seems equally desperate for it. Her arms wrap around my neck, and her mouth opens to me with the sexiest goddamn moan I've ever heard. Groaning, I slide my tongue between her lips to deepen the kiss.

The second it touches hers, a new level of desperation sparks. I can't stop myself from grinding down on her, driven by an all-consuming need. Nothing else exists right now.

I'm mindless with hunger for her. I want everything, to kiss her, bite her neck, suck on her nipples. But more than anything else, I want to taste her pleasure on my tongue.

She tears her mouth from mine to gasp, "I need you," her hips rocking against mine as her nails sink into my shoulders. "Please, Dominic, *I need you.*"

I think it's the sound of my name on her lips that fully does me in.

I shift back to get a grip on her spandex shorts and yank them off of her hips. She doesn't even get a chance to lift her ass as I pull them off her legs, narrowly keeping from ripping them apart.

Thankfully, her underwear comes with the pants. Making it one less barrier between my mouth and the forbidden space between Skylar's legs.

I don't even hesitate. I just drop my mouth to Skylar's cunt, and I *feast*.

I can't tell which one of us moans first: it's a symphony of a sound, so it might be both of us. But the second I get her taste in my mouth, I go weak with relief.

She melts like butter on my tongue. She's drenched, giving away that she's been just as turned on as I've been through this lesson. As I lick the length of her, swirl my tongue around the swollen, pink bud, I take pleasure in the fact that I can feel her essence spread all over my mouth. I even love that I can taste her sweat, only emphasizing our desperation and impatience. I love knowing she wants me as much as I want her.

"I've been dreaming about the way this pussy tastes," I groan against her skin. I wrap my arms around her thighs, holding her tight against my face as I look up the length of her body to watch her.

"Fuck," she groans, arching her back in ecstasy as my tongue spears inside her. Her hand slides into my hair and grips the strands hard enough to send a bite of pain into my scalp.

My movements become frenzied, my mouth punishing. I want Skylar to come on my face more than I want to breathe.

As her hips start to rock against my mouth, her moans and gasps become more wanton. I figure out the quick side-to-side motion on her clit that seems to make her suck in a breath and start to shake, and I settle in with hungry desperation.

For a second, her hand tightens in my hair and her whole body freezes. Then...

She *shudders*.

I'm groaning through her orgasm, licking up every drop of her ecstasy and trying to memorize the taste of her.

Because even though we've given in, there's still a nagging thought in the back of my mind that's telling me this is temporary. That this is, and will always be, off-limits and forbidden.

I shove that thought to the back of my mind by absorbing Skylar with every sense I have: the feel of her soft skin beneath my hands, the taste of her on my tongue, the sounds of her gasping breaths as she tries to suck oxygen into her lungs. The sight of her lost in the force of her pleasure.

And before the first one has even ended, I'm sliding my fingers inside her and driving her to a second orgasm that has her crying out my name.

She's trembling by the time she comes down. She still has a death grip on my hair, and just enough strength to weakly tug on the strands.

"Come up here," she gasps. "Come here, come here, please..."

I straighten from between her legs, automatically sliding my tongue across my lips to gather every drop of her that I can. *Fuck, she's like an aphrodisiac. I just want more and more and more of her.*

When I'm close enough, she fists a hand in my shirt and pulls me down over her. I manage to catch myself with a hand next to her head before I crush her with my weight.

She doesn't seem to care, though—she's too focused on my mouth.

She lets out another sexy-as-sin moan when our lips meet. Licking her juices off my lower lip, she then angles her head to slide her tongue inside against mine. The second I kiss her back, she's sucking on my tongue and silently begging for more.

"Fuck," I gasp, completely overwhelmed by the bolt of lust that shoots through me. I've *never* wanted a woman like this. I want Skylar in a carnal, hedonistic way that I didn't even know was possible.

She whimpers when I bite her bottom lip in anger. Not anger at her, just anger at the universe for making *this* fucking woman the one that I want this badly.

"I want you," she breathes against me. "I want you inside me. Please, *please*, oh God please—"

I take her mouth again, the sound of her begging too much for me to handle. I'm already scrambling to push my shorts down, so desperate to feel her that my hand is shaking when I finally grip my cock and stroke it. And when she feels my hand between our bodies, my tip just barely brushing along her soaked skin, her desperation spikes. She wraps her legs around my waist and pulls me flush against her body.

And I realize there's no way I can stop this anymore.

I have just enough of my sanity left that I manage to croak out, "I don't have a condom."

She's already pulling at my hips and trying to get me closer. "I don't care, I'm clean. I need you inside me."

My tip sinks inside her. "Are you on anything?"

Her eyes spark, head shaking, like I might stop what's about to happen. "No, no, but—" She whimpers as I push another inch deeper.

"Fuck it, I'll pull out," I grit out.

And then I plunge all the way inside her, clapping a hand over her mouth as she screams.

She's so *fucking* tight, warm, wet. My eyes roll to the back of my head.

I try to slow down, give her time to adjust, but when she tugs at my hips to move, I drop my head into her neck with a groan and let the last of my sanity go.

I pull back far enough that only my tip is inside her... and then I start to fuck her.

And the harder I fuck her, the more my mouth starts to run.

"Is this what you wanted? To drive me out of my mind until all I can think about is fucking you?" I take her mouth in a filthy kiss. "I've been dreaming about how this pussy would feel. I should've known I wouldn't be able to resist."

She gasps against my mouth, her nails digging into my back. I relish the pinpricks and reach down to hike her legs higher around my ribs.

"Knees up. Let's see how deep I can get."

On that first drive, her eyes widen. On the second, she starts to squirm.

Christ, I shouldn't be fucking her this hard. She's probably used to slow and sweet.

But I've been driven too far, too deep into this hunger.

I slip one hand between us, desperate to see her reach the same level of madness that I have. Pressing my thumb to her clit, I start to move it in circles in the way I discovered she likes.

I lean down so I can take her mouth in another kiss. I can't get enough, can't get close enough.

"I hated myself for wanting you," I say against her lips, my hips never slowing in their movements. "But no matter how hard I tried, I couldn't stop thinking about what it would feel like to sink inside this tight cunt."

"And d-does it feel good?" she stutters.

"It's perfection," I growl, driving into her even harder. "But it would feel even better if you'd come. I'm dying to feel you squeeze my cock." I circle my thumb faster. "You want to come for me, baby?"

By the time I ask, she's already coming. Her lips pop open in a silent scream, and her whole body tenses for half a second before she shudders, thighs clenched around my hips. I pull back just enough so that I can see the pleasure that *I* gave her ravage her body.

And I was right, no level of fantasy could have imagined what it would feel like to have her come on my cock.

I groan at the feeling of her muscles squeezing me. With every second, I get closer and closer to giving in to my own release.

Thankfully, the ripples of her orgasm slow just before that happens. Before they can stop completely, I'm pulling out of her and flipping her onto her stomach, then pulling her onto her hands and knees.

Gripping her hips, I slide back inside her.

"Oh *God*," she moans, dropping onto her elbows. I let out a hiss at the change in angle, at the sight of her perfect ass arching even higher. I can't help dropping a slap onto one of her cheeks, just to watch it pinken under my hand.

"Fuck, you're perfect." I grip her hips so hard, I know I'm leaving her with bruises in the shape of fingerprints. "Look at you, taking me so well. Did you fantasize about this, too?"

"Yes," she sobs, pushing her hips back and begging for more. "I wanted you so bad."

I slap her other cheek, hard enough to make her moan. "And does it feel like you thought it would?"

"It feels...s-so much b-better," she stutters as she gasps for air. "I d-didn't know it would feel like this with y-you."

And suddenly, I know what I want from her. I know how I want her to come again.

Reaching down, I guide her upright so her back is against my chest. She moves easily, and her pleasure-drunk compliance is like another shot of lust to my groin.

I knock my knees against the inside of hers to widen her stance. When she moves, and when my next thrust goes even deeper because of it, she lets out a surprised moan.

Wrapping a hand around her throat, I tilt her head back so I can press a biting kiss along her jaw. The touch causes her muscles to squeeze around me.

"Say my name," I say, my voice like gravel. "I want you to admit who you just begged to be inside you."

Her lips pop open as she pulls in gasping breaths. One of her hands grips onto my forearm, not quite holding me against her throat, but hanging onto me for dear life as she starts to spiral from the pleasure. She has just enough mental energy to let out a breathy, "Dominic."

When my other hand slides down the front of her stomach to settle in on her clit, another one. "*Dominic.*"

And when the fourth orgasm consumes her body, it's a desperate, soul-deep shout. *"Dominic!"*

With a groan, I drop my forehead to her shoulder as I feel her come around me again. She feels fucking *exquisite*. I can't hold out any longer.

I only manage to wait long enough for Skylar to fall forward onto the mat with a tired, but satisfied, sigh. The second she's bent over in front of me again, I thrust into her two more times, then hurriedly pull out and shuttle my hand over my cock. I stripe her ass cheeks and lower back with my cum, reveling in the sight of marking her like this.

"Fuck," I let out on a final groan. For a moment, the only sound in the gym is the sound of us both trying to regain our breaths.

While she's still on forearms and knees, forehead pressed to her hand, I stumble as I stand and walk the three feet to the sidelines where the paper towels are. I rip one off and hurry back to Skylar, dropping back to my knees so I can wipe the proof of what just happened off her skin.

Skylar lets out a sound of contentment and drops onto her back. Arching in a shameless stretch, she smiles and says with a sigh, "That was amazing."

And *fuck*, what seeing her perfect body splayed out like this does to me. My cock is already getting hard again and I'm *thisclose* to doing something about it. Knowing that *I* brought her pleasure and made her this happy... it's intoxicating.

She's everything I've ever wanted, and I'm helpless against this pull between us.

Wrongness be damned.

18

DOMINIC

The fifteen-minute drive isn't exactly awkward, but I do have to turn on the radio to cover up the silence. I think fucking her so thoroughly is the only reason she accepted my ride without argument, but her hesitation beside me is palpable, and it's making me uneasy. Clearly, neither of us knows what to say from here.

When I pull up in front of her house, it's with the intention of being honest with her and hoping like hell she feels the same way.

But just as I'm about to open my mouth to blurt it out, I see her eyes track over my shoulder, brow furrowing.

"What..." is all she says as I turn to see what she's looking at.

I don't notice anything out of the ordinary. Her house is what caught her attention, but I have no idea why. All the lights are on, which stands out, because it's almost midnight and every other house is almost completely dark, but that's not enough to warrant her reaction. When I turn back to ask her what's wrong, I realize her frown has been replaced by a look of panic.

"Skylar, what's—?"

But she's already scratching at the door handle, fumbling to get out of the car. When it finally opens, she's out like a shot.

I don't question the reaction; I just jump to follow her.

She's rushing up the steps, shaking so bad that she can barely get her key in the front door. I reach past her to help, but then the lock clicks and the door swings wide open.

To reveal an older woman crumpled at the bottom of the steps, a young boy crouched over her.

"Oh my God, *Mom*," Skylar breathes. Then she turns toward the boy. "Joey, what happened?!"

He's obviously in shock, his eyes wide and his body frozen as he turns slowly toward Skylar.

It takes him a few seconds to answer. By the time he does, Skylar has already rushed over to her mom and begun checking her vitals, her hands skillfully making sure not to move her body too much as she does it.

"She... she fell," the boy answers. "It just happened. I heard her come out of her room, so I came out to check on her, and right as I opened my door, I saw her trip at the top of the stairs." His voice takes on an anxious edge. "Skylar, I was taking care of her, I swear. *I swear*. It just happened so fast... I didn't even have enough time to call to her, or grab her, and now she's... now she's—"

Skylar finishes her checks just in time to stop the boy from spiraling. Which he's clearly about to do. His eyes have turn crazed, and his skin has paled. He looks like he's barely a teenager, way too young to be dealing with this.

"Joey, listen to me," Skylar says, grabbing him by the shoulders and shaking him, hard, just once. "This isn't your fault. Do you hear me? It was an accident. She fell. It happens with her disease. It is *not your fault*."

Her tone is both forceful and comforting. Forceful enough to make him believe, and comforting enough to convince him she's not lying. It breaks through the fog of his shock, and he gives her a small nod.

Skylar sees it and lets go of him to turn back to her mother.

"But I need your help," she says, her hands checking over the rest of her mother's body. "I need you to call 911, right now. Put them on speaker so I can talk to them. She's breathing, and her heart rate is normal, but she might be concussed, or hurt somewhere else. I need you to help me."

Again, the direction is self-assured. Probably one who's done this before, who's used to taking control of a situation and leading others through it.

Joey immediately reaches for his phone and follows her instructions.

"911, what is your emergency?"

"I need an ambulance to 921 Poplar Street, right away," Skylar says. "My mother has fallen down the steps and she's unconscious. I don't see any visible injuries or obvious deformities, but I need her taken to the hospital imme-diately."

"Sending EMS to your address. What's your name?"

"Skylar Vega. Please hurry."

I'm still standing in the doorway when their conversa-tion ends, stunned by not only the situation before me, but also by the sight of Skylar falling so quickly into the role of matriarch. I knew she had responsibilities just based on the way she carries herself, but seeing her in action gives me a whole new understanding.

Once Skylar has answered the operator's questions and has finished treating the immediate situation, I finally feel like I can step in.

"Can I do anything?" I ask, stepping closer.

Skylar's eyes dart to mine, as if she completely forgot I was here.

She probably did. If I'm going by the looks of things, she's used to being on her own.

Where is her dad? Is she really the only other adult here?

Skylar's focus travels back to the boy, who looks on the verge of tears now that the shock has worn off.

"Can you get my brother some water, please?" Skylar says, then releases a heavy breath as her eyes meet mine briefly. "I need to stay with my mom while the ambulance gets here."

I nod immediately. Stepping forward, I gently take the phone from her brother's hand and place it beside Skylar. Then I'm guiding him to his feet and pulling him toward the kitchen that I can see behind the living room on this floor.

He moves as if he's in a trance, although walking even a short distance seems to help. I quickly fill a cup of water in the sink and hand it to him.

"Drink. And then take a deep breath."

He does as I say. When he downs the water, I fill it again and hand it back to him.

"She's going to be okay, kid," I tell him in what I hope is a soothing voice. "Skylar wouldn't be that calm if there was something really wrong."

When he looks at me, and it's like he's finally noticing that a stranger is in his house.

"Skylar always sounds like that," he says. "Even when things are at their worst, she sounds that calm." He pulls in a stuttering breath, then drinks half of his water. "It shouldn't work—her using her parent voice on me. I should see through it by now. But somehow..." His gaze travels back to his sister, who we can still see from where we're standing.

"I still believe her when she says everything is okay. How is that possible?"

Now I'm the one frozen in place. I have no response to that. I'm so far out of my element here.

Jesus, is this the life Skylar's had to live? For how long? Was she ever *able to be a kid?*

We both jolt when we hear sirens in the distance. Before I can even say a word or take a step, Joey's leaving his cup on the counter and rushing back to his sister.

It's a whirlwind of activity after that. Three EMS workers push through the still-open door, immediately doing their standard checks on Skylar's mom. I hear Skylar quietly speaking to them, and see one of the workers nod at whatever she's saying. It seems the fall didn't affect the spine, because after a moment, they place her on a gurney and roll her out the door.

Skylar's mom gains consciousness as she's being lifted into the ambulance, zeroing in on her children.

"Skylar? Joey? What happened?"

"You fell, Mom," comes Skylar's voice. She's holding her hand, Joey right beside her. "They're going to take you to the hospital."

The woman looks at her son. "Oh, honey. I'm so sorry I scared you."

That's when I notice Joey is crying silent tears, the fear and the pain evident on his face and in the way he grips his sister's hand with white knuckles.

Skylar sees it, too. Lifting her brother's hand to their mother's, she moves aside so he can stand beside the gurney.

"Do you want to go with them in the ambulance?" she asks him softly.

He's nodding before she's even finished the question.

"Okay. You go with them, I'll be right behind you." She wraps an arm around his shoulders. "Joey, I promise she's okay. This is just a safety precaution." But she must know her brother doesn't fully believe her, because she looks at one of the paramedics. "Right? You don't see any serious injuries."

The woman nods, sending him a smile. "She's okay, I promise. We just want to get her fully checked out."

Hearing it from a third party seems to finally convince him. Enough that he dries his tears with his sleeve.

Once they've lifted their mom into the ambulance, Joey and the paramedics climb in after her. Skylar gives him one last reassuring nod as they close the doors.

"I'll be right behind you. I'll meet you at the hospital."

In a matter of minutes, we're all alone. It almost feels like a fever dream, it happened so fast.

I follow Skylar back into the house. It looks like she's on autopilot as she starts cleaning up and collecting her things. She's reaching for a sweatshirt when I realize she's talking out loud to herself.

"...last time the ambulance cost $2,400. If I open a new credit card, I can use it for groceries and pay off the hospital bill with cash. I'll need to pick up more shifts at the restaurant, and probably get a third job, but if I can pay it off this month, then the interest shouldn't be too bad—"

"Skylar," I interrupt. I can't listen to this, can't listen to her talk about a life *this* hard in such a detached tone. I wish I could just wrap her in my arms right now, but I know she isn't ready to lean on me.

She looks up at me with a blank stare. Not because she forgot I was here, but because she's falling into some kind of fucked-up pattern that she's used to living in.

"You're still here," she says simply. She pulls the sweatshirt over her head. "You didn't need to stay. Thank you for the ride home, though. If I had gotten home later—"

She swallows thickly, the severity of the situation breaking through her emotional walls for the first time. And her voice is rougher when she says, "I have to get going. I'll see you at the gym next week."

For a moment, I can only stare at her. But then I realize it doesn't matter what I do or say, she's going to keep pushing me away to stand on her own.

And I can't bring myself to stand by as she does that.

I reach for her backpack and sling it over my shoulder. "Come on, I'll give you a ride to the hospital." When she opens her mouth to protest, I add, "Taking the bus or even waiting for an Uber at this time of night will take too long."

Still, she stares at me. And my heart breaks a little when I whisper, "Please, don't make me leave here knowing your brother is alone at that hospital waiting for you."

That finally breaks through her defenses. Her eyes well with tears, but then she's blinking them away and nodding.

The sight of her like this, vulnerable yet strong, fills my chest with a maelstrom of emotions I'm not prepared for: awe, pride, respect. But most of all, affection.

19

SKYLAR

The rest of the weekend goes by quickly, despite Mom being kept overnight for observation in the hospital. Since she's on blood thinners I was worried about a brain bleed, but a head CT didn't reveal any trauma, and thankfully, she only has a bruised hip from the fall.

Overall, it wasn't the worst weekend we've had. There have been plenty of other emergencies that didn't end with our family smiling and laughing. Even the discussion about needing to finally move out of the townhouse, to an apartment that's safer for Mom, didn't kill the mood. Mom was told to take it extra easy for a few days, but other than that, everyone is back to their usual schedule.

Everyone except me, because I'm no closer to knowing what to say to Dominic when I walk into the gym on Monday.

And, of course, he's the first one I see when I step through the doors. He's sitting on the couch in the reception area, and when he sees me, he immediately stands and moves toward me, making me wonder if he's been waiting for me.

"Hey," he greets me, brow furrowed in clear concern. "How's your mom?"

I give him a genuine smile. "She's good. Little sore from the fall, but no real injuries. It just seemed bad because she knocked herself out on the way down."

He seems to deflate in relief at the news. "Good. That's good to hear."

I fidget with the hem of my sweatshirt for a moment. "Thank you again for the other night," I say quietly. "For the ride, and for helping me with my brother." I suck in a shaky breath. "You didn't need to do any of that, but I'm grateful that you did."

For a moment, he only stares at me, his expression giving away nothing. But then he speaks, his voice quiet but deep. "You're welcome. You never have to thank me for that. I'm just glad your family is okay. I'm glad *you're* okay."

His words fill my chest with warmth. He makes me feel cared for, in a way that's not overwhelming. And yet, I still have no idea how he feels about everything *else* that happened the other night. We have so much to talk about, to figure out, but he's giving me zero hints about how he's feeling or which direction he's leaning.

I feel wanted, yet completely lost.

Classes are the usual mix of therapeutic, challenging, and exhausting. By the time they're over, I feel a sense of overwhelming peace that my life is back to normal. And that the gym still feels like my safe space.

But as soon as I start to clean, and I'm left alone with my thoughts, reality hits. Because I realized after the other night that there's no way I can be with Dominic.

It's not because of *him*. And it's not because of the professional boundary, or his age, or any of the other things. It's because *I* can't be in a relationship.

I tried dating once when I was in high school. I said yes to a boy in my class, went on a few movie dates, I even liked him enough to lose my virginity. But a month after we started dating, my mom was diagnosed with early onset Parkinson's. We found out when she cut herself making dinner—for the third time in a week. And while 11-year-old Joey was crying in the corner watching his blood-soaked mother tremble so hard that it took her ten minutes to call 911, I was out with my boyfriend. Being selfish.

That was the last time I dated. Because not only is another person not worth the sacrifice of my family, but bad things also happen when I do things for myself. This weekend proved that. Even though Mom is completely fine, I'm still shaken up.

While my mother was hurt and my brother was scared, I was busy having sex.

This guilt is suffocating. Every time I think of my recklessness, the pressure in my chest makes it hard to breathe.

So, whether Dominic is getting ready to end things or not, *I* need to end things.

Sucking in a deep breath, I knock on the doorframe of Dominic's office.

He turns around from where he's digging through a box of gym T-shirts. As soon as he sees me, his throat bobs on a rough swallow.

"Hey," he says, his voice tight.

"Hey. Umm, mats are done. Gym's all clean for you."

Dominic gives me a stiff nod and drops the shirt in his hand back into the box.

"Skylar, I think we should—"

"The other night was a mistake," I blurt out.

His eyebrows rise in surprise, but he doesn't contradict me. It's enough of an opening for me to continue.

"We're both adults. We can be honest about what this is and isn't. And the truth is, that night was amazing, especially after a month of should-we-shouldn't-we, but it's not something that can ever happen again. We both have our reasons."

Goddamnit, his expression is always so unreadable. I can't tell if he's relieved, or sad, or if he agrees with me. And he's not saying anything.

Nerves bubble in my stomach. I just want this over with—I want to get all of this out, and then I want to go home.

The rest of the words tumble from my lips, each one tripping over the last. "It's a bad idea for both of us. You, because you're my coach and clearly you don't like mixing business and pleasure, and me, because my life is already a shitshow that needs my full attention. I don't have time to add even a physical relationship into it. So, I think it would be better if we just went back to coach and student. You don't need to worry about me making anything weird. I promise I'll go back to being the annoying student who asks too many questions. It'll be like nothing ever happened between us."

Throughout my entire speech, Dominic doesn't let on to what he's thinking. There's only a flash of something at the very end—something that resembles hurt. But it's there and gone so quickly, I'm sure I imagined it.

There's no way he wanted a relationship with me. He doesn't strike me as the type that only wants sex, but the thought of him wanting to date *me* is equally laughable. I'm a nobody with too much baggage.

"So...yeah. Deal?" I awkwardly stick out my hand, as if we're really going to shake on a *no more fucking* agreement.

To my surprise, he takes a step closer. But he doesn't

shake my hand yet, he just studies me in that all-seeing way of his.

"And you're sure this is what you want?" he asks in a deliciously deep voice. Half of me wants to say *fuck no, I changed my mind* just from the sound of it.

But I force myself to nod. My feelings before I stepped into this room were the honest-to-God truth—the fact that Dominic's presence makes me want to melt into a puddle can't detract from that.

Another flash in his eyes, but he's gripping my hand before I can question it.

"Okay, then," he says, shaking my hand once, and then stepping away, as if he was scared to touch me for longer than necessary. "If that's what you want, then I'll honor it. We'll go back to Coach and Skylar."

God, I'm a mess. Hearing him say that hits me like a stab to my stomach. And then it swirls with the guilt of sacrificing my family for a man, and the emotional concoction makes me about ready to throw up. I need out of here.

"Great, I'm glad we talked that out," I say hurriedly. "I'll see you on Saturday, then? I'll be here for open mat."

He only nods in answer. I manage to send him a stiff smile, and then I'm awkwardly waving my goodbye and disappearing through the front door.

For the next three weeks, I only train at the gym two nights a week.

Ending things with Dominic was only the first of my attempts to eliminate anything selfish from my schedule: training also fell under that category. And if I hadn't committed to cleaning two nights a week, I probably would have convinced myself that I needed to quit entirely. But because of that verbal contract with Dominic, I justified being at the gym for a few hours on nights I wasn't working.

Dominic honors the distance between us. It's almost sad how easily we go back to coach and student, how natural it feels. On the rare occasion, I think I catch a flash of regret in his eyes when his stare lingers a few beats too long, but for the most part, he treats me like any other athlete.

I keep my distance from the fighters, too. They either don't notice the change, or they're ignoring it, because Remy and Lucy make plenty of attempts to pull me into their conversations. I can usually start cleaning before they try, but tonight, I'm too slow getting into the cleaning closet.

"Hey, Skylar," Lucy calls. "You coming to Aiden's fight at the end of the month?"

I shake my head, feeling robotic in my answer. "Can't. I have to work."

She frowns as she studies me. She's looking for a lie, but there isn't one—it's just not the full truth. I haven't gotten my work schedule yet, but I need every shift I can get. Especially because we got the first ambulance bill yesterday.

"Alright, well...if your schedule opens up, we'd love you to come with us," Lucy says. "We're hosting a pregame at my house, too."

There's a pang of something in my chest. *What would it be like to have friends? To not feel guilty about going to a party with them?*

I force a smile. "Thanks, Lucy. I'll let you know if anything changes."

She nods and starts up the stairs, leaving me alone in the bag room. I reach for the disinfecting wipe so I can clean the heavy bag in front of me. But before I can swipe it over the leather, I get an overwhelming urge to punch it.

So I do. I haul back my right fist and unleash it on the bag.

I barely feel the sting in my knuckles, even without gloves on. So I punch it again.

And again.

And again.

Until I *do* feel the sting. And the soreness in my shoulder. And yet, none of that physical pain compares to the emotional agony that has taken up residence in my chest.

I'll never be able to take a Saturday off. My Saturday nights are spent working, or taking care of my sick mother, or being a parent to my little brother. I can't just blow off my responsibilities to watch fights with my friends. That's not the kind of life I have.

And it'll never be a luxury I can afford. The bills will never stop, not until—I can't even think about that. And Joey is still young enough that I'll be his only parental figure for a few more years, and the only adult he can count on forever. I have years of schooling left, and God only knows how long it will take me to pay off my student loan debt, and it doesn't matter how much I work, or how hard I try, I'll never be able to catch up. I'll never be able to live in a way that *isn't* this perfectly planned-out, fragile version. And *God*, I'm so tired. I'm just *so*—

I feel arms come around me, gently but effectively stopping me from throwing any more punches. *Dominic.* I try one last time to throw one, but end up choking out a sob and collapsing into his arms, limp with exhaustion.

"Skylar. Baby, look at me."

I don't know what's happening. I don't know how long I've been lost in my thoughts. But suddenly, my environment registers, and my brain slowly settles back into reality. Maybe it's the sound of "baby" on his lips that does me in.

Dominic is sitting on the mat, and I'm sitting sideways in his lap. His hands are soothing as they rub up and down my arms. My face feels wet, and my chest is still so tight that I realize I'm raking in loud, strangled breaths, but Dominic's touch makes the inhales come a little bit easier. My erratic heartbeat also begins to slow.

He looks so worried. Like he wants to pull me into his arms, but also like he's trying to give me some space. He doesn't stop rubbing my arms, but as soon as my breathing is under control, he asks quietly, "What happened?"

"Sorry, I—" I clear my throat and try again. "I just...had a moment. I'm sorry."

There's a storm of emotions swirling in my stomach as Dominic comforts me. Shock that I just lost my mind a little in front of Dominic, embarrassment that I let him see it— vulnerability as I try to rebuild the walls that just came crashing down. I've *never* lost my mind in front of someone like that. Not at my father's funeral, not when Mom got sick —Joey's never seen me shed a tear. I've been an impenetrable fortress since the day I overheard Dad's diagnosis at the age of nine.

And yet, I expose myself all over again when Dominic asks, "Do you want to talk about it?" Because as soon as the question leaves his lips, I instantly throw myself into his arms. Vulnerability be damned.

Wrapped around Dominic with my face pressed into his neck, I allow myself to soak in his warmth, his strength. The feeling of his hand stroking my hair is calming. Taking a deep breath, I try to vocalize what I'm feeling.

"I guess it just hit me that I'll never have the kind of freedom to be happy that other people have at my age," I murmur into his skin. "I have too many responsibilities to be selfish."

But how can I possibly say that I don't have anything in my life that I chose on my own? When did I become so self-absorbed? Not only did I pick up a sport that I love, but it also came because of a financial break that made my entire family's lives better. A break that made it possible for me to do things that bring me joy. Today is the perfect example.

"Actually, forget I said that," I hurry to say, pulling back from Dominic. "I'm feeling sorry for myself. I don't know why I'm being so dramatic." I try to force out a laugh to play it off, but Dominic sees right through me.

His eyes never leave my face. When his thumb brushes over my cheek, any remaining semblance of a mask falls to the wayside.

"It's okay to feel overwhelmed sometimes," he says. "You've lived a hard life, Skylar. No one would judge you for that." I can't answer, because my eyes once again fill with tears. I hurry to blink them away, very aware of the fact that Dominic is still wiping the rest of my tears from my face.

"Everyone needs to be a little selfish," he tells me gently. "We all need to find our happiness. It doesn't make you a bad person."

"It feels like it," I whisper.

"Skylar, you are so far from being a bad person that I kind of want to shake you just for thinking it."

I duck my head to hide my smile. Sweet Dominic is disarming.

Peeking at him through my eyelashes, I try to get a read on him. He hasn't tried to cross the line I drew after I cut things off between us, to the point that I've wondered if he even cared. But with the way he's looking at me...

I know he does.

A sad smile appears on his face when he catches me looking. Tucking a strand of hair behind my ear, his hand drops to the side of my neck, his thumb rubbing gentle circles on my skin. "It breaks my heart that you think you don't deserve good things," he says softly.

I swallow the whimper that wants to escape. My defenses are crumbling, and every reason I had for not going after what I want is slipping away. Suddenly, all I want is to give in, and to lose myself in Dominic. Without the guilt.

"Tell me what would make you happy," he whispers. "Tell me how I can prove to you that you deserve it."

His eyes never leave mine. And even with his arms around me, the honesty and vulnerability heating the space between us, I can see in his face that he doesn't mean it in a physical way. He just wants to make me happy. In whatever way that means.

So I kiss him.

Because even though we both still have reasons we shouldn't be together, nothing can contend with the joy that comes from being Dominic's. Even if only temporarily.

20

SKYLAR

He kisses me back for several seconds, and I soak up the warmth and comfort that comes from being in his embrace. *God*, I missed this. I missed *him*.

Any doubts I may have had about this instantly disappear.

But Dominic must feel differently, because he pulls back, just far enough to touch his forehead to mine.

"That's not what I meant," he says breathily.

"I know," I whisper, sliding closer and tightening my arms around his neck. "That's why I did it."

Sensing his hesitation, I put some distance between us. Just enough that he can see the truth in my eyes. "I want this, if you do. I know I said I wanted to put space between us, but...you're right. *You* make me happy. And I don't want to fight this anymore."

His gaze travels over my face, clearly looking for any doubt. When he doesn't find any, he pulls me in for another kiss.

And this time, he sinks into it.

His arms wrap around my waist, his head tilting to

deepen the kiss. The second his tongue touches mine, a whimper slips out, and I try to slide even closer.

Instead, he pulls back again, breathing heavily. "You're sure?"

I nod, already tugging him back. As soon as our lips connect this time, my hips start to rock. *God, I want him so badly.*

Seemingly convinced, he rolls me until I'm lying under him on the mat, his lips never leaving mine as his hands start to explore.

But before he can do any more, I push against his chest. "Wait," I gasp.

He lifts off of me. "What? What's wrong?"

"Nothing, it's just... I smell like cleaning supplies. I don't want to get it all over you."

It only takes him a second to make a decision, and another to lift me into his arms as he stands.

"Where are we going?" I ask, my legs wrapping around his waist as if it's the most natural thing in the world. My lips land on his neck, pressing kisses along his skin.

I feel the shiver that runs through him, and the way his steps quicken. "Shower," he grunts.

My lips travel up to his ear. "Good idea," I hum, nipping his earlobe.

And if there's any question about Dominic's level of desperation, it's answered when he kicks open the locker room door, steps us fully clothed into the shower, and blindly turns the water on as he takes my mouth in a scorching kiss.

His kiss is *everything*. Every desire I saw on his face a moment ago, he shows me with his mouth, and his tongue, and his hands.

His touch becomes greedy. Despite the water soaking

our clothes, he manages to peel my shirt over my head and my shorts down my legs. Strong hands smooth over my ass, down my thighs, up to squeeze my waist. It feels like he doesn't know where to touch first. He groans every time he tilts his head and slides his tongue across mine.

"Fuck," he murmurs. "I told myself that if I got the chance to fuck you again, I'd look at you and take my time. You're making a liar out of me, baby."

Hearing him call me *baby* again has a whimper slipping from my lips and my hands scrambling to pull his shirt off. The second the drenched fabric passes between our lips, I'm back to kissing him, flattening my body against his and getting as close as possible. When his chest hair brushes against my nipples, a full-body shiver runs through me.

Suddenly, all I want is him inside me.

Reaching down, I slide my hand inside his shorts and wrap my fingers around his cock. One impatient stroke has him groaning and flattening me against the shower wall once more.

"I'm going to want to fuck you all the time now, aren't I?" he muses, as he kisses and nips along my jaw. "This torture is going to be a regular thing. Every time you walk into the gym, I'm going to want to drag you into the office and bend you over my desk. And I'm going to be in pain until I do it." He quickly pushes his shorts down, the soaked material landing on the shower floor so he can kick them away. Then he grips my thigh and lifts it to hook around his hip.

The new position has me on my toes, and him at the perfect height to slide his cock against me. Which he does, even before I let out a moan and grind down on his length.

"*Fuck*, Skylar." That's all he gets out before he's driving inside me with one hard thrust.

I cry out at the stretch. He's just so *much*. It doesn't

matter that I already knew how big he was, I have a feeling I'll never get used to the way he fills me.

"*God*, you feel so good," I say on a moan, my head dropping back as he starts to pump into me. From this position, I can grind down on him every time he thrusts, adding pressure against my clit.

He kisses along my neck as he fucks me. But then they become bites, his hands squeezing at my thigh and waist, and the need to get even closer to him, to get him *deeper,* becomes an absolute need.

He reads my mind and reaches down to lift my other leg to wrap around his waist.

"Oh my God," I gasp, my thighs squeezing around him. "Oh my God, that's so deep. D-Dominic, *oh my God...*"

He drops his forehead to my shoulder and lets out a deep groan. In this position, with him bracing my back against the tiled wall and his hands gripping my ass to rifle me up and down on his cock, he's impossibly deep inside me.

"Fuck, Skylar, your pussy's so *tight.*"

I let out a whimper and arch against him, my eyes fluttering shut. Between how deep he is and the way he's grinding on my clit, I'm already burning up inside. His words are going to be the light to the match.

My eyes pop open when I feel him drop his mouth to my nipple. He suctions his lips over it, the pull echoing in my core. Arching again, I silently beg him for more.

He latches onto the other nipple with a growl. But this time, his touch comes with a bite of pain. I cry out when I feel him worry the pink bud between his teeth.

Suctioning over it again, he pulls once, twice, swirling his tongue around it until I'm shaking with the need to come.

"Dominic, *please*," I whimper. "I'm so c-close…"

He straightens and takes my mouth in a blistering kiss. His hips never stop moving, but now they pick up in intensity until my breaths come in gasps. Where his hands dig into my ass cheeks, I can already feel the bruises forming.

"I've been dying to feel you come on my cock again," he says against my lips. "I've been fucking my fist all week at the thought of it. Are you going to let me feel it now?"

I'm frantically nodding. I can feel the orgasm roiling inside me, threatening to incinerate me any second. I'm so close, so close, I just need—

Dominic's hand slips between us, his thumb fastening to my clit and rubbing quick, hard circles. And the next time he drives deep, *deep* inside me, my orgasm explodes, and I cry out, shuddering against him.

I've never been so full of someone, so full to the brim of pleasure and so overwhelmed by feeling them *everywhere*. My body becomes one giant live wire as the sensations roll through me.

I've just come back to reality when Dominic groans and his hand disappears from my clit. He pulls out and I watch as he wraps his hand around his length. And right as he stamps a hard, desperate kiss to my lips, I feel a splash of warmth on my stomach.

Eventually, the sounds of our sex are replaced by only the sound of the running water, interrupted only by our heaving breaths.

My arms are still wrapped around him, my legs tight but trembling around his waist. I don't know how he's still holding me up—if his heartrate that I can feel beating against my own chest is any indication, he was just as overwhelmed by that release as I was.

He sets me down gently. The shower is just big enough

that he can take a step back from me, and I watch as his gaze trails slowly over my body, his pupils expanding with every inch covered.

"Fuck, Skylar," he murmurs under his breath. When his eyes meet mine, there's still heat simmering in them as he says, "I'm already looking forward to tasting every inch of your body. You're an addiction."

My cheeks warm with pleasure at his words.

The corner of his mouth lifts with a fleeting expression of adoration. Then he sighs and tugs me under the water spray.

"Come on, let's get you cleaned up."

He's efficient but sweet in his movements. He lathers up the body wash in his hands and massages it over my skin, never making it sexual but seemingly enjoying touching me. Because he stops me when I try to do it myself.

He does, however, let me wash *him*. He lets out a chuckle when I eagerly rub the body wash over his muscles, my excitement obvious. Dominic's just so...*hot*. I haven't really been able to freely look at his muscles, let alone touch them. Exploring his body like this is almost as good as the sex.

"Keep looking at me like that, and I'm going to turn you around and take a second fuck," he says in a deliciously deep voice.

A shiver runs through me, and he chuckles at my reaction. With every inch of him soaped up, he steps under the water to rinse himself.

"Let's get you dried off," he says.

We step out of the shower, and he hands me the towel he brought in for himself. Ass-naked and completely unashamed, he walks out of the bathroom to grab a second towel from the changing room.

We're silent as we towel off. With our clothes in different

places in the gym, we separate when we leave the bathroom, me heading for my bag along the mats and him going into the office for a change of clothes. I throw on a pair of leggings and an oversized sweatshirt, and watch Dominic through the cracked door of the office as he tugs on jeans and a T-shirt. I love how he looks in casual clothes, but especially when he's barefoot wearing jeans.

"Want to watch some fights?"

I'm startled out of my ogling. For a moment, I can only blink at him.

"I... What?"

He seems amused by my reaction. "I asked if you wanted to watch some fights. It's not that late, so I figured we could watch a fight or two. I'll let you pick."

Still, the only thing I can do is stare at him. *He wants to hang out?*

"Did you think I only wanted to fuck you?" he asks, his tone softening along with his expression.

My cheeks flush hot when I realize *yes, that's exactly what I thought he wanted.*

He moves closer to me, close enough to take my hand and press a kiss to my jaw.

"This doesn't just have to be physical," he says. "I like hanging out with you. I was hoping we could do both. If... you have time."

I shouldn't be surprised when he adds that last part. But just hearing him be so considerate—hearing that he wants to spend time with me, but understands why I might not be able to—is enough to make my decision.

"I'd love that." I hesitate, then ask, "So this wasn't just a one-time thing?"

His brow furrows slightly as he shakes his head. "Not unless you want it to be."

I try to imagine this being the last time I get to touch Dominic like this, and be close to him, and immediately hate the idea.

"I don't want it to be."

His grin is almost boyish in its charm. "Good. Now come hang out with me so I don't feel like you only like me for my dick."

21

DOMINIC

I tug her over to the couch in the welcome area, my fingers threaded with hers. Taking my usual seat on the far side, and before she can second-guess what this is, I prop one leg up on the couch so my back is to the armrest, and I pull her down between my legs. She sits with a cute *oomph*.

Pulling her back against my chest, and then wrapping an arm around her waist to hold her to me, I reach with my other hand for the remote on the coffee table. Watching the fights with her was just an excuse, but I'm going to put them on anyway.

What I really want is to talk to her for a little bit.

But I can't exactly launch into invasive questions about her family and home life, so for now, both of our attention is focused on the fight on the TV screen.

We're only pulled away from it when we feel the couch dip with another weight as Brutus climbs up beside us.

Skylar lets out a giggle as he plods toward her. She, too, opens her legs to give him a space to sit, and he takes the offered spot. With a loud grunt, he collapses in her lap, planting his big head on her thigh. Almost immediately, the gym fills with the sound of his snores.

Skylar starts to pet his head. Warmth fills my chest at the sight of them together.

"Is he a cuddly dog?" she asks after a moment.

"Not really," I answer, reaching around her to scratch between his shoulder blades where I know he likes it. "He reminds me of a grumpy old man for the most part—always wants his space."

She peeks over her shoulder at me, a smile lighting up her eyes. "Sounds like someone else I know."

That warrants a pinch to her side. She yelps, the sound causing Brutus to lift his head and blink at us in sleepy confusion.

"Sorry, buddy," Skylar coos. "I didn't mean to wake you. Your daddy doesn't like to hear the truth."

Another scolding, this time by nipping at her neck. The sound of her giggle soothes me.

"Have you ever had a dog?" I ask curiously, my touch moving from Brutus to Skylar, where I rub lazy circles on her thigh.

She shakes her head. "We couldn't ever really afford one. Not only that, but we also weren't sure we could commit to taking care of one. Good days would be fine, but my parents were hospitalized plenty of times, which would've left us scrambling to find dog sitters. Even when we were home, the priority was always taking care of Dad, and then Mom. I just... I knew we wouldn't be able to give a dog the life it deserved."

The tone of her voice makes me sad. I can't imagine living the life Skylar's lived, the pressure on her shoulders.

She's given me the perfect opening to ask about her

family, but I want to be careful. I want to understand her better, but not at the price of making this place and my company anything less than a safe space for her.

"Your dad was sick too?" I decide to ask.

She nods. But when she doesn't say more, I settle for making myself vulnerable instead.

"I don't know what it's like to have a parent get sick like that, but I took care of my mom before she passed," I explain, my hand caressing up and down her arm. "I moved her in with me when she got older. It was always just me and her when I was growing up, so making her comfortable when her body started shutting down at the end was the least I could do."

"She raised you by herself?"

I nod against her hair. "I never knew my dad. He left us when I was still young."

Skylar's finger traces soothing patterns on the arm that's wrapped around her. "Your mom must've been a strong woman," she says quietly.

"The strongest."

"When did she pass away?"

"Three years ago. Right after I stopped fighting. Any time I wonder if I retired too early, I think about how I got to spend time with her and be there to take care of her because of it." My arm tightens around Skylar. "She would've loved you. You might be the only woman I've ever met who could match her for strength."

That makes her go quiet. But sharing that with her must've made her comfortable enough to open up to me with the rest of her story, because she starts talking.

"My dad was diagnosed with lung cancer when I was nine," she says, and I squeeze her leg in a silent show of support. Taking a deep breath, she continues. "They found it early, so the trips to different doctors were always hopeful. He went through the usual radiation, chemo, everything. Nobody seemed surprised when he went into remission. It spread to his brain two years later. That time, nobody sounded positive when they talked about it."

For a few minutes, the only sounds in the gym are Brutus snoring as she pets him and the faint hum of the TV. I give her the space to take the time she needs, pressing a kiss to her head.

"When he died, it was like my whole world froze. I don't even remember the sadness; I just remember feeling like I was living in an out-of-body experience. Everything felt surreal, like it was happening to someone else. I went through the motions every day, but that's all everything felt like."

She lets out a shaky exhale. "I had been taking care of my little brother since Dad was first diagnosed, because all of Mom's attention and efforts went to helping Dad. Not in a bad way, and I never resented her for it—they had just had this great love story that seemed to transcend everything else. I didn't mind taking care of Joey, not if it gave her a little more peace of mind. I was happy to do it. But...when Dad died, it felt like...like I lost *her*, too. She became a shell of a person. Nothing I did could snap her out of it, and suddenly instead of caring for one other person, I was caring for two. And doing it at thirteen."

She slumps down in my lap, though I can't tell which emotion is weighing her down. I'm almost scared to hear what comes next.

"Do you know that's the thing I feel most guilty about? That one year when I was so *angry* with her, and every day I wished she would just *grow up*. I was *thirteen*, and acting like a parent to two kids. Every time I sent in a rent check, or cooked dinner, or forged her signature on Joey's field trip slip, I hated her. And now..." She lets out a sound like a hiccup, but that could very well be a sob. I wrap both arms around her. "And now I would do anything to go back to that year and shake myself. Because on my worst days, it feels like *I* caused her disease."

"Skylar, no," I finally say, tightening my arms around her and speaking softly beside her ear. "You were a *kid*. What you felt was completely normal. Anyone in your shoes would have felt sad, and hurt, and angry. You didn't 'bring on' anything. Sometimes, bad things just happen. It's nobody's fault."

She traces the seam of my jeans for a moment, her voice defeated when she finally speaks.

"I know you're right. It's just hard to get rid of the feelings I internalized back then."

I kiss her neck in answer. "That's valid, too."

Part of me wonders if Skylar has anyone to talk to about these things. The idea of being a support system for her—of being a safe space—has me pushing just a little more. Just enough so I can understand the whole picture.

"Skylar, what disease does your mom have?"

"Parkinson's." Her hand goes back to stroking Brutus's head. "We found out a year after Dad died when she started having serious mobility issues. She's young for the disease, which is why it took them a little while to diagnose. But when she had to quit working because her balance was off and her hands wouldn't stop shaking, it became pretty obvious it was a neurological issue."

Suddenly, I'm remembering how Skylar talked to Lucy when she got concussed. She said the knowledge was because she's in nursing school and likes the brain, but...

First brain cancer, then a neurological disease.

"They're why you're in nursing school, aren't they?"

She nods. "I always knew I'd end up doing something in healthcare. Nursing was the logical answer because of cost, but if I had it my way, I'd be on a straight doctorate track. I love the idea of nursing because I love helping people, but being a doctor would let me solve problems. I could actually treat the disease and help people like Mom. My dream would be to become a neurologist but..." She lets out a shaky exhale. "It's just not really in the cards. So, I'm in nursing school."

I think about how much of a hard worker Skylar is, and how determined she can be when she has a goal. "You'd make an incredible doctor," I tell her. Because I think she needs to hear it. And *God*, I hope I'm not the first to say it.

She gives me a small, grateful smile over her shoulder.

"I think I would, too," she says quietly, turning back toward the TV.

Then just as quickly as she launched into her life story, she ends it by changing the subject. "Did you ever consider a career outside of fighting?"

I turn my own attention back to the fight. "Not really. I got into fighting early, and I've been coaching for almost the same amount of time, so owning a gym was always the end goal. Of course, it helps that I still love the sport and that it makes me money."

"Did you make good money as a fighter?"

I let out a snort at that. "Feeling a little bold, are we?"

She shrugs. "You almost just killed me with your big dick—it's a side effect."

My head tips back with a laugh. "I'll keep that in mind for the next time."

From over her shoulder, I can see the way she bites into her lower lip to control her smile.

That's right, baby. This thing between us is only starting.

I run my fingers through her hair as I answer. I could touch her all night. "It wasn't an astronomical amount, but it was enough to let me live comfortably. A lot of fighters at that time couldn't say the same, so I was thankful for what I had." I hesitate before adding, "It was enough for me to support me and my ex-wife."

That startles her enough to turn slightly in my lap so she can see my face. I let her, wanting her to see I want to be transparent with her the same way she was with me.

"You were married? When?"

"Early in my fighting career. We weren't even that young, but I was too young for marriage. I was a terrible husband."

Her brow furrows as her eyes search mine. "I find that hard to believe."

I shrug. "It's true. Not that I'd do anything differently now, beyond not getting married in the first place. I was not ready for marriage. At all."

"Explain, please," she says, almost sternly, as her frown deepens.

My lip twitches at her adorable expression. I return my hand to her hair, focusing on the strands flowing between my fingers as I explain.

"When you're a fighter, when you want to be the *best* fighter, you have to be selfish. Selfish with your training, selfish with your time, selfish with everything. Your entire world revolves around fighting." I sigh. "It's a really bad quality for a husband."

Skylar's forehead smooths out slightly. "So...you got divorced during your career? *Because* of your career?"

I nod. "I don't blame her for leaving. Regardless of the fact that we weren't a good fit, no one should feel like they come second to anything in their marriage."

"Have you dated anyone since?" she asks, absentmindedly rubbing circles on my leg.

"Not really," I admit. "Nothing's ever felt as fulfilling as fighting."

Until now.

I don't say that out loud, of course. Not just because I know Skylar doesn't feel the same, but also because *Skylar* being the thing I finally like as much as fighting is too complicated to wrap my head around.

I can't tell if she reads it in my eyes, though. Because after holding my gaze for a moment, her attention drops down to my mouth, her tongue swiping across her lower lip and immediately making blood rush to my cock.

But she doesn't initiate a kiss. Instead, she hurriedly looks back to the fight, and then promptly reaches for my ankle.

"Why haven't I done leg locks in class, yet?" she asks, wrapping her arm around my leg. "I feel like I'm at a disadvantage when I'm rolling with the higher belts."

I chuckle at her eagerness. "Because I don't trust white belts to not break other people's legs."

Her gasp is outraged. "I'm offended. Show me right now, I'll prove you wrong."

My eyebrow rises. "Putting my legs in your hands seems like a worse idea than putting my life in them."

She sends me a glare and pokes my foot in impatience. "Just *show* me."

I let out a heavy sigh. "Fine. Turn to face me. I'll show you a straight ankle lock."

She scoots to follow my instructions. The position change causes Brutus to have to move, which he does—with a *humph*. As soon as he plods to the other end of the couch, Skylar settles by my legs like I asked.

I lift one leg and drape it over her lap. "Okay, now wrap your arm around my ankle and grab your other hand at your chest. Your wrist should be against my heel. You're going to pull your hands up toward your chin, raising my foot as much as possible, and then you're going to lean back to put pressure on the arch of my foot."

Slowly and methodically, she follows my instructions. She goes through each step one by one, until she's finishing the submission.

"Tighten your hold on my leg. That's it, now lean back and stretch out my foot." I wait for the telltale ankle pain, then tap against her leg. "There you go, now you know ankle locks."

She stares in wonder at my foot, which just brings a smile to my face. And now I want to kiss her again.

"How would you get out of this?" she asks.

"I would try to stand up and put weight on my foot so you couldn't bend it."

But instead of doing that, I jerk my leg back toward my chest. Since she still has her arm wrapped around my ankle, she jerks forward with it. And as soon as she lands on my chest, her hands bracing against me, I wrap my arms around her waist to hold her in place.

She lets out a startled gasp at the sudden proximity. Almost immediately, her eyes darken with lust and drop to my lips.

Leaning forward, I close the distance between us and take her mouth in the way that tells her exactly how eager I am for her taste.

Once she's panting for breath, I slow the kiss, lazily swiping my tongue along her bottom lip. When I let her go, she gasps out, "I don't think that's a legal ankle lock defense."

I bark out a laugh at that. "Strictly speaking, you're right. I don't want to see you using it in class."

She lets out a dazed sound of agreement, her focus on my mouth again.

And when I kiss her this time, I can't decide which I like better: her taste, or...*her.*

22

SKYLAR

I'm walking on cloud 9 for the rest of the week. I get offered a few extra shifts at the restaurant that I can't turn down, so I don't get back to the gym for three days, but mentally, I spend the entirety of those days on the mats.

Despite Dominic giving me his number the night my mom fell, we don't really talk on the phone. Not only is he not a big texter, but I'm also so swamped with work and schoolwork that the one time he *does* call me to see how my day was, I end up yawning three times in one minute. Plus, talking to him just reminds me of how much I miss him.

And when I finally walk back into the gym, and Dominic is the first person I see, all of that comes roaring to the surface.

"Hi," I say, a giddy smile overtaking my face.

"Hey, Skylar." He stands from the couch and walks over to the reception desk, giving me a small smile of his own. At the sight of him, my body wants nothing more than to hop this counter and into his arms. "How are you? How's your week been?"

"Busy. Worked a lot. Studied a lot. The usual." I swear it

feels like my smile is going to crack my face, and I catch his eyes drifting down to my lips before meeting my gaze again, our minds clearly in the same place. "How's your week been?"

His lip twitches as he leans forward slightly. "Good. Taught a lot. Trained a lot. The usual."

I huff out a laugh, trying to ignore the tension brewing between us.

"So, what are we doing today?" I ask.

For some reason, that question triggers a nervous reaction. His eyes dart around the gym, and then into the office, before taking a step closer to me and speaking in a hushed voice.

"About that... I wanted to talk to you. We didn't exactly discuss boundaries last time, or about how we're going to play this in the open. I don't want to assume what kind of relationship you want here, but for me, I'd prefer if we keep things professional during gym hours. My focus needs to stay on my fighters, and I need to be just Coach when I'm here." His expression becomes apologetic. "I hope you can understand that."

For a moment, I can only blink. Then...

I have to bite down on my lip to smother a smile.

"I meant, what are you teaching in class today..."

He stares at me. And then the faintest pink appears on his cheeks.

"Oh...uh, it's kick week in Muay Thai, and armbar defense in jiu-jitsu." He clears his throat.

I finally take pity on him and release the giggle I've been holding back. "That sounds good. And so does the clarity on our relationship." He might go pinker at that, so I flatten my expression. "Okay, in all seriousness, I appreciate the honesty. I *was* on the same page as you, but it's good to say it out loud. And I would never want to risk your name, or make you any less committed to your fighters, so I'm in complete agreement." I lower my voice even more. "During gym hours, we're nothing more than coach and student."

He looks relieved when he nods. "Okay, then. So, we're on the same page."

I nod but then realize I missed the most important clarifying point. My tone is careful when I say, "But even after gym hours, I need this to stay casual. I think we both have our reasons, but on my end, it *definitely* can't be a full-blown relationship. You've seen my life outside of here... I can't let anything take my focus from that."

"I understand," he says, soothing the last of my worries. "Let's just say we're...enjoying each other's company. Sound good?"

A grin stretches across my face. "Yes, Coach," I purr.

His eyes heat at my tone. Laughing, I turn and make my way toward the changing room.

When jiu-jitsu finishes, I'm happy and exhausted. By the time the last bell rings, I collapse on the mat with a content sigh.

"I feel like my brain is going to explode from all the steps we have to remember in this goddamn sport," Aiden groans from the other side of the mat.

"You *better* remember the steps to an armbar defense," comes Tristan's voice. "Your next opponent loves the arm, so I can pretty much guarantee he's going to go for yours."

Aiden flexes his bicep with a grin. "I mean, can you blame him?"

There's a collective eye roll around the gym.

"But seriously, I've been concussed too many times to have a good memory." I'm surprised when he turns his attention to me. "Hey, Miss Perfect Student, you got any notes I can borrow? I bet you've got a little notebook in that bag with all the steps listed."

I raise a disbelieving eyebrow at him, which just makes his grin grow.

"You can tease all you want, but she's already better at armbar defense than you," Tristan shoots across the room. "I give her a few months and she'll be submitting you."

Aiden holds up his hands in surrender. "Hey, it was a *compliment!*"

Tristan points at the heavy bag room. "Whatever you say. Now go start your bag work. You're fighting in a few weeks." He looks around at the other fighters. "That goes for everyone. Fighter training starts in five minutes."

As Aiden stands and begrudgingly heads toward the bag room, I call after him, "I'll make a copy of my notes for you. If you'd had them last year, maybe Banker wouldn't have submitted you in the second round."

His only response is to turn and gape at me.

Tristan lets out a bark of laughter and smacks him in the shoulder as he passes him. "I think that's the first time I've seen you speechless, pretty boy. She *did* tell us she looked up everyone's records before she signed up. Looks like she's not afraid to use it, either."

Aiden's mouth snaps shut as Remy pushes him, chuckling under her breath.

I'm smiling as I start toward my gym bag on the sidelines. Since the next class is an hour fighter training that I can't attend, I'm going to use the time to do homework. I don't normally clean after, since one of the fighters does it, but I think part of me is dragging my feet with leaving.

I glance toward the office where I know Dominic is working right now. With a wistful sigh, I turn back to my gym bag.

But just then, the door to the bag room opens.

And Jax walks in, with Craig by his side.

"And this is our mat room," Jax says, giving a tour of the gym. "This is where we teach the jiu-jitsu and sparring classes." He notices me and adds, "Skylar here just got finished with jiu-jitsu. Good class, Skylar?"

It takes me a moment to reply because I'm still in shock that my classmate is standing in my gym right now. *Is this a small-world kind of thing? He just* happened *to walk into the gym I train at?*

I fumble my way through an answer. "Um...uh, yeah, it was a great class. Tristan always teaches great classes." My confused focus shifts to Craig. "What are you doing here?"

I get a half-smirk in response, which all but confirms my theory that he's here because of me. *Goddamnit.*

"I'm looking for a new sport," he says, his tone nonchalant. "You raved about this place so much that I thought I would check it out. You're right, it *is* amazing."

Jax, looking every bit as confused but, seeming to sense my tension, asks carefully, "How do you two know each other?"

"We go to school together," Craig answers for us. "Skylar convinced me that training MMA is better than lifting boring old weights. She's the reason I set up this consult."

Jax gives him a look I can't read and doesn't respond. The room fills with an awkwardness that no one knows how to break.

Suddenly, the door to the office opens. And Coach walks in. When he sees us all standing there, his steps slow.

Jax hurries to make introductions. "This is the owner and head instructor, Coach Dominic."

Dominic extends his hand to Craig. "Hey. Nice to meet you."

Craig shakes it, still looking completely at ease. "Hey, man, I'm Craig. You know, your students love to sing your praises."

A slight frown creases Dominic's forehead. "I'm glad to hear that," he says slowly. His attention shifts to Jax. "Which of my students was singing?"

A huge grin appears on Craig's face as he gestures toward me. "Skylar, of course. She's obsessed with this place. I couldn't *not* come check it out. It seemed too good to be true."

At that, Dominic doesn't meet my gaze, but I can sense that his eyes are now solely on me.

Craig is oblivious. When he turns to me, that grin hasn't faded even a little. He looks downright *giddy*.

"You were right, Skylar. I think I'm going to sign up. It'll be so fun training together! We'll finally get to hang out, even with your ridiculously busy schedule. And since you're *so* into this, I'll even do extra work with you. I've got plenty of space at my house, so we can get some extra practice in whenever you want."

In an instant, Dominic stiffens.

"I wouldn't recommend practicing these techniques outside of the gym, especially when you're still new," he grits out. "A lot of the things you learn are dangerous and should only be practiced under professional supervision."

Craig actually *waves him off*. Like he knows more than the literal legend standing next to him.

"We'll be fine," he says, his tone and his stance still relaxed. "How hard could it be? I'll make sure she's safe."

And if I thought Dominic looked tense before, it's nothing compared to the marble statue he becomes now.

"I'm sorry, I don't think you'd be a good fit for our gym," he says, his words like ice. "Our students take this sport very seriously, and not doing so puts others at risk of harm. If you're already planning on ignoring the gym rules, I can't have you sign up here."

My jaw drops at the reprimand. I've never seen him turn a new student away, and I definitely never thought he'd be capable of doing it like *this*. One look at Jax's shell-shocked expression confirms he's never seen anything like this, either.

The silence in the gym is loud. Craig stands there gaping at Dominic, completely unprepared to be shut down so definitively. His mouth opens and closes a few times, clearly trying to come up with a response, but nothing comes out.

Dominic puts him out of his misery by shifting to face me, effectively turning his back on Craig and ending the conversation.

"Do you have time to do a little extra work?" he asks me, his expression stone. "Tristan's teaching the fighters, so I can help you with that combo we were working on last week."

Too stunned to speak, the only thing I manage is a jerky nod and some kind of stammered agreement.

"Good. Grab your things. We're working in the cage today."

With a final glance at me, Dominic turns and strides toward the cage. Leaving us all in an uneasy silence.

I'm the first one to make a sound, because I want *out* of this situation. I don't know how I'll ever look Craig in the eye after this—not that I really want to. I'm not too fond of him these days. But I have no idea what to say to him right now.

Sorrynotsorry that my coach just kicked you out of his gym. See you in Anatomy class next week.

Jax finally snaps himself back to reality. "Uh, well, I appreciate you coming in to check out the gym—"

I don't hear the rest of it because I'm hurrying past them to follow Dominic into the cage.

His tone is hard and flat when he speaks. "Start with the four elbows we learned last week. Then we'll work them into combos."

I hesitate, long enough for him to notice.

"What?"

Finally, I look up to meet his eyes. Tossing everything that just happened out the window, I let out a noisy exhale and admit, "I was actually wondering if we could focus on jiu-jitsu. I... Well, I was thinking about doing a jiu-jitsu tournament."

That's the first time I've said that out loud. I know plenty of people do competitions not long after starting, since jiu-jitsu isn't physically dangerous and there's no record-keeping, but I still have no idea how Dominic will react to me wanting to compete.

He gives me no reaction. The only reason I know he doesn't hate the idea is because he's quick to agree.

"Good. Let's start with your takedowns, then."

I nod, some of the nerves leaving my body. But as I get into my ready stance, I can't help glancing over to the reception area, where I can see Craig finally leaving.

I feel Dominic's arms come around my waist. Distantly, I hear him say something like *have to get a better grip when you shoot for the takedown.*

But just as I have the vague thought that Dominic isn't usually so quick to touch me, I also catch the flash of Craig's expression as he walks through the door.

It's there and gone in a millisecond. And I can't read it, I don't understand it, but I feel the shiver of dread that runs through me at the sight of it.

I'm torn out of my thoughts when Dominic knocks me over. I land on my back with an *oomph*.

"Got it?" he asks. *Nope.* But I nod dazedly.

He helps me to my feet, his touch lingering for a moment. Then he jerks his chin at me and says, "Now you try."

I don't know anything that he just said, but I settle into my wrestling stance and move for the takedown as best I can. I get Dominic to the ground, but I have a sneaking suspicion that he's more distracted than he's letting on, because he doesn't make any corrections.

Thankfully, Jax chooses that moment to walk out of the office and toward the cage. I notice the wary way he looks at Dominic as he nears.

"Anything you want me to do with the fighters?" he asks.

Dominic pulls me to my feet as he answers. "Run the offense versus defense drills after their bag work."

Jax nods as he turns toward the heavy bag room. "You got it, Coach."

The second he's through the door, Dominic leans down and tosses me over his shoulder.

I let out a squeak, gripping onto his shirt. "What are you—?"

"Quiet," he orders, as he carries me toward the office. He strides inside and closes the door behind him. And before I can consider his intentions, he's dropping me on top of his desk.

"Wait, I thought you said—"

He cuts me off with a hard kiss.

I'm too surprised to react. But he doesn't seem to mind,

because he takes ownership of my mouth by gripping the side of my neck and deepening the kiss. By the time his tongue grazes mine, I'm too dazed to even attempt to match him.

He uses both hands to grip my thighs and spread my legs—and when he steps between them, he moves close enough that his cock rubs against my already-drenched center. With a hard roll of his hips, he sends an electric shot of lust through my veins.

I can't stop the loud moan that escapes my lips at the contact.

He claps a hand over my mouth, his eyes boring into mine. The heat in his stare lights me on fire all over again.

"You're not allowed to talk until you've come on my hand," he says, and my core clenches in response. "Do you understand?"

I'm too stunned by what's happening to do anything other than nod.

Letting his hand slide from my mouth, he wraps it gently around the front of my throat. My pulse picks up at the possessive gesture.

His other hand goes back to my hip. He squeezes once, then I feel his touch slowly drift across my stomach, along the hem of my shorts. One finger dips enticingly under the material.

He holds my stare the entire time. I don't know what he's looking for, but I can't bring myself to look away.

Finally, his hand slides down the front of my shorts. He doesn't tease me any longer, just goes right under my thong and runs his fingers over my drenched skin.

My lips pop open at the sensation, but a scolding look from him traps the moan in my mouth. I have to bite down on my lip to keep my sounds inside as he starts to tease me.

His fingers slide between my lips once, twice, but on the third pass he drives them deep inside. And maybe he knew I wouldn't be able to stop myself from making a sound, because he takes my mouth in another heady kiss as he does it.

I'm clinging to him now. With both hands fisted in his shirt, I'm glad he's still holding me up by the throat because the feel of him inside me, of his need for *me*, is making me weak in the knees. I can barely return his kiss.

As his fingers start to pump into me, I feel the moment he curls them and brushes the spot that sends electricity through my veins. I think I try to gasp again, but he just swallows the sound again with his mouth.

And when he puts his thumb on my clit at the same time, I know I'm not going to last much longer in his hands like this. His tongue slides across mine, his fingers drive deeper, and I *explode.*

I'm shaking, weak and overwhelmed, when the sensations finally die down. After a moment, I realize his grip on my throat has shifted to cup my neck and run his thumb soothingly along my jaw.

I sound dazed and out of breath when I ask, "I thought you said no hooking up at the gym."

There's not an ounce of regret in his voice when he says, "I know what I said. But I hated that guy thinking he had any claim to you in *my* space."

It takes a second for his meaning to sink in. But suddenly, his greedy touch, his harshness, makes sense to me. And the fact that he was even a little bit jealous spikes a new heat in my blood.

"He *didn't* have any claim to me," I assure him. "Even if you hadn't kicked him out, I never would have given him the time of day."

Dominic looks skeptical. "I had no way of knowing that."

My lip twitches with a smile. "You could've just asked me."

He doesn't respond. So I push off the desk and stand, taking pleasure in the fact that he stays right where he is, just lets me flatten my body against his as he waits for what I'm about to do.

Pressing up on my toes, I let my lips brush against his as I whisper, "Would you like me to prove to you that you're the only one with any claim to me?"

A heartbeat passes. Then another. And then...

My stomach flutters with excitement as he drops one hand to cup his hard cock straining through his shorts.

"On your knees."

23

DOMINIC

I'm out of my fucking mind by the time she drops to her knees.

I hadn't intended to let it get this far. I told her barely two hours ago that I wanted to stay Coach during training hours, but that piece of shit who walked in here tonight snapped every piece of iron restraint I possess. I wanted to wring his neck just for *looking* at Skylar, let alone hitting on her right in front of me. And I know we agreed on keeping things professional during gym hours, but the second he hit on her, my brain screamed *MINE.* There wasn't a chance in hell I wasn't dragging her in here to put my hands on her.

Between the scene in the gym and then watching Skylar come on my fingers, my body is vibrating with need. I feel possessive and jealous, and I'm not in control of my actions anymore. I feel fucking insane. But I need to calm down a little before I do something I'll regret.

She keeps her gaze locked with mine as I push my shorts over my hips. I can't take my eyes off her, off the smile on her face and the eager sparkle in her eye. Even as I pull my length out and guide the tip to her mouth, we never look away from each other.

But then I sink an inch between her lips, and her eyes close on a moan.

Groaning at the feel of her hot, wet mouth, my head drops back. A surge of possession roars through my body again, and I can't stop from thrusting forward harder than I intend to.

She doesn't push me away, though. She just swallows me deeper and swirls her tongue around my length.

"Christ," I gasp. I knew her mouth would feel good, but I didn't know watching her *love* it would set this to the next level. My remaining control, if it even existed before this, is dissolving right onto her tongue.

Fuck it.

Giving in to the urge, I grip her ponytail with one hand.

"Put your hands behind your back. You're going to open your mouth and take everything I give you."

And she's so goddamn perfect that she does it immediately, without question. Her hands lock at her lower back, and her mouth goes slack. When her eyes meet mine again, it's with a silent plea.

"Grab my leg if you need me to stop." That's the only warning I give before I start to fuck her mouth.

And *God,* she looks so beautiful when I do it.

I sink into her on the first thrust. Deeper on the second. By the third, her eyes start to water. I don't go so deep that she chokes on me, but I want to find her limit. I'm feeling too much like an animal to *not.*

She takes every bit of me with her hands locked behind her back, her mouth open and inviting. I can see the lust in her eyes as much as I can feel it on my cock when her tongue flattens under it. She wants this just as much as I do.

"*Fuck*, you look so pretty like this," I murmur, brushing a tear from her cheek. "Do you feel like mine yet?"

She nods as much as she's able. And just that has the heat spiking in my body, and my hips moving even faster. I want my imprint on every part of her. I want my taste on her tongue, and for her to remember this moment every time she licks her lips today. I want her to think of only *me*.

Every muscle in my body tightens. I can feel the orgasm crawling up the base of my spine, threatening to explode at any second. Her mouth is way too fucking sweet.

I'm about to tug on her hair and tell her to get ready for my cum, when I hear it. Voices getting closer to the office door.

I have to drag myself back to reality. It feels like I'm moving through quicksand as I do it, like everything is working in slow motion. As I shuffle Skylar a few inches back to be under the desk, and as I drop into the seat and move forward so my exposed cock isn't visible.

Tristan opens the door right as it hits me what's happening.

I'm fucking my student's mouth. And one of my instructors just walked in.

Tristan pauses in the doorway. His expression, as always, is unreadable. But after a moment, he says simply, "Hey. Everything good?"

I manage a stiff nod. "Yeah. I'm coming out to hold pads for you in a minute. I just…needed to take a call."

I have no idea if he believes me. Especially when he simply moves on to what I assume is his reason for coming in here.

"Jax said you kicked some guy out of the gym. Need me to do anything? Do we need to cover ourselves?"

The reminder of that asshole has my hand tightening in

Skylar's hair. I didn't even realize I still had a hold of it. But I suddenly become aware of the fact that she's sitting quietly between my legs, trying just as hard as I am to not get caught.

I turn my attention back to Tristan, wanting to get him out of here as quickly as possible. "No, we're fine," I answer him. "The guy was an asshole. Would've washed out quickly, but also would've made every class a living hell while he was here. I just saved us the two months."

Tristan accepts that answer with silence. God knows we've seen the type enough times over the years that it's a believable answer.

"Jax said he hit on Skylar, too?"

My jaw clenches. I wish I could bring the guy back in here just to go a round with him in the ring. "Yeah, he—"

I choke on the next word when I feel Skylar's tongue lick along the underside of my length.

Arousal flames in my blood. I didn't go soft from the initial interruption, but the feeling of Skylar's mouth takes me right back to rock hard and ready to fuck my claim into her.

Tristan quirks an eyebrow and I realize I need to finish my sentence. Wiping away the sweat that I can feel beading on my brow, I say, "Sorry, I think I took too much of that new preworkout. My heart's beating out of my chest."

I swallow roughly when I feel Skylar's mouth close over the head of my cock. She starts to slowly and lazily suck me, and it takes all the willpower I have to continue the conversation.

"He was the toxic alpha type," I offer by way of explanation. "He would've leaned into it to hit on every girl in the gym. I—" I clear my throat with a cough when I hit the back of Skylar's throat. "I don't need that kind of bullshit in my gym."

Finally, Tristan nods, accepting my answer. Kicking someone out isn't *completely* out of character for me, since I've been known to subtly weed out assholes, so it's not the hardest sell. Thankfully, he moves on.

"Jimmy just called me. He heard Hill has been seen in a boxing gym a lot lately. I know we prepared for him to strike a lot, but I was hoping we could work some extra kicks today."

Skylar's mouth continues to slide up and down my length, lazy and silent in her movements. I want so badly to hold her head in place and drive my cock as deep as she can take, but I force myself to keep my attention on Tristan.

"We'll go heavy on the kicks today, then." And I'll admit I'm a little proud of myself when I manage to focus and actually coach. "Get the kick shield ready. We'll do leg kick burnouts, too."

Tristan's nod is more enthusiastic this time. "Sounds good. I'm just warming up, so I'm ready whenever."

"I'll be out in a few minutes," I assure him. "We'll work in the ring today."

Thank God, he's not a man of many words. The second the door closes behind him, I'm shoving my chair back and pulling Skylar out from under the desk.

With my hand still gripping her hair, I slide my cock between her lips without a second's hesitation. When she lets out a whimper and opens for more, I start to fuck her mouth with abandon.

"You little tease," I growl. "Did you want us to get caught? Were you hoping you'd suck me so good, I'd give away what was happening under my desk?"

She shakes her head as much as she can while I'm filling her mouth over and over again. I don't know how she doesn't gag, because I've devolved into a caveman. I feel my release waiting on the fringe of my awareness, and it's ten times more powerful than it was before we were interrupted.

"I'm going to come in your mouth, and you're going to swallow every drop," I force out, my thrusts becoming less smooth. I'm fully fucking her face at this point. "I want to know you're walking around with my cum inside you today."

She moans her assent, staring up at me expectantly. The fact that her cheeks are wet with tears and her hair a mess from my grip just makes me want her even more. I haven't even finished yet and I already want her again.

But then she flattens her tongue under my cock and lets out a needy whimper, and my climax comes barreling down my spine.

With a groan, I explode in her mouth. Feeling her throat muscles flex as she swallows heightens the sensations by a thousand.

"Christ, baby," I gasp, reaching down with my other hand to pull out just enough that I can shuttle my hand over the base of my cock. And when she opens her mouth wide so I can see the last drops of my release on her tongue, I think I lose my mind all over again.

I get so lost in the sight of her closing her swollen lips over my tip and sucking the last of my cum off my length with a sexy little moan that it takes me a few seconds to catch my breath. My hand's still tangled in her hair with a death grip and I'm still gazing down at her like I've never had a woman on her knees in front of me before. I'm pretty sure I haven't. Or at least, I can't remember a single time that I did.

She finally unlocks her hands and leans back, and I begrudgingly let go of her. When she winces as she pushes off her knees, a wave of regret hits me. For her discomfort, for being rough, for probably crossing a few lines. Not to mention, I'm sending mixed signals by fucking her in the gym.

I reach for the paper towel roll on top of one of the boxes. "Are you okay?" I ask softly as I hand her a piece, then hurriedly tuck my softening cock away. "That was too rough. I'm...sorry."

But she just gives me a sweet smile, so at odds from how she looked a minute ago. I can't decide which version of her I like better. "I like when you're rough, Coach," she purrs.

"Jesus, don't start," I mutter. "I'll have you back on your knees in thirty seconds."

Her eyebrows shoot up, gaze dropping to my crotch. "Thirty seconds? So much for the old guy not having stamina."

I let out a growl and step forward so I can fist my hand in her hair again. "Careful, little girl. I've got plenty of ways to prove I'm not old."

She just grins, pleased with herself.

And I can't stop from stamping a hard kiss to her lips.

She stiffens in surprise, which just makes me slide my tongue in her mouth and make it dirty. I take my time scandalizing her.

When I pull back, her eyes are wide. "But...you just came—"

"I know where I came. My own cum isn't going to stop me from kissing you, Skylar. You're fucking a man, not a teenager."

If possible, her eyes go even wider. And her voice is filled with wonder when she whispers, "You're so *dirty*."

Now I'm the one grinning. Pressing another quick kiss to her mouth, I put some real distance between us.

"We should get back out there before someone else comes looking," I say, my tone sullen. "I know I'm not exactly standing by my own rules, but this is exactly why I didn't want anything to happen in the gym."

Skylar disappears into the bathroom. Thank God, we have one in here. "Hey, I agreed with you," comes her voice through the open doorway. "I like you *because* you're Coach. I would never want to take away from that."

For some reason, that soothes something within me.

When she comes out of the bathroom, her face has been washed and her hair has been smoothed back into a new ponytail. She no longer looks like she was just face-fucked by her coach.

Jesus. What has my life turned into?

"I'll go out first, and make sure no one's around," I tell her. "We should be good, since all the fighters are supposed to be in the heavy bag room, but let me just make sure." My stomach drops with dread—though I'm not sure if it's from the prospect of being found out, or the fact that I have to hide her in the first place. "If someone *does* see us, we'll say we were discussing your membership. I did actually pull you in here for that."

She nods in understanding and waits patiently. Taking a deep breath, I listen for anyone at the reception desk, and then push the office door open.

When I see no one is around, I let out a breath of relief and wave for Skylar to hurry out. She does, and suddenly I'm in my normal place behind the desk, and she's beside her gym bag on the sidelines.

We're back to coach and student.

———

By the time I head home for the night, I'm physically and mentally drained. Working with Tristan when he's in fight camp is always exhausting, and Monday is my hard training day as it is. But it's the emotional rollercoaster of the day that has me ready to crash.

Pulling Skylar into the office was a bad idea. I knew it before I did it.

So why couldn't I stop myself?

Getting caught by Tristan would've been...bad. Really bad. I know he respects me as a coach, and I know he knows who I am as a person, but there's no way he would keep me as his head coach if he found me with a student. A *young* student.

I throw myself down on the couch with a weary exhale. Brutus jumps up next to me, clearly sensing my negative emotions tonight, and settles with his big head in my lap. I absentmindedly pet him, my head dropping back against the couch as conflicting thoughts roil in my brain.

But thinking about what I *shouldn't* be doing with Skylar just makes me think about her *more*.

Slowly, my nerves and worries surrounding everything Skylar morph into happiness and excitement. In the back of my brain, it occurs to me that she always seems to have that effect.

Reaching for my phone, I scroll to her number and press *Call* before I can second-guess myself.

"Dominic?"

A smile immediately comes to my face when I hear her voice, even though her confusion is obvious.

"Yeah, it's me." In the background, I hear the sounds of dishes clattering and people yelling. "Sorry, are you at work? I assumed you went home after the gym."

"I'm not working, I just came in to grab my paycheck." A door slamming shut cuts off all background noises. "I'm actually leaving to walk home right now, so you caught me at the perfect time."

Just as it always does, the thought of her walking the streets of a big city by herself fills me with unease. Even though she's smart about staying safe. But I know how important independence is to Skylar, so I force down my need to protect and care for her.

Still, I can't help asking, "How long's your walk?"

"Ten minutes. I work close to home."

"Want to stay on the phone with me while you walk? Or will that distract you too much?"

"I can talk. My coach taught me well when it comes to self-defense."

A smile comes unbidden to my face. It also has me admitting, "I wanted to hear your voice."

There's a pause on the line. And I can tell she's smiling when she finally says, "You know, none of your students would be scared of you if they knew how sweet you are."

"Well, don't be giving away my secrets, then."

"Yes, sir," she purrs. And the heat that stays barely banked when Skylar is on my mind roars right back to life.

I'm desperate to see her again. Talking to her isn't enough.

"Are you coming to open mat tomorrow?" I ask. "You could stay after if you're not busy."

"I'm not in tomorrow," she answers, regret lacing her tone. "I have a commitment tomorrow night."

Curiosity gets the best of me. "What's tomorrow night?"

"Joey has a basketball game. I always try to support him as much as I can, since...since Mom can't."

This girl is too loyal for this world.

"Can I come?"

"You...want to come to a high school basketball game?" Skylar asks, her confusion evident. "Why?"

"Well, *obviously* because I have a lot invested in the local high school basketball scene. I follow it religiously."

Fuck, I love the sound of her giggle.

"It's not going to be very exciting," she warns. "Joey hasn't been starting so there's going to be some downtime. It could get boring."

"I'm sure I can find a way to entertain myself," I say, deepening my voice in that way that I know makes her shiver.

I can't hear any kind of reaction, but she sounds a little breathless when she says, "Yeah, your students have *no* idea who you are."

I chuckle at that, and she quickly changes the subject.

"I'll get there at seven when it starts," she says. "I usually stay for the whole game, but you obviously don't need to do that. Just come whenever, I guess?"

One corner of my lip twitches.

New goal: make Skylar understand that there's a reason people vie for her company.

"Alright, I'll just come whenever," I repeat, knowing full well I'm going to be there before seven o'clock. "Just text me the address, and I'll meet you there."

"Okay," she agrees, and the sound of a door opening can be heard in the background. "I just got home, so I'll text you in a minute." There's a pause, and then she adds softly, "I don't know why you'd want to suffer through a high school basketball game, but I'm excited to see you."

And just hearing the change in her voice—from confusion to happiness—is enough to make me feel like a kid on Christmas.

24

SKYLAR

The third time I catch myself craning my neck to look the length of the hallway, I have to acknowledge that I'm a little nervous.

I'm nervous. Because of a guy. A guy is making me nervous.

But it's not just *any* guy. *Dominic* is making me nervous. *Dominic* is the one who got a *yes* out of me after an offer of hanging out.

I've said no to my coworkers so many times, it's become a running joke, complete with an exaggerated mimic of my voice. If I ever said yes, they'd likely be too shocked to react.

I *wanted* him to come hang out with me. If I had given myself time to think about it, I probably would've second-guessed everything and drawn my usual boundary. Instead, I'm standing in a high school hallway, twisting my jacket in my hands as I wait for the man I'm sleeping with to appear at my little brother's basketball game.

What has my life turned into?

But before I can disappear down a whirlpool of doubts and stress, a familiar head of black hair appears at the end of the hallway. And the second he catches sight of me, a smile lights up his eyes.

God, that man is beautiful.

Usually, when we leave the gym, he's wearing joggers and a T-shirt or gym hoodie. And he's still hot enough to melt iron then, but Dominic in real clothes is enough to stop traffic.

He's wearing faded jeans and a white t-shirt, with a blue flannel unbuttoned over top of it. And I don't know if it's because of the blue of his shirt or because I'm mesmerized by the sight of him, but the blue in his eyes pierces right through my soul. I can't look away from him.

He strides toward me, his gait confident and his eyes never moving from mine. I'm too hypnotized by his appearance and attention to even muster a smile when he stops in front of me.

"Hey," he says, his lip quirking in response to my frozen expression.

"Hi," I squeak.

"You look cute when you're out of your element," he says with a chuckle. "You'd think fighting would bring it out of you, but apparently it takes a date to a high school basketball game."

I don't know whether to be offended that he called me out on my nerves, or shocked that he just referred to this as a date.

His smile turns into a grin, seemingly delighted to be making me feel this way. "Let's go find our seats. Before I pull you into an empty classroom and we miss the whole game."

That finally draws a reaction out of me. Because I'm tempted to let him do it, especially since I probably shouldn't kiss him out in the open.

"Look at that blush," he murmurs, the pad of his thumb lightly brushing over my warm cheek. "You'd think I had you on your knees again."

My breath whooshes from my lungs, all thoughts rushing back to my brain. "Jesus," I gasp. "Are you going to be like this all night?"

Dominic throws his head back with a laugh, then slings his arm around my shoulders. "Come on. Let's go watch a basketball game."

As soon as we walk into the gymnasium, the reality of my decision to say yes to Dominic fully sinks in.

I realize quickly that my usual habit at these games is to pull out my textbooks and finish some homework while I wait for Joey to get tagged into the game. And it's not that I *want* to do that right now, it just never really hit me that I'm so locked into my routines that *not* following them feels startling. Which once again just emphasizes that I was reacting instinctively when I agreed to this. Switching things up shouldn't stress me out this much.

"So..." Dominic drawls. He leans his elbows back on the bleacher behind him, his focus on the basketball game that's now starting. "Are you freaking out about this?"

My head whips to the side to stare at him. "How on *earth* did you—"

"I've learned you only get stressed about two things," he interrupts, still not looking at me. "Money, and being thrown out of your routine. And since I haven't even offered to buy your pretzel yet, I'm going to assume it's the latter."

I can only gape at him.

He turns his head to look at me and grin. "I'm right, aren't I?"

Finally, my mouth snaps shut as I glare at him instead. "And they call *me* the know-it-all," I grumble. But even though he chuckles, he still waits expectantly for my answer.

I sigh. "It's the being *here* with you. When we're at the gym, I know what we are and how you fit into my day-to-day. I have times and places in my life for everything I do. This is new to me, and I'm trying to make sense of it. I'm just a little off-balance right now, that's all."

Dominic nods in understanding. "Well, what would you normally be doing while you wait for Joey to play?"

"Homework," I answer with a shrug.

"Do you *want* to do homework?" he asks. "If this time is important to you and I'm a distraction, I won't be offended if you ask me to leave. I wanted to spend time with you, but not if it makes you uncomfortable or makes things harder for you."

"I don't want you to leave," I blurt out. Just as quickly as I said yes to this date. Only, the fact that my gut has reacted this way to Dominic *twice* now is oddly comforting. I feel some of the tension deflate from my shoulders.

Dominic notices. And he seems to relax just as much.

"Okay, you're right," I admit on an exhale. "I need to chill out. My brain is on overdrive."

"I like your brain," he says. And it's so immediate, so genuine, that I soften even more.

Deciding to cut my overthinking short for the night, I turn to Dominic and ask curiously, "Did you play sports in high school?"

He nods. "I played football in the beginning. Then picked up wrestling one off-season and never went back. It was pretty much a snowball into jiu-jitsu and MMA after that."

I hum thoughtfully. "You really did make it your whole life, didn't you?"

Another nod, but this one's stiffer. I want to ask him about it, ask him if he regrets it in any way, but he cuts me off.

"What about you? Did you play any sports?"

I shake my head. "Dad was sick by then. I couldn't stay after school for practice because I had to pick up Joey and take care of him at night."

As if hearing his name, Joey chooses that moment to turn in his seat on the bench and start looking for me.

A smile comes to my face automatically. I love that he does that. I love that he can assume I'm going to be at his games. Any time I'm struggling—with work or school, with Mom, with anything—these are the moments I try to remember. The moments I see all my hard work pay off for my family's well-being.

When he finally spots me, a big grin appears on his face. And my heart warms another few degrees. But then I see his gaze track to my right, and his expression becomes a look of confusion. Which is when I realize just how close Dominic and I are sitting.

Before I need to mime some kind of explanation to my brother, there are loud shouts of dismay from all around us. My attention snaps back to the court just in time to see the opposing team's breakaway and score.

"Would you rather be in a zombie apocalypse or a robot apocalypse?"

My head jerks toward Dominic. "What?"

To my surprise, he seems to be blushing.

"I was trying to think of the most ridiculous question to ask that would put you at ease," he admits.

My lip twitches with amusement. "And a zombie apocalypse is what you came up with?"

He sits up a bit straighter and clears his throat. "I was watching *28 Days Later* last night. It stuck with me."

I huff a laugh as I face forward again. "Probably robot apocalypse," I answer, trying to get comfortable in my seat. "Omniscient beings scare me a little less than cannibals." When I hear Dominic's chuckle beside me, the tension releases from my muscles once again. It empowers me to ask a question of my own.

"Would you rather always be stuck in traffic, or have to take public transportation everywhere?"

He actually *shudders*. "The public transportation one. Sticking me in traffic would be a genuine form of torture if I was ever captured." He says it so seriously that a laugh bursts out of me.

"Alright, smartass," he growls, "I've got one for you. Would you rather have everyone be able to read your thoughts, or everyone have access to your Internet history?"

Heat flames my face at the things I've googled.

"Guess that answers *that* question," he says with a chuckle, leaning back to brace his forearms on the bleacher behind him, behind me. My eyes follow the line of his muscles that his white shirt reveals. He's so effortlessly attractive that it makes my throat dry up. I have to clear my throat before my next question.

"Would you rather be the absolute best at fighting but no one knows it, or wear the UFC championship belt and have everyone think you're a joke?"

His eyes widen and his jaw drops as his face swivels toward me. "You're a *monster*," he whispers. This time, when I laugh, it feels like the most effortless thing in the world.

And that's how it goes. Back and forth, until I completely lose track of time.

When he asked to come, I wasn't worried that we wouldn't have anything to talk about, or that it would feel weird spending time with him outside of the gym, but I never expected it would feel this *easy* to be with him. I could sit here for another six hours. It wouldn't matter if we're talking about pointless topics or discussing the secret to greatness. I feel like I would never get tired of picking Dominic's brain.

And *that* is terrifying.

I'm distracted from my impending nerves when I see Joey jump up from the bench and stride onto the court when his coach gestures him forward. My heart starts to beat twice as fast.

We've talked through the entire game. Looking up at the scoreboard, I realize it's the end of the fourth quarter and the score is tied.

I'm silent as I watch the next few minutes unfold. Joey gets the ball a few times, but he doesn't get the opportunity to shoot. He runs as fast as he can on the opposing team's breakaway, and manages to get the rebound when their shot doesn't go in. I think I let out a shout and a cheer when that happens.

Joey's coach is screaming for a play, the urgency thick in the air. I can't breathe from the anticipation.

Both teams struggle to score. When one of the opposing team's shots just barely tips off the rim, our side of the crowd audibly lets out the breath we were holding. And when the same thing happens to one of our shots, they groan.

Then, with twenty seconds left in the game, Joey gets the ball. I suck in a breath and grab Dominic's arm in a death-grip. Joey fakes to one side and then drives in when the kid guarding him trips in that direction. He lifts the ball, aims, and shoots.

The crowd is so silent, we can hear the sound of the ball swishing through the net.

And then the gymnasium erupts. I'm screaming so loud, I can't hear a thing from anyone else. Still latched onto Dominic, he cheers as I start jumping up and down, my heart exploding with happiness and pride as I watch my brother lifted onto his teammates' shoulders.

"Holy shit, that was incredible!" I throw my arms around Dominic's neck without a second's hesitation, squeezing him in a tight hug. "He did it!"

His arms wrap around me, his chuckle warm in my ear. "Yeah, he did."

The feel of his embrace is too good to let go of. Especially when his hold tightens, and his intoxicating scent invades my senses. I love that he's here for this.

I love that he's here.

Begrudgingly, I unwind my arms from around his neck and slide down his body. But I can't quite let go of him completely, because my hands stay flat on his chest. His stay on my hips. When I finally glance up at him, his stare hits deep into my soul.

I can't look away. But I still have to muster up the courage to whisper, "I'm glad you came."

My words soften him. Still holding my gaze, he says quietly, "Me too."

And I wonder if this feeling in my chest is the tight circle of my world expanding a little more.

25

SKYLAR

"Skylar!"

I spin around on the basketball court to see Joey coming through the big doors. He's got a huge grin on his face, and has every bit the swaggering confidence of a winner when he spreads his arms out wide and says, "Game-winning shot, baby!"

Laughing, I wrap him in a hug. He lets out a whoop and spins me around.

"Honestly, that might be the coolest thing you've ever done," I say breathlessly when he finally sets me down.

"I don't know, I think blowing up a volcano in the sixth-grade science fair was a little cooler."

"You only think that because you weren't on the receiving end of your science teacher's scathing phone call," I respond dryly.

Joey throws his head back and lets out a bark of laughter. "Okay, okay, you're right. Scoring the game-winning basket as a sophomore is way cooler."

I'm still chuckling when Joey notices Dominic standing behind me, just close enough to make it obvious that he's with me. I watch as my brother's giddy mood fades into wariness.

Dominic decides to meet this challenge head-on by stepping forward and extending his hand before Joey can say anything. "Hey. I'm Dominic."

Joey shakes his hand, but doesn't introduce himself. "And who exactly are you to my sister, Dominic?"

I make a sound of surprise. Joey has never once been protective over me in front of a friend. But before I can smooth this over, Dominic says, "I'm Skylar's coach. She trains at my MMA gym."

Now my head whips toward Dominic, shocked that he went with that title. But before I can comment on *that*, Joey asks, "And why would my sister's MMA coach be at my basketball game?"

"Okay, okay, I think I need to be the one doing the talking here," I say hurriedly. Turning toward Joey, I say, "Yes, he's my coach. But he's also a friend. And I wanted to spend some time with him. So now we're here. Is that okay?"

Joey's eyes narrow as he studies Dominic, looking every bit the skeptic. But my answer seems to have reassured him, because after a moment, he says, "Fine, I'll allow it."

I roll my eyes and throw my arm around his neck, yanking his head down under my armpit. "Since when do you make the calls here?"

He pokes me in the side once, and again, until I squirm. "Since I scored the game-winning basket and became the more successful sibling."

I let him go with a haughty sniff. "Fine. If you're so successful and mature now, you can buy *yourself* a pizza at Santucci's."

At the mention of his favorite pizza, Joey brightens.

"Seriously? We're going to Santucci's? But it's a school night."

I shrug, my smile too big to hide. "Special occasion."

Joey turns toward Dominic. "I take it back. I'm officially your biggest fan now. Whatever you said to my sister, keep it up."

Dominic chuckles. "I just suggested—very gently—that she should step out of her routine a little bit."

I quirk an eyebrow at him. "*Gently?* I'm pretty sure you jedi mind-tricked me into inviting you here tonight." That earns me a wink in return.

"Well, whatever you did, you have my support," Joey says. "I swear, I've never met a person who needs to relax more than her."

Turning a glare on my brother, I lightly slap his head. "Hey!"

"Skylar, you put *robots* to shame."

I let out an exaggerated gasp of outrage and open my mouth to make a retort, but I'm cut off by Dominic chuckling again.

"Alright, alright, easy, Big and Little Vega. The sibling love is blinding me. Why don't you two go bury the hatchet with that pizza?"

"You're not coming with us?" Joey asks, sounding surprised. My chest warms at him already welcoming Dominic.

"Maybe another time," he says politely. "I got my time with Skylar, and I don't want to intrude on your time together."

Joey rolls his eyes in that way that only teenage boys can. "Trust me, dude, I don't need one-on-one time with my sister."

That earns him another glare and a slightly harder smack. "Just go get your stuff, you jerk."

When he bounces away, I turn my full attention toward Dominic. "You *can* come, you know. I was going to invite you." I only hesitate for a moment before adding, "I want you to."

If he's trying to hide how pleased he is, he's failing miserably. "Yeah?" he asks softly, a smile on his face. I can only nod. "I'd love to."

I'm pretty sure we're both standing there, just stupidly smiling at each other, when Joey bounces up next to me again.

"Okay, enough yapping. Let's goooo!"

"Holy shit, you're eating *another* slice?"

I snicker at the sight of my brother's gawking face, even though I'm just as shocked by the fact that Dominic can eat a whole pizza.

"I'm a growing boy, I need sustenance," Dominic quips, taking a huge bite that makes a third of his slice disappear.

"Yeah, right. You're, like, sixty years old," Joey claps back. "Shouldn't you be worried for your metabolism?"

Dominic quirks an eyebrow, then drops the pizza onto his plate and lifts his t-shirt up to reveal washboard abs. "Do I look like I need to worry about my metabolism?"

I have to cover my sound of surprise with a cough. Dominic catches it anyway, and shoots me a knowing wink. I just reach for my water and take a big mouthful.

"Yeah, okay, you have abs, big deal," Joey grumbles. But his curiosity is piqued. "So do you have a specific lifting workout? Or that's just because of fighting?"

"I lift more now that I'm retired, but most of these muscles are just because of throwing people around," Dominic answers, demolishing the rest of his slice. He gives Joey a curious look. "Why, you want to get into lifting?"

Joey shrugs, not wanting to seem overeager. Dominic sees right through it.

"You have a weight room at your school?" he asks. Joey nods. "I can set you up with a basic lifting routine, if you want. Something that compliments basketball."

Excitement lights in my brother's eyes, and the sight is so rare, and sometimes feels so foreign, that I want to throw my arms around Dominic just for making it appear.

"Really? That would be awesome! My season's almost over, and I really want to be a starter next year, but I feel like I can't keep up with the seniors. If I could bulk up over the summer, though, I bet I could impress my coach."

"Well, now, wait a second," Dominic says, leaning back in his seat. "Bulking up and doing sport-specific workouts are two different things. Do you want muscles, or do you want to be in peak physical condition to play basketball?"

"Both."

I huff a laugh, and Dominic shakes his head with a chuckle of his own. "Why don't I put a starter workout together for you, and then we can go from there," he says. Then he glances my way. "And maybe we can set a goal to get you strong enough to beat up your sister."

"Hey!" I exclaim, startled by the turn in conversation. "That should absolutely *not* be a goal."

But Joey just rolls his eyes. "I can already do that. I'm taller and quicker. She doesn't put up much of a fight anymore."

"She *is* pretty slow," Dominic agrees. "Sometimes I get

off three punches in the time it takes her to get off one." The corner of his mouth twitches with a smile as he glances my way.

I can only gape at them both.

"I know," Joey says. "You ever watch her throw a body shot? It looks like she's in slow motion."

My head whips toward my brother. And then back toward Dominic. "How did *I* just become the group punching bag?"

"Easy target," they say in unison. Grinning, they reach for a fist bump.

"You guys are jerks," I mutter, falling back in my seat.

But inside, I love that they're getting along.

It should be surprising how easily Dominic fits into our dynamic, but it's not. We walked in here thirty minutes ago, and immediately settled into a comfortable conversation. Dominic asked Joey about his basketball season, and Joey asked Dominic about the gym. I just sat back and watched happily. I don't know what I expected when I decided to put them in a room together, but there's been an undeniable loosening in my chest the longer they talk.

"Alright, we should probably get going," I say, somewhat unhappily. I can't remember the last time I didn't want a night to end. But it's late, and I need to get Joey home.

"I can give you guys a ride," Dominic says, then tosses his napkin onto the empty pizza pan. These two ate almost *two* whole pizzas together. "You're on the way, anyway."

I quirk an eyebrow at him. "Are we really?"

I just get a grin in response.

But I don't fight him on it. I know Joey would rather get a ride than take the bus—my pride doesn't need to come into play here. Plus, Dominic already proved earlier that he respects my boundaries when he didn't offer to pay for everyone. He didn't say anything when I ordered first and paid first; he just waited for his turn to place his own order.

The ride home is a quiet one. I see Joey nodding off in the backseat, so Dominic and I settle into a comfortable silence. I can't seem to wipe the happy smile off my face.

When we pull up in front of the house, Joey wakes with a startled snort. Dominic doesn't bother to hide his chuckle. I expect him to stay in the car, but instead, he shuts off the engine and steps out.

Once we're all standing on the sidewalk, I look at my brother and jerk my head toward the house. "Go to bed. No video games. It's already way too late on a school night."

Joey rolls his eyes. "And here I thought you were loosening up," he says, unable to smother his yawn.

"I *am* loosening up. I just took you out for your favorite pizza *despite* it being late on a school night."

"Yeah, yeah," he grumbles. Then he sighs. "I guess it's nice to see you having a little fun, though. You should do it more often."

I don't miss Dominic's grin out of the corner of my eye. "Just go inside," I weakly scold my brother. "I'll be in in a second."

Dominic extends his fist toward Joey, who returns a fist bump of his own. "Good game tonight," Dominic tells him.

Joey nods his thanks. "Good job getting my sister out of her shell."

That earns him a glare. "*Inside.*" Swinging his gym bag onto his shoulder, he turns toward the house. And then I hear the obnoxious kissing sounds that he starts to make.

He's close enough that my kick can still reach his ass.

Letting out a yelp, he disappears through the front door.

The shyness that only seems to appear around Dominic creeps back as soon as my brother's out of sight. I turn toward him, lifting my eyes to finally meet his gaze.

"Thanks for hanging out tonight," I say softly. "And for the ride home."

"Thanks for letting me tag along." He nods toward where Joey went. "He's a really good kid."

I smile. "Yeah, he is."

He steps closer, close enough that he can wrap his arm around my waist. I'm sure there are stars in my eyes when I tilt my head up toward him.

"It was fun spending time with you outside of the gym," he says, his opposite hand lifting to brush along my jaw. "No MMA, no fighters—I feel like I got a whole new side of you."

"Yeah?" I breathe. "Still like me enough to keep seeing me?"

Leaning down, he brushes his lips against mine, not quite kissing me, just letting us breathe each other's air. And suddenly I'm wondering how I survived the past few hours without Dominic's hands on my body and his lips on my skin.

"I think I like you more now," he whispers.

And then he's kissing me. And I forget about everything that *isn't* his lips on mine.

Right away, he sinks both hands into my hair, his tongue prying my lips open so he can deepen the kiss. My hands clutch onto his shirt, and I kiss him back with just as much passion.

I feel my back hit the side of his car. The entire length of his body flattens against mine as he devours my mouth. When a moan slips from my lips, he swallows it with a growl and presses into me even harder.

I don't know if I've ever been this turned on in my life. Every time Dominic touches me, it feels like a new level of attraction, a new level of *need*. I don't know or care where we are right now, I just know I need him closer. I need him *closer*.

Which means when he pulls back, a whimper slips from my lips. Then I notice with a start that I've wrapped my leg around his hip and am shamelessly grinding against him.

"Easy, baby," he breathes. I love hearing his raspy breath, and feeling his chest heaving against mine. It gives away how much he got caught up in it too. "That's not why I kissed you."

"No?" I ask on an exhale, dropping my leg back down. "Then why?"

A heavy breath bursts out of him as he slides his hands down to my hips and drops his face into my neck. "Because you've been adorable all night and there's no way I was letting you go without a goodnight kiss." I feel his lips press a kiss to the place where my neck and shoulders meet, making me shiver. "But you're too tempting for just one sweet kiss. I can't help myself with you."

My lips curve into a smile, and my arms tighten around him.

I miss the heat of his body as soon as he straightens. "I meant what I said, though," he says, tucking a strand of hair behind my ear. "I liked spending time with you that had nothing to do with fighting. I'd like to do it more often."

"You'd rather go to a high school basketball game than fuck me against a heavy bag?" I ask with a chuckle.

It's an automatic deflection. Because including Dominic in my life for a night is one thing, but making it a regular thing, and potentially making this relationship more serious, makes me nervous.

Dominic sees right through me. He doesn't laugh, just brushes a thumb over my cheek and says, "I'd love anything that got me time with you."

And then he kisses me again, and suddenly I'm not over-thinking anything.

26

SKYLAR

"*TIME!* Let's bow out of class and then you can roll."

Silently, the entire jiu-jitsu class lines up on the mat and waits for Dominic to dismiss us. The second he does, everyone rushes for their water on the sidelines.

The cold water sliding down my throat is a relief after that grueling class. And yet, I can't wait to get back on the mat for some live rounds. I've been working hard on my jiu-jitsu in preparation for the tournament, and it's been fun trying to implement the skills I've been learning.

But right before I get back on the mat, I glance at my phone and notice a text from my boss at the restaurant. Frowning, I swipe to open the notification. I never get texts from my boss.

> Boss: Hey Skylar. Sorry for the last-minute text, but I don't need you for your shift tonight. The owner just hired his daughter so I might need to take you off a few shifts to make room for her.

My stomach drops through the floor.

"Skylar?" comes Dominic's voice from beside me. "What's wrong?"

In a daze, my face turns up toward his. He looks worried.

I turn back to my phone, as defeat settles heavily on my shoulders.

"My shift tonight got canceled," I say, no emotion in my voice. "Maybe a lot of shifts."

Out of the corner of my eye, I see his hands twitch before he shoves them in his pockets.

"I'm sorry to hear that," he says quietly.

"I needed that shift," I say, desperation now bleeding into my tone. "The bills from Mom's fall have started coming in, so even *one* shift lost is—" My voice cracks, and I can't finish the thought.

I can never catch a break. Nothing I do is ever good enough, and I'm just so *tired*.

"I'm sorry, Skylar." I feel him stepping closer and can only nod miserably in response.

"What are you going to do?"

I let out a dejected breath as I stare at the mat. "Start looking for another job, I guess. I don't know, it sounds like this might not be the only shift I lose. I probably shouldn't stick around for open mat right now." My shoulders drop, and I let my phone fall from my hand into my gym bag.

"When was the last time you took a break?" Dominic asks. "Like, *really* took a break from your responsibilities."

I turn toward him, my brow furrowing. "Uh, being here is my break."

"Okay...but that's three times a week for maybe two hours. When was the last time you took a break from your life entirely?"

Still, I can only stare at him in confusion.

"How about this," he starts. "Put your phone on Do Not Disturb so only emergency calls come through, and stick around to roll. Don't look at the time, don't worry about when you're getting out of here, just...take an afternoon to yourself. No work, no school, no pressure."

I...don't even know what that looks like.

"And then what? I go home and bask in my defeat?"

An amused half-smile appears on his face. "No, then you let me take you somewhere. Give me one afternoon, Skylar. Give *yourself* one afternoon." When I still hesitate, he adds softly, "It's okay to find your happy, remember?"

I glance back at my phone, at the still-open notification on it. And I try to look at its face-value: one shift, not canceled by me, and there's nothing else I can do about it tonight. I can tackle this problem tomorrow.

Taking a deep breath, I turn back to Dominic. "Alright. One afternoon."

He's beaming when we step onto the mat.

"So...where are we going?"

It's been ten minutes since we got into his car and pulled out of the city. Ten minutes of recapping training and avoiding the obvious subject. The only hint he gave me at the gym was to say he hopes I brought comfortable clothes to change into.

He seems downright giddy behind the wheel. Or as giddy as he's capable of looking. But he's clearly proud of himself for getting me to agree to come with him.

And if I'm being honest, I'm a little giddy myself. I've never been surprised with something like this.

"Are we going somewhere fighting related?" I ask, too curious to let it drop.

He shakes his head.

"Are we road tripping?"

"Okay, no more guessing," he finally interrupts. "A surprise is a surprise. I'm not giving it away before we get there."

I pout as I lean back in my seat, even though I'm secretly delighted. He glances over at me and sighs when he sees my expression.

"How about this. You can ask me any questions you want, but nothing related to this."

I raise an eyebrow in his direction. "You're giving me free rein to ask you whatever I want?"

"Yes. For the next thirty minutes."

I have to bite down on my smile that he gave away even that much, but he does too, so I know he did it on purpose.

"Okay, fine." I tap my chin in thought. *I can ask him any question?* "Tell me about the worst fight of your career. Why was it your worst and how did you feel about it afterwards?"

A pause. Then...

"I lied. You can ask any question that isn't about where we're going, fighting, school, or work."

I frown. "Why not?"

"Because the whole point of today is to separate from our everyday lives. No talking about anything we think about on a normal day."

I let out an exaggerated huff. But secretly, I don't mind— I love the idea and I'll take any excuse to get to know him better.

I start to pepper him with every random question I can think of.

"Favorite music genre?"

"Favorite food?"

"Most embarrassing moment?"

But those questions soon morph into me asking about things I'm curious about.

"Have you ever hated any of your opponents?"

"Did you like being an only child?"

"What's your favorite childhood memory?"

In the end, that's the question that we get lost in. I love hearing the nostalgia in Dominic's voice as he reminisces about that one memorable summer, as he talks about the family and friends that he spent it with. I inhale every detail that he reveals about himself. I could listen to him talk like this for hours, and I'd still be greedy for more.

I don't realize how much time has passed until suddenly we're pulling into a big parking lot. Part of me is disappointed that our conversation has to end, but a bigger part of me is curious about where he's brought me. Squinting, I look around and try to figure out where we are.

iFly Indoor Skydiving

My jaw drops at the sign on the building. I had a lot of guesses for where we were going, but this wouldn't have been in my top hundred. I didn't even know this was a thing.

"We're going skydiving?" I squeak.

He gives me a gruff nod. "I've always wanted to try it, but it's not exactly something you do by yourself. I figured you might like it. But I only want to do it if this sounds fun to you," he hurries to add. "If it doesn't, there are plenty of other things we can spend our time with. Movies, bowling, axe-throwing—"

"Let's definitely table the axe-throwing idea, because that sounds amazing," I interrupt. I never take my eyes off the massive building in front of us, trying to imagine what indoor skydiving looks like. Actual skydiving has never crossed my mind as a possibility in my life, but a simulation sounds...

I take a deep, steadying breath. "Okay. Let's do it."

27

DOMINIC

I let out a breath of relief as I open the door for Skylar and guide her inside with a hand on her back. Skydiving was a random, slightly panicked idea and I had no clue how she'd react to it. I just knew I wanted to get that sad look off her face.

Thankfully, she's practically bouncing as we walk over to the front desk. The receptionist greets us with a smile.

"Hi there, welcome to iFly. Do you have a booking today?"

"Uh, no." *Fuck, I didn't think this through.* "Is there any way you have space for one person?"

Skylar's startled gaze flies to mine. "What? I don't want to do it without you. You're what makes this fun."

I barely process *that* before the receptionist intercepts.

"Actually, you're both in luck. We just had a cancelation from another group of two, so we *do* have space for you. If I could just get you both to fill out our waiver of liability, I'll get you signed up."

We fill out the paperwork, and then we reach the point that I'm slightly dreading.

"Okay, great, thank you," says the receptionist. "Now, are you paying separately or together?"

I'm not surprised when Skylar reaches for her wallet. But she seems surprised when I push her hand away.

"What're you doing? I can pay for myself."

I keep my voice gentle. "I know you can. But I want to pay. This was my idea."

A flash of panic appears in her expression. "I can pay. I told you, I don't need you to take care of me."

I lean in beside her ear, close enough that the receptionist can't hear me when I say, "I don't need to take care of you. I just want to make you happy."

She looks stunned when I pull back. But thankfully, the panic is gone, replaced with an emotion I can't name, but that looks like it's on the happy side of the spectrum.

Finally, she nods.

I turn back to the receptionist and slide my card across the counter. "Together, please."

The next thirty minutes fly by. We meet our instructor, go through some academics to understand the physics of everything, and then suit up with all the necessary gear.

Finally, we walk over to the air tunnel in the middle of the building. I look over at Skylar, taking in her outfit of a one-piece flying suit and a gigantic helmet, and I can't help smirking. "You know I didn't think I'd say this, but you look adorable in that getup."

She looks up at me from behind goggles that take up half her face. Taking the time to give me a blatant once-over, she says, "I don't think you look quite as adorable."

I bark out a laugh at her indignation. I don't get a chance

to make a dirty comment about getting her out of that one-piece, because the instructor chooses that moment to wave her into the tunnel.

I can sense her slight nervousness, but she's also fearless as she steps inside. The instructor grabs her hands and moves her to the center, and then she shows her how to lay on her stomach to simulate the default skydiving position. When her feet fly up under her to suspend her in midair and she lets out a shriek of delight, I can't help smiling. Gone is the nervousness, in its place is the picture of pure joy.

As I watch her find her balance and rhythm in the air tunnel, her excitement only grows. By the time she's flying on her own, there's no sign of the dejected girl from a few hours ago.

I don't even mind that I feel like a total moron when I get in the tunnel. Twenty years spent in a sport where balance and athleticism are literally a life-or-death skill, yet I feel as awkward as a day-one student who's never done a workout in their life. The only thing that makes the embarrassment worth it is the sight of Skylar's downright glee as she watches me.

As I touch down and right before I walk out of the tunnel, I ask the instructor if I can pay for Skylar to have another spin. He gives me a knowing smile and agrees.

When she gets out of the tunnel, her grin looks permanently plastered on her face. She latches onto my arm as she bounces over to me and squeals, "Oh my *God*, that was the most fun I've ever had. This was such a good idea!"

I don't even attempt to contain my own smile. "I'm glad you enjoyed it. Worth the afternoon off?"

"*So* worth it," she gushes. "Now I want to go real skydiving, though."

"You might be on your own for that one," I say with a chuckle. "I'm not sure I could talk myself into jumping out of an actual plane."

She presses herself closer to me, her eyes twinkling. "I wonder if I could talk you into it."

And as I look down at her adorably freckled, smiling, flushed face, I realize no part of me is lying when I say, "I don't doubt that you could, baby."

She beams up at me. I swear I could stay here for another ten hours, just watching her smile and shriek and laugh, but our time slot is way past over by now. Begrudgingly, I jerk my head toward the changing room.

"Come on, let's get changed out of these onesies."

By the time we walk out of the building and near my car, the mood has sobered. Because I only asked her for an afternoon, and technically we've reached the end of that.

But I'm kind of dying to keep her with me for a little bit longer.

"Are you hungry?" I hurry to ask as soon as we're both seated in my car. "There's a good burger spot right around the corner that I like to eat at when I'm out this way."

I'm sure she senses the same urgency I do, but she doesn't let it show as she agrees. All I know is I'm grateful that I get her for another hour.

"Alright, I have more questions for you," she says as soon as we sit down at the table, her playful mood back in effect.

The corner of my lip twitches in amusement and a bit of relief. "Fine, but I get to ask questions this time, too. I shouldn't be the only one baring my soul."

"Fine." And before she can do any more than open her mouth, I rush out, "What's your most embarrassing moment?"

Her eyes narrow, both at the question and the interruption. "No repeating questions."

I shrug with a smirk. "Set that rule too late. Answer the question."

Sighing, she leans back in her chair as she mulls over her answer. After a moment, she says, "I fell in the water during a first date at a mini golf course."

I let out a bark of laughter. "What? How does that even happen?"

"I shot the ball into the water and tried to go after it, but I slipped. I got drenched head to toe." She pouts. "He said it's why he didn't kiss me at the end of the night."

"Idiot," I grumble. Even though the idea of Skylar kissing some limp-dicked teenager makes me slightly feral.

"It's okay, his best friend was a better date anyway," she quips. My eyebrows rise, but she's already adding, "Okay, no more repeats from now on. We ask all new things."

"Yes, ma'am."

Her nose scrunches at that, and I'm pretty sure it's the cutest fucking thing I've ever seen.

"I've got a few—at least ten—years before anyone calls me ma'am, thankyouverymuch. You on the other hand..."

"You can just call me sir," I say in a low voice only she can hear.

Her cheeks pinken in that way that I love. And when the waitress appears beside our table to take our order, Skylar is so flustered that it takes her a second to get the words out. She has to avoid my eyes to collect herself, because I can't wipe the cocky smirk off my face.

"You are so inappropriate," she grumbles when the waitress walks off.

My grin widens. "Baby, you asked for it."

That makes her blush all over again. *God, she's cute.*

I decide to take pity on her. "If you could have any super-power, what would it be?"

She collects herself with a big inhale. "Omniscience."

I sigh. "Guess I walked into that one. Were you as knowl-edge-hungry in kindergarten as you are at the gym?"

"I'm sorry, that question seems to be outside of the game parameters," she says in a robotic voice. I chuckle and gesture for her to ask her question.

"Favorite holiday?"

That, I actually mull over. *Do I have one? I don't even know which ones I celebrate.*

I don't have any family since my mom passed away, so I usually spend Thanksgiving and Christmas with Brutus. And as far as the other holidays... I can't say I go out of my way to celebrate any of them.

"Uh... New Year's, I guess?" It's the only holiday I 'cele-brate,' and actually sit down to set my business goals for the year.

"Ooh, I love New Year's," Skylar gushes, oblivious to my inner turmoil. "Joey and I always spend it doing a 24-hour marathon of some sort. Last year, we watched an entire season of the show '24.' And even though you're not allowed to ask, I'm going to tell you anyway because I love it so much. Mine is Christmas."

And she looks so giddy about it that I can't help asking, "Why? What is it about Christmas?"

She shrugs, looking down at the napkin she's fiddling with. "I don't know, I guess it's because...it's the only full day of the year when *everything* is closed. With other holi-days, I'm always working because they pay time and a half. With Christmas, I *can't* work. I can actually be at home with my family without feeling guilty. I get a whole day to hang out with Joey and my mom, and we just sit around watching Christmas movies and stuffing our faces."

The mood sobers with her answer.

We shift back to easier questions for a few minutes. Skylar's gotten much more comfortable with opening up to me, but pushing those serious topics can be a delicate balance.

So for now, we go back and forth about trivial things— favorite subject in school, hidden talents, weirdest dream she's ever had—until the waitress shows up with our food. Between a hard training session this morning and the adrenaline of skydiving, both of our appetites are raging, and we scarf down our burgers.

But by the time we're lazily popping fries in our mouths, exchanging playful smiles and easy laughter all throughout, I wonder if it's ever felt like this. I've based all of who I am around fighting, which comes naturally. In the past, talking about anything that's not fighting was *not*.

So why does Skylar asking if I like sunrises or sunsets better make my chest warm?

I use the excuse of still being hungry to order another side of fries, just so I can sit at this table with her for another twenty minutes. It isn't until the restaurant fills up with their dinner rush and the waitress starts giving me impatient looks that I finally call the meal over.

Using the excuse of needing to use the restroom, I walk over to our waitress and pay the bill before she can bring it to the table.

I'm not quite slick enough, though, because the second I get back to the table and ask Skylar if she's ready to leave, she stands from her chair, then frowns and looks around. "But we haven't paid yet."

"I already paid," I say nonchalantly, hoping that'll be the end of it.

That scared look is back in her eyes. "Dominic..."

I place my hand on her lower back and nudge her toward the exit. "Well, I can't exactly call this a date if I don't pay, can I?"

And once again, my honesty and forwardness win me the battle with her. That starstruck look is back in her eyes, and she lets me guide her outside.

When we get to my car, I reach for the passenger door. But she stops me before I open it, turning to face me. I don't need to rack my brain for another excuse to keep her with me, because she makes the decision for us.

Going up on her toes, she presses her mouth to mine. It's a quick kiss, and it doesn't give me enough time to press her back against my car so I can *take*, but her next words ratchet the heat between us in a whole other way.

"So, if it's a date, does that mean you're going to invite me back to your place?"

28

SKYLAR

I'm not sure what I expected walking into Dominic's home, but I shouldn't be surprised that it's a plain one-bedroom loft apartment. Nothing about it screams bachelor pad. There's no pool table and no pizza boxes left out—in fact, the space is noticeably neat. The two things that stand out the most are the big kitchen and the even bigger, very comfy-looking couch.

I smother the urge to dive headfirst into the cushions that look soft as a cloud, and instead take a seat as Dominic walks into the kitchen. Brutus happily plods over to me for some scratches as I take my time looking around the open space.

"How do you feel about some dessert?" Dominic asks from the kitchen. "I've got a new flavor of ice cream that I've been dying to try. Do you want some? Or just some water?"

"Ice cream sounds good," I say distractedly, taking in every detail of his space.

I hear ceramics clinking as Dominic reaches into the cupboard. "I can see the thoughts running through your head right now," he says. "Is this what a thirty-six-year-old divorcé's home is supposed to look like?"

"My life experience with thirty-six-year-old divorcés is admittedly kind of limited. But my experience with *you* says this is exactly what it's supposed to look like. Clean. Simple. Biggest TV money can buy."

He chuckles. "Guilty. The only thing I spend time doing in my apartment is cooking, sleeping, and watching fights. A big TV was a necessity."

I chew on my bottom lip as I contemplate my next question. But I figure if he's letting me into his home, we're close enough that I can at least ask.

"That's *all* you do here?" I ask. He cuts me a confused look as he pulls the ice cream out of the freezer. "Typically, a bachelor pad veers a little more toward female comfort. I can picture the ladies being a big fan of the loft aesthetic."

He grins when he realizes what I'm getting at, scooping the ice cream from the gallon container. "It's been a while since I've concerned myself with female comfort. I can't remember the last time I even had anyone over. But well done on the sleuthing."

I let out a huff of laughter as I go back to petting Brutus. "Can't blame a girl for asking."

Dominic rounds the couch, two bowls clutched in his hand. He gives me one, then takes a seat beside me. Before he starts in on his ice cream, he reaches for the remote and turns on the UFC fight card that's live right now.

They're in the middle of a fight, so for the next few minutes, we just watch and eat our ice cream, the silence a comfortable one.

I take another bite as the fight finishes. With a groan of approval, I say, "You're right, that coffee chip hit the spot. This is so good."

Dominic places his bowl on the table. "As soon as the waitress said milkshakes at the restaurant, I started thinking about how I had this in my freezer." When he leans back in his seat, I'm a little disappointed that he doesn't make any move to touch me.

"I think this might be my favorite kind of Saturday night," I muse. "Ice cream and watching fights? Literal paradise."

Dominic sends me a lazy smile. "This is my every Saturday night, so I never really thought about it. But I can't imagine doing anything else, so yeah, I don't know what would be better." Stretching his arm across the back of the couch, he shifts his body to face me. "You should work it into that airtight schedule of yours. I bet a night off watching fights would do wonders for your stress levels."

Despite how nice today was, and how much I enjoyed essentially playing hooky with Dominic...it's never going to be my norm.

I send Dominic a tight smile and try to make light of the situation. "But then who would serve food to the couples on their once-a-month date night?"

He sees right through it, of course. He studies me for a moment before saying thoughtfully, "You're going to treat today as a one-off, aren't you?" I push around the last bit of melting ice cream in my bowl so I don't have to respond.

"How about this," he says, taking the bowl from my hand and setting it on the coffee table. When he shifts to give me his full attention, he also forces mine to be on him by pulling my feet into his lap. "Tell me one big thing and one little thing that you'd like to be able to do, and we'll see what we can do to make them more likely to happen in your day-to-day life. What do you think?"

It takes a second, but I nod. "Okay."

A small but pleased smile appears on Dominic's face. "Okay, then. We'll start easy: what's one *little* thing you'd like to do?"

The usual guilt and vulnerability trickles back. "I feel selfish saying anything because I already get to train at the gym—"

"And people get to have more than one thing that they love, Skylar," Dominic interrupts. "So pick something that isn't getting twisted into a pretzel by people who are trying to kill you."

A smile comes unbidden to my lips, softening me enough to answer honestly. "Going to the movies. I... I never have enough time to just sit in a theater and waste two hours watching a mindless action movie."

Dominic lets out an approving hum. "And how hard would it be to catch a matinee and go into work a little bit later than usual?"

"Not that hard, but—"

"What *specifically* would happen if you worked two less hours?" His hard look demands a real answer.

Thoughts and figures fly through my head. It would mean less money, obviously, but if I force myself to really think about it, I have to acknowledge that I've managed to create a sophisticated enough system that I'm not *quite* living paycheck to paycheck. Technically, two hours wouldn't make or break the bank.

He must know I'm not going to tell him out loud that he's right. "How about this: set a goal to go to the movies once a month. Doesn't even have to be with someone else, I just want you to put a movie afternoon into that carefully curated schedule of yours. Deal?" I nod my assent, stomach fluttering at his thoughtfulness.

Then his expression sobers. "What about a big goal?" he

asks, his thumb rubbing soothing circles on my ankle. "I want to know what kinds of hopes and dreams you have, baby."

Although I suck in a big, stuttering breath before I can speak, this answer comes easier. "I want to be a doctor," I whisper.

"Not a nurse?" His eyes search mine, head tilting slightly as he listens intently.

"I'd love to be a nurse," I say. "I'd be *happy* to be a nurse. But...after everything with my parents...if I could pick, I'd really want to be a neurologist."

Dominic never looks away from me. I watch him catalogue every reaction that flits over my face, every thought that flashes in my eyes. "Do you ever imagine yourself as a doctor? When you think about the future?" I shake my head. "You should. You work hard and you're more than smart enough for it. Don't you think you should visualize the things you truly want?"

"Visualizing isn't going to change anything," I mumble. "The bottom line is, it's completely unattainable. I don't have the money for medical school."

He quirks an eyebrow. "I'll let you in on a little secret, Skylar." He crooks a finger at me and leans in as I do. When I'm close enough, he whispers, "No one has the money for medical school. That's why everyone graduates with a mountain of debt."

I huff a laugh and lean back. "Okay, touché. Still not a great financial decision, though."

Dominic shrugs. "Medical school is never a good financial decision. Until you become a successful neurologist and make double that in salary."

I chew on my lip as I digest what he's saying. That's pretty much the norm for a doctorate financial landscape.

He sees the victory in my eyes. "See? You know I'm right. So you shouldn't feel bad about wanting it."

I nod, my answer sounding breathless even to my ears. "Okay."

That smile returns to his face, and with it, I melt all over again. Sitting here with him, his hands on my body, I'm content. I feel like I'm right where I need to be—both physically and emotionally.

"I really did have a nice time today," I whisper. "Thank you for taking me out."

"You're welcome." He breaks our eye contact, but only because his gaze drops to my lips. And I can tell he doesn't want to be the one to disrupt this serious moment between us, but all I can think about is how much affection I feel for this man.

Leaning forward, I press my lips to his. "You're a good man, Dominic," I whisper against him.

And then there's no more talking.

29

SKYLAR

He tugs me into his lap, his mouth never leaving mine. It's like he wants to eliminate every last inch between us. When his tongue slides over the seam of my lips to silently demand entry, he tilts my head to deepen the kiss. I moan at the taste of him and wrap my arms around his neck—it's like a switch has been flipped, and we suddenly need as much of the other as we can possibly get.

As my hips start to rock against him, I can feel him hardening between my legs, and I can't stop from pressing against it through our jeans. Ripping his lips from mine with a muttered curse, he stands, with me still in his arms.

My legs automatically wrap around his waist and my lips move to his neck. "What are you doing?" I manage to ask between kisses.

He starts to walk. "I don't relish the idea of not fucking you in a bed when there's one nearby."

I hide my smile in his neck, tightening my arms around him as I nip at his ear. "You don't like fucking me at the gym?"

"I like fucking you everywhere," he clarifies. I feel us

246

ascending stairs. "But given the option...I'd much rather lay you out and lick every inch of you."

A flash of heat runs through me at his words, my legs tightening around his waist and my core grinding against him again.

He chuckles, and I can feel the sound rumble through his chest. When he reaches the landing at the top of the steps and stops, he tugs my head back again so he can meet my eyes. The half-smirk on his lips is the sexiest thing I've ever seen.

"I think you like that idea," he says thoughtfully, his gaze traveling over my flushed face. "Hmm, yeah, you definitely like that idea."

When he lays me on the bed, he follows me down, his body staying pressed against mine and settling between the cradle of my thighs. The second my head hits the soft mattress, his lips are on mine once more.

It's so easy to get lost in his kisses. Every time he sucks on my tongue, or nips at my lip, my desire for him ratchets and I become singularly focused on his mouth. I almost don't notice when his hands travel down my sides to grip the bottom of my tank top and slowly start to slide it up my body. But when it passes over my chest and exposes my bare breasts to the cold air, a whimper slips from my lips to Dominic's. I start to tug on his shirt, desperate to feel his skin under my hands.

This feels different. *I want this to be different.*

Wordlessly, he abides by my silent request. He does that ridiculously hot thing where men grab the neck of their shirt and pull it over their heads, and my pussy clenches at the sight of his body. As soon as the fabric is off, my mouth is back on his, my hands tracing over as much of his skin as I can touch.

He ends our kiss so that he can pull back just enough to look down at me. His eyes light with a hungry fire when he sees my half-naked body, and he drops his head immediately to latch onto a peaked nipple.

I moan as I arch into his mouth and sink my hands into his hair. God, I have *never* felt attraction like this. Every time I think I can't want him any more, he does something that sets me on fire all over again.

"So sweet," he murmurs, switching to my other nipple so he can lick a circle around it. "I'm going to enjoy tasting every inch of you."

It distantly registers that that's the second time he's said that. I manage to lift my head up so I can give him a questioning look, but he's already shifting his focus.

My tank top, which only made it as far as exposing my breasts, is now dragged over my head and along my arms. But right before I can pull my hands back down, I feel the fabric being tied at my wrists.

Knotting the tank top, he holds my hands on the mattress as he looks down at me. "I want to take my time. Do you think you can keep your hands up here while I do that? Or should I tie the other end of this to my bed?"

The idea of being restrained and completely at this man's mercy sends a bolt of pleasure directly between my legs. But part of me also wants to be a good listener, a good student for him, so I find myself nodding my agreement.

"I'll be good," I whisper, pleased to see a flash of satisfaction in his eyes.

Which immediately morphs right back to hunger when he realizes he now has free rein over me. His gaze drops over me, from my tied hands, over my exposed breasts, and down to my stomach. I'm still covered from the waist down, but I have a feeling I won't be for very much longer.

I'm so, so wrong.

Apparently, Dominic meant it when he said he wanted to taste every inch of me. With his hands still braced next to my head, he leans down to place a gentle kiss to my wrist. Then to the other one. Then he drags his lips down to press a kiss to the inside of my elbow.

Then the other one.

He takes his time dragging his lips over my skin. By the time he reaches my shoulders, I'm squirming. When he lavishes my breasts with more kisses, I'm vibrating with anticipation. As he finally sucks my nipple into his mouth, I'm trembling with need.

"Dominic," I gasp, wriggling as I try to get every part of my body closer to his. "Please."

His lips slide between my breasts, down to my stomach. "That's going to be my favorite word for the next ten minutes," he murmurs, circling my belly button with his tongue.

And *God*, he's not kidding. He kisses across my stomach, his movements so lazy that by the time he teases his tongue under the hem of my leggings, my begging is constant.

"Dominic, *please*...touch me. I need you."

For the most part, he ignores me. He's on *his* schedule right now. But he does grip either side of my leggings and pulls them down my legs. I expect him to slide back up my body, to either fuck me or touch me, but Dominic doesn't do either of those things.

As soon as he tugs my leggings past my feet, he's lowering his head and pressing a chaste kiss to my ankle.

Then the inside of my knee.

Then up the inside of my thigh, with dizzying gentleness.

When his lips finally near my pussy, I'm trembling with

anticipation. And when he moves back to repeat the process on my other leg, I become a babbling mess.

"Please, *please* touch me. I need you to touch me. I need you inside me. Dominic, *please*, I can't stand another second—"

I'm so wound up that by the time he presses a single kiss to my clit, I'm on the verge of an orgasm. And when he roughly shoves my legs wider, latches onto my pussy with his mouth, and drives two fingers inside me, I detonate like a bomb.

I think I scream through it, my muscles tensed as euphoria consumes me. When the sensations finally abate, my throat is sore and my hands are no longer dutifully held above my head, but sunken into Dominic's hair to hold him against me. He doesn't look in a hurry to go anywhere, though—when I glance down, he's almost reverent in the way he kisses and licks me.

Eventually, he moves up my body and takes my mouth in a kiss. When I silently beg for his tongue, for the taste of my pleasure, he groans and guides his cock inside me. His thrusts don't start gentle, he doesn't wait for me to get used to his size. He just fucks me.

The closeness of our bodies does something to me. With every drive of his hips, his chest slides along mine, the subtle hair on his chest brushing against my nipples and sparking another wave of arousal. And with the way he's flat against me, it also means the base of his cock is grinding into my clit.

I've never come without someone's hand on my clit, but Dominic is about to blow that right out of the water.

"Christ, you feel so good," he groans into another kiss. He hasn't stopped kissing me—it's like he's starving for the taste of my lips.

"You're going to make me come," I gasp, my nails digging into his back as I hold him to me. I'm *so. close.* I just need a little more.

He must read it in my face, because he immediately starts to thrust with harder, measured strokes that massage that spot inside me. And I come apart on his cock.

He stops kissing me long enough to watch my face as it happens. His expression looks awed, and despite the filthy way he's fucking me, it makes me feel beautiful.

"Beautiful," he breathes, again proving how in sync we are. His thrusts slow as he fucks me through the last ripples of my orgasm.

Grabbing a pillow, he slides it under my lower back, propping my hips up for a better angle. I feel exposed, especially when he pushes my legs wide, but seeing his eyes light with hunger all over again makes any insecurities vanish. I drop my knees even wider and arch my back.

"*Fuck*, you're so hot," he groans, looking down to watch as he slowly fucks into me, and I can hear how wet I am. "I swear I could come just from looking at you."

One hand leaves my thigh and grips the base of his cock, pulling it out and guiding the tip to rub against my clit. I whimper at the touch, already overstimulated from everything he's done to me, yet finding myself eager for more.

He slides his length between my lips, then traces his tip down my slit. I expect him to push inside me and start fucking me again, but his touch suddenly slips even lower.

I freeze, my eyes widening at the feel of it. I've never had anyone go near my ass, so the touch is a shock.

Dominic notices my reaction and quickly moves back to my clit. "Sorry," he murmurs.

But...now I'm kind of curious.

"It's okay, you just surprised me," I admit.

He meets my eyes. Looking for honesty, after a moment, he finds it. "Yeah?" he asks.

I bite into my lower lip and give a small nod in answer. After a second's hesitation, he reads the consent for what it is and lets go of his length to instead slide two fingers inside my pussy. I'm drenched after two orgasms, so when he moves one down to my ass, his finger is coated and can easily rub a smooth circle around the puckered hole.

I squirm a little, trying to get used to the feeling. Even when he starts to press a little bit, it doesn't feel uncomfortable, just odd.

When the tip of his finger breaks through the barrier, I suck in a breath. But then his other hand starts to play with my clit, and my body immediately relaxes into the sensation. Dominic uses that as an opportunity to slide in a little bit deeper, and I find myself moaning and spreading my legs wider.

I pout in disappointment when he does the opposite of my silent request. He leaves me empty and climbs off the bed, but it isn't until he pulls a small tub of Vaseline out of his gym bag that I realize what he's doing. I start to feel the tingles of nervousness.

Dominic sees it, leaning down to press a sweet kiss to my lips. "If you want to stop, we stop. I don't want to do anything you don't want to do. Okay?"

Looking into his eyes, I can see he's being genuine. Not just about the stopping part, but also about him only wanting to do things that *I'm* sure of.

My nerves abate, and a trickle of excitement takes their place.

"Okay," I whisper. "I trust you."

He groans and takes my mouth in a kiss. "You're amazing."

I smile against him. "You're just saying that because I want you to play with my ass."

He huffs a surprised laugh and kisses me again. "Smartass. No, that's not why."

Reaching down, I wrap my hand around his cock. "Mmm, okay. Can you touch me anyway?"

"Fuck," he groans, dropping his face to my neck. "You're going to make me come like a goddamn teenager."

I let out a laugh at the irony, but he's already moving down my body. Opening the tub of Vaseline, he coats his fingers before returning them to my ass. His other hand goes back to my clit.

"So sweet to let me play with this ass," he purrs in appreciation. "Spread your legs for me, baby."

His words eliminate all remaining tension in my body. Spreading my legs for him, I sink into the sensation of his forbidden touch.

He circles and presses against the tight bud, then eventually slips the tip of his finger inside. When I don't tense up, he slowly starts to work his finger deeper. By the time the entire length of it is inside me, I'm moaning and pressing against his hand for more.

"Good girl," he praises, slowly giving me a second finger. "Do you like it?"

I nod quickly. I don't know at what point his touch went from feeling weird to feeling good, but now, with his thumb on my clit and two fingers inside me, I just want *more*.

"Do you want to keep going?" he asks, his dark gaze trained on my face.

Another nod. I'm too turned on to speak.

But he braces a hand next to my head so he can lean over me and meet my eyes. "Give me your words, baby."

So, I hold his gaze and give him what he wants, meaning

every word so much that I think I might die if he doesn't give me what I need.

"I want you to teach me," I say breathlessly. "Teach me how to take your cock in my ass."

For a moment, he only stares at me, the only movement that of his pupils growing so big that his eyes are almost wholly black. Then...

"Get on your hands and knees," he demands. And the gravel of his voice has me flushing all over again.

I scramble to follow his directions. I don't know anything about anal, but I trust Dominic, so the tinge of nervousness that comes from trying something new is over-shadowed by the excitement of letting him show me a new kind of pleasure.

He folds his body over me, his hands bracing beside mine and his lips going to the skin below my ear. The kiss he places there is comforting.

"From this position, you'll be able to control everything," he explains. "How deep, how slow, all of it. I won't move until you ask me to. You're in complete control, understand?"

I nod, arching my neck for more kisses. He grants my silent request instantly.

Feeling his mouth along my neck and jaw is so distracting that I don't even startle when his fingers slide between my cheeks again. I just close my eyes and savor the sensation of his lips on my skin and his fingers sliding inside me.

It's only when I start pushing my hips back for more that he replaces his fingers with his cock. He's drenched in lube already, and presses between my cheeks when I try to center his tip against my hole. I see his hand disappear from beside mine and feel his length line up where I need it.

"Slow," he murmurs. I wonder if he's more nervous than I am.

Taking a deep breath, I push my hips back just a little bit. Just until I feel pressure against my ass. I have a split second of doubt, but then...

The head of his cock breaks through the muscle.

I suck in a startled breath and freeze. *God, that feels weird.*

"Slow," Dominic says again. I think I feel him trembling against my back. "Only when you're ready."

I swallow roughly and nod. I want this.

After a few seconds, I push back another half inch. It burns—not in a painful way, necessarily, but definitely in an unused way.

"Squeeze down on me," Dominic coaxes. "When you relax, it'll relax the muscle."

I let out a heavy exhale and will myself to follow his directions. And I squeeze against him.

The second I stop squeezing, every muscle in my lower body relaxes, and Dominic easily slides in another inch.

"Oh," I breathe. Without my tenseness, that feels...good.

Dominic lets out a groan against the back of my neck. "You're so fucking tight."

My moan vibrates through my chest, my eyes sliding shut as I arch my hips and press back another inch. The heat of this moment swirls around me, taking me higher and higher, making something that's taboo feel so good *because* of how wrong it is.

I don't fully understand why this feels good, but I know...*I want more of it.*

I take another inch of him. And then one of his hands arrows between my legs and circles my clit, and I moan so loud that I feel more than hear his curse against my skin when I drive my hips back and take the rest of him inside me in one thrust.

"Oh, God," I gasp, freezing in place as the weight of the moment hits me. I feel so *full*.

"That's my girl," Dominic praises, his fingers still moving in soothing circles. "Such a good little student. So sweet taking my cock in your ass."

His words have a shiver running through me, the dirty sentiment making me crave more of this.

Experimentally, I shift my hips slightly. Just enough to feel Dominic move inside me.

"Oh," I breathe. And then I move again, this time with a tiny forward and back motion. "*Oh.*"

To his credit, Dominic stays stock-still as I fuck myself on his cock. He lets me get used to his size and figure out what feels good.

But the more I move, the more my own movements aren't enough. As I push my hips forward and back, riding Dominic's length, need thrums beneath my skin. I need more. I need *him*.

"Fuck me," I beg, my voice sounding raspy and foreign to my own ears. "Dominic, *please* fuck me."

He shudders against me. Then his hips pull back, before slowly driving into me on a long slide.

"*Yes,*" I breathe. "Oh my God, *more.*"

"Christ, Skylar," he groans, straightening up behind me and gripping my hips so he can fuck into me again. "*Look* at you."

I whimper and fuck back into him. I don't think I've *ever* felt this needy.

He abides by my silent request and starts to rut into me, his movements becoming harder, more carnal.

But the angle doesn't feel quite right. Normally, to get

deeper I would drop to my elbows and arch my hips up as much as I can. But right now, the angle feels like it would be better if I were upright.

So, I push off my hands and flatten my back to Dominic's chest. He immediately wraps an arm around my waist to hold me in place.

"You're the sexiest thing I've ever fucking seen," he growls in my ear, fucking into me even harder. "I'll never get enough of you."

Suddenly desperate for his kiss, I turn my head and search for his lips. He falls on my mouth like a man possessed.

An orgasm starts to build, but it doesn't feel like anything I've ever experienced before. The magnitude of it is makes my breaths come quicker, and I latch onto Dominic's arm that's banded across me in an effort to anchor myself to this moment. The bigger it gets, the messier my kiss becomes.

His thrusts become hard, deep fucks that take me to the very edge. And then his hand goes back to my clit, his tongue fills my mouth, and I'm lost to this new pleasure.

My orgasm explodes through every nerve of my body. Shaking, shuddering through it, clenching down on Dominic as he swallows my gasp with his mouth. I've never felt anything like this. I vaguely register his own groan, and the stuttered movement of his hips. Right as my pleasure is dying down, he pulls out and comes in stripes over my thighs.

We're both trembling and breathing heavily when everything finally slows. But for long moments, I can only clutch Dominic to my back and catch my breath against his lips.

"Fuck, baby," he groans, his forehead dropping to my shoulder. "You've ruined me."

I'm trembling too hard to tell him *I'm the one who's ruined.*

Slowly, he untangles himself from me and lays me down on the bed on my stomach. Then he stands and quickly searches for a towel to clean me with.

His touch is gentle as he wipes off the back of my thighs. As soon as he's done, he grabs a blanket and drapes it over my body.

"Are you okay?" he asks. "Do you need anything? Water? A shower? More ice cream?"

I smile against the pillow. *Is this what it's like to be taken care of? I was right, this is what paradise feels like.*

"I'm okay," I mumble. "I think you fucked me into a coma, though." Sure enough, my words are overtaken by a yawn. I hurry to blink my eyes open and lift my head. "Sorry, I don't want to fall asleep on you."

Dominic lets out a soft laugh. "Skylar, I'd love nothing *more* than for you to fall asleep on me. Do you have anything in the morning? Can you stay over?"

I force myself into a sitting position and rack my brain for these kinds of important details. "I have work tomorrow, but not until noon. Joey's home tonight, so I could probably ask him to keep an eye on Mom."

I feel guilty about that last part, but when Dominic presses my phone into my hand and I text my brother, his response is a simple: *Thank god, I thought you'd never get a life.*

I smile, and my guilt disappears—well, most of it. But then I look at Dominic, stretched out beside me like some kind of naked Greek god, and I just feel...*happy.*

"Actually, that shower sounds nice," I tell him, sliding close enough that I can press a kiss to his chest. And then another one, slightly lower. "You *did* make me dirty, after all."

He immediately scoops me into his arms. "I'm about to make you even dirtier. If for no other reason than to dispel any old jokes about my refractory period before you make them."

I'm still laughing when he drops me under the cold spray.

30

SKYLAR

I can't knock the damn smile off my face for the rest of the weekend.

My coworkers notice, my brother notices, even my mom makes a comment about me seeming happier lately. I can't even bring myself to deny it—when she says it, the only thing I respond with is a kiss on her cheek and an even bigger smile.

I carry it through the weekend and to the gym on Monday, where it grows, knowing I'm going to see Dominic. And sure enough, he's got a twinkle in his eyes when I walk through the front doors.

"Hey, Skylar," he greets from beside Jax. "Did you have a good weekend?"

"I had a great weekend," I respond, trying not to appear downright giddy at the simple question. "Actually got to do something besides work, for once."

"I'm happy to hear it. Anything fun?" He has to fight to keep the smile off his face.

I shrug. "It was more the company than anything else."

"You know, if you want to bring your friend to the gym,

this month we're doing Refer-A-Friend discounts," Jax interjects. "Do they like MMA?"

Now *I'm* the one trying not to grin and give it away. "Uh...I'm not sure. I'll ask."

Jax gives me a big smile. "Awesome. Just let me know."

I have to start toward the locker rooms to hide my laughter. I have no idea how Dominic contains his.

When I walk into the changing room, Remy and Lucy are already in there getting ready for class. Their heads pop up when they see me.

"What's got *you* so happy to be here?" Remy asks with a chuckle. "Not that you aren't always happy to be here, but that's a big smile you've got on today."

I scramble to think of a reason they'll accept. Because I've gotten close enough with the girls—and I know Remy well enough now—that I know they'll push for a real reason.

"I...finally signed up for that jiu-jitsu tournament this weekend," I blurt out.

Remy's eyebrows shoot to her hairline. "No shit? That's awesome. Congrats on making the leap. You'll do great."

Nerves immediately start to seep in. I *did* sign up for the tournament, but I have yet to feel good about it. Most of the time when I think about it, I just feel fear.

"You think so?" I manage to ask. "You don't think I'm doing it too early?"

"No way," Lucy assures me now. "You train harder than any other white belt and you've already got a crazy competitive spirit. It'll be a good test and a great learning experience, no matter which way it goes."

I nod, feeling comforted by their belief in me.

"Plus, the officials of that tournament love Coach," she

continues. "So being a Bulldog MMA competitor practically gives you a leg up on the competition."

I pause in pulling my rashguard on. I've been dying to ask about Dominic outside of my relationship with him, but couldn't figure out a way to do that stealthily.

"So, his name is pretty respected in the fight world?" I ask carefully.

Remy snorts. "Respected is putting it mildly. He's like the golden boy of Philly MMA and the poster child for the ideal fight career. Came up early, fought to get recognized, made a dent in the MMA world at the peak of his career, and then became the best kind of coach when he retired. He's the coach everyone wishes they could have."

Pride swells in my chest at hearing that. Not just because of his illustrious fight career, but because he's *respected* in this world. He's everything I hoped he would be when I first walked through the gym doors.

"I swear, sometimes I want to shake the newbies who walk in here and complain about his coaching style," Lucy says with an eye roll. "They think because he pushes them hard and demands more than they want to give, that he's an unfair coach. They have *no idea* what a bad coach looks like."

I turn to her, startled. "You started somewhere else?"

She glances at Remy. "I did. Remy was lucky enough to start here. She never had to go through what I did."

I glance between them. "Do you mind if I ask what happened?"

Lucy avoids looking at me by stuffing her sweatshirt into a cubby. "The usual. Unfortunately, being a woman in a sport as male dominated as this one can open you up to some sexist experiences." She sighs in defeat and turns toward me. "Look, I trained at two gyms before this one.

Neither were good. The first one just treated me as inferior to the boys and never gave me any attention or opportunities, but the second one...that one was bad. Like, sexual harassment bad."

My eyes widen. "Holy shit, seriously?"

She nods stiffly. "Turns out, he—he being the owner—had done the same thing to every female who wanted to fight. It's not uncommon, unfortunately. When there's such a power imbalance between male coaches and female fighters, a lot of times the women end up in situations where they feel they need to...*do things* to earn the right to fight. One of the girls actually got pregnant. That's when everything about him came to light."

Somehow, my eyes go even wider. "Jesus. He got shut down, though, right?"

She shakes her head, sadness in her eyes. "Nope. He still has a gym, and he's still coaching fighters."

I blink, speechless.

"Do you know that we had a woman sign up here last week who signed up *because* Coach didn't ask her out at the end of the consultation?" Remy says. "Apparently, at the last gym she tried, both of the instructors asked for her number after class."

My stare turns to Remy.

She gives me a sad smile. "We're really lucky with Coach. Not all women in this sport have it as good as we do. You know how nice it is to learn from someone who *doesn't* try to fuck you as payment for private lessons?"

My heart plummets. *Fuck.*

That's not what he's doing with me, right? No, of course not, that's insane. I can read people well enough to know that's not why he's interested in me. Besides, I made the first move. And he fought too hard against giving in to be playing that kind of game with me. Is this what the rest of the fight coaching world looks like? Is this what he's setting himself *apart* from?

Is this what he's risking, being with me?

Guilt sours my stomach.

"None of that is to scare you," Lucy hurries to say, seeing my shift in mood. "It's just to point out that we have it good here. And that his name carries far in most tournaments. You'll do great this weekend."

I force a smile onto my face. "Thanks. I'm nervous, but I'm excited for it."

"And you'll have Coach there to coach you," Remy says. "I don't know if you've ever seen a jiu-jitsu tournament, but the coaches sit four feet away from you on the sidelines and can practically talk you through a submission from where they're sitting. He'll have your back the whole time."

I hate that that's not as comforting as it was ten minutes ago.

My brain isn't as present as it normally is during class. I'm listening to instructions and following directions, but my body seems to be on autopilot and detached from my passion for it. Dominic notices and tries to catch my eye a few times, but I don't return the attention. I just go through the motions.

I'm not on duty to clean the mats tonight, so thankfully, I don't need to clear my jumbled head and have a conversation with Dominic about what's bothering me. I do respond to his worried text, though, just to assure him everything is okay and that I'll see him tomorrow.

I just need to get out of here and think.

I toss and turn all night, and I'm still distracted when I walk into my anatomy class the next day. So much so that I don't realize when Craig sits down next to me.

"Hey, Sky," he greets with a charming smile. "How's your week going?"

I force a smile of my own. "Good. You know, busy. How are you?"

"You mean since your crazy coach threw me out of the gym? Nursing my bruised pride, but I'll live."

I wince. *Shit. I forgot about that.*

I don't have to fake the guilty look on my face. "Yeah, about that... Sorry that made things awkward. I think he's a little protective of his students' safety."

Craig hums a non-answer.

An ice-cold feeling of discomfort washes over me. I don't like the way he's looking at me right now.

He moves on from the subject in a way that's way too forgiving for having brought it up in the first place. His eyes are sparkling with excitement when he starts to talk, but not in a healthy way. "Listen, I've been wanting to ask you something, but didn't want to do it in the middle of your midterm craziness. Since, you know, I know how 'busy' you are."

I hate the way he acts like I'm using "busy" as an excuse. But I hate even more that his tone makes dread drop like a stone into my stomach.

"But now that we're in the eye of the storm between midterms and finals, I figured it was safe to ask." He laughs, but it doesn't reach his eyes. "Maybe try not to make a liar out of me."

"Craig, I don't think—"

"Have dinner with me."

I blink in surprise. I can't believe he just came out and *said it*, when I've been trying to be gentle but obvious about the fact that I'm not interested in him. Why would he think I'd suddenly say yes? Did he think cornering me after midterms would actually work? That I'd suddenly find him charming?

"I appreciate the offer, Craig, but I'm not really interested in dating right now."

"It's *one* date," he pushes. "Who doesn't have time for one date? I promise I'll make it a fun night."

I can't stop my wince at the creepy, sexual undertone of his comment. But he sees it, and suddenly, that dread starts to feel a whole lot like fear. Because his expression turns a little crazed.

"Go out with me," he says again, taking a step closer. "I tried to meet you halfway at the gym, but your precious *coach*," he spits the word, "wasn't very welcoming. Take a break from your little hobby and your side jobs and have dinner with me."

It takes a second for my mouth to form words. I'm frozen in place, stunned by what's happening. I have no problem being firm in my decisions, or communicating my opinions, but I've never had to reject a guy. And Craig's reaction to my *no* is filling me with an unease I've never felt.

"I said no, Craig," I say carefully. "I'm sorry if that's hurtful, but my answer's no. I don't want to go on a date with you."

"Come on, Skylar," he whines, sounding every bit his young age. "You know you want to. You've been flirting with me all semester."

My eyes go wide at that, and this time I don't care about preserving his feelings. "Are you delusional? I haven't been flirting with you. I've just been *nice* to you."

He takes another step closer, and now he's entirely too close for comfort. I look up at him, forcing myself to hold his gaze, but my stomach churns with unease. His eyes are flashing with an energy I've never come face to face with.

"That's what they all say," he says with a manic grin. "I like playing the hard-to-get game as much as the next guy, but it's getting a little old. You can stop playing now and give us both what we really want."

He must take my silence as consent because he steps impossibly closer, close enough that he can place a hand on my hip, and then slide it around me and down to my ass.

That snaps me out of the shock-fear-confusion tornado I've sunken into. Even after only being at the gym for a few weeks, my training kicks in, and I shove Craig away from me. Then my hand whips out to slap him across the face, hitting with the heel of my hand, the way Dominic taught me.

"Don't ever fucking touch me again," I bite out at a stunned Craig. He doesn't seem hurt, just surprised that I reacted physically.

Honestly, so am I.

Craig recovers quicker than I expect him to. He shoots forward and grabs me by the wrist on the hand that's curled into a fist by my side.

"You're a stuck-up little bitch," he snarls. "You've been teasing me all semester. And now you're going to act like you don't want me? Fuck you."

Before I can jerk away from him, he drops my hand and steps back, his gaze traveling the length of my body.

"*You're* delusional if you think you're going to get a better offer. You're not as hot as you think you are, and everyone thinks you're fucking weird. I was doing you a favor, asking you out."

I swallow roughly and stand in place, hoping if I don't respond, that he'll go away.

But then his tone goes from hard and angry to soft and mocking, and dread drops like a stone into my stomach.

"But maybe I'm just not your type," he says in a lilting voice. A pleased-with-himself grin stretches across his face. "Maybe I'm just not old enough for you."

Every ounce of blood freezes in my veins.

He can't know. He can't know. No one knows.

I force myself to respond. Steeling myself, I say, "After this childish display, yeah—there's a good chance I'll date older from now on."

The fact that my answer makes his grin *grow* makes me feel even colder.

He's just guessing. He can't know. And he has no proof.

"Good luck with that," he says with a chuckle that has no warmth.

And as I watch him walk away, that dread inside me tangles with a sense of foreboding.

31

DOMINIC

I spend so much time thinking about why Skylar may have run out of the gym yesterday that when Joey walks in the next day, part of me wonders if I've started to hallucinate Skylar-things into my environment.

And then I take in his expression. And any concern for my sanity evaporates.

"Joey? What's wrong? *What happened?*"

"Skylar's fine," he hurriedly assures me. "I'm not here because of her."

The squeeze in my chest deflates, and I can breathe again. "So then why are you here?"

Now he seems nervous. His eyes dart around the gym, looking everywhere but at me. I soften my voice and ask again, "Joey, what's going on? I promise, if I can help, I will."

Shoulders slumping, his words are mumbled. "I need help finding a job."

That's...not what I expected.

"A job? What kind of job?"

When he finally locks eyes with me, it's pleading. "Any job. Just something that makes money. But..." He shuffles awkwardly. "No one wants to hire a fourteen-year-old. I get turned away before I can even ask for an interview."

My next question is spoken carefully. "What do you need a job for, Joey?"

"You already know," he says, his voice sad. "I hate that Skylar stresses so much about money—I want to help."

Fuck, my heart aches for this kid. For Skylar, too. They don't deserve to have these kinds of worries at this point in their lives.

"I know you gave her a job," Joey continues. "I know she cleans and does stuff around the gym for you. I can do that, too. Whatever you need, I can help with. I'm almost fifteen, and I swear I'm a hard worker, you can trust—"

"Joey, Joey, slow down," I interrupt. He swallows the rest of his urgency and nods. Sighing, I tell him the truth.

"Your sister probably wouldn't like you working here—I practically had to beg *her* to take the job. And I'm assuming she's not a fan of you looking for work in general, am I right?" His guilty expression tells me everything I need to know. I know how hard Skylar works for her family, and how much she wants to keep Joey a teenager.

But I also understand him wanting to help. These two love each other so much that they'd do anything to relieve some of their sibling's stress. I can't fault Joey for his feelings, just as much as I can't fault Skylar for hers.

Unfortunately, Skylar isn't the one whose hopes I'm crushing.

I must have been his last resort, because hearing me say no seems to have taken all the fight out of him. Now, he just looks...resigned.

"Okay, you're right. I just thought I'd ask, I guess. Thanks for being nice about it and not just kicking me out." He gives me a tremulous smile and turns to leave.

"Hold on," I blurt out. "Just wait a second."

I pinch the bridge of my nose, my brain buzzing with ideas. *Who do I know that would hire a fourteen-year-old?*

It hits me so hard, I practically bolt from the gym, gesturing for Joey to follow me.

I blow into the pizza pub three buildings down, my rushed entrance attracting the attention of Big Tony behind the counter. His eyebrows shoot to his hairline when he sees me.

"Well, fuck, look who it is," he says in that heavy South Philly Italian accent. "Dominic. What the hell are you doing in my pizza shop? You finally decide to add some carbs to that dry-ass diet of yours?"

Normally, I'd enjoy the back-and-forth. I like to come in here between training sessions to grab a salad and shoot the shit with him. But I don't have a lot of humor left in me today.

Tony's eyes dart to Joey as he walks in behind me, just as I say, "I need a favor."

His expression becomes skeptical. "Oh, yeah? What kinda favor?"

"The job kind." I hear Joey suck in a breath. "You were looking for a dishwasher, right? Well, I found you one."

Tony's attention drifts back to Joey. "This my new dishwasher?"

Joey steps up beside me and answers strongly, "Yes, sir. My name is Joey Vega."

"Well, Joey Vega," Tony says, coming around the counter to stand in front of us with crossed arms. "You ever wash dishes before?"

"Uh, yeah." Joey's voice wavers. "Not...at a restaurant this nice, but I'm great at...scrubbing, and rinsing, and, uh, drying—"

"Relax, kid, anyone could see you've never had a job before." Tony turns his attention back to me. "Why am I hiring a kid who's never worked a day in his life?"

"He's never been *paid* a day in his life," I correct. "I can vouch for him. He'll do whatever job you need done around here."

"Yeah? Any job I give you?" When Joey nods, he says, "What if I ask you to clean the bathroom?"

"Whatever you need, sir," Joey responds without hesitation.

"What if one of my idiot cooks accidentally throws a pizza cutter in the dumpster out back? Would you get it back for me?"

That draws a wince out of Joey, but even still, he says, "I'd— Yeah, I'd get it back for you."

"I can only pay you minimum wage," Tony warns.

"That's fine."

"And I need you here every weekend."

"I can do that."

"And if you fuck up, you're out. I don't need to be babysitting in my place of business."

"That's totally fair, sir."

A flash of admiration appears in Tony's eyes. And I knew I was right to bring Joey over here.

"Alright, you're hired," Tony says. "Come in Saturday morning at 9 a.m. and I'll get you trained."

I expected to see excitement as I look over to Joey, but all I see is relief.

I catch Skylar as soon as she steps through the gym doors.

"Hey." I gesture for her to step around the desk and into the office. "You got a minute?"

Her gaze darts over to heavy bag room where Jax is teaching a private class. For now, we're alone out here. "Yeah, sure."

"What's up?" she asks as we step into the office. There's none of the same uncertainty that I saw on her yesterday, when she looked lost in her head and wouldn't meet my eyes, but there's still a level of stiffness in her posture.

That's what I want to get rid of.

"Is everything okay?" I ask without preamble. All day, I've been trying to decide if I want to ask her about yesterday or tell her about Joey first, but as soon as I have her in front of me, I can't not check on her well-being. "I don't want to overstep if it's something at home, or if it's none of my business, but...I just want to make sure you're okay. Something happened under my roof yesterday, and if it's something I can fix, I want to know about it. Please."

She blows out a heavy breath, and I'm suddenly on high alert at the look in her eyes.

"It's about us," she admits quietly.

As much as it doesn't make sense to feel this way after such a short time with her, the words form an ache in my chest. *She's going to end it.*

I force myself to sit still and wait for her to speak. I promised myself I would walk away with no questions asked if she decided she didn't want this anymore. That I would respect her decision and not push her on it.

But the idea of walking away from her never truly crossed my mind, and now I'm finding it hard to breathe around it.

She fidgets with her bag strap, but then she finally meets

my eyes again with a sullen expression. "Are you sure you want to keep seeing me?"

My brow furrows. "What? Of course."

Another shuffle with the strap. "Seeing me isn't too risky? You know I would never want to hurt your reputation."

"Skylar, what is this about?" I ask quietly, and she shakes her head, seeming to struggle with what she wants to say.

"I just feel selfish. I mean, I'm the one getting all the perks here."

Before she's even finished, I'm relaxing, and my lip is curling with a small smile. Now I understand her concern. And *this* concern I can appease.

She keeps talking, not even noticing my reaction. "I mean, I get to hang out with you, and ask you all kinds of questions about fighting, and don't even get me *started* on the mind-blowing orgasms—"

"You're welcome for that." I try to lighten the mood.

"And I know you won't admit it plays into our relationship, but giving me a free membership is definitely a part of this—"

"Whoa, that has *nothing* to do with—"

"What do *you* get out of this?" she continues, ignoring my alarmed interruption. She's stuck in her head and gaining more speed. "What do you get from me that you couldn't get from any other woman, that *wouldn't* come with a huge risk to your name and your business? I just don't—"

Finally, I've had enough. I step close to her and grab both of her arms, anchoring her in place and forcing her eyes on mine.

"Skylar," I say gently, but firmly. "I don't know what triggered this, but let's get rid of these doubts right now. I get *everything* from being with you. I get your heart, and your brain, and your humor, and your passion. I *love* watching how excited you get about the things that you love. You have no idea how much lightness you've brought into my life. *You* do that. Not anyone else. *You*. So don't tell me I get nothing out of being with you."

Skylar looks down, but not before I catch the smile on her lips or the pink on her cheeks.

"Don't forget the mind-blowing orgasms," she murmurs.

I huff a laugh. "I did not forget the mind-blowing orgasms. But if I added those, I'd be here all day listing the things I like about you in bed." My voice softens. "And I think the other things were more important for you to hear."

That has her smile shining up at me. And I hate that I didn't make it more obvious to her that she makes me happier. I vow to tell her more often.

"So, I'm not too much of a risk for you?" she asks.

I frown. "Of course not." With a sigh, I add, "I mean, eventually, we'll have to talk about...what this is, but Skylar... You're worth way more than any of the risks."

She bites down on her lip. "Yeah?"

I sink a hand into her hair that's still down for once and tilt her face up. "Yeah," I whisper as I kiss her.

"Okay," she whispers back, her grin too big to tamp down on anymore.

Reluctantly, I untangle my hand from her hair and step back. "No more doubts. Not about that. If you're worried, we talk about it. Okay?"

"Yes, Coach."

I force myself toward the door, grumbling, "Little tease." Opening the door, I peek out and see that no one's here yet. But before I nudge Skylar out, I press a hungry kiss to her lips. "Now get out of here before I cash in on my mind-blowing orgasms."

Her sensual purr floats back to me as she walks toward the changing rooms.

"Yes, Coach."

I have to keep my eyes off of Skylar while I'm teaching the rest of the night. I have this unquenchable urge to smile, which would definitely draw unwanted attention from my students who know me better than that. Even when I'm *not* looking at Skylar, I still want to smile.

I meant everything I said to her earlier today. The difference she's made in the past few weeks has been like going from colorblind, to suddenly walking into an amusement park and seeing the whole spectrum lit up and all around you. She's breathed life into days that I had no idea were dull.

Which is why it's insanely hard not to spend every second that she's near me staring at her.

Somehow, I make it through my classes. By the time she starts cleaning and I retreat into my office to do some paperwork, I've managed to keep my distance for almost three hours.

I finally lose the battle to stay away from her and stride from the office, fully prepared to rip the mop from her hands and carry her back to the couch in the welcome area. But right as I step out into the gym, she's coming out of the storage closet in the back corner, no cleaning supplies in hand.

"Done?" I ask.

She nods and quickly washes her hands at the sink. "I

can't stay too long tonight. I promised Maria I'd relieve her early. Joey's at his last basketball game."

The reminder of her brother is enough to make my need for Skylar recede to the background for a moment. I don't know if Joey wanted to be the one to tell her what happened, but I also don't want to spend even a single second lying to Skylar about something I've done that will affect her carefully constructed life. So once she's done drying her hands, I take them in mine.

"I saw your brother today," I start.

Skylar's eyebrow quirks. "What? Where?"

"He came in here. He asked me for a job."

That makes her eyes widen in alarm. "He did *what?* I *told* him he doesn't need a job. Why would he be looking for one? And why would he think it's okay to come to you?"

"Skylar, he's trying to help," I say, as softly as I can manage. "You should be proud of the kid you've helped to raise because he sees his sister struggling and wants to take some of the burden off."

Skylar's lower lip wobbles, and it takes everything in me not to sweep her into my arms and soothe her. Especially when she presses her lips tightly together to try to stop the trembling.

"He's too young to be working," she says firmly. "He should be out with his friends, and ignoring homework, and being a regular kid. He doesn't need to be worrying about this kind of stuff."

I lightly brush my thumb over Skylar's cheek, her eyes filling with tears at my touch. "It's okay to ask for help, baby," I whisper.

She doesn't let the tears fall, of course. "I don't want him to have to help," she says on a breath. "He's just a kid. He doesn't deserve this."

I finally wrap my arms around her and hold her tight to my body, relieved when she melts into me. "Neither of you deserves this. You're both just trying to deal with the hand you've been dealt."

Her arms wrap around my waist and her face buries into my chest. She doesn't say anything, she just lets me hold her.

"I think it would make him feel better if he could help," I say after a few moments, murmuring the words into Skylar's hair. "I know you're trying to protect him, but this doesn't have to be a bad thing."

When she pulls back, there's no sign of tears, no sign of grief. She just seems tired and a little reluctant. "What kind of job would it be?"

I tuck a strand of hair behind her ear. "I took him next door, to the pizza place. They needed someone to help with dishes and cleaning."

"And they hired him?" she asks.

I shrug. "I vouched for him. I've known the owner for a long time."

Skylar swallows roughly, but nods. "Okay, that doesn't sound so bad. With his season over, he'll have time for it, and if you know the guy, then…"

"I'll keep an eye on him," I assure her. "But I promise he's in good hands. And this is a *good* thing."

Another nod, this one less shaky. "You're right. I can do this. *He* can do this."

Pressing a kiss to her temple, I whisper a quick, "Proud of you."

That brings a smile to her face. I wonder how many times she's heard it, and how many times I can get away with saying it. Because *fuck*, I'm so amazed by her.

She cups my face and presses a sweet kiss to my lips. "Thank you."

My hands curl around her waist to pull her tighter against me. "You're very welcome."

"So, what was your first job?" she asks after a moment, propping her chin on my chest so she can look up at me.

"Cashier. Well, technically, I was a bagger first, then I worked up to being a cashier."

"That doesn't sound so bad. Scanning things and swiping cards? I bet your brain stayed on jiu-jitsu the whole time."

"You're forgetting I grew up in the era of cash and checks. If I didn't stay focused, I was risking fucking up money-things. Not a good idea."

She sighs and drops her forehead to my chest. "I always forget how *old* you are."

Chuckling, I tug on her hair. "I thought you said I was experienced."

When she raises her head to look at me again, that familiar playful sparkle is back in her eyes, her stress from earlier forgotten. A sensual smile curves her lips. "You're that, too."

My lips drop to her neck as my other hand drifts under the hem of her tank top to brush teasing lines along her stomach. "Sounds like you might need a lesson to differentiate between the two," I murmur against her skin.

I feel the shiver that runs through her body. "Well...you *are* the coach," she mumbles. "You're basically required to teach me."

I nip at the line of her neck, loving the sound of that. Wrong or not, there's something insanely hot about the teacher/student thing.

Unable to stay away from her mouth any longer, I

straighten and take her lips in a heated kiss. She opens for me instantly, like the good student she is. When she tangles her tongue with mine, a bolt of lust courses through my body, and I can't help but groan.

It's not lost on me that we're standing at the entrance of my gym, visible from the street. It's late, and we're not on a main street, but anyone could peek through the large windows and see me making out with a younger woman.

And suddenly, I want to play into the *wrongness*. Just for tonight.

"I'm not a very good coach with you," I tell Skylar, backing her toward the mat where, barely an hour ago, we had been training with thirty other people. "Do you know what I was thinking of when I was teaching you tonight?"

I can feel her smile against my mouth before she shakes her head. "Tell me," she whispers.

The hand that was teasing along the edge of her tank top smooths down the front of her shorts, under her thong and arrowing directly to her clit. I swallow her gasp with a desperate kiss.

"The whole time we were working submissions from the mount, I couldn't stop thinking about the one I would kill to have you try on me."

As my finger moves in circles over her slick skin, her breaths come quicker. "Which one?"

I draw out the moment by slowing my fingers and taking my time kissing her. She looks almost ready to snap at me when I finally say, "Mounted triangle. I want you sitting on my face with your legs wrapped around my head."

"Oh my God, yes," she moans. "I want that, too."

I take her mouth in another, filthy kiss. "Yeah? You want to mount my face so I can taste this sweet pussy?"

She nods hurriedly, clutching at my shirt as her tongue swipes mine.

"Say it," I demand, pushing her shorts down her legs before dragging her down to the mat with me. I settle her over my face, inhaling her intoxicating scent but not touching her yet. Instead, I grip her hips, holding her in place, and look up the length of her body to meet her eyes. "You know what I want to hear."

She's almost too dazed, too eager for my touch, to understand. But then the sexiest smile brightens her face. And my dick gets so hard, I'm worried I might come without even touching it.

"Yes, Coach," Skylar purrs.

I smile against her inner thigh. "Good girl," I murmur with a kiss. Then I turn my head so my mouth is centered beneath her pussy, so close that I can smell the wetness shining on her skin. "Now sit on my face, baby."

She doesn't hesitate. And just like every time I touch Skylar, I become so lost in her that the flash from outside doesn't register in my subconscious until days later.

32

DOMINIC

The day of the jiu-jitsu tournament, Skylar is the first person to show up, to no one's surprise. When she walks into the arena, my heart stutters at the sight of her.

Fuck, I think I'm more anxious for her to compete than I ever was during my own fights.

"Hey," she says when she eventually spots me and walks over. There's a smile on her face, but I can see the tension sizzling beneath it.

I return the smile, wishing I could kiss her hello. "Hey. You ready? Feeling okay?"

She shrugs, the tension in her shoulders obvious. "As ready as I'll ever be. I managed to get some sleep last night, though, so that's a win in itself." She hesitates, then admits, "I'm just a little nervous."

God, I want to touch her so bad. I just want to hug her and assure her that she's going to do great.

I stick my hands in my pockets to curb the impulse. "I'd be worried if you *weren't* nervous, Skylar. But don't worry, the nerves go away after the adrenaline of the first match. You're going to do great."

"Then let's hope I *win* the first match," she grumbles.

"You will," I say confidently. "I'll be right there with you. I'll coach you straight to the gold medal."

That earns me a warm smile, and my heart trips over itself.

Before I can do something foolish—like taste her smile on my tongue—I say hurriedly, "I have to go, the coach's meeting is up next. You'll probably start in an hour, since the women's divisions go before the men's. I'll try to catch you for some warmup drills, but if I'm running late, just warm up with your jump rope and stretch out on the mats."

She swallows thickly with a shaky nod.

"You're going to do great," I tell her quietly. Glancing around to make sure no one can hear, I add, "We'll celebrate your victories tonight."

She smiles knowingly, and then she's jerking her head toward the mats. "Go. I'll see you soon."

The next hour flies by. These tournaments are always hectic and exhausting, with long rules meetings and dozens of matches throughout the day. Not to mention, constantly being stopped by fellow coaches and old training partners. When I glance at my watch for the fifteenth time and realize Skylar's match is starting soon, I have to rush through the arena to find Mat Eight.

She's already there warming up when I duck under the rope blocking off the competitors' space.

"Alright, you ready?" I ask, stepping up beside her. "All I want you to do is grab hold of her when the match starts, and get her down to the mat with that takedown you like. Don't overwhelm yourself, just focus on one thing. I'll talk you through the rest."

She nods her understanding. But before I can get a read

on where her head's at, the ref calls the two girls onto the mat.

"Let's go, Skylar! You got this!" I recognize Jax's and Remy's voices and feel instantly grateful that Skylar has some gym support from her peers.

The match starts the way most first-time white belt matches start. With both competitors circling, then eventually grabbing a hold of each other, and then spending the next three minutes attempting a takedown.

"Grab her collar, Skylar, try to snap her down!" I'm sitting at the edge of the mat, only three feet away from the competitors, but I'm so amped up that my voice comes out too loud.

Still, Skylar follows my directions. I see her knuckles turn white as she grips the other girl's gi lapel and tries to drag her to the mat.

"One more time. Let's try it again, Skylar."

Again, she yanks down on her opponent. She doesn't get her to the ground, but she does manage to cause the girl to stumble. I see the moment Skylar's eyes light up and she capitalizes on the advantage by sticking her foot out and tripping the girl.

It works. She goes down, with Skylar on top of her. Two points for a takedown.

A loud cheer sounds from behind me: the Bulldog team. Glancing at the clock on the table beside me, I see there're only thirty seconds left of the match.

"Hold your position, Skylar, just hold it for thirty more seconds!"

Though the girl struggles and tries to push her off, Skylar doesn't budge. Finally, the ref calls time on the match.

Skylar has a huge smile on her face when she stands up.

It gets even bigger when the ref raises her hand up in victory.

"Nice job," I tell her as she steps off the mat. Jax and Remy both lean over the barricade to slap her shoulder in congratulations.

"You'll have this next match to rest and then you're up again," comes the official's voice from beside me.

"Alright, ten-minute break," I tell Skylar. "Shake it off and get ready for the next one." I automatically unscrew the cap on her water bottle and hand it to her. "I want you to do the same thing this next match, but I want you to get that takedown earlier. Go for that leg sooner."

She nods, taking a small sip of water. Now that her victory has died down and she has to focus on the next match, some of the nerves have come back. I can see them in her face.

"You're doing great," I tell her quietly. "I'm so proud of you."

Some of the tension loosens from her shoulders, and she sends me a tremulous, grateful smile.

"Skylar Vega? You're up."

Skylar hands me her water and then steps back on the mat for Match #2. She still looks nervous, but slightly more comfortable than she did fifteen minutes ago.

The match starts the same way her first one did, with both girls unsure of how to get their opponent to the mat, and ending up grabbing hold and yanking each other around.

But halfway into the five-minute match, Skylar's opponent gets her off balance. And then capitalizes on it the same way Skylar did in her first one.

The ref lifts two fingers for two points. Thankfully,

Skylar quickly wraps her legs around the girl's waist to keep her from scoring any more points.

"Get control of her first, then let's go for a sweep," I call out, leaning my weight forward onto my knees. "We've got to get some points this time, Skylar."

To her credit, Skylar tries her hardest to reverse their position. But every time she unlocks her legs to use them for a sweep, her opponent jumps on the opening and tries desperately to get out from between her legs. Twice, she almost gets it. And twice, Skylar has to lock her legs back up and yank down on the girl's collar so she can't sit up straight.

For three minutes, Skylar has every muscle engaged as she tries to keep control of her opponent. She's tiring, I can see it in her eyes and in her body. Her breaths are starting to become choppy from all the energy she's exerting and from the constant stress of another person's weight fully on top of her. With only forty-five seconds left, it looks like she might end up too tired to try for a Hail Mary.

But I should know my girl better than that. Skylar would have to be dead to not try her hardest with something that's important to her.

With a final burst of energy, Skylar scissors her legs and knocks the girl onto her back. And when she scrambles on top of her to get the dominant mount position, the ref holds up six fingers just as the match ends.

Our team erupts with cheers around the mat. Skylar quickly climbs off her opponent, and then helps her up. Once on her feet, she sucks in a big breath before letting it out with a stuttered exhale. She's too tired to smile when the ref holds up her hand in victory.

Her steps drag as she makes her way off the mat. She's barely reached me before I've twisted the cap off her water and lifted it to her lips for another drink. She looks in shock, like she can't fully comprehend what's happening.

"She's got five minutes before her finals match," comes the official's voice from beside us.

Jesus, fuck. That's barely even a break.

I turn my attention back to Skylar. She's shaking from muscle overexertion, and she seems too overwhelmed to be able to focus on specific instructions. So I focus on cheering her on instead.

"Hear that? You just made it to the finals. How's *that* for your first jiu-jitsu tournament?"

She smiles up at me, but it's tremulous.

She's still shaking, and I want like hell to make it stop. Without a single thought about how this might look, I grab her arm so I can push up the sleeve of her gi jacket and start to massage her forearm muscles.

"Listen to me, I want you to leave everything on the mat during this next match," I tell her, my hands never stopping the motions on her arm. Slowly, her shaking slows, and I switch to the other arm. "I need you to get that takedown early so you can focus on staying on top and racking up points. It'll be way less tiring that way."

She gives me a jerky nod.

"You can do this, Skylar," I tell her, relieved when her eyes focus on me. "One more match, and then you're done. This is it. This is the one that counts."

A pause, and then another nod, this one with more determination. I let out a breath at the sight of it.

"Skylar Vega and Emily Samson, for the finals," comes the ref's voice.

"Let's go, Skylar, you got this!!" Jax shouts from the sidelines. "For the gold, baby!"

Skylar shakes hands with her new opponent, and right

before the ref starts the match, I watch her take a deep breath.

"Come on, Skylar, last one!" I yell in encouragement.

Another deep breath in, but this time, it's followed by her shooting forward to grab onto her opponent's lapel.

"Atta girl, get a grip on her," I call out. "Let's try to take her down now."

She tries, I know she does. But she's tired, and this girl is heavier. It doesn't take her very long to manhandle Skylar to the mat.

Skylar quickly locks her legs around the girl's waist, though. She's not deterred by the fact that she's now down two points, only a minute into the match.

"Get control of her body, Skylar. Grab her neck, her arm, something."

Somehow, she manages to get two hands on the girl's arm.

"There you go." My voice rises in pitch, excitement roiling in my stomach as a submission slowly comes into view. "Lock up that armbar, Skylar."

It's like watching a *How To Do An Armbar* training video. Step by step, she sets up the submission. And with every movement, her opponent's expression becomes more and more worried.

Skylar swings her leg around to lock it into place. And her hips press against the girl's elbow to force the tap.

The next thirty seconds happen in slow motion. I feel frozen in place, watching everything unfold, unable to do anything about it.

In jiu-jitsu, submissions shouldn't be painful. They simulate a choke, or an arm crank, or a leg crank, but the whole point of the sport is to tap out when you feel the pressure of it, *before* it turns into an actual choke or break. It's the *threat* of violence, not the practice of it.

But in a competition, where the adrenaline is high and everything is happening at warp speed, sometimes that instinct to tap out disappears.

The second Skylar's opponent feels pressure on her elbow from the submission, her expression explodes into panic. And I watch in horror as her reaction becomes that of a cornered animal trying to physically fight their way out.

With Skylar hanging onto her arm and completely wrapped around it, the girl summons every ounce of energy and power inside her to stand up.

And then she slams Skylar to the mat to try to dislodge her grip.

White noise fills my ears. People are moving and things are happening, but all I can see is Skylar's head being slammed. Her grip on the girl's arm slackens and drops to the mat, and then she's just lying there. And I can't tell if she's conscious or if she broke her neck, and I can't *see*, I can't *get to her*—

I don't know what snaps me back to reality. I think it's the shrill sound of the ref's whistle because, all of a sudden, I realize I'm surrounded by chaos. There's screaming, and someone rushing the mat, and everyone on nearby mats has turned to see what the commotion is.

I feel like I'm moving through quicksand. Slamming is illegal, and one of the most dangerous moves in jiu-jitsu. There are a million ways to get hurt from a slam, and my brain keeps replaying the sight of *Skylar* getting slammed—

I drop to my knees beside her, my hands traveling over her body, checking for injuries without touching.

"Skylar," I breathe. "Breathe, baby. Are you hurt?"

For the first time, my eyes focus on her face. She's

conscious, thank God, and breathing, though her breaths are clearly labored. Her eyes are wide, and she looks dazed.

"I'm okay," she wheezes. "I think—" She winces. "I think she just knocked the wind out of me."

Relief flows through my body like rainwater after a drought. *She's okay. She's okay.*

I still can't bring myself to touch her, but my eyes travel over her one more time, checking for myself that she's not hurt. As soon as I assure myself that she *is* fine, my relief flips to rage.

Her opponent is still standing on the mat, looking shell-shocked as she stares at Skylar. I round on her before I can think better of it.

"What is *wrong* with you?" I yell. "You could have *killed* her!"

Her eyes dart to mine and widen. "I'm sorry, it was a gut reaction—"

"That's no excuse!"

Someone grabs my arm from behind and tries to pull me back. "Look, it was an accident. No one is blaming—"

I spin to find the ref, and my anger rachets.

"And where the fuck were you?" I shout in his face. "Your job is to protect the competitors! What the fuck kind of ref are you if you can't do that?"

His expression shifts from being irritated by my outburst to stunned by it. Jacob's been my friend for over a decade, and I've never once raised my voice at him.

When he speaks, his words are quiet. Just between us.

"Jesus, Dom. It's just a white belt match. What's gotten into you? The girl's fine."

His words snap me out of my panic-stricken haze. Immediately.

When I look around, I realize this entire corner of the

arena is quiet, every person staring. I've been to hundreds of tournaments in my career, and none of them have ever been brought to a standstill because of me.

I don't know what to do beyond rushing back to Skylar. "Are you sure you're okay?" I ask, pulling her to her feet now that she doesn't seem winded or dazed.

"Yeah, I'm fine," she assures me. "I promise. I'm okay."

The awkwardness hits me with full blast. Jacob senses it too, because when I turn back to him, he snaps back to referee mode.

"Competitors, back on the mat," he orders. I move back to my coach's chair and watch as the girls take their spots in the center of the mat.

"Due to an illegal slam, I'm ruling the match a disqualification. Blue Team is officially the winner of the white belt division." He raises Skylar's hand, but the only celebration heard is a smattering of hesitant clapping.

To her credit, Skylar's opponent doesn't seem annoyed by the decision. I begrudgingly admit to myself that she looks apologetic when she shakes Skylar's hand.

That expression turns to fear when she approaches me. It's common practice for fighters to shake the hands of their opponent's coaches, but after everything, I wouldn't have been surprised if she had forgone that step.

When she does stop in front of me, she immediately apologizes. I've cooled down enough to be able to respond like a rational human being, not an insane, overprotective bastard.

"I'm sorry I yelled at you," I murmur.

She nods. "It's okay. I understand."

I'm still tense as the division ends and everyone moves away from the mat. I follow Skylar to the podium where the medals are given out, refusing to meet anyone's eyes as we move through the crowd. And I can definitely feel eyes on me.

I take the usual picture of my student winning a medal, but afterwards, I have no idea what to do with myself. The next division my fighters are in isn't for another hour, so I have nothing else to distract me from my loud overreaction that was completely out of character and noticed by way too many people. Including my own instructors. I don't see Jax or Tristan anywhere, but I'm already anticipating a few odd looks in the gym next week.

I don't know if I'm thankful or worried when Skylar finally takes a long look at me, sighs, and then drags me out of the arena.

33

SKYLAR

Thankfully, it's pretty easy to find an empty room in this place. Away from the open arena of the building, there are plenty of locker rooms and meeting rooms for coaches and players, so it takes me no time at all to drag Dominic into one of them. When I close the door behind us and turn to face him, he doesn't even look surprised that I pulled him aside.

"Dominic," I start gently. "I promise I'm okay. I wouldn't lie to you if I was hurt."

He looks over me for the millionth time, his skepticism obvious. "Not even a headache? Ribs don't hurt from where she slammed you?"

I shake my head. "She didn't slam me on my head. She knocked the wind out of me when it happened, but I swear I'm okay." I wince. "Although, there's a good chance my forearms will be so sore tomorrow that I can't lift any plates at work. Why didn't you tell me grip-fighting is so exhausting?"

Finally, he huffs a laugh, and some of the tension melts away. After a moment, he lets out a heavy breath and closes the distance between us to pull me into his arms.

He holds me tight against his body, his cheek pressed to my hair. Wrapping my arms around his waist, I let him anchor himself how he needs to.

"I had a fighter get slammed once," he says quietly. It's been minutes, and by the obvious sound of pain in his voice, it took him that long to work up the courage to say it.

"What happened?" I whisper.

Another hesitation. More pain.

"He's paralyzed from the waist down."

I pull back in shock to meet his eyes. "What?!"

His normally expressionless face looks grief-stricken. *This is why he freaked out.*

"He's paralyzed from the waist down," he repeats. "He was the best fighter I ever had, and coming up on the peak of his career, and…" He swallows roughly. "It was a freak accident. MMA barely ever has long-term injuries. But it's been almost two years, and he still can't— I mean, he's still in a wheelchair, and when that girl slammed you, all I could think about was that happening to *you*, and I just—I couldn't—"

I cup his face and push up on my toes to bring our foreheads together. "It *didn't* happen to me," I whisper. "I understand now why it scared you, but nothing happened. I'm fine." Bringing his hands to my face, I will him to feel my beating heart through my pulse point.

His heavy breath washes over my face. *Finally,* he seems to have found relief, free of the event and the resulting memory. He holds me like something precious that he wants to protect.

With the tension finally gone from his body, I voice the question that's been running through my mind since my match ended. The one that could potentially change a lot of things.

"Do...do you think you think you shouldn't coach me? If it scares you this much?"

He pulls back with a frown.

"Because it's still a violent sport," I hurriedly tack on. "And chances of me getting hurt sometimes aren't small. Will it scare you like that every time? Should you not be in my corner?"

He shakes his head, hard. "No. No, I *want* to be there. I want to be your coach. I'll be fine, I swear. It just... It caught me off guard how much I—"

When he swallows and looks away, my brain can't help coming up with the end of that sentence. *How much I wanted you to win? How much I fear for your safety?*

How much I care about you?

God, I wish I could know what was going through his mind. I wish I knew how he feels about me. Because, in his arms and this empty room, after a scary moment where he cared for me in a way no one ever has...I feel more connected to him than I ever thought possible.

I didn't know I could feel this way about a person. I didn't know I could be *drawn* to someone like this. To feel so protected, so safe, that for the first time in my life, I feel like I can actually take a breath. And let my guard down.

With Dominic, I can just...*be.*

I swallow roughly and force my muscles to relax. This is the worst time to realize I'm developing real, big feelings for someone that I shouldn't be developing feelings for. Especially because we had a clear understanding between us about what this was, and I have zero read on whether that's changed for him.

My hopeful, youthful brain immediately points out that he just freaked out in front of everyone because he thought I was injured—of course, he cares about me.

But the realistic, cynical part of my brain immediately counters with the reminder that fighters getting slammed is simply a sore spot.

"I *do* want to be your coach," he says firmly, pulling me out of my thoughts before I can spiral. "This was just a freak occurrence. I'll be okay next time, I promise." He gives me a tremulous grin, obviously trying to lighten the mood. "Besides, I got you the win, didn't I? My coaching must not have been *that* bad."

I narrow my eyes at him. "*You* got me the win? I'm sorry, did you have someone sitting on top of *you?*"

The corner of his lip twitches, amusement shining in his eyes. "No, I did not. That was all you."

I sniff. "Personally, I think the anal sex was good luck."

He barks out a laugh, looking happier and more relaxed than I've ever seen him.

"You're such a little weirdo." Chuckling, he grips me by the waist and pulls me close. "I would never guess half the thoughts in your head."

"You love it," I quip, wrapping my arms around his neck with a grin.

His smile softens. "I guess I do."

God, I don't even care if his feelings aren't developing like mine are. Even if I only get it behind closed doors, I'll take this happy, carefree version of Dominic any day.

He takes my mouth in a slow, sweet kiss. It's different from the way he usually kisses me, but no less mind-melting. In barely a few seconds, I've gone breathless and limp in his arms.

Eventually, he pulls away. "I should probably go corner the rest of your teammates."

I hum in agreement and steal another kiss.

"But maybe I can convince you to come home with me afterwards?" he asks.

I try to tamp down on my grin and fail miserably. "I think that can be arranged."

He looks like he might be trying to hide his elation as he nods.

But I see it. Because I feel the exact same way.

On the way to Dominic's place, we stop at my house to pick up a change of clothes. I know Joey is at one of his friends' houses tonight, but I have no idea what Mom and Maria are up to. I can't decide how I feel about them meeting, or even spotting, Dominic.

But the nerves bubble as we pull up in front of my house. I open my mouth to ask Dominic to stay in the car while I run in, but that plan evaporates almost immediately. Because Maria is walking up the sidewalk right beside us, her arms full of so many groceries that I have no idea how she can see through the half a dozen brown paper bags. And then one of them slips, and a bag of apples falls, and Dominic is jumping out of the car before I can make a move.

He scoops the apples from the ground before taking the bag they fell from right out of Maria's arms. And then he takes another. And another.

"Here, let me help you carry those in," he says in that deliciously deep murmur. "I swear, they make these bags thinner and thinner every year."

"Why, thank you," Maria says, a pleased smile on her face. She turns to me and, in that blunt way of hers, says, "I don't know who this man is, but I like him already."

I let out an awkward chuckle. Beyond Joey, I haven't told

anyone about Dominic. I have no idea how anyone is going to react to him.

"Maria, this is Dominic. My...friend."

Dominic smiles over top of the bags. "It's a pleasure to meet you, ma'am."

Maria waves him off. "Oh, please, ma'am makes me feel old. Just call me Maria." But she gives him an appreciative look as she moves toward the steps to our house. "But your manners are impeccable. I like you more and more by the second."

I could swear a blush warms Dominic's cheeks. He seems almost...*eager* as we all walk into the house.

"Where's Mom?" I ask as I start to unpack the bags of groceries.

"She had just laid down for a nap when I left," Maria answers as she does the same. "She said it was her first one today, so I'm expecting her to be out for a while."

My head snaps up. "Her *first* one? What did she do all day?"

A smile tugs at Maria's lips. "Read a book, crocheted a bit, met a friend for coffee. The usual."

"She *what?*"

Maria stops trying to hide her excitement. She looks up and meets my gaze, and we share a silent moment of surprised glee. Because even though Maria's been an incredible help these past few months, Mom's disease unfortunately still gives her more bad days than good ones. Which means this news has me wanting to both scream in excitement and break down sobbing in Maria's arms.

"I was going to let her sleep," my little miracle worker says, turning back to the ingredients in front of her. "Meanwhile, I figured I'd whip up a little dinner so Joey has something he can grab before his work shift tomorrow." Her eyebrows rise in Dominic's direction. "Unless I can interest you in staying for dinner? I assumed Skylar would be at work tonight, but since you're here... You look like you'd appreciate some homemade gnocchi."

Dominic lets out an appreciative groan. "I haven't had homemade gnocchi since I was a little boy. My grandmother used to make it." His eyes brighten when he turns to me. "I haven't made any family recipes in years. We should stay in one night, and I'll cook for you."

"Ah, *and* he's Italian." Maria looks to me, nodding her approval. "I told you I liked him more by the second. You should definitely ask him to stay for dinner."

Dominic looks like he's already salivating over the offer, but all I can think about is how badly I want to be alone with him tonight. Maria, bless her heart, sees right through me.

"Listen to me, trying to take over your whole night." She waves me off. "Ignore me. You kids probably already have plans."

I chew on my lip, debating how much to reveal. But when I lock eyes with Dominic, I find myself admitting, "I was actually thinking of staying at Dominic's place tonight. Since Joey will be home."

Maria's smile takes over her face. "I think that's a great idea! You're long overdue for a night off. I've been telling you that you need to take time for yourself."

Dominic gives me a look that screams *I told you so.*

In answer, I send him a playful glare. But when that makes him chuckle and press a kiss to my temple, I can't stop the giddy, girlish smile from appearing on my face.

"Get out of here, you two, we'll be just fine here," she says. Then she points a finger at Dominic. "But I'm going to make enough gnocchi to feed an Italian family, so I expect you to take some of it the next time you're here."

"Yes, ma'am," Dominic says with a grin. "Can I help you while Skylar packs her bag?"

Maria doesn't seem surprised by the offer; she just points at the pot on the stove. "You sure can. You can start by boiling those potatoes."

While Dominic sets to work, I hurry upstairs. I grab a quick shower to scrub the sweat from my skin, and the entire time, I can't wipe the giddy smile off my face.

I'm throwing random clothes into a bag, when my mom appears in the doorway.

"Mom," I say in surprise. "I didn't think you'd be awake. Maria said you had a busy day today."

Her smile is tired, but not in a pained way. I rush over to her and help her take a seat on my bed.

"I heard you come home, and I wanted to ask you how your tournament went," she says.

"It was great. I won gold in my division."

Pride lights in her eyes. "That's amazing, Skylar. Congratulations." Her focus shifts to my bag. "Are you going somewhere to celebrate?"

Guilt immediately floods my veins. I shouldn't leave her. I need to be *here*. She needs me.

Her skin is cold against mine as she takes my hand and pulls me down beside her. I turn my conflicted gaze toward her, doing nothing to hide the war in my eyes.

"Skylar, you *should* be celebrating," she says softly. "You just accomplished something incredible, and you deserve to have some fun. You don't need to take care of me all the time."

"Yes, I do," I whisper. "I love you— I need to be here to take care of you. Nothing is more important than that."

"Oh, honey." Pulling me closer, she wraps her arms around me. "You've always been the most caring person. Even when you were a little girl, you'd always give the last piece of your snacks to anyone that looked like they wanted a bite. You've always thought about others more than yourself."

I turn my face into my mother's shoulder, not knowing how to respond but soaking up her comfort anyway.

"It's the most lovable and admirable thing about you," she says. "It's what I've *always* loved about you. But...I should've taught you a long time ago that there's a limit. That your happiness is always going to be more important than others. Than me."

I startle and straighten. "How can you say that? *Nothing* is more important than you. Than our family. That's all we have!"

Her smile is sad as she cups my cheek in her hand. "Family and obligation can't be your whole life, Skylar. That's no life at all."

My lower lip starts to tremble. Because how can she say that? If my family isn't what I base my life and every decision around, then nothing makes sense in the world.

"I don't know how to live any other way," I admit on a whisper.

"I know," she soothes, her eyes shining with tears as she strokes my hair. "But you owe it to yourself to try. You *deserve* to be happy. Taking time for yourself doesn't make you a selfish daughter, or a bad sister. It makes you *human*."

I look down at my lap, trying to choke back my emotions. Part of me knows she's right. It's the same thing Dominic, and even Joey, have been trying to tell me. I just never expected it to be this hard.

"Will you tell me what your plans for tonight are

supposed to be?" she asks. "I should know what my daughter's idea of fun is." When I lift my eyes to meet hers, I see her make a face. "Not that I'm likely to understand it: it doesn't matter how many fights I watch, I can't understand the appeal of rolling around with sweaty men while they try to kill you."

A laugh bursts out of me, and a warmth fills my chest. I had no idea my mom did any research into MMA. I never doubted that she loved me, or that she would support me if she could, I just always assumed her life revolved around her sickness, the same way that mine did. But hearing that she's happy enough about my new hobby to do some research into it...it lifts one of the thousand weights on my shoulders.

"Well, you probably won't understand *this* idea of fun, either," I tell her, mischief infusing my words. It feels good. "I started dating my thirty-six-year-old coach."

I think I expect surprise, or some kind of scolding—maybe a part of me is hoping for it, for some normalcy.

But if there was any remaining doubt in my mind that my mom truly wants me to be happy, it disappears when she says with delight, "Are you kidding me? That sounds *exactly* like my idea of fun. If I could stop falling long enough to go on a date, those would be the *only* parameters I would put into that Hinge app."

By now, I'm laughing through my words. "Why do you know what Hinge is, Mom?"

She winks at me. "Don't ask questions you don't want the answers to. But stop trying to change the subject. Is it serious? Is he good-looking? What's his name? How dare you not share the hot tea with me."

"Mom," I chuckle. "First of all, it's just tea, not hot tea. But I'll tell you all about him, I promise. Maybe tomorrow?

When I get home? I'll pick up our favorite snacks and we can make an afternoon of it."

"That sounds perfect," she says with a warm smile.

And then she's hugging me, squeezing me for long seconds. "You deserve to be happy, Skylar," she whispers into my hair. "*Go be happy.*"

I squeeze her back, unable to do anything but nod my acknowledgement, my gratitude, my love for her. I had no idea how badly I needed to have this conversation with her. But in only a few minutes, I feel lighter than I have in months.

When we separate, we're both smiling. But then she smirks and says, "So you're staying out all night, huh? Guess I don't need to worry about you having fun, then."

"Mom!" I shriek.

She feigns innocence. "What? I just told you I support it."

I'm shaking my head as I stand and help her to her feet, but I can't tamp down on my smile. "You're ridiculous. Come on, I'll help you back to bed."

We start toward her room, but then something occurs to me, and I stop in the doorway.

"Actually, you feel up for a meet-and-greet right now?"

———

I wake up to the sun streaming through the two-story windows of Dominic's loft apartment. I reach beside me for his body, but at the same time my hand only hits pillow, the sounds of someone in the kitchen registers in my brain.

Arching, I stretch my arms over my head, the sheets brushing against my naked body. Dominic was gentle with me last night after the tournament, but I still feel sated and slightly sore. I also feel well-rested—I can't remember the last time I slept in.

All that has me feeling more content than I ever have.

That feeling multiplies tenfold when I hear the creak of Dominic coming up the stairs.

When he appears, he has a mug of coffee in one hand and a plate in the other, piled high with scrambled eggs and avocado toast. But I barely notice any of that, because I can't take my attention off of the man himself.

He's shirtless, every one of his mouth-watering muscles on display from the waist up. I'm so glad he doesn't train shirtless at the gym because there's not a doubt in my mind that I wouldn't be able to focus if he did.

Although, that focus is nowhere to be found right now, either. Because the man is barefoot and wearing sweat-pants. This casual look is enough to make me combust as is, but add in the coffee mug and breakfast plate, and this relaxed, domesticated version of him is beyond intoxicating.

When he sees me and smiles, my heart stutters its next beat. And I realize that I've fallen completely in love with this man.

Maybe it's because he was such an incredible support yesterday—caring and helpful, but without being over-whelming. Maybe it's because my conversation with my mom eliminated the last of my guilt over being happy.

Maybe it's because of the way he's looking at me right now.

Whatever it is, the full force of the emotion hits me. And it doesn't feel stifling, or heavy, the way I always thought it would.

It feels like a warm blanket—comforting and protective.

And just like every other time I'm in Dominic's presence,

the tension I live with leaves my body, to be replaced by more happiness than I ever thought I was capable of.

"Morning," he greets in a deep, sleep-roughened voice.

"Hi," I respond with a giddy smile. When I push myself to sit up, I wince at the soreness in my muscles.

Dominic chuckles as he places everything on the night-stand beside me. "Yeah, I figured you'd be sore." He leans over to press a sweet kiss to my lips. "Don't worry, I'll give you a massage after breakfast."

My body warms at the thought. "Something tells me I'll end up sore in *other* places if you do that."

He looks like a naughty teenager when he grins and says, "Guilty."

He hands me my coffee and takes a seat on the bed beside me. When I take a sip, I'm not surprised to realize it's exactly how I like it: strong, with a splash of creamer and too much sugar. In typical Dominic fashion, he silently memo-rized my coffee preference.

"So how long do I have you for today?" he asks, pulling me from my swooning thoughts.

I take another sip before I answer. "I have to leave at noon. I want to check in with Joey, but I also told Mom we'd hang out before I go into work at the restaurant tonight."

Dominic nods, his hand starting to caress my thigh. The corner of his lip twitches with a grin as he says, "Joey blew up my phone yesterday. He was pissed he couldn't get off work, and he wanted to know every detail of your match, but he didn't want to bother you with it."

I startle and turn toward Dominic. "What? Really? Since when do you two have each other's numbers?"

"I gave it to him when he got the job at the pizza place. I wanted him to have it in case he needed it." He doesn't look at me when he says it, which gives away more than his words do. He wanted to be able to help if something happened with Mom or with me.

He wanted to stay close enough to take care of me. Of us.

I place a hand on his arm to signal my answer. That I know him well enough to know he's not doing it because he thinks I *can't*—he's doing it because he *cares*.

"I'm glad Joey feels like he can rely on you," I say softly.

I *feel* the tension leave his muscles. He gives me a relieved smile, his hand landing on my thigh and caressing my skin. "You're a good daughter, Skylar," he says. "And sister. Your family is lucky to have you."

My throat constricts from the weight of emotions. He must sense how hard it hits me because his expression softens when he looks at me.

"I'm really glad I got to meet your mom last night. I'm glad your family knows about us." He pauses, searching my eyes and making my stomach flip. "I want more people to know about us."

Suddenly, my throat tightens for a whole other reason. "You want to tell other people about us?"

He never looks away from me. He just nods. He doesn't look scared by the idea.

"Are you honestly ready to go public at the gym?" I ask, a little incredulously.

Finally, he sighs and lets me into his thoughts. "Okay, fine, probably not today. I need to figure out the best way to tell Tristan and Jax. But...do I want to stop hiding you in my house and sneaking around the gym? Yes." He gives me a possessive look. "Do I want to hold your hand in public and make it clear that you're mine? Also, yes."

The warmth of love entwines with the heat of passion, filling every corner of my body and turning into an overwhelming *need* for this man. In every sense. Physically, emotionally, spiritually, all of it.

I place my mug on the nightstand so I can slide my leg over Dominic's and settle in his lap, my arms winding around his neck to pull myself as close as possible. I want everything he's saying, but I also know there are enough things at risk and that we need to be careful. "Are you sure?" I ask quietly. "This will change a lot."

His hands settle on my waist, and I'm relieved when he takes a few moments to think about the question again. But I'm not surprised when he says, "I'm sure. Because I realized yesterday that it killed me when I couldn't pull you into my arms when you got hurt, or kiss you when they put the gold medal around your neck. I hate hiding you away, Skylar— you don't deserve it, but also, I don't *want* to. I want you with me. I want you as *mine*. I don't care about what anyone else thinks."

I can only stare at him. This is huge, and *he's* making the first step, because he feels this too.

"We don't need to decide anything today, I just wanted to put it out there," he interrupts my thoughts. And I realize I haven't given him an answer, I've just been staring at him.

"I want that too," I rush to tell him. "I want to tell people. I want to tell *everyone*."

The smile that stretches across his face is blinding. And then he's kissing me, showing me every ounce of his happiness, his adoration—maybe even his love.

34

DOMINIC

When Monday morning comes around, I'm still stuck in the haze of the weekend. Normally, I'm up early so I can get to the weightlifting gym for a session before I have to teach the pros class at noon. I've always made sure I start my week off on a proactive, productive tract, so Mondays have always been busy.

Looking back, I think part of me was running from the loneliness of the weekend.

Today, though, I don't want to rush to the gym. I want to spend the last few hours before the week starts remembering my time with Skylar. I even slept in this morning just so I could spend a few extra moments soaking in her scent that she left on my sheets.

She wants me. She wants more.

I feel the millionth smile lift my lips at the thought. The usual terror—at the thought of a relationship, or at the thought of making *this* a relationship—doesn't come.

By 10 a.m., I can't keep procrastinating with memories of Skylar's taste, or the look on her face when I said I wanted to tell people about us. I have to get to the gym and be a functioning human being again.

I'm grabbing my keys and donning my coat when I realize I never took my phone off *Do Not Disturb* after Skylar left.

The second I switch off the setting, my phone starts pinging with alerts. Calls, text messages, notifications across multiple social media sites... My phone *blows up*.

I don't even know where to start. I rarely get texts, and my social media presence for the gym is meager. I have no idea what could spur notifications like these.

I settle on my text messages. I see Tristan's and Jax's names at the top, so I click on Tristan's first.

Tristan: Call me ASAP

Jax's is slightly wordier.

Jax: Coach, call me AS SOON as you get this. Don't check socials, just call me or Tristan. It's an emergency.

So, of course, I click over to Instagram.

It's riddled with comment notifications and tags. My stomach had already started filling with dread, but the second before I click the first notification, it eats up my whole body, too.

The gym is tagged in a picture of Skylar winning her gold medal over the weekend by the tournament organization. Underneath it, there are over twenty comments already.

Is this the gym that's run by that creepy instructor?

I heard she's one of his older girls. He probably likes them underage.

So do you think he fucked her before or after she won the gold medal?

Bile fills my throat. My head spins, and I have to grab onto the back of the couch to keep from collapsing.

No, no, no, this can't be happening. They can't know. No one can know.

I can barely make my fingers work enough to switch over to the gym profile. Under our latest post, there are similar comments.

Was that girl even legal?

The fact that women can't catch a fucking break in the MMA world. Men are pigs.

Bulldog MMA: where you send your daughters and girl-friends to get mounted.

I fight the urge to dry heave. This is... This is insane. This is so much worse than anything my brain could have conjured up.

I don't know what makes my rational brain turn on again. It feels like I stand in the middle of my living room for hours, frozen in horror and shock. But eventually I remember the texts.

My hands are trembling when I call Tristan. He picks up on the first ring.

"Hey." I can't hear anything in his voice. "Where are you?"

"Home," I reply in a monotone voice. "I was about to leave for the gym."

There's a pause. Then, "Have you checked your email?"

My eyes slide closed. "No. I got stuck on Instagram."

"Stay on the phone with me while you check it."

My motions are robotic as I follow someone else's orders for once. Putting Tristan on speaker, I switch over to my Gmail app.

It was sent at 11 p.m. last night, from an anonymous sender.

My gut already senses what's in the email before I open it.

And I'm right. There are pictures of Skylar and me at the gym. In some, we're only kissing, but in a few, the sexual undertones are clear—the worst one is a picture of me on top of Skylar on the mat, my teeth latched onto her nipple through her tank top and my hand down the front of her shorts.

There's no nudity, but it's explicit enough to make it obvious that we're about to have sex.

There are half a dozen images at the top of the email. It's the first thing I see when I open it. But as I start to scroll down, my lungs constricting with every inch, I realize there's more.

This is Dominic Caruso, owner and head instructor of Bulldog MMA in Center City Philadelphia. You've likely heard his name before, as he was a well-known fighter in the professional MMA circuit until he retired and opened a gym. For years, it's been a well-respected, successful gym. But only because no one knew what was lurking beneath the surface.

Pictured above is Skylar Vega, one of Bulldog MMA's newest students. Skylar is a freshman at Temple University. As a pre-nursing student, Skylar was looking for a way to de-stress outside of work and classes, and decided to pick up MMA. She had no idea she was about to walk into every young woman's nightmare.

It took no time at all for Dominic to take advantage of this young, helpless student. Being seventeen years her senior, Dominic made quick use of their power imbalance, alienating her from the gym's other instructors and even going so far as to offer Skylar a job so he could further tie her to him. Skylar might not even really see his monster behavior for what it is—as a skilled predator, Dominic may have even brainwashed her into thinking 'he's never done this before,' and that he 'only loves her.' We can only guess how deep the horrors of Bulldog MMA go.

I can't read the rest of the email. I skim the second half, my eyes landing on a few phrases that make acid rise up my throat.

Predator... grooming... underage girls...

In the end, I do throw up. I rush to the bathroom and vomit every bit of the breakfast I made myself this morning. I have a bizarre, errant thought about the irony that I made that breakfast while thinking about Skylar, barely twenty minutes ago.

I don't remember that I kept Tristan on the phone until I'm sucking in water from the faucet and see my phone on the sink beside it. Somehow, he stayed on the line through all of that.

Leaning both hands on the sink, I let my head hang between my shoulders. "Tristan," I say, my voice sounding like it's been dragged over gravel. "You there?"

"I'm here, Coach," he says. And his voice is gentle. He stayed on the phone with me because he knew he needed to, and I feel a wave of gratitude.

"It's not what it looks like," I tell him. "It's not... I'm not *fucking* her. I mean...it's more than that. I think I—I couldn't —and *Christ*, there are no other girls, I would never—"

"Take a deep breath, Dom," Tristan interrupts. "You have to stay calm with this. We're going to figure this out, but you have to keep your head on for me, alright? You with me?"

I suck in a deep, shaky breath. "Yeah, I'm here. I'm good."

"Jax and I are trying to get the Reddit thread taken down, but I don't know how long it's going to take. We—"

"It got posted to Reddit?" Nothing should horrify me at this point, so I don't know why that does.

"Yeah. Whoever sent the email last night also posted it at the same time. We can't figure out where it came from. I just need you to hold tight, okay?"

I nod, even though he can't see me.

"Go to the gym, Jax and I are on our way over. We'll figure out what to do, I promise."

"Okay," I answer in a daze. "I'll meet you over there." And then I hang up.

When my phone rings a few seconds later, I think my brain assumes it's Tristan again. I don't know, I can't think straight. I hit answer.

"Dom?"

I frown. *That's not Tristan.*

Pulling the phone away from my ear, I realize it's one of my friends who owns a gym himself over in New Jersey about an hour outside of the city.

"Andy?"

"Yeah, it's me."

But he doesn't say anything else. And it hits me immediately.

"You saw it, didn't you?"

A pause. "Yeah. I did."

I swallow roughly and force myself to ask, "Was it... Was it sent to you?"

Another hesitation. "Yeah. We all got the email."

"*We?*" I choke out.

"Yeah. All the Philly and Jersey coaches. We got the email last night. And then... We saw all the comments on social media."

Fuck. Fuck fuck fuck.

"Jesus, Dom, a *teenager?* What the hell were you thinking?"

"It's not... It's not what it looks like." *Is this what my whole day is going to be like? That on repeat?*

Suddenly, I need out of this conversation. I need air.

"Andy, it's not what it looks like. I swear. Just...trust me a little, okay? I've gotta go."

I hang up before he can respond.

And then I'm grabbing my keys and Brutus and leaving for the gym.

I don't remember any of the drive, because parts of me are still running on autopilot. But I think I'm hoping I'll snap out of it at the gym, or somehow magically figure out how to fix this. *Because I have to fix this.*

Jax and Tristan are already at the gym when I get there. When I walk in the door, their conversation stops, and their heads turn toward me.

I stop where I am and just stare at them. I have no fucking clue what to say.

What are they thinking? Do they think less of me? Do they believe any of that post?

"It's not what it looks like," I blurt out. *Definitely on repeat.* I focus on Jax and tell him the same thing I told Tristan. "I'm not just fucking her. None of it is true."

Jax, the kind soul that he is, recognizes my desperate need to be comforted. "We know. Coach, we know. We're not judging you, I swear."

It's only a fraction of what my body is filled with, but some tension leaves my shoulders. I give him a nod.

He turns to look at Tristan. "We're trying to get the thread taken down on harassment grounds, but it's taking a while. We know the pictures were taken without consent, but there's no way to prove that. And since there's no nudity, and Skylar isn't actually underage, the pictures aren't technically an issue. So, we're pushing hard on the bullying and harassment violations."

Another nod, because that's apparently all I'm capable of. I shuck my jacket off and collapse on the couch, with Brutus climbing up next to me and dropping his head into my lap only a moment later.

"We canceled pro training," Tristan says. "The guys who are fighting are coming in tonight, but I assumed we'd want to use the day to figure out what to do."

When I don't respond, Jax is the one to speak, shooting Tristan a nervous glance. "Should we...make a statement?"

Tristan immediately shakes his head. "We have to wrap our heads around it first. Get the post taken down, figure out who leaked it and *why*, and *then* we can figure out what to post publicly. We're not in any condition to say anything right now."

His glance at me obviously translates that to *I'm* not in a condition to say anything. And he's right—I'm so fucked, I don't know which way is up.

I barely register Jax's voice when he says my name. He has to repeat it twice before I lift my gaze to his.

His expression is sympathetic, and his voice calming. Typical Jax. "Do you want to talk about it?"

I blink in answer.

He tries again, and I realize for the first time that these two have been actively fighting the urge to ask me about Skylar. *I don't deserve them.* "Can you tell us something about how it happened? If we know what the relationship is like, we can fight this a little better."

"I..." I swallow and try again. "It just...happened. I tried not to, but she's..." *Fuck, I can't get anything out.*

"Do you love her?" Jax asks quietly.

My eyes widen. How is it that, out of everything, *that* feels like the most bizarre question?

"I don't know," I respond in a monotone. "And I'm not going to figure that out in a mess like this."

Cutting his losses, Jax nods and turns back to Tristan. "Let's just get that post down. We can figure out what to say to the other gyms later."

They don't ask me any other questions. But as soon as they walk away, Jax's question starts ringing in my head. And it hits me that this is the first time I'm thinking of Skylar in all this.

Fuck. Skylar. Does she know?

I fumble for my phone in my pocket. I have to scroll through way too many notifications, on way too many apps, before I can pull up my text messages and scroll through those, too. Part of me hopes to see Skylar's name pop up, but a bigger part hopes it doesn't.

Nope. No text. Thank God. Maybe she hasn't seen it?

My thumb trembles over her name. Even if she hasn't seen it yet, there's no way she won't eventually. We need to talk about it. We need to figure out what to do.

We need to figure out what this means for us.

I hit the *Call* button next to her name before I can think better of it. I have no idea what I'm going to say to her, I just know I need to hear her voice. I need to know she's okay, and that we're going to survive this.

Four rings later, I get her voicemail. My eyes slide closed at the sound of her voice, so close to what I need, but also so, so far. I hang up before the beep, not wanting to leave a voicemail of me stammering through a chaotic non-message.

Instead, I open our text messages. I'm barely a texter, so all of our exchanges so far have been matter-of-fact messages with questions and one-line answers. There are no *good morning* or *how was your day?* messages, because every time I had those thoughts, I just wanted to see her and say it in person. A text wasn't nearly enough.

But it hits me in this moment that I might never get any more contact with Skylar. This might be the thing that changes her mind about us, that alienates her from me and removes her from my life. Because who would want to be with someone whose relationship causes you to be ridiculed and judged by an entire community? Hell, maybe even the city. If the social media comments are this bad from a single picture, what are people going to say in public when they see us together?

I would never want Skylar to experience that. Never.

So I force myself to type out a text that I never let myself think I would ever send. And I think my heart breaks a little as I send it.

> Dominic: Hey. I'm sure you'll see the post and comments at some point, so I wanted to

I delete the message. *Fuck, I have no idea what to say here.*

Just wanted to reach out and see where your head's at? See if you still want me, even though this is so much fucking worse than what we were scared of?

I try again.

> Dominic: Hey. Give me a call whenever you can. We need to talk.

I hit send before I can second-guess it. But then I realize how cold that sounds, and I type another one.

> Dominic: I'm so sorry. About everything. I never wanted you to get hurt in any of this. Pain is the last thing I wanted to bring to your life.

I hesitate, then slowly type another and send.

> Dominic: Whatever you want to do, I understand. I'll support your decision.

And now I just...wait.

I manage to distract myself with a workout, and with watching some fights with Brutus. Though I can't remember any fighters or any of the results.

Jax comes over at one point to tell me the post got taken down. When I don't respond with any kind of relief, he tells me he'll take over teaching classes tonight. That I should go home. But as tempting as that is, I can't do it. Not just because my pride in being a good coach is the only thing I'm hanging onto for dear life, but also because I know Monday is Skylar's training day.

And even though I suspect it's highly unlikely she'll come in, I can't bring myself to potentially miss the opportunity to see her.

So, I stay. I stay and I teach my classes, ignoring the occasional whispers and frequent glances. I numb myself to all of it. Because there's nothing else I can do.

I need to get out of here. I need this day to end. I need *out*.

By the time I'm driving home, I think I'm done taking hits for the day. But when I walk into my house, I realize there's one more coming.

Because there's an email in my inbox from the UFC with the subject line: *Hall of Fame Induction Rescinded.*

35

SKYLAR

Of course, I saw the post.

I saw the comments, too. As soon as my phone started blowing up with notifications from comments on a tagged photo, I knew something was up. My heart dropped into my stomach before I even opened any of them.

And when I finally did, my heart broke.

"No," I breathe, clicking through social media and then the Reddit thread on my break at the café. "No, no, this can't be happening. This isn't happening."

Who did this? Who took those pictures? And why would they want to hurt me?

But then it hits me that I'm not the one who's being hit right now. I mean, there are a few comments about me being a whore, but I've gotten that comment based on an outfit choice—that's not unusual. What's bad is the way Dominic is being painted. *Dominic* is carrying the brunt of this attack.

And it's so much worse than I thought it would be. I know we talked about what we were risking by being together, but in my head, I only pictured a few judgmental looks and maybe some whispers in the very beginning. I never, ever thought it could be like this. With words like *predator* and *grooming* being thrown around, this could very easily be a career-ender for Dominic.

And me? I just get pity. I'm seen as the victim, with no consequences whatsoever.

While Dominic loses his reputation.

How was I ever naïve enough to think I was worth it for him?

I see Dominic's call and texts come through on my way to class. I've been trying to work up the nerve all day to call him, but every time my thumb would hover over his name, I would chicken out. There's nothing I could say that would make this better for him. Why does he even want to talk to me?

But typical Dominic, his texts show that he's worried about *me*. That he's sorry about causing me pain.

How could anyone question his character? Accuse him, *of all people, of something this heinous?*

Sorrow churns like acid in my stomach, clashing with the love I feel for Dominic, the love that's been blooming inside me for this caring, intelligent, protective man who I couldn't keep from falling head over heels for. The rush of emotions, both positive and negative, are enough to make me dizzy.

But they pale in comparison to the crushing guilt. I can't *breathe* from it. Because all of this is my fault.

I was the one who came onto Dominic in the first place. It doesn't matter that we had a clear and honest conversation about it or that he agreed to everything—I was always the one with the power between us, because I never had anything to lose. *I* should've protected him.

I won't let him down again.

I'm sitting in class when I finally make my decision.

I don't respond to Dominic's texts. And I don't go to the

gym after class, even though Mondays are my usual gym nights. Knowing what I need to do is one thing, but I couldn't handle doing it in person.

Instead, I distract myself with work. I swap a shift with a coworker at the restaurant, working Monday but freeing up my Tuesday.

Dominic isn't at the gym on Tuesdays. It's the only night I know he's not there, because Tuesday afternoon is the time he goes to the inner-city park to teach the kids boxing.

Even that thought makes me want to cry. Why isn't *that* the story that goes viral?

So, I don't go to the gym on Monday. But I go after class on Tuesday, hoping I'm early enough that there aren't any students in the building. I didn't even think about how other fighters might look at me—although looking at the comments still coming in on social media, I should expect dirty looks, at the very least.

Thankfully, when I walk into the gym, Jax is the only one there. He looks up from the reception desk and does a double take.

"Hey," he greets quickly as he stands up. "You're here."

I force a smile. "I'm here."

I have no idea what to say to him. I'm sure going public with my relationship with Dominic would've been a little awkward and stressful, but no one is ever prepared to have it happen with intimate, personal photos of yourself. I hate that this is how Jax found out.

The look he gives me is one of mostly worry, and some pity. "Are you... Are you okay?"

I bark out a laugh. "No."

He nods and looks down. "I know. I'm sorry."

I've had plenty of moments in my life where I thought

about giving up, but until this moment, I've never actually wanted to. I want this to be over.

"Look, I need to terminate my membership," I tell Jax in a flat tone. "I know I'm not paying anymore, so there's no card to cancel, but I wanted to let the gym know that I won't be coming back. I'm sorry if that messes up the cleaning work, but I think it's better for everyone if I'm not here."

Jax's eyes widen. "Skylar, no. Don't do this."

"I have to," I say, my voice breaking. I clear my throat and try again. "It's bad enough that he has to deal with this at all, but if I stay here? If anyone sees me around him again? He'll never be able to overcome it. At least this way, he can do some kind of damage control before he moves on."

I know I'm right when Jax immediately looks panicked. He knows I'm right.

"The only way to make this better is if I leave. It's not like there are any other teenage girls in the gym, so he doesn't have to worry about the rumors growing. Everything will die down. But I can't be around for that to happen."

"But...you love it here," Jax says, eyes searching mine.

I love him more.

I look away from Jax's sad expression. "It doesn't matter," I say quietly. "Some things are more important. I'll find another hobby."

"Skylar—"

"Thank you for everything," I interrupt, giving him a tight smile. "I loved training here. You guys have a really great gym here, you know?"

I can barely get the words out without my throat closing at the threat of tears. But Jax nods. "Yeah, I know."

I force myself to revert back to an emotionless voice,

blinking back the tears burning the backs of my eyes. "Anyway, that's all. I just wanted to tell you in person."

I turn toward the exit, intent on leaving as quickly as possible. But I don't make it through the door before I slow and look over my shoulder at Jax.

"Can you tell him I said I'm sorry?" I ask.

That look of panic appears on Jax's face again. "Skylar..."

"Please," I beg in a whisper.

Panic morphs to heartbreak, then to acceptance. "I'll tell him."

I manage a grateful smile before rushing out the front doors. I haven't broken down yet, but that...seeing the gym, and seeing what I'm giving up...that has the dam breaking. It doesn't matter that I knew subconsciously this whole time that it was going to end like this, or that I know I'm doing the right thing by distancing myself from Dominic, it's still tearing me apart.

As I walk down the street for the last time, I say a silent goodbye to Bulldog MMA, the place that became my home and my second family, and to Dominic, the man who, even if it was for a little while, brought a happiness into my life that I never knew enough to wish for.

36

DOMINIC

I'm convinced this is rock bottom. It can't get any worse than this. My social media is still being slaughtered with awful comments, and I can't get an answer back from the UFC Hall of Fame Induction Committee about my status in the Hall of Fame. But worse than all of that is I still haven't gotten Skylar to talk to me. I haven't texted her any more, but I tried calling her again yesterday, with no response.

The silence is worse than any kind of 'this is over' message that I half-expect her to send. At least with that, I'd have enough information to figure out what I need to do next. But having no idea where she stands, I'm stuck in this limbo of hope and heartbreak, and it's wearing me down.

So, I'm convinced things can't get worse. And it takes the universe five minutes to prove me wrong.

I know something happened when I walk in and see Jax already there. He never beats me to the gym. But clearly, he needs to talk to me about something, because the second I walk in with Brutus, he's jumping from the reception desk.

"Hey," he rushes out.

My eyes narrow in his direction as I drop my bag on the

floor and let Brutus off his leash. "What's going on? Why are you here early?"

Nervousness blankets his expression. *Fuck.*

"Two things," he says. "And you have to stay for the second one after you hear the first."

"Just spit it out, Jax," I bark. I can't handle any more this week. I've been bled dry.

"Skylar quit last night."

I lied. There's more of me to bleed.

My voice is stone-cold when I finally speak. "Why didn't you stop her?"

"I tried," he assures me. "But she's not a paying member, so there's not really anything to cancel. It was basically her coming in to let us know she won't be coming anymore."

I curse internally. I knew I shouldn't have gone to the local middle school yesterday. A part of me *knew* she was going to choose the one day she knows I'm not in to show up. If I didn't love working with those teenagers as much as I do, I would've skipped it. But I couldn't bring myself to take away the one day a week I know they look forward to.

"What did she say?" I ask instead.

Jax's expression is pained. "She said she feels like she has to quit. Because you might be able to do damage control on your own, but you'll never be able to move past the rumors if she's still here."

I thought my heart was already broken—turns out, *this* is what true heartbreak feels like.

Because that's my answer. She doesn't want to be around me. She doesn't want *me.* And the worst part is, it's such a *Skylar* decision. Of course, she'd be this selfless, even in a situation like this.

"Fuck," I mutter, looking around the gym as thoughts buzz through my brain. *Do I force her to talk to me? Clearly, she doesn't want to, if she came here when she knew I wouldn't be here. But I need to talk to her. And I have no idea where she even is right now.*

"She said she's sorry," Jax adds, almost apologetically. "She made me promise to tell you that."

And that decides it for me. "I have to go find her. Can you teach today?"

"Yeah, but—"

I'm already grabbing my keys and turning toward the door.

"Wait, Dom—"

I'm not listening. I have to go fix this.

"The committee is meeting right now about your Hall of Fame induction," he blurts out.

I freeze in the doorway and slowly turn my head toward him.

"They're...what?"

He looks relieved to have my attention back. "The committee is meeting right now to discuss your induction. My friend on the board just called me. The president scheduled a last-minute meeting to have everyone vote on whether they're still going to admit you."

"Jesus Christ," I murmur, dragging a hand down my face.

I kind of figured that's what they were going to do, based on their email to me. It was a very professional email, never outright addressing the rumor or saying they're going to kick me out, but I could read between the lines. They don't want a "predatory" coach in their Hall of Fame—especially since it directly contradicts the reason I was nominated.

There are multiple reasons to be inducted into the Hall of Fame: being a pioneer for the sport, having an impressive fight career, or being part of a historically important bout.

Ironically, I was nominated because of my contributions to the sport *outside* of it.

When I was fighting, I always spent a lot of time helping up-and-coming fighters. So much so, that I had plenty of people tell me that I was wasting time and energy that could be better spent making me a better fighter. But I never listened, because mentoring fighters the way I didn't really have when I was young was far more rewarding than any win I ever got. Sometimes I would even do seminars and donate the money to local schools that needed additional funding for their sports programs. The same program I spent last night teaching.

To get the induction for a reason that's bigger than my fighting talent was the best gift I could ever ask for. And the fact that it completely contradicts what I'm now being accused of is devastating.

Fuck. I have to talk to the induction committee. If they vote me out for this, my whole career disappears.

If I lose the Hall of Fame nomination, and for a reason this public, it won't just be the Philly MMA community that will shun me, it'll be the whole country. I'll lose my name, my career, everything.

"Where's the meeting?" I ask Jax.

"Downtown in the Frederick Green Building. They're starting in ten minutes."

I don't wait for anything else. Passing the first student to walk into the gym for 11 a.m. class, I beeline to my car so I can make it to the meeting will undoubtedly determine the rest of my career.

The receptionist is too stunned by my presence to stop me from entering the conference room where the meeting is being held. So, I brush right past her.

As the doors slam open louder than I intend them to, every person's attention snaps to me, and I immediately freeze in place.

The room is filled with older men. None of the board members were professional fighters themselves, but all of them have too much money and love to give their opinions about the sport and its athletes. Deciding who goes into the Hall of Fame is the ultimate power move.

And I'm now standing in front of them, ready to beg them to use that power to let me in.

Unfortunately, I didn't think this through, and now I have no idea what to say.

The president saves me the trouble of starting. "Dominic, this is a closed meeting. You aren't allowed to be in here."

I swallow roughly and start toward him on the other side of the long conference table. "I know, sir, and I'm sorry to interrupt. But I believe what I have to say directly affects your meeting."

He looks uncomfortable as he clears his throat. I don't blame him; it would be much easier for them to make a decision based on facts on paper, and without the consequences of that decision staring them in the face.

I have no idea how to convince them that I'm not some creepy old man going after a teenager without seeming like a creepy old man who's just trying to defend his actions.

"Sir, all I'm asking for is five minutes of your time. Just let me say what I need to say, and then you can make your decision with all the necessary information, and I promise, I won't contest it."

For a second, I think I have him. I think he'll let me at least say my piece, so at the very least I can feel like I *tried*.

But then he looks down at the papers in his hand, shaking his head. "I'm sorry, Dominic. That's just not appropriate."

My stomach drops. I knew this was a long shot, but I thought...if they just heard why I did it...

"But it's not what it looks—"

"I promise we will make a fair decision based on facts, but we need to make that decision without your bias," the president continues. "So please leave the room immediately. We'll notify you of our decision as soon as it's been made."

I hang my head, all hope and all energy immediately deflating from my body. *This is it. I lost.*

Just then, a muted commotion sounds from behind the door I just blasted through. Everyone turns their attention toward the loud arguing outside of the conference room.

The doors open with another bang, and a furious Tristan steps through them. Behind him are Jax and Kane, and hidden behind the three large men, I can also make out Remy, Aiden, Max, and Lucy. Each of them wears their own expression of outrage.

The pale and terrified secretary beside Tristan is trying fruitlessly to keep the group out of the room. "I'm so sorry, Mr. Barton, I told them they couldn't come in here, but—"

"It's alright, Samantha, I'll handle this," the president responds. Then he turns his focus to Tristan. "Mr. West, this is highly inappropriate behavior. Not to mention, this can only hurt your position in the UFC."

"With all due respect, Mr. Barton, I couldn't give a fuck about my position in the UFC. Not when you're unfairly jeopardizing my coach's place in it, too."

The president raises an eyebrow. "Unfairly? May I

remind you that this board has plenty of evidence to support the claims made. We're not judging based on gossip."

"You might as well be," Jax interrupts. "Because none of what was said is true."

Mr. Barton sighs. "Look, I appreciate what you all are trying to do. I respect your loyalty. But the fact of the matter is this board has decided that Dominic is no longer representing the organization in an appropriate manner—"

"He's *exactly* the kind of man you want representing your organization!"

Although the room was quiet before, Tristan's outburst stuns it into a different kind of silence. His chest is heaving, his eyes are sparking, and he's commanding everyone's attention in a way that I'm proud to see.

He takes a deep breath, gathering that iron-clad control of his. His voice is more controlled when he speaks.

"That man is the best person in this entire city's history of MMA. Forget how impressive his career was, and how good of a fighter he is, he's the best *man* in this sport." He takes turns making eye contact with every single person in the room. "You nominated him because of the mentoring he did while he was fighting, and the public fundraisers by his sponsors. Well, you have *no idea* how much more he does in private.

"He gives free private lessons to those who love this sport but can barely afford the membership, let alone the extra help. He gives jobs to those who need it. He provides mentoring to kids, teenagers, amateur fighters, literally *anyone* who needs the help. And none of it is for money. Do you know how many times I've tried to pay him extra for coaching me? And every time, the only way I win the argument is if I donate it to a charity for underprivileged city kids in his stead. But that's not written on your little piece of paper, is it? Because he refuses to put his name on those. All of his contributions are anonymous."

Hearing the way he's standing up for me makes my chest tighten as I take a shaky breath. Tristan turns his attention back to the president at the head of the table. "That man is the best coach I've ever had, and the most honorable man I've ever known. He is *exactly* who you want representing your organization."

To his credit, Mr. Barton looks properly chastised. But after a look around at his colleagues, it's obvious he's not quite convinced. "Look, son, I understand that you think highly of your coach. But one person isn't enough to—"

"He saved my life," Kane interrupts.

Everyone's focus zeroes in on the large, tattooed-from-the-neck-down man behind Tristan. His presence is foreboding as it is, but on top of that, Kane's always been the silent one of their group, speaking only when he has to. So, when he does, everyone listens.

He doesn't look thrilled to have everyone's attention, but that doesn't stop him.

"I've been kicked out of three gyms in two years. I was the worst type of student and fighter that no one wanted, and everyone treated me like trash because of it. Until Dominic." He locks eyes with me. "He took a chance on me. He gave a shit about me that I didn't deserve. And he saved my life because of it." His attention shifts back to the president. "You don't get to call him dishonorable. Because I've seen dishonorable men, and Dominic is not one of them."

Suddenly, it becomes hard to breathe through the sting of tears. Taking Kane under my wing and helping him through a tough time in his life had been important to me, but I never expected anything from him. I was just happy to make a difference. I knew he was grateful, just from reading Kane's body language in moments that others weren't looking, but saying something like that out loud...

It makes my whole career worth it.

"He's the best man I know," Jax says quietly. And by now, everyone's too stunned to do anything but listen. His eyes meet mine. "The best coach I've ever had, the best mentor I've ever learned from...the best *friend*. You have no idea how honored this organization should be to have someone like Dominic Caruso representing it."

Attention automatically travels to Remy and Lucy, as they step up beside Jax. And it's Lucy who speaks for them.

She makes strong eye contact with Mr. Barton, and her voice is loud and sure when she says, "I know the story that you heard about Dominic this week. And believe me, if there were any truth to it, I would applaud you for taking steps to protect young women. Because sometimes it's really hard being a woman in the MMA community. But...when I tell you that Dominic is the *protector* of women in this sport, I mean it with every fiber of my being. I've *seen* the type of coach that the gossip in your hand is talking about. I've even been on the receiving end of it, terrified and confused and hating myself *so much* for giving in to the manipulation of an authority figure." Her eyes dart to me. "Dominic was the first one to make me feel safe. Everything you read in that post? Dominic is the one who *protects* women from men like that. You've got this whole thing backwards."

There's a low murmur of voices around the room. I can't make out any words, or figure out who's talking, because my eyes are stuck on my fighters, my students who came in here, outraged on my behalf.

"Look, we all know what this is about," Tristan says loudly. "We all saw the post—the person who wrote it made sure of that. And I can tell you that it was posted out of revenge, specifically to ensure *this* kind of fallout for Dominic, but that won't matter to you, will it? Because you still saw the pictures, and you still need to protect your organization. So, let's nip this in the bud. Let's talk about it."

"Tristan..." I warn, nerves vibrating through my body. I know he's right, to an extent, because I can't just keep saying *it's not what it looks like*, but I'm a private person, and this is not something I ever wanted to talk about.

Especially without having Skylar here.

But Tristan must have seen something in the president's eyes, something that looked like an opening, because Mr. Barton slaps his papers on the table and looks to me.

"Fine. Let's talk about it, then. Dominic, do you deny starting an inappropriate relationship with a student?"

I clench my hands into fists before forcing myself to relax again. "No," I say tightly. "I don't deny it."

There are murmurs around the room again. I'm losing them.

"But I *do* deny every conclusion you falsely drew from that information and from those pictures."

Mr. Barton quirks an eyebrow. "Really? Then let's talk about those conclusions. Did you initiate the relationship with Miss Vega?"

"No." But again, I force honesty. "But being the authority figure, I should have stopped it. So yes, I accept all the blame. Since that's what you're really asking."

There's a flash of admiration in his eyes. *Did they expect me to put it all on Skylar?*

"Have you had other relationships with...*young* female students?" he asks. Though it looks like it pains him to do it.

"*No*. God, no. I have never, ever crossed a line like this with any student, young or otherwise. I pride myself on being a coach and mentor, and being someone women especially can feel safe coming to. Hall of Fame induction aside, I hate that that's even being questioned right now."

I wince and rub my temple, desperately trying to figure out what to say, *how much* to say, and how much I'm even capable of admitting.

Resolve hardens my spine. Straightening, I glance around the room. "Look, I should probably wish that it had been anyone else but Skylar to walk into my gym. I know how it looks to see us together. I've known this whole time. And yeah, if she was older, we probably wouldn't even be having this conversation, because it's the age gap that's fueling this fire. I know how this looks, believe me."

Awareness trickles in, and for the first time since Skylar came into my life, I don't feel guilty about the decisions I've made.

My gaze locks on Mr. Barton's. "But the truth is, I wouldn't change a thing about Skylar. I wouldn't have her pick a different sport, because her love for *this* sport is what makes her eyes light up. And I wouldn't make her a day older, because every single thing she's gone through in her life has made her into the person that she is today."

Mr. Barton's softening expression shifts finally to pity. "Dominic, I can appreciate that you think so highly of your students, but the fact of the matter is that there isn't really a good reason to be dating a nineteen-year-old—"

I love her. That's the good reason.

It hits me like a ton of bricks. The piece I've been missing. I've been wondering why I couldn't stay away from her? Why being with her always felt more important than any possible risk we faced? This is why. Because I *love* her.

This isn't just some passing infatuation because she's young and pretty and forbidden.

I love *her*.

As soon as the realization takes over, desperation seeps from my pores. Because I need them to understand. "I know you think I'm just some creepy older guy chasing a young girl," I rush to say, the words tasting like acid on my tongue. "But you're so, so wrong. I'm not just sleeping with her, I'm *with* her." I shake my head as I drop my gaze. "And I'm not with her *because* she's nineteen. I just...happened to fall in love with a woman who was born nineteen years ago."

Admitting the truth feels equal parts cathartic and terrifying. Because realizing I'm in love with her might make things clearer in my situation, but it doesn't tell me where I am with hers.

Suddenly, I know exactly where I need to be. And it's not here. Because this award, and this community's opinion of me, is no longer the most important thing in my life. I don't care if they judge me for who I love.

Nothing is worth losing Skylar.

"I need to go," I tell the board. "I'm sorry for interrupting your meeting. You make whatever decision you feel is right. Take the Hall of Fame award, take my career, take my 4th degree blackbelt. I don't care. She's worth all of it."

As I stride out of the room, I slow as I pass my fighters. I don't know what to say to them that could ever properly express my gratitude, so I settle for looking around the group and telling them quietly, "I'm so proud to be your coach."

Tristan and Jax both clap me on the shoulder, and Kane gives me a nod that says more than his words could. The girls send me tremulous, tear-filled smiles.

It's Aiden who pushes through the group and throws his arm around me. "Aw, shucks. We love you, too, old man."

"*Aiden!*"

He looks at his teammates in shock. "What? It's an endearment!"

I let out a loud laugh at the same time they pile on top of him and drag him out of the room. Following them out, I can't help thinking that despite everything else being chaotic and undetermined...I'm glad I have *this*.

I just hope I can still give Skylar the same.

37

SKYLAR

When I walk into the building, half of me expects to be immediately recognized and laughed out of the arena. Black clothes and my red hair tucked under the hood of my sweatshirt be damned. With the amount of drama I caused last week, I thought for sure the entire city would remember me.

But nothing happens. After I get my ticket from Will Call, and I'm scanned through to the center of the building, I make my way through the crowd without anyone's head turning my way. No one knows who I am.

I breathe a sigh of relief. I wanted to be here so badly, but it's only been ten days since everything went down, and I didn't think that was enough time for everyone to forget. And the last thing I wanted was to make things any worse for Dominic.

Actually, the last thing I wanted was to run *into* Dominic.

At the thought of him, I quickly scan the area around me. With Aiden fighting tonight, I know Dominic is here, but he never leaves the backstage area. So, the chances of running into him are slim to none.

I glance down at my phone and reread Aiden's message for the fifteenth time. He's the reason I'm here, after all.

> Aiden: SKY. You still coming to the fights this weekend? Please still come to the fights this weekend. You know you don't want to miss out on the chance to see me kick some guy's ass.

> Aiden: Lucy already bought you a ticket. I left it at Will Call for you. Whether you come to the Bulldog section or not, just know that we want you there. We miss you.

> Aiden: Aaaaand with that I'm maxed out on my sentimental quota. Guess Dani doesn't get any more I love yous this month.

My lips twitch with a smile. Aiden's message is the only thing that's brought one out lately, and for that, I'm grateful. The past ten days have been awful.

I hate not being at the gym. Not just because I'm missing the stress relief that comes with it, but also because I miss the excitement. The learning, the physical workout—the people. I miss my teammates. I miss *Dominic*.

I haven't let myself think about him too much. When throwing myself into my studies didn't work, I took on as many shifts at the café and restaurant as I possibly could. Distracting myself with customer service became the only thing that would exhaust me to the point of not thinking about him.

Because every time I thought about him, I got eaten up by the guilt that came with it. I'm responsible for everything that happened to Dominic, and I hate myself for it.

It doesn't matter that the post got taken down quickly, or that the social media posts and comments eventually slowed. The damage is done. And the rumors of the UFC withdrawing their Hall of Fame election didn't help, even though their decision hasn't been made public yet. All it took was one post to shred Dominic's reputation. And it was my fault.

I force myself to brush all of that off. What's done is done, and there's nothing I can do about it. I'm only here because I want to support a friend.

A friend who is being called to the cage right now.

The announcement of Aiden's name is a welcome distraction. I'm at the back of the arena, hidden in the crowd, but even from here, I can see where the fighters making their entrance.

Aiden walks through the smoke, his walkout song making him bob his head to the beat, an eager grin on his face. I take a deep breath and look for his corner.

But to my surprise, it's Tristan and Jax who follow behind him.

Dominic is nowhere to be seen.

I frown. *Why wouldn't Dominic be in his corner? Did something happen? Is he okay?*

The only thing that keeps me from spiraling into a panic is knowing that Tristan and Jax wouldn't be here if something was wrong with Dominic. Coaching and working relationship aside, I know how much those guys care about him.

So, I focus my attention on Aiden. He seems excited to be in the cage for his second pro fight, so much so that he's maintained his playful persona in the face of his determined opponent. When the ref asks the fighters to touch gloves, Aiden mimics rock paper scissors instead.

Whether that's meant to confuse his opponent or not, the tactic throws off the Red corner enough that the fight quickly goes downhill. As soon as the bell rings,

Aiden is out of the Blue corner like a shot, taking his opponent down before the guy even knows what's happening.

Thirty seconds into the fight and the two men are already on the ground, Aiden in a dominant position. His opponent puts up a valiant fight, but he's never able to regain the momentum. Every time he tries to get off his back and to his feet, Aiden drops a few punches to his ribs, an elbow to his face, and stuns him enough to put him right back on the mat.

On Red's third attempt to push Aiden off, Aiden grabs the guy's arm and swings his leg around to secure the armbar submission. Dropping his own back to the mat, he pushes his hips up and forces Red to tap.

The arena erupts into chaos. That was a dominant, two-minute fight that ended in an impressive submission by the favored fighter. It was a perfect fight.

I let out a loud cheer, bouncing on my toes and clapping for my friend's victory. I'm so glad I came.

There's cheering inside the cage, too. Jax is lifting Aiden up and even Tristan is grinning and clapping for his friend. The whole team is so supportive and elated.

I miss them.

I force that thought from my head and absorb the excitement in front of me. Aiden is still grinning from ear to ear when his name is announced as the winner, and as the announcer pulls him aside for his interview.

"Aiden Reeves, what a victory! Did that fight go the way you expected it to?"

Aiden grabs the mic and looks out at the crowd. "I'm sorry, Bob. I'm going to interrupt you for a quick second. Can we get all the lights on in here, please?"

A murmur runs through the entire arena, everyone

confused about what's happening. But after a few seconds, every light in the arena flips on.

The rumblings grow louder, and my head whips around, as does everyone else's. With his hand shielding his eyes so he can scan the crowd, Aiden is clearly looking for something. Or someone.

"Skylar."

I freeze in place when I hear the voice behind me.

Aiden spots me at the same time. With his grin becoming impossibly wider, he points me out in the crowd and says, "There we go, found her. Do your thing, Coach."

Then, as if that was the most normal thing in the world, he turns back to the announcer. "So, Bob, you asked if that fight went the way I expected it to. Well, obviously, I planned on winning. So, I'd say it did."

A chuckle sounds from behind me, and the whole situation is so bizarre that I find myself turning around.

And coming face to face with Dominic.

He looks...*happy*.

Well, actually, he looks tired. There are dark circles under his eyes, and he looks a little worn down, but...he looks happy *now*. A genuine, warm smile sits on his lips, and there's an air of relief about him.

"Hi, Skylar," he says quietly.

"Hi," I reply, feeling breathless.

Suddenly, it registers that even though Aiden is still answering questions in the cage, we've become the center of attention in this part of the arena. Plenty of people have turned toward us, and I can hear them whispering.

"What are you doing?" I chance a glance around us. "Everyone's staring."

Dominic never takes his eyes off me. "Good. That's what we wanted."

I frown. "We?"

His smile grows. "Yeah. Me and Aiden. Turns out, the guy's a really good wingman. Go figure."

Still, I can only blink in shock. "What is happening right now?"

Dominic's expression sobers slightly. He starts to take a step closer to me but suddenly hesitates, gauging my reaction before he moves. When I don't retreat, he takes another one.

There's about a foot between us now. He's close enough to make my heartrate accelerate, but far enough that he's still giving me space. Yet his eyes never waver from my face.

Desperation sets in. I don't know why he's here, but I think a part of me *does*, and I can't handle being wrong. I can't handle him asking me to come back to the gym to be his student again. I'm already barely hanging on after the loss of him, I wouldn't ever recover from him asking me that question.

I look around at the crowd again as my nerves grow. "You shouldn't be here. People are going to talk."

"Let them."

My eyes widen and lock onto him at the quick response. "You don't mean that."

He doesn't hesitate in his answer. "I do."

My brow furrows, shaking my head. "People talking is bad for the gym. Bad for *you*. Being seen talking to me will hurt your reputation."

Dominic takes a step closer. "I don't care."

I can feel my heart now pounding in my ears. "Of course, you care. Your reputation is everything. Your business, your fighters—MMA is the only thing you care about. You said it yourself."

When he takes another step toward me, he's finally close

enough for me to feel the heat of his body—close enough that my fingers itch with the need to touch him. It takes everything in me to *not*.

"That used to be true," he says. "But not anymore."

I start to tremble—with disbelief, unease... but most of all, crippling hope.

"For as long as I can remember, MMA was the only thing I cared about," he says softly. "Everything I did, every decision I made—that was my reason why. Anything to make me a better fighter. Anything to make me a better coach. And I was *proud* of the persona I built with my years of experience. Being a good fighter and a good coach meant I had a lot of knowledge to use and give. Being a good gym owner meant I had a lot of people I could help by intro-ducing them to this sport I loved. I centered my entire life around my brand."

When he looks at me, it's not with his usual unreadable gaze. Now, he's got his whole heart in his eyes.

"But then you walked into my gym," he whispers, and I hold my breath. "And I realized all that pales in comparison to what *you* bring to my life."

I let out a whimper and try to wrap my arms around my waist to somehow anchor myself to this moment, but Dominic reaches for my hands and lifts them to his chest, holding them tight.

"You asked me once if what we had was worth the risk. There *is* no risk. Baby...you're worth everything."

My lower lip starts to tremble, and my hands fist in his shirt. It's unbelievable, too *easy*. Things felt way too impos-sible at the beginning of this for it to be this simple.

"You don't mean that," I choke out. "You *can't* mean that. You just said you built your entire life around being a fighter and coach—look at what one picture with me cost you! Your social media, your Google reviews...and *God*, when I heard about the Hall of Fame—"

"They inducted me. They're announcing me tomorrow night."

I blink in surprise. "They...what?"

Sliding one arm around my waist, he pulls me flush against his body. "They inducted me into the Hall of Fame. I told them the truth, and they made their decision."

It takes me another second to digest that. With the way people responded to the accusation, I thought for sure the UFC was going to do anything they could to cover their asses.

The fact that they didn't is...huge.

"But... But what about..."

Dominic strokes the back of his knuckles against my cheek. There's not quite a smile on his face, but he seems so content, I can't help but relax a little against him.

"But what? What other worries are rolling around in that beautiful, self-sacrificing brain of yours?"

"But what about what everyone said?" I whisper, my eyes stinging with tears. "All the comments, and the whispers—what about what everyone is going to think?"

Dominic sobers and cups my cheek. "I don't care about any of it. I just want *you*. I—" He swallows roughly, looking nervous for the first time. "I love you, Skylar. I love you because you're kind, and smart, and so goddamn strong. I love you because, even with everything you've gone through, you haven't let any of it change you as a person. You bring a lightness into the room that everyone is better for. You make *me* better for it—you taught me how it feels to truly love someone."

A tear slides down my cheek. When a second one follows, Dominic wipes it away with his thumb.

"And I'm not worried about what other people think. Because I don't care about anyone's opinion who looks at the way I love you and questions *why*."

A sob escapes as I throw my arms around Dominic's neck, lifting up on my toes so I can press my mouth to his in a kiss that feels like home. The relief is overpowering.

"I love you, too," I cry against his lips. His arms tighten around my waist as he lifts and kisses me back. "I love you so much."

When he places me on my feet and brings his forehead to mine, I'm still trying to catch my breath, both from the emotions and the feel of Dominic's claiming touch. "I hated that I was bad for you," I admit. "I hated how everyone reacted, and knowing that I was the cause of it—"

"Hey, no, never." Dominic brushes a kiss to my forehead, then to both sides of my temple. "We didn't do anything wrong. You could *only* be good for me."

I look up at him and finally take in the sight of Dominic as *mine*. My gaze travels over his dark tousled hair, his sparking blue eyes, his kiss-swollen lips.

He's more than I ever imagined for myself.

"Are you sure about this?" I ask one final time. "If last week was any indication, this isn't going to be easy."

With perfect timing, a few whispers from the crowd around us can be heard over whatever the announcer is saying in the cage. One quick glance to the side confirms people are still staring.

"I don't want easy," Dominic says. "I want you. And everything that comes with that."

I'm smiling deliriously when his lips claim mine again. None of his kisses have been tame, but this one is nowhere near appropriate. When he coaxes my mouth open and slides his tongue inside, we hear a few catcalls sound out around us.

We both huff a laugh when we separate. "And on that note..." I ask, "why on earth did you decide to do this *here?* In front of everyone?"

"That's exactly why—I wanted to do it in front of everyone." He seems proud of himself too.

"I had no idea you were such an exhibitionist," I say with a quiet chuckle, making sure no one else can hear.

He nips at my lower lip with a growl. "Only when it comes to showing off how much I love you." Then he sighs and steps back, taking my hand as he turns toward the cage. "Speaking of exhibitionists..."

Shifting my attention toward the cage, I see Aiden has finally finished with interviews and pictures and is now standing at the top of the cage steps, his arm around his girlfriend's shoulders as they both watch us over the crowd. Aiden even looks like he's on the verge of tears.

When he sees us looking at him, a huge grin splits his face. He pumps a fist into the air and yells, "Attaboy, Coach! I knew you could do it!"

There's a ripple of laughs in the crowd, including from Dominic. Shaking his head, he squeezes my hand and says, "Come on. Let's get you back to the family."

38

SKYLAR

I'm walking across campus, mentally cataloguing my upcoming tests and scheduling when I can study for them, as I run into Craig.

"Skylar. Hey."

His tone is hesitant when he stops me. And when I turn to face him, his expression matches.

"Hey, Craig," I respond just as carefully, a cold shiver running down my spine. "What's up?"

The tension seems to release from his shoulders when I give him my attention.

"Not much, just heading to the library. Are you...going to the study group tonight?"

My eyes never leave his. "No, I'm only on campus for a quick meeting today."

He simply nods. "What about tomorrow? I heard our anatomy final is killer. We're all meeting up every night this week to study."

"Nah, I'm good on my own," I say, my voice flat. Why would he think I'd want anything to do with him after our last interaction? "And anyway, I'm training at the gym tomorrow night."

His spine stiffens and his eyes narrow.

"You're still at that gym?" he spits.

I knew it.

I don't answer. I don't need to, because he's revealing everything about himself with the way he's looking at me.

And he knows it, too. His fists clench and his face reddens, maybe from anger, maybe from embarrassment at being found out.

"Why the fuck would you still be training with that creep? And how is his gym even still open?"

For a moment, I only stare at him, feeling nauseous. Then I let out a tired sigh. "So, it *was* you. I was hoping I was wrong."

Craig reddens even further. "I don't know what you're talking about."

"Why would you do that, Craig?" I ask quietly. "Why would you try to ruin someone else's life like that? You don't even know him."

"He deserves it, Skylar," he rushes to convince me. "He's a *predator*. I know you can't see it because he's brainwashed you, but—"

"Don't you *dare* talk down to me," I snarl, taking a step forward into his space. "Who do you think you are? Who the *fuck* do you think you are?"

Craig falls back a step, his eyes widening.

I close the distance between us with another step. "Let's ignore the fact that you clearly did this because your ego was bruised by my rejection." Anger laces every one of my words. "If you were honestly worried about me being taken advantage of, you should've just talked to me. Not taken pictures of me like that to prove a fucking *point*."

That's when something occurs to me. And I tilt my head as I freeze in place once again, this time with *fire* running through my veins.

"Did you stick around while we had sex? Is there revenge porn on your phone, Craig?"

Panic has him paling.

He shakes his head so hard, his teeth chatter as he answers. "N-no, of course not, I—"

I take another step, so close now that there's barely any space between us. Despite the people around us slowing when they notice the scene, only Craig can hear me.

"Tell me the truth right now, Craig, or I swear to God, I'll go to the police and press charges, if for no other reason than to tie a paper trail to you. Are there more pictures of us besides the ones you posted?"

"Jesus, no, I wouldn't do that to you, I just wanted to ruin *him*—"

I hold up a hand to stop his tirade. "You better hope I believe you, or your future as a shitty personal trainer is no longer going to include a Bachelor's degree."

"You can't prove anything," he hisses, but I hear the fear in his voice.

I hold his gaze, and I let him see the truth in my eyes. He might be right, but I don't care. "Maybe. But I'll let the dean decide that. Fuck you, Craig."

I turn and walk away from him, mentally and emotionally done with the conversation. I had a suspicion that Craig was the one who leaked the pictures. After it happened, and after Dominic and I got back together, we sat down and tried to figure out who hated us enough to do this. And since Dominic was the one who was truly threatened, we guessed that it was someone who hated him but wanted to, in their own twisted way, protect me—since the fallout mostly avoided me. Even the fact that the pictures weren't fully nudes showed a level of protection.

I was the first to bring up the possibility of Craig. And immediately, Dominic agreed that it would make sense. When I told him about my history with Craig, and about how he reacted the last time I turned him down, we both agreed that it fit with his fragile ego.

But that didn't mean we had agreed on what to do about it. Dominic immediately wanted to take the case to the police. I wanted to talk to Craig first. A part of me wanted confirmation that he had done this. And I just got it.

I think I believe him about the only pictures being the ones he posted. Maybe it's naïve of me, but I saw the emotions in his eyes; I know how he reacted to my accusation. And I don't think it was an act.

My pace is brisk as I stride across campus. I have a meeting with my anatomy professor in ten minutes, and then after that...straight to the dean's office. I wasn't lying about reporting Craig. Regardless of what happens to him after I disclose everything, I need to do the right thing. I just haven't decided if that also includes a police report.

By the time I knock on my professor's office door, I've somewhat managed to push all thoughts of Craig from my mind. But I still have to urge a smile onto my face when I'm called inside.

"Skylar! I'm glad you're here. Have a seat."

I settle into the chair in front of my professor's desk. Unlike mine, his smile seems to be brighter than the sun as he sits across from me with folded hands.

"Skylar, I wanted to talk to you about something, but I have to preface this with an apology in case I've overstepped. That is certainly never my intention."

Wariness shifts to confusion. "Professor?"

"You see, I know you told me you were set on a nursing path," he continues. "But you'll forgive an old man for seeing through a pile of shit."

My mouth twitches, but I tamp down on it. That reaction only seems to spur him on.

"I know passion in a student when I see it. And I know when it's focused on something specific, and when they're not giving everything to that passion." His voice softens as he adds, "You want to work in neuroscience, don't you?"

All humor drops from my expression, and my breaths come quicker. *I'm not prepared for this conversation.*

He studies me for a moment, then nods. "I wrote the letter of recommendation that you asked for," he says, sliding a sheet of paper toward me. "And if you really want to go down the RN route, I'll sign it right now and hand it over, wishing you nothing but the best of luck. But..."

He opens a drawer and pulls out a second sheet of paper. This one he doesn't hand over just yet. Not until I finally work up the nerve to meet his eyes.

"But I'm hoping that you're strong enough—strong enough to be *honest* with yourself—to go after what you really want."

For a moment, I can't breathe. This is not what I expected when I walked in here today. But I'd be lying if I said this hasn't been at the forefront of my mind.

Ever since Dominic and I had the doctorate conversation, I've been thinking about what I'd need to do to go after the career I really want. Not the career that I've been letting myself settle for, but the one where my true passion lies.

The kind that...might let me assist in finding a cure for my mom's disease.

Even though I know that everything I've done in my life has been for my family, somewhere along the way, I forgot that I could help them with more than just a paycheck. Honoring my mom by finding a career that I love would make her happy. And if that passion also helps her disease on top of that? I shouldn't have any kind of hesitation over this decision.

Medical school would extend my education years and add on more loans than I want to think about, but it would be worth it.

The clarity hits me so hard, I recoil in my seat. I lean back, my eyes wide as I stare at my professor.

He smiles, something like relief shining in his eyes. "I think I just got my answer," he says.

I think I just got my *answer*, I think to myself. Because I've never been more sure of a decision as I am right now.

I can make this work. I can take the risk, and make the sacrifices, and ask for help, all so I can do this incredible thing that I never let myself want. *I can do this.*

I glance down at the paper in my professor's hand, watching in shock and amazement as he signs it. When he hands it to me, I take it without another thought.

"When you're ready, come talk to me about medical school applications. I'll help you through the process so it doesn't feel so overwhelming."

I have to blink back my tears as I nod, but I still force myself to say, "Thank you. This... This means everything to me. Thank you."

"You don't have to thank me, Skylar," he says with a kind smile. "You deserve every bit of success that comes your way. You just have to believe you're worth it."

And...I think I finally do.

39

SKYLAR

My professor's words stick with me the entire way back to the gym. But it isn't until I'm splayed out on Dominic's desk a half hour later that the thoughts take a backseat. And for good reason.

"That's it, baby, come all over my hand for me," Dominic growls, his thumb on my clit and his fingers driving inside me.

My lips pop open, my gasp loud in the office. When my orgasm hits, my whole body shudders with the force of the pleasure.

I haven't even begun to catch my breath when Dominic pushes his shorts over his hips and impales me on his cock.

"Oh *God*," I whimper, my hands coming up to scratch at his abs. He doesn't start slow, just grabs under my thighs and pulls me into every hard drive.

My eyes slide shut on a shaky moan, my back arching and my hands sliding up my body to cup my breasts. I'll never get enough of him.

"You're so fucking sexy," he grits out, as his thrusts

become more powerful. "I could come from just the sight of you."

I open my eyes so I can take him in as he inevitably loses control.

"You feel so good," I whisper. "I love the way you fuck me."

His groan sounds pained. "I want you to come again. Give me one more, baby."

I hum a non-answer, a smile sliding across my face as I pinch my nipples in a tease. "I want to feel you come, Coach," I purr.

Another groan, this one a sound of defeat. Because I know exactly what sets him off, and I love being the one who makes him unravel.

He pulls from my body, his fist barely shuttling over his cock before he's coming on my bare stomach.

He's breathing heavily, likely trying to decide how to punish me for making him come before me, when his gaze catches on my hand as I slide it down my body.

I'm running purely on instinct when I swirl my fingers in the cum splattered on my stomach. Then I move them even lower, down to my sensitive clit, my lips popping open on a heady sigh.

"Fuck," I hear Dominic breathe. I've never done anything like this before, but I've loved exploring with him in the bedroom. I usually follow his lead, but I'm feeling a little bold today.

I swirl my fingers over my clit once, twice, and then I slide one inside myself.

Dominic looks like his head's about to explode. He's frozen in place, his eyes glued to the place between my legs as he watches me finger myself with his cum.

354

"You know, Coach," I purr, sliding another finger inside. His gaze jumps to my face, his expression *ravenous*.

"I'm on the pill now," I continue, pausing at how good this feels. "So, you can come inside me if you want. You can fill me up, make me messy—"

I break off with a gasp. Because Dominic has apparently decided he's done with watching, and drops his head to suction his lips around my clit.

"What are you—" I breathe.

He ignores me, his hands holding me to his face and his tongue swirling around my clit. The fact that he's going down on me, that he's tasting his own pleasure—

My fingers are still inside myself, but my other hand slides into his hair with a moan. *God,* this is so hot. My breaths start to come in gasps. I don't realize I've started to finger myself again until Dominic's fingers slide in beside mine and I'm suddenly *so. full.*

I come on a soundless cry.

When he eventually takes pity on my overstimulated body and lifts away from me, I'm sated and limp on his desk. But as soon as he leans down to take my mouth, I sigh into the kiss and wrap my arms around his neck.

"Dirty old man," I whisper with a smile.

He stamps another hard kiss to my lips. "You love it," he says with a grin.

I hum in agreement and pull him in. I could spend hours with him just kissing.

But eventually, he lifts off me with a sigh. Grabbing a paper towel, he wipes the cum from my skin, his touch reverent and his expression thoughtful.

"So what had you so distracted when you walked in here that I had to get your attention with an orgasm?" he asks after a moment.

Eyes closed and melting onto the desk from the soothing touch of the cool towel, I mumble, "I can't remember a single thing that happened outside of this room."

His chuckle has me cracking an eye open. "You're good for my ego, baby."

I sit up and stretch my arms over my head. "Fighters already have the biggest egos," I answer with a yawn.

Smiling, he presses a kiss to the side of my neck and rights the straps of my sundress. He can say he jumped me when I walked in here because I looked distracted, but it's more likely that it was the dress. I recently discovered it as his kryptonite and have enjoyed tormenting him with it.

"Fine, keep your secrets," he says, lifting me off the desk. I move right into his arms.

"I just had a nice conversation with my professor," I admit quietly. "About...medical school."

He tips my chin up with a finger, his eyes shining with surprise and delight. "Yeah? That's amazing." He's still smiling when he leans down to kiss me. "I want to hear all about it later."

My brow furrows. "Later? I thought we were going out to dinner."

When he steps back and takes my hand, he's grinning. "We are. But I've got some surprises of my own before that. Now go freshen up, we're late."

I don't understand until he leads me out of the gym, and into the pizza shop next door.

Sitting at one of the tables is Maria and my mom, Joey standing behind them in his work uniform.

"What is this?" I breathe.

With his arm wrapped around my waist, Dominic gestures toward my family. "I wanted to surprise you. Dinner and your monthly movie."

"We're all going to the movies after this?"

He nods. "Joey's shift ends in an hour, and then we're all going over to the theater. If your mom gets tired, Maria might take her home, but I wanted to get everyone together for a little bit."

My eyes fill with tears. *How does he always know what I need? How is it possible for someone to be this perfect for me?*

Dominic sees my reaction and nuzzles into my neck, his lips brushing a kiss to my skin. "Happy?" he murmurs.

My nod is immediate. "Perfect," I whisper, turning my head to catch his lips with mine.

He wastes no time taking over, and I sink into him with a content sigh.

"Hey, lovebirds, get a room! You're ruining everyone's appetite."

I break away with a huff of laughter.

"Remind me to annoy the crap out of you when you get a girlfriend," Dominic grumbles, guiding me over to my family's table. "If you *ever* get a girlfriend," he adds with a playful glare as he drops into his seat, Mom and Maria laughing.

Joey quirks an eyebrow in our direction. "Says the forty-year-old bachelor who couldn't find a girl to date him until my sister took pity on him."

I smack him upside his head with a glare of my own. "Watch it, hotshot. You're not so big that I can't still beat you up."

"This is familial abuse," Joey says dramatically, rubbing the back of his head. "I liked you better when you two weren't dating."

Dominic pulls me down into his lap and wraps his arms around my waist. "No, you didn't."

Joey sighs, dropping his hand. "No. I didn't." He

357

begrudgingly adds, "I guess it's kinda nice to see Skylar happy."

I hide my smile in Dominic's neck, who presses a kiss to my temple and squeezes me even tighter. I catch Mom's adoring smile from behind my hair.

"So we're decided on the movie we're watching, right?" Maria asks. "The newest Liam Neeson movie?"

Joey lets out a groan only a teenager is capable of. "Nooo, come *on*, his movies aren't good anymore. He's so *old*."

Maria and my mom exchange a look. And it's Mom who says, "That's exactly the appeal, my sweet summer child."

I burst out laughing at the look of disgust on my brother's face. "Ewww, *Mom!*"

The restaurant echoes with our laughter, the sound of it filling me with a warmth that's become entirely familiar these days.

Finally, Mom takes pity on Joey. "Alright, alright, fine. We'll see the newest *Fast and the Furious* movie, instead. Satisfied?"

Joey grins. "Very. At least there're hot girls in that one."

Now we're the ones groaning. But it's Maria who balls up her napkin and chucks it at my brother's head.

Resting my head on Dominic's shoulder, I take a second to soak in the sight of my family. They're happy, as healthy as possible, and together. There's not much more I could ask for.

Dominic presses another kiss to my hair. Lifting my head, I look up at him with what I know has got to be a giddy, love-drunk expression. And like always, he reads my mind.

"I'm glad you walked into my gym, baby."

My lips brush against his as they lift into a smile. "Me too, Coach."

EPILOGUE
DOMINIC

Six years later

"Doctor Skylar Caruso!"

The cheers from our row almost drown out the sound of my racing heart—almost. Every one of us is clapping, screaming, cheering for my wife as she walks across the auditorium stage to collect her degree.

From medical school.

When we finally quiet down, I catch the sound of a sniffle from beside me. Glancing over at Joey, I realize his eyes are shining with tears.

I don't want to embarrass him, but it makes me want to hug the kid. He's always been the most incredible support for his sister.

Disguising my hug, I reach around him to squeeze his mom's shoulder, who's sitting beside him. She, on the other hand, is not worried about hiding her tears. With her eyes on her daughter, pride radiating, she's silently sobbing into a tissue.

"She's going to cure something someday," Joey says in quiet wonder.

I give up on not hugging him and move my hand from his mom to the back of his neck. "Yeah, I know," I breathe.

I spend the rest of the ceremony choking down my own emotions and trying to figure out how this much love can fit inside a person.

It's crazy to look back at how our relationship started. Six years ago, we were both worried that it wasn't worth it to take the risks. Now looking back, I can't believe the thought ever crossed our minds.

We did experience judgment, in the beginning. The whispers and side glances were there for a while. Thankfully, though, I didn't see a huge effect on the gym. I think the UFC granting me the Hall of Fame award helped a lot. But once the community figured out we were in this for the long haul, our drama became old news.

Skylar figured out how to juggle a relationship in her busy life way quicker than she gave herself credit for. She still worked sixty hours a week, still pushed herself in school, but she also learned how to accept help, from all of us, and stopped feeling bad about doing things that brought her joy. She even let herself move in with me— though I made the decision a lot easier when I moved her mom into the apartment building right next to my townhouse.

By the time she started medical school, we both knew this was a forever thing. She didn't even seem surprised when I popped the question on a random Tuesday night, Brutus sleeping between us and her textbooks spread out all over the couch. It didn't matter that she was twenty-three; our commitment to each other had already been made when we initially went public with our relationship. Going down to City Hall with our close family and friends and exchanging rings was just a formality.

Memories of the months after, of my nights spent helping her study and her nights spent helping me grow my business even more, flit through my mind. Skylar is the best partner I never imagined for myself, and every day, I'm in awe of how much better she makes my life. The fact that she was able to earn her doctorate at the same time is just Skylar in a nutshell.

When the ceremony finally ends, we're quick to stand from our seats and move over to the courtyard, eager to congratulate Skylar in person.

The moment she spots our group, the biggest smile brightens her face, and she runs over to us, completely unbothered by the dress and heels that she's wearing. Nothing could delay her from wrapping her arms around her mom.

I give the women some space, the sounds of soft cries filling the air. Joey quickly swipes at his face, trying to hide his tears, then I watch as he gives up entirely and throws his arms around his family.

To no one's surprise, all three of them have achieved some pretty incredible things these past few years. Skylar's mom has good days and bad days with her health, but through it all, she's still her kids' number one cheerleader. She's the only one I know who rivals Skylar in strength.

Joey accepted an offer to play D2 basketball at an in-state college—with a full scholarship. He also found a girl to go out with him.

And Skylar...she did everything she set her mind to.

Her cheeks are wet, eyes shining, when she eventually separates from her family and locks eyes with me. *God...* she's the most beautiful woman I've ever seen.

"Hi," she whispers as she steps over to me.

"Hey, baby," I say quietly, wasting no time wrapping one arm around her waist and pulling her to me. With the other hand, I wipe the tears from her cheeks. "I believe congratulations are in order."

She lets out a laugh and throws her arms around my neck, squeezing me against her. I squeeze right back.

"I'm so proud of you," I whisper in her ear. "So, *so* proud of you."

When she pulls back, there are new tears on her cheeks. "Thank you for being the most incredible man," she says. "I couldn't have done it without you."

I smile down at her. "Yes, you could have. But I'm happy I got to love you through it anyway."

The rest of the day is one giant celebration dinner. I booked a long reservation at Barcelona, Skylar's favorite restaurant. We have enough time for two dinners: one for family and one for the fighters.

I watch Skylar smile for hours. I knew bringing Joey home for the weekend and getting the family together would be the only way she'd want to celebrate. Tacking on a second dinner reservation with the Bulldog family was just a bonus.

We somehow get every fighter and their significant other to the restaurant—Jax even shows up with his six-month-old daughter strapped to his chest in a baby carrier. It's rare to get everyone together nowadays, what with everyone's lives and fighting careers changing. But they're all just as proud of Skylar's accomplishment as I am, so they made the time.

Because the one thing that's never changed at the gym is the family sentiment.

Despite our dinner starting at an early hour, it's late by the time we get home. Skylar looks tired, but so happy, as she collapses next to Brutus on the couch.

"Hi, old man," she coos as she pets him. Immediately, his head lifts and tail wags. She's still the one that gets the biggest reaction out of him.

The sight of them together puts a smile on my face that I've never been able to get rid of. She must feel my gaze on her because she stops fawning over Brutus and follows me into the kitchen, a twinkle in her eye. When she hops up on the counter in front of me, I step between her legs and brace my hands on either side of her hips.

"Hi, wife," I murmur, pressing a kiss to one side of her neck. "Or should I call you Doctor Caruso from now on?" Another kiss, this time to the other side.

She hums thoughtfully as she wraps her arms around my neck and pulls me closer. "That does have a nice ring to it," she muses.

I make a sound of agreement as I take her mouth in a kiss. "Yes, it does," I murmur, my hands already traveling over her skin.

Her arms tighten around my neck and her body arches against mine. "I *am* partial to being called your wife, though," she whispers against my lips.

Another sound of agreement, another kiss—this one greedier. I nip at her bottom lip. "*Wife.*"

A shudder runs through her body under my hands. "God, you're making it so hard to have this conversation. All I want to do is hear you call me that while you fuck me on this counter."

I almost do just that. But I somehow manage to filter

through the lust-drunk thoughts and zero in on the first part of what she said.

I pull back slightly. "What conversation?"

A little bit of the haze clears from her eyes.

"I was thinking...maybe we could try for a baby."

My eyes widen. "Right now?"

Her lips stretch into a grin. "I mean, your hands are already up my dress. We're practically halfway there."

I shake my head—more to clear the cobwebs from my brain than to refute her. "No, I mean...you're about to start your intern year, and then you have three years of residency. Isn't that the hardest part of the doctorate track?"

She shrugs. "It's all hard."

"Yeah, but..." I study her closely. "That's a big hurdle, baby. Are you sure you're not just saying this because I'm getting old?"

Her nose crinkles in that way I love. "You're not *that* old. You're forty-two. Plenty of men have babies into their seventies."

"So, then we can wait until you're done your residency."

Her arms tighten around my neck to pull me closer. "But I don't want to wait that long."

My gaze travels over her face, cataloguing every emotion for any hint of hesitation. Not because I'm looking for a hole in her argument, but because I'm desperate for there not to. The idea of having a baby with my wife, of Skylar pregnant with my child—

She must see my need for reassurance because, after a moment, she lets out a heavy breath and explains, "Every woman I've talked to in the medical field says the same thing: there's no such thing as 'the right time' to try for a family. My next four years—and then my starting years as a doctor—are always going to be busy. Plus, no one ever knows how long it'll take to conceive. And besides..." Her expression softens, love and vulnerability and desire shining up at me. "I love you. I want to have your babies. That's the only reason I need."

My chest constricts from the weight of her words. My arms go around Skylar, and I hold her to me as I try to swallow down the emotions choking me. "That's the only reason I need too, baby."

When she smiles, my heart trips over itself. Six years later, and I still find myself falling in love with this woman every single day.

"So that's how you want to celebrate your graduation day?" I ask, my voice sounding scratchy to my own ears. "Trying for a baby?"

A twinkle of mischief appears in her eyes. "Don't act like we weren't going to do that anyway."

I huff out a laugh. "Touché."

She pulls me down to her, her lips brushing against mine in a tease. "Only difference now is that I won't take my birth control pill tonight. I'll just go to bed with your cum still inside me."

A heavy breath whooshes from my lungs. "Christ. I'll never get over your mouth." And then I can't keep my hands off her for any longer. Pulling her off the counter, I throw her over my shoulder and head for our bedroom.

"You have no idea what you just started," I growl. "I hope you're ready for a long night, wife."

Her delighted laugh is still my favorite sound in the entire world.

But in a close second place...

"Yes, Coach."

ACKNOWLEDGMENTS

I loved every moment of writing this book. It's not that it was easy, but Coach and Skylar's story came together so naturally that I felt like I flew through this one. To date, this was my favorite book to write.

My first and most important thank you is to my very own Coach Dominic. Every day I think I can't love you more than I already do, and every day I'm wrong. Thank you for being the best husband, and the most incredible support.

To my sister, who continues to be my sounding board throughout every book release, and who never complains about the rollercoaster of emotions that comes with being an author. Thank you for never letting me convince myself that my manuscript is trash.

To my editor Kenzie, who continues to be my lifeline during every book release. I've said it before and I'll say it again: there is no Nikki Castle without you. Thank you for helping to shape my books into the stories they're meant to be.

To Amanda, Nicole, and Sam, who are my beta readers, graphic designers, therapists, and friends all rolled into one. You three are my rock, and I shudder to think about what these books would look like without you. Thank you for always being honest, and for being the most incredible support.

To my beta readers: Brittany, Jessicah, Rebecca, Stephanie, and Maria. Thank you for helping to shape this story into its best possible version. Your feedback is invaluable.

To my family, friends, readers, *everyone* who has supported me throughout this writing journey, all I can say is *THANK YOU!* As I say with every book, without you, a book is just some ink on a dead tree. Thank you for loving this story as much as I do.

TRIGGER WARNINGS

This book contains a sick parent but not the death of that parent. There are also brief mentions of the deaths of other parents.

ABOUT THE AUTHOR

Nikki Castle is a wife and dog mom from Philadelphia who writes spicy love stories about alpha MMA fighters and the women that melt their badass, playboy hearts. She's a full-time romance author during the day and spends her evenings running a Mixed Martial Arts (MMA) gym with her husband, who is also a retired fighter.

Nikki has been writing in one way or another since she was a teenager. She pursued an English and Philosophy degree in college, and finally decided to sit down and fulfill her longtime dream of writing a novel when quarantine began in 2020.

Nikki loves to hear from her readers on Instagram or through email. Message her on any social media platform @nikkicastleromance or email her at nikkicastleromance@gmail.com!

ALSO BY NIKKI CASTLE

The Fight Game Series

Book One: 5 Rounds

Book Two: 2 Fights

Book Three: 3 Count

Book Four: 1 Last Shot

The Just Tonight Novella Series

The Stranger in Seat 8B